Jens Lapidus

EASY MONEY

Jens Lapidus is a criminal defense lawyer who represents
some of Sweden's most notorious underworld criminals.
He lives in Stockholm with his wife.

EASY MONEY

EASY MONEY

Jens Lapidus

Translated from the Swedish by Astri von Arbin Ahlander

Vintage Crime/Black Lizard
Vintage Books
A Division of Random House, Inc.
New York

FIRST VINTAGE CRIME/BLACK LIZARD EDITION, NOVEMBER 2012

Translation copyright © 2011 by Pantheon Books, a division of Random House, Inc.

All rights reserved. Published in the United States by Vintage Books, a division of
Random House, Inc., New York. Originally published in Sweden as *Snabba Cash:
Hatet Drivet Jakten* by Wahlström & Widstrand, Stockholm, in 2006.
Copyright © 2006 by Jens Lapidus. This translation originally published in
hardcover in the United States by Pantheon Books, a division of
Random House, Inc., New York, in 2011.

Vintage is a registered trademark and Vintage Crime/Black Lizard and colophon are
trademarks of Random House, Inc.

The Library of Congress has cataloged the Pantheon edition as follows:
Lapidus, Jens.
[Snabba cash. English]
Easy money / Jens Lapidus ; translated from the Swedish by
Astri von Arbin Ahlander.
p. cm.
1. Organized Crime—Fiction. 2. Stockholm (Sweden)—Fiction. I. Title.
PT9877.22.A65S6313 2011839.73'8—dc22 2011003721

Vintage ISBN: 978-0-307-39023-3

Book design by Laura Crossin

www.vintagebooks.com

Printed in the United States of America
10 9 8 7 6 5 4 3 2 1

I looked at him and nodded. "Tough day," I said.
   He shrugged. "Me, too," he said and pulled onto the expressway.

—DENNIS LEHANE

It worked. It happened. It cohered. He did it—he made white horse.

—JAMES ELLROY

EASY MONEY

PROLOGUE

They took her alive because she refused to die. Maybe it made them love her even more. That she was always there, that she felt real.

But that's also what they didn't get, what would be their mistake. That she was alive, thinking, conscious. Plotting their demise.

One of her earbuds kept falling out. The sweat made it slippery. She wedged it in at an angle, thought it might stick, stay in place and continue playing music.

The iPod Nano bounced in her pocket. She hoped it was safe. No way she could drop it. It was her favorite possession and she didn't even want to think about the scratches it could get from the gravel on the road.

She groped with her hand. No worries: The pockets were deep enough; the iPod was secure.

She'd treated herself to the iPod as a birthday present and loaded it with as many songs as it could hold. It was the minimalist design, the brushed green metal, that'd tempted her to buy it. But now it meant something else to her, something more. It gave her peace. Every time she picked up the iPod, it reminded her of these moments of solitude. When the world didn't force itself on her. When she was left alone.

She was listening to Madonna. It was her way of forgetting, running to music and feeling the tension slip away. Burning fat at the same time was obviously a perfect combo.

She flowed with the rhythm. Almost ran to the beat of the music. Lifted her left arm a bit higher to check her time on her wristwatch. Every time she went jogging she'd try to break her own record. With the competitive obsession of an athlete, she checked her time, memorized it, and later wrote down the results. The route was a total of four miles. Her best time was thirty-three minutes. During the winter months, she trained only indoors at the gym. Weight machines, tread-mills, and StairMasters. During the summer months, she kept going to the gym but traded the treadmill for side roads and gravel paths.

She was heading toward Lilla Sjötullsbron, a bridge at the far edge of Djurgården, a park on the fringe of Stockholm's inner city. A chill rose from the water. It was eight o'clock and the spring evening was beginning to give way to dusk. The lights along the path hadn't yet been lit. The sun that shone on her back no longer gave any warmth. She was chasing her own long shadow and thought that soon it would completely disappear. But in a moment, when the path was lit up, her shadow would flicker and change direction in time with the lampposts she passed.

The trees were beginning to sprout crisp leaves. Closed buds of whitewood anemones pushed up through the grass beside the path. The banks of the channel were lined with old, dry reeds that'd sur-vived the winter. Flashy villas rose up to the left. The Turkish embassy with its barred windows. Farther up the hill was the Chinese embassy, surrounded by tall iron fencing, surveillance cameras, and warning signs. By the rowing club was a mansion with a yellow picket fence around it. Fifty or so yards farther up was a rectangular home with an outdoor pavilion and a garage that looked like it was built right into the bedrock.

Ritzy private houses with sheltered gardens spread out all along the running path. Every time she jogged, she'd check them out, massive hidden villas protected by bushes and fences. She wondered why they tried to appear unassuming when everyone knew only heavy hitters lived in Djurgården.

She passed two girls who kept a high pace. They sported that spe-cial Östermalm look for power walking in the Djurgården Park: down vests over long-sleeved shirts, yoga pants, and, above all, baseball caps pulled down low. Her own workout outfit was more serious: black Nike Clima-FIT windbreaker and tight running pants. Clothes that breathed. It sounded clichéd, but it worked.

Memories from that weekend three weeks ago came flashing back again. She tried to push them away and think about the music in-stead, or concentrate on running. If she focused on making good time around the channel and the Canada geese she had to veer for, maybe she could forget.

Madonna was singing in her ears.

There was horse shit on the path.

They thought they could use her any way they liked. But she was the one using them. That attitude protected her. She was the one who chose what she did and how she felt. To the world at large, they were successful, wealthy, powerful men. Their names appeared on the front pages of the daily business sections, on the stock market tickers, and in the highest income tax brackets. In reality, they were a bunch of pathetic, tragic losers. People who lacked something. People who obviously needed her.

Her future was staked out. She'd continue to play along in the charade until the time was right to stop and expose them. And if they didn't want to be exposed, they'd have to pay. She'd prepared herself, gathered information for months. Lured confessions out of them, hid recording devices under beds, even filmed some of them. Felt like a real FBI agent, except for one difference. Her fear was so much greater.

It was a high-stakes game. She knew the rules, and if things went wrong, it could be the end. But it would work. Her plan was to quit when she turned twenty-three. Leave Stockholm for something better, bigger. Cooler.

Two young girls, straight-backed, came riding over the first bridge by Djurgårdsbrunn Tavern. They still hadn't seen life with a capital *L*. The same way she'd been, before she left home. She straightened up, because that was still her goal. To ride with her head held high through Life. She'd make it.

A man stood with his dog by the bridge. Spoke into a cell phone while he followed her with his gaze. She was used to it, had been the center of attention since early puberty, and after a boob job at twenty, it'd been like an invasion of constant male staring. She got a kick out of it, but it grossed her out at the same time.

The man looked built. He was dressed in a leather jacket and jeans, with a round baseball cap on his head. But something was different about him. He didn't have that ordinary horndog look in his eyes. On the contrary, his senses seemed elevated, calculated, concentrated. As if it was her he was talking about on the phone.

The gravel ended. The road leading to the last bridge, Lilla Sjötullsbron, was paved but riddled with deep cracks. She considered running on the trail that was trudged up in the grass instead. But there were too many Canada geese there. Her enemies.

She could hardly make out the bridge anymore. Why weren't the lights coming on? Didn't they usually turn on automatically when it got dark? Apparently not tonight.

A van was parked with its back toward the bridge.

No people in sight.

Twenty yards farther up was a luxury villa with a waterfront view. She was familiar with the owner, who'd built the house without a building permit inside an old barn that'd already been on the property. A powerful man.

Before she could turn onto the bridge, she noted that the van was parked weirdly close to the gravel path, only a few feet from her as she turned right.

The van's doors swung open. Two men jumped out. She didn't have time to realize what was happening. A third man came running toward her from behind. Where'd he been a second ago? Was he the man with the dog who'd been watching her? The men from the van grabbed hold of her. Put something over her mouth. She tried to scream, scratch, strike. She gulped for air and became dizzy. There was something in the rag they were holding over her mouth. She threw her body around, yanked at their arms. It didn't help. They were too big. Built. Brutal.

The men pulled her into the van.

Her last thought was that she regretted ever having moved to Stockholm.

A shit city.

* * *

Case: B 4537-04
Tape 1237 A 0.0–B 9.2
Transcript

Case B 4537-04, *the People v. Jorge Salinas Barrio,* count 1. Direct examination of the defendant, Jorge Salinas Barrio.

District Court Judge: Would you please tell us in your own words what happened?

Defendant: There isn't a lot to say. I didn't really use the storage unit. My name was just on the lease as a favor to a friend. You know, sometimes you gotta give a bro a hand. Sure, I'd stored stuff there sometimes, but my name was really just on paper. The storage unit's not mine. That's pretty much all I got to say, actually.

District Court Judge: Okay, if that is all, you may proceed with your questions, Mr Prosecutor.

Prosecutor: When you say the "storage unit," you are referring to the storage facility at Shurgard Self-Storage near Kungens Kurva?

Defendant: Yeah, sure.

Prosecutor: And you're saying that you're not the one who uses it.

Defendant: Right. I signed the lease, and I did that to be nice to a buddy who can't rent property and stuff. He's got bad credit. I'd no idea there was so much shit in there.

Prosecutor: So, who does the storage unit belong to?

Defendant: I can't say.

Prosecutor: Then I would like to bring the Court's attention to page twenty-four of the preliminary investigation. It is a statement you, Jorge Salinas Barrio, gave after questioning by the police on April fourth of this year. I will read the fourth paragraph, where you say the following: "The storage unit is rented by a guy named Mrado, I think. He works for the big guys, if you know what I mean. I signed the lease, but it's really his." Did you or did you not say that?

Defendant: No, no. That's wrong. There must've been a misunderstanding. I never said that.

Prosecutor: But it says so right here. It says that the statement was read back to you and that you approved it. Why didn't you say something, if they misunderstood you?

Defendant: I mean, I was scared. It's hard to keep everything straight when you're being interrogated. There was a misunderstanding. The police were putting pressure on me.

I was freaked-out. Guess I said that so I wouldn't have to sit there and be interrogated anymore. I don't know any Mrado. I swear.

Prosecutor: Really. Well, Mrado told us, in a statement, that he knows who you are. And you just said that you didn't even know there was so much "shit" in the storage unit. What do you mean by "shit"?

Defendant: You know, drugs. The only thing I stored there was, like, ten grams of cocaine for my own use. I've been using for years. Other than that, I used the storage unit for furniture and clothes 'cause I move around a lot. The other stuff wasn't mine and I didn't know it was in there.

Prosecutor: So, whom do the narcotics belong to?

Defendant: I can't talk about that. You know, I might have to face reprisals. I think it could be the guy I usually buy drugs from who put the cocaine there. He's got the key to the storage unit. The scale's mine, though. I use it to measure out my fixes. For my own use. But I don't sell. I have a job; I don't need to deal.

Prosecutor: So, what line of work are you in?

Defendant: I'm a courier driver. Mostly weekends. It pays well. Under the table. You know.

Prosecutor: Let me see. If I've understood you correctly, you're saying that the storage unit does not belong to someone named Mrado, but to someone else. And this someone else is your dealer? But how did six and a half pounds of cocaine end up in there? That's a lot of cocaine. Do you know what that's worth on the street?

Defendant: I don't know exactly, since I don't sell stuff like that. But it's a lot. Maybe a million kronor. The guy I buy from puts the drugs in the storage unit himself after I pay him. That way, we avoid direct contact and being seen together. We think it's a good system. But now it seems like he's screwed me. Put all that shit in the storage unit so I'd take the hit.

Prosecutor: Let's go over this one more time. You're saying that the storage unit does not belong to someone named Mrado. It actually doesn't belong to you, either. And it doesn't belong to your dealer, either, but he uses it sometimes for transactions between the two of you. And now you believe that he's the one who stored all the cocaine there. Jorge, you actually want us to believe you? Why would your dealer want to store six and a half pounds of cocaine in a storage unit that you have access to? What's more, you keep changing your answers and you refuse to name names. You are not reliable.

Defendant: Come on. It's not that complicated, I just get a little confused. This is how it is: I hardly never use the storage unit. My dealer hardly never uses it. I don't know who all that cocaine belongs to. But it seems probable that it's my dealer's shit.

Prosecutor: And the baggies, whom do they belong to?

Defendant: They must be my dealer's.

Prosecutor: Well, what's his name?

Defendant: I can't say.

Prosecutor: Why do you keep insisting that the storage unit is not actually yours and that the narcotics in it are not yours? Everything points to that.

Defendant: I'd never be able to afford that. Anyway, I've already told you, I don't deal. What more do you want me to say? The drugs aren't mine.

Prosecutor: Other witnesses in this trial have named another person, too. Isn't it possible that the narcotics belong to a friend of Mrado whose name is Radovan? Radovan Kranjic.

Defendant: No, I don't think so. I have no idea who that is.

Prosecutor: Yes, I think you do. During the questioning by the police, you mentioned that you know who Mrado's boss is. Isn't it Radovan you mean?

Defendant: I already told you, I never talked about no Mrado, that shit's wrong, so how would I know what you're talking about? Huh? Can you answer that?

Prosecutor: I'm the one asking the questions here, not you. Who is Radovan?

Defendant: I already told you, I don't know.

Prosecutor: Try—

Defendant: For FUCK's sake, I don't know. You slow or somethin'?

Prosecutor: It seems like this is a sensitive subject. No more questions. Thank you. The defense may ask their questions now.

* * *

Case B 4537-04, *the People v. Jorge Salinas Barrio*, count 1. What follows is a questioning of the witness Mrado Slovovic in regard to the matter of narcotics in a storage unit by Kungens Kurva. The witness has been sworn in and reminded of his rights. This is the prosecution's witness.

Prosecutor: You have been mentioned in the preliminary investigation in connection with the accused, Jorge Salinas Barrio, as the person who rents a storage unit with Shurgard Self-Storage by Kungens Kurva in Skärholmen. What is your relationship to the defendant, Jorge Salinas Barrio?

Witness: I know Jorge, but I'm not renting any storage unit. We've been acquainted in the past. I used to be involved with drugs, too, but quit a couple of years ago. I run into Jorge now and then. Last time was in the Solna Mall. He told me he runs his drug operation through a storage unit across town now. He said he'd come up in the world and started selling a whole lotta cocaine.

Prosecutor: He says he doesn't know you.

Witness: That's wrong. We're not exactly friends. But we know each other.

Prosecutor: Okay. Do you remember when you saw him? Can you tell me more in detail what he said?

Witness: It was in the spring sometime. April, I think. I was in Solna, visiting some old friends. I'm not usually around there much otherwise. On the way home, I went into the mall to play the horses. I ran into Jorge in the bodega. He was well dressed and I almost didn't recognize him. You know, when we were buds, he was on his way down, straight shot to the shitter.

Prosecutor: And what did he say?

Witness: He said he was doing well. I asked him what he was up to. He said he'd done some good business with snow. He meant cocaine. Since I quit that stuff, I didn't want to hear any more. But he kept bragging. Told me he kept everything in a storage unit south of the city. In Skärholmen, I think he said it was. That's when I told him to stop talking 'cause I didn't want to hear about all the shit he was into. He got pissed at me. Told me to go to hell or something.

Prosecutor: So, he was angry?

Defendant: Yeah, he got pissed when I, like, thought he was talking smack. Maybe that's why he's made up some story about me being involved with that storage unit.

Prosecutor: Did he say anything else about the storage unit?

Defendant: No, he just said he kept his cocaine in it. And that it was in Skärholmen.

Prosecutor: Yes, thank you. I have no more questions. Thank you for your time.

PART I

1

Jorge Salinas Barrio learned the rules fast. The gist of *número uno:* Never pick a fight. He could count the long version on five fingers. Never talk back. Never stare back. Always stay seated. Never snitch. And finally: Always take it nicely up the ass—no whining. Figuratively.

Life shat on Jorge. Life blew horse cock. Life was tough. But Jorge was stronger than that—they'd see.

The joint stole his energy. Stole his laughter. Rap life remade as crap life. But what only he knew was that there was an end to it, an idea to realize, a way out. Jorge: homeboy you couldn't keep down. He was gonna get out, break out, escape from this shithole. He had a plan. And it was thick as cream. Whipped.

Losers—*adiós.*

One year, three months, and nine days in the slammer. Which is to say, more than fifteen months too long behind a twenty-three-foot concrete wall. Jorge's longest time yet. He'd only done short stints before. Three months for theft, four months for possession, speeding, and reckless driving. The difference this time: He had to create a life for himself on the inside.

Österåker was a close-security prison, a correctional facility of the second degree. Specialty: those condemned for drug-related crimes. Heavily guarded from both directions. No one and nothing got in that wasn't supposed to. Drug dogs sniffed through all visitors. Metal detectors sniffed through all pockets. COs sniffed out the general mood. Shady types needn't apply. They only let in mothers, children, and lawyers here.

And still they didn't succeed. The place used to be clean—during the previous warden's days. Now bags of weed were catapulted over the walls with slingshots. Dads got drawings from their daughters that were actually smeared with LSD. The shit was hidden above the inner roof in the common areas, where the dogs couldn't smell it, or was dug down in the lawn in the rec yard. Everyone and no one could be blamed.

A lot of people smoked up every day. Drank four gallons of water so it wouldn't show in the urine test. Others freebased heroine. Lay in their rooms and played sick for two days until the piss wouldn't come back positive.

People stayed for a long time at Österåker. Grouped off. The COs did their best to split up the gangs: the Original Gangsters, the Hells Angels, the Bandidos, the Yugoslavians, the Wolfpack Brotherhood, the Fittja Boys. You name it.

A lot of the screws were scared. Threw in the towel. Accepted the bills thrust at them in the chow line, on the soccer field, in the shop. The prison administration tried to be in the know. Break things up. Send members to other institutions. But what did it matter. The gangs were in all the prisons anyway. The lines of demarcation were clear: race, housing project, type of crime. The white supremacist gangs didn't measure up. The heavy hitters were the Hells Angels, the Bandidos, the Yugos, and the OG. Organized on the outside. Worked heavy shit. The operational description clear: Make thick cheddar through multicriminal work.

The same gangs controlled the city outside the walls. Nowadays tiny smuggled cell phones made it as easy as zapping channels with a remote. Society might as well surrender.

Jorge avoided them. After a while, he made friends anyway. Got by. Found mutual points of interest. Chileans connected. People from Sollentuna connected. Most blow connections connected.

He hung out with an old Latino from Märsta, Rolando. The guy came to Sweden from Santiago in 1984. Knew more about snow than a gaucho knows about horse shit—but wasn't totally chalked up himself. He had two years left for smuggling cocaine paste in shampoo bottles. Good guy to know. Jorge'd heard his name already when he was living in Sollentuna. Best of all: Rolando was connected with the OG guys. That opened doors. Gave privileges. Guaranteed golden gains. Access to cell phones, weed, blow if you were lucky, porno rags, pruno. More smokes.

Jorge was drawn to the gangs. But he also knew the danger. You tie yourself down. You make yourself vulnerable. You give them trust— *They* screw you.

He hadn't forgotten how he'd been burned. The Yugos'd sold him out. Wrapped him at the trial. He was doing time because of Radovan—cocksuckers' cocksucker.

They often sat in the chow hall and shot the shit. Him, Rolando, and the other Latinos. No Spanish. There was a risk that those who belonged to gangs be mistrusted by their own. Go ahead, talk to your countrymen and have a good time—but not so that *They* can't understand.

Today: a little over two weeks before he hit play on the plan. Had to be cool. It was impossible to escape *totalmente solo*, but he hadn't even told Rolando anything yet. First, Jorge had to know the guy could be trusted. Had to test him somehow. Check up on how strong their friendship really was.

Rolando: a homeboy who'd chosen the hard way. Good snow flow wasn't enough to become a member of the OG. You had to be able to kick the shit out of anyone your leader thought had an ugly mug. Rolando'd done his part: The tattoos around the scars on his knuckles told their own loud, aggressive story.

Rolando took a bite of rice. Talked broken Swedish with a mouth full of food: "Yo, paste even betta than powder. Like, it middle product, not finished. Get you in higher up. Don't have to deal with them boys on the street. Yeah? Do business with real gangstas, fo' real. Homeboys without heat on their ass all damn day. And, move easier. No fucking dust. Easier to hide."

Even if Jorge'd heard all of Rolando's half-baked ideas by now, the slammer offered a first-class education. Jorge, receptive. Had learned. Listened. Knew a lot already, before he went in. After fifteen months in Österåker, he knew the business inside and out.

J-boy: proud of himself. He knew all about the cocaine routes from Colombia via London. Where to score, what the price was, how to distribute, which middlemen to use, where to unload the shit. How to bulk it without the junkies knowing and how to cut it without the rich Stureplan set catching on. How to package it. Who to bribe, who to avoid, who to stay tight with. One of the latter: Radovan.

Fuck.

The chow hall was a good place for private talk. Enough noise so that no one could really hear what you were saying. What's more, it wasn't seen as hush-hush. No sneaking. Just chatting, openly.

Jorge had to steer the conversation in the right direction. Had to know Rolando's stance.

"We've talked about this a thousand times. I know you're into it. But I'm gonna stay away from the shit for a while. When I get outta here, I'm gettin' the hell outta this cold-ass Nazi country. And I got no plans of becoming some fuckin' flake myself."

"Winnin' points. Never use. Only sell. Wisdom of the day."

Carefully, he tested Rolando.

"You got good channels. Heavy hitters got your back, right? No one's gonna touch you here. Fuck, you could break today and make it easy."

"Break? Not my game plan right now, *hombre.* Speakin' of, yo you heard? Know that dude, OG guy, Jonas Nordbåge. Got done."

Jorge caught on. "I know who he is. Used to bang that centerfold chick, Hannah Graaf. The guy flew custody in Gothenburg, right?"

"S'right. Same day the sentence. Seven and a half years for two simple robberies and third-degree assault. Dude a real CIT pro."

"What the fuck man, he fucked it up."

"Still a king. Listen. *Muchacho* broke a window and lowered down from the eighth floor. Fifty-six long feet. Five torn blankets. Beautiful, ey?"

"Real pretty."

Jorge told himself, Keep going, Jorge-boy, keep going. Lead the discussion, read Rolando. Get him to say how he feels about me and breakouts. Subtly.

"How'd they get him?"

"Respect to 'im, but dude ain't real slick. Hung out at bars in Gothenburg. Partied. Guess he wanted to meet a new Hannah with fat tits. Felt like a baller. Only thing he did, dyed his hair white and wore shades. Like, homey wanna get locked up?"

Jorge silently agreed: totally *loco* to only dye your hair. Him, he was gonna play it safe. He said, "Had nothing to lose. Bet he thought, Fuck, even if they get me, I won't get more months. They won't add to seven and a half."

"Playa almost made it. Got him in Helsingborg."

"Pushing the exit?"

"'Parently. Checked into a hotel with a fake name. When the Five-Oh plucked him, playa had a fake passport. Coulda worked. First to Denmark, then on. Homeboy probably got a stash somewhere. But somebody snitched. Tipped the Five-Oh off where he be. Probably somebody saw him at the bars."

"Anyone in the OG know he was gonna fly?"

"Sorry, Jorge, can't talk about shit like that."

"But wouldn't you back an OG if he broke out?"

"Does Pamela Anderson sleep on her back?"

Bull's-eye. Jorge-boy, get closer. Test him.

Jorge knew how it was: Friends on the inside are not like friends on the outside. Other rules apply. Power hierarchies are clearer. Time inside counts. Number of times inside counts. Smokes count; roaches count more. Favors grant relationships. Your crime counts: rapists and pedophiles worth zero. Junkies and alkies way down. Assault and theft higher. Armed robbery and drug kingpins on top. Most of all: Your membership counts. Rolando, a friend according to the rules on the outside. According to the principles of the slammer: Playa batted in the major leagues, Jorge in the minor.

Jorge swallowed a gulp of his soda. "One thing to support someone already out. But would you help someone escape?"

"Depends. On risk and shit. Wouldn't help just anyone. Would always support an OG. Fuck, *amigo*, I'd help you, too. You know. Never I'd keep my mouth shut for some fucking skinhead or Wolfpack *puto*. They know it, too. They'd help me never, neither."

Jackpot.

Three-second silence.

Rolando did something Jorge had never seen him do before. He put his utensils down properly on his plate. Slowly.

Then he grinned and said, "Ey, Jorge, got plans or what?"

Jorge didn't know what to do. He just smiled back.

Hoped Rolando was a real friend, one who didn't betray.

At the same time he knew: Friends on the inside play by different rules.

2

Four guys sat in a living room, pumped to party.

JW with a backslick. And yes, he knew a lot of trash resented his hairstyle. Looked hatefully at him and called it a "jerkoff coif." But Communists like that were clueless, so why should he care.

The next guy had slicked-back hair, too. Boy number three sported a shorter style, every strand immaculately in place. A carefully chiseled side part cut through his hair like a ruler. The classic New England look. The last guy's hair was blond, medium length, and curly—a tousled charm.

The guys in the room were fine, fair kids. Creamy white. Clean features, straight backs, good posture. They knew they were sharp-looking boys. Boys in the know. They knew how to dress, how to carry themselves, how to act appropriately. They knew all the tricks. How to get attention. Girls. Access to the good things in life—24/7.

The general vibe in the room—electric: We know how to party; it's going no way but our way.

JW thought, This is a good night. The boyz are on top. Fit for fight.

As usual, they pregamed at Putte's, the guy with the side part. The apartment, an attractive one-bedroom on swanky Artillerigatan, had been a gift from Putte's parents on his twentieth birthday, the year before last. JW was familiar with the family. The father: a finance shark who brown-nosed his superiors and kicked down at anything and anyone beneath him. The mother: old money—the family practically owned half of Stockholm, in addition to hundreds of acres of farmland at a country estate in Sörmland. As one ought.

They'd finished eating. The Styrofoam containers were still on the kitchen counter. Takeout from Texas Smokehouse on Humlegårdsgatan: high-end Tex-Mex with quality meat.

Now they were drinking on the couches.

JW turned to the curly-haired boy, nicknamed Nippe, and asked, "Shouldn't we go soon?"

Nippe, whose real name was Niklas, looked at JW. Replied in his shrill pretty-boy voice, "We've reserved a table for midnight. We're in no hurry."

"Okay. Then we have time for another round of Jack and Coke."

"Yeah, well, when are we gonna taste the other coke?"

"Ha, ha. Clever. Nippe, relax. We'll have our hits when we get there. It'll last longer."

The baggie with four grams burned in the inner pocket of JW's jacket. The boyz usually took turns getting the weekend fix. The goods came from a darky, a *blatte*, who, in turn, bought from some Yugo gangster. JW didn't know who the top dog was but guessed. Maybe it was the infamous Radovan *himself*.

JW said, "Boys, I really went for it tonight. I brought four grams. That's at least half a gram for each of us and still enough to give the girls."

Fredrik, the other guy with slicked hair, took a sip of his drink. "Can you imagine how much that Turk must make on us and all our friends?"

"I'm sure he makes out fine." Nippe smiled. Pretended to count money.

JW asked, "What do you think his margins are? Two hundred per gram? Hundred and fifty?"

The conversation moved on to other, more familiar topics. JW knew them by heart. Mutual friends. Chicks. Moët & Chandon. Certain things were always a given. It's not like they couldn't talk about other things. They weren't idiots; they were verbally well-bred winners. But their interests didn't expand unnecessarily.

Finally, the talk landed on business ideas.

Fredrik said, "You know, you don't need that much money to start a company. A hundred thousand kronor's enough. I think that's the lowest capital stock. If we come up with a sweet idea, we can totally do it. Try to do some business, register a cool company name, appoint a board and a CEO. But, above all, buy stuff tax-free. How awesome would that be?"

JW amateur-analyzed Fredrik. The guy was completely uninterested in people, which, in a way, was a relief. He'd never even asked where JW came from or anything else about his background. Mostly, he talked about himself, luxury brands, or boats.

JW downed his Jack and Coke. Poured himself a strong G and T. "Sounds supersweet. Who'll get the hundred thousand kronor?"

Nippe interjected, "That's easy enough, right? I like the idea."

JW was quiet. He thought about where he could get a hundred thousand from and already knew the answer. Nowhere. But he didn't say anything. Played along. Grinned.

Nippe changed the music. Putte put his feet up on the coffee table and lit a Marlboro Light. Fredrik, who'd just bought a new Patek Philippe, played with the wristband and recited aloud to himself, "'You never actually own a Patek Philippe. You merely look after it for the next generation.'"

The latest hit gagaed from the stereo.

JW loved these pregames. The conversation. The mood. These were boys with class. Good-looking boys. Always well-dressed boys. He checked them out.

Button-down shirts from Paul Smith and Dior, and one specially made by a tailor on Jermyn Street in London. One from the brand A.P.C.—French—with an American collar and double cuffs. Two of the guys wore Acne jeans. Gucci on another: intricate designs on the back pockets. One wore black cotton slacks. The blazers were elegant. One from Balenciaga's spring collection: double-breasted, brown; a somewhat short model with double flaps in the back. One was a charcoal pinstripe from Dior, a slim model with double pockets on one side. One was ordered from a tailor on Savile Row in London: visible seams at the cuffs and with a red silk lining. The wool was super 150s, no higher quality anywhere. The telltale sign of a nice suit: the fluidity of the lining, that it didn't sag. This particular jacket's lining was softer, more fluid, and had a better fit than anything that could be found in the stores in Sweden.

One guy wasn't wearing a blazer. JW wondered why.

Finally, the shoes: Tod's, Marc Jacobs, Gucci loafers with the classic gold buckle, Prada's best-selling rubber shoes with the red logo on the bottom of the heel. Originally developed for Prada's sailboat in the World Cup.

On top of it all: slim black leather belts. Hugo Boss. Gucci. Louis Vuitton. Corneliani.

JW appreciated the total value: 72,300 kronor. Excluding watches, cuff links, and gold signet rings with family crests stamped into them. Not bad.

On the table: Jack Daniel's, vanilla vodka, some gin, a half a bottle of

Schweppes tonic water, Coca-Cola, and almost a full decanter of apple juice—someone had come up with the idea of making apple martinis but then only had one glass of it.

The general consensus: This is not where we get drunk. We'll get trashed at the club. A drinks table at Kharma was already reserved. Chicks were basically included.

JW thought, What atmosphere, what buildup, what wonderful camaraderie. These were chill guys. The Stockholm night was theirs to conquer.

He let his eyes scan the room. The ceiling was over ten feet high. Rich moldings. Two armchairs and a gray couch on top of a real Persian carpet. Four hundred thousand tiny knots tied by some shackled kid. A couple of *Maxims*, *GQs*, car and boat magazines were tossed on the couch. Against one wall stood three low bookshelves from the luxury design store Nordiska Galleriet. One was filled with CDs and DVDs. The second housed the stereo, a Pioneer—not big, but with good power in the four small speakers that were installed in the corners of the room.

The last bookshelf was filled with books, magazines, and binders. A bound catalog of the Swedish aristocracy was among the books, as was *Strindberg's Collected Works* and a bunch of high school yearbooks. *Strindberg's Collected* had to have been a present from Putte's parents.

The TV was wide, extremely flat, and disgustingly expensive.

Everyone wore their shoes inside—classic. The shoe question divided the Swedish indoor world. There are three types of people. The type who always walks in with shoes on and has the right attitude—is there anything worse than walking around in party attire and socks? The second type of person is the one who becomes insecure and checks out what everyone else is doing, who might keep them on if everyone else does. Wishy-washy, a turncoat. Finally, there's the third type, who thinks you should always take your shoes off, who walks around soundlessly in sweaty socks, who only has himself to blame.

JW hated people who walked around in only their socks. Even worse if there were holes in the socks. His suggestion for a solution was simple: a bullet to the back of the head. Seeing an errant toe grossed him out. So Sven-style. So coarse. A true sign of plebs. A recap of the rules of the sock world: Keep your shoes on, never wear tube socks, and make sure there's never any skin showing between pant and sock. The color should be black, or possibly fun socks in loud colors if matched with an otherwise-somber look.

To be safe, JW always wore kneesocks. Black. Always Burlington brand. His theory: Much easier to sort after washing if they're all the same.

The plan for the night was simple. Bottle service was always a sure win. They easily fulfilled the requirements to make a reservation. You had to booze for at least six thousand kronor.

Straight shot from there. Drink, snort, drink, check out chicks, maybe dance for a while, converse, flirt, unbutton more shirt buttons, order bubbles, definitely hit on girls, snort again. Fuck.

JW couldn't let the matter drop. Kept returning to it. The questions popped up in his head. How much can the dealer darky make? Does he have to work long hours? How dangerous is it? Who does he buy from? What are the margins? How does he get customers?

He said, "So, what do you think he makes a month?"

Fredrik, surprised: "Who?"

"The Turk. The *blatte* we buy C from. Is he a little Gekko, or what?"

Referring to *Wall Street* was standard among the boyz. JW'd seen the movie over ten times. Enjoyed every second of it: the simplicity of greed.

Nippe laughed. "Damn, you go on about money. What does it matter anyway? I'm sure he makes plenty, but, like, how cool do you think he is? Ever seen his clothes? Hick leather jacket. Thick Gypsy gold chain that he wears outside his shirt, baggy pants from an outlet or something. Huge cuffs on his shirts. I mean, he's a real tool."

JW let rip a belly laugh.

They dropped the subject.

Two minutes later, Putte's cell phone rang. He held the phone close to his ear as he talked, while grinning broadly at the boys. JW couldn't hear what he was saying.

Putte hung up. "Boys, I have a little surprise for us tonight. They're just looking for a place to park."

JW had no idea what he was talking about. The other guys leered knowingly.

Five minutes passed.

The doorbell rang.

Putte went to open the door. The other guys stayed put in the living room.

Nippe lowered the music.

A tall girl in a trench coat and a bodybuilder type in a black jean jacket entered the room.

Putte glowed, "Voilà, the evening's warm-up."

The girl went over to the stereo as if she were walking down a cat-walk. Self-assured and steady, almost gliding, in sky-high stilettos. She wasn't a day over twenty. Stick-straight brown hair. JW wondered, Is it a wig?

Changed the music. Raised the volume.

Kylie Minogue: "You'll never get to heaven if you're scared of get-ting high."

The girl dropped the trench coat. Underneath, she was wearing a black bra, a thong, and nylons with a garter belt.

She began to dance to the music. Provocatively. Invitingly.

She gyrated. Smiled at the boys as though she were doling out candy. She rolled her hips, played her tongue across her top lip, put one foot up on the edge of the coffee table. Leaned forward and stared into JW's eyes. He chortled. Yelled, "Damn what a fine bonus, Putte. She's better than the one we had before the summer."

The stripper moved in time to the music. Touched herself between her legs. The boys howled. She approached Putte, kissed him on the cheek, licked his ear. He tried to pinch her butt. She danced away from him with her hands on her back. Thrust her crotch back and forth rhythmically. Unclasped her bra and tossed it toward the bodybuilder, who stood motionless against the wall. The music kept pumping. She moved faster. Humped. Breasts bobbed. The boys sat as though in a trance.

She grabbed hold of her thong. Moved it back and forth. Put one leg up on the coffee table again. Leaned forward.

Little JW flexed.

The show went on for five more minutes.

It only got better and better.

Nippe joked when it was over: "I swear that was the loveliest thing I've seen since my confirmation."

Putte settled the bill in the hall. JW wondered what the damage was.

When the stripper and the guard'd left, they each had another drink and put on more music. Kept talking about the experience.

JW wanted to hit the town. "Come on, boys. We're walking, right?"

"No, let's fucking cab it!" Putte roared.

It was time to get going.

Putte called a taxi.

JW wondered how he would be able to afford the whole night with the boyz.

3

The gym: Serb hangout. Anabola-fixated. Bouncer farm. *Summa summarum:* Radovan-impregnated.

Mrado'd hung out at Fitness Club for four years.

He loved the place even though the machines were shitty. Made by Nordic Gym—an old brand. The walls weren't too clean. From Mrado's perspective: didn't matter. The free weights and the clientele mattered. The overall interior: ordinary gym kitsch. Plastic plants in two white buckets with fake dirt. A TV tuned to Eurosport screwed into the wall above two stationary bikes. Constant Eurotechno from the speakers. A poster of Arnold Schwarzenegger posing from 1992, another of Ove Rytter from the 1994 World Gym Championships. Two posters of Christel Hansson, the chick with a six-pack and silicone tits. Sexy? Not Mrado's style.

Niche: big guys. But not the biggest training freaks—those guys weren't made of the right stuff.

Niche: guys who care about their bodies, size, and muscle mass but who also realize that some things trump training. Work can take priority. Honor takes priority. The right stings have priority. Highest priority always—Mr. R.

Radovan was in on 33 percent of the gym. Brilliant business concept. Open 24/7, all year round. Mrado'd even seen guys roaring in front of the mirrors on New Year's Eve. Putting up big plates while the rest of the country watched fireworks and drank bubbly. Mrado was never there on nights like that. He had his business to run. His own standard times were between nine-thirty and eleven at night. The gym then: perfect.

The place was an asset in other ways. Recruitment base. Information magnet. Training camp. Mrado kept his eye on the meatheads.

The moment right after the workout in the locker room—one of the day's best for Mrado. Body still warm from the workout, hair wet. The steam from the showers. The smell of shower gel and spray-on deodorant. The ache in his muscles.

Relaxation.

He put on his shirt. Left it unbuttoned. They didn't make shirt collars wide enough for Mrado. The definition of a bull neck.

His workout for the day: focus on back, front of the thighs, and biceps. Worked a machine for his back. Slow pulling motions for the muscles in the small of his back. Important not to pull with your arms. Then back-ups. Training for the back, lower region. After that, thighs. Seven hundred and seventy pounds on the bar. He lay on his back and pushed upward. The angle between your lower leg and foot isn't supposed to change, they say. According to Mrado: crap they tell rookies—if you know what you're doing, you can stretch it out a little more. Maximum results. Concentration. Almost shat himself.

The last part: biceps. Muscle of all muscles. Mrado only used free weights.

Tomorrow: neck, triceps, and back of the thighs. Stomach: every day. It couldn't get too much.

He kept a log with daily notes from every workout session at the reception desk. Mrado's goals were clear. To go from 270 to 290 of pure muscle before February. Then change up his strategy. Shred. Burn fat. By summertime: only muscle. Clean, without surface fat. Would look damn good.

He trained at another place, too, the fighting club, Pancrease Gym. Once or twice a week. Guilt got to him. Should go more often. Important to build muscle power. But the power had to be used for something. Mrado's work tool: fear. He went far on size alone. In the end, he went even further on what he learned at Pancrease: to break bones.

He usually hung around for about twenty minutes in the locker room. Soaked up that special amity that exists between big guys at a gym. They see each other, nod in recognition, exchange a few words about the training schedge for the day. Become friends. Here also: a gathering of Radovan honchos.

Big boy talking points: BMW's latest 5 series. A shoot-out on the city's south side over the weekend. New triceps training exercises.

Two dudes were shoveling tuna fish from one-pound containers. A third sipped on a gray protein drink. Bit into a PowerBar. The idea:

to scarf as much protein as possible directly post-workout. Rebuild broken muscle cells into even bigger ones. An unknown face among the guys, a newbie.

Mrado was big. The new dude: gigantic.

He defied the regular ritual: Come a few times. Keep to yourself. Check out the scene. Show humility. Show respect. This guy, the giant, sat right smack in the middle. Seemed to think he was one of the guys. At least he'd kept his mouth shut so far.

Mrado put on his socks. Waited. Was always what he put on last. Wanted his feet to be completely dry.

"I've got a job this weekend, if anyone's interested."

"What is it?" Patrik asked. Swede. Ex-skinhead who'd left his own and been working for Mrado instead for a year now. His Nationalist tattoos were all over the place. Hard to distinguish. A green mess, mostly.

"Nothing too big. Just need a little help. The usual."

"How the hell're we supposed to work if we don't know what it is?"

"Relax, Patrik. Don't get so worked up you shit yourself. I said it's the regular."

"Sure, Mrado. I'm just fucking around. Sorry. But what's the deal?"

"I need some help collecting. You guys know my routes through town."

Ratko, a countryman, Mrado's friend and squire, raised an eyebrow. "Collecting? Something more than the usual? Aren't they paying up every weekend like they're supposed to?"

"Yeah, most of 'em. But not all. You know how it is. Might be some new bars who want us, too."

One of the few Arabs at the gym, Mahmud, was smearing wax in his hair. "Sorry, Mrado, I gotta work out. Do another session every night."

"You work out too much," Mrado replied. "You know what Ratko says. There are two things that'll give you blisters up the ass: being too small in the slammer, so you have to take cock, and always pressing at the gym 'til you shit your pants like a toddler."

Ratko laughed. "The job, will it take all night?"

"I think it might take a while. Ratko, you in? Patrik? Anyone else? I just need some backup. You know, just to make sure I don't look like I'm alone."

No one else offered.

The new giant opened his mouth, "Seeing how fucking tiny you are, you probably need an entire army of extras."

Silence in the locker room.

Two possible alternatives. The giant thought he was funny, trying to become one of the guys. Or the giant was challenging him. Seeking a confrontation.

Mrado stared straight out into nothing. Poker-faced. The music from up in the gym was clearly audible. Mrado: the man who could paralyze an entire bodybuilding club.

"You're a big guy. I'll give you that. But lay low."

"And why's that? Is joking not allowed in here, or what?"

"Just lay low."

Ratko tried to defuse the tension. "Hey, you, take it easy. Sure, you can joke around, but—"

The giant cut him off. "Fuck yourself. I'll say what I want, when I want."

The mood in the locker room like at a wake.

Same thought in everyone's head: The new giant is playing Russian roulette.

Same question on everyone's mind: Does he want to be carried out on a stretcher?

Mrado got up. Put his jacket on. "Hey, man, I think it's best you go upstairs and do what you came here to do."

Mrado walked out of the locker room. No problem. Nice and easy.

Twelve minutes later, in the upstairs gym area. The giant was standing in front of the mirror. A one-hundred-pound dumbbell in each hand. Swaying slightly and rhythmically. Veins like worms along his arms. Biceps as big as soccer balls. Arnold Schwarzenegger—you can hit the showers.

The guy grunted. Growled. Groaned.

Counted lifts. Six, seven . . .

It was eleven-thirty at night. The gym was practically empty.

Mrado was standing by the reception desk, writing down the day's workout in his notebook.

. . . eight, nine, ten . . .

Patrik came up. Talked to Mrado. Told him, "I'll call you on Friday about the job. I think I'm in. That work?"

"Thanks, Patrik. You're in. We can talk more when you call."

. . . eleven, twelve. Pause. Rest a minute. But don't let the muscles contract.

Mrado walked over to the giant. Stood next to him. Stared. Arms crossed.

The giant ignored him. Began the count over again.

One, two, three . . .

Mrado picked up a sixty-five-pound dumbbell. Did two lifts in time with the giant. Heavy on freshly worked biceps.

. . . four, five.

Dropped the dumbbell on the giant's foot.

He screamed like a stuck pig. Dropped his dumbbells. Grabbed his foot. Jumped on one leg. Eyes teared up.

Mrado thought, Poor, stupid oaf. You should've taken a step back and raised your guard instead.

Mrado swung with full force at the guy's other leg. Three hundred and thirty pounds hit the floor. Mrado over him. Unexpectedly quick. Careful to keep his back to the window. Pulled his gun. Smith & Wesson Sigma .38. It was small but, according to Mrado, functional: It could easily be worn under a blazer without being seen.

People outside couldn't see what was happening. To flash a live weapon—unusual for Mrado. Even more unusual at the gym.

The barrel pushed into the giant's mouth.

Mrado released the safety. "Listen up, kiddo. My name is Mrado Slovovic. This is our club. Never so much as set foot here again. If you have any foot left, that is."

The giant as passé as a reality TV celeb three months after the fact. Realized he'd lost face.

Maybe forever.

Maybe he was done for.

Mrado got up. Angled the gun down. Aimed at the giant. His back to the window. Important. The giant remained lying on the floor. Mrado stepped on his bad foot—265 pounds of Mrado on fresh-crushed toes.

The giant whimpered. Didn't dare wriggle away.

Mrado took note: Was that a tear he saw in the corner of the guy's eye?

He said, "Time to limp home, Tiny Tim."

Curtain.

4

———

Life dr*aaa*gged.

When you're locked up from eight every p.m. to seven every a.m., there's a lot of time to think in your cell. One year, three months, and, now, sixteen days on the inside. Escapeproof, they said. Forget that.

Jorge was walking on eggshells. Craved smokes. Slept like shit. Back and forth to the crapper. Drove the screws nuts. Had to unlock his cell every time.

Slow nights brought serious thoughts. Memories.

He thought about his sister, Paola. She was doing well in college. Had chosen a different kind of life. *Suedi*-style with security. He adored her. Prepared things to say to her when he was out, when he could see her for real. Not just stare at the photo he'd pinned up over his cot.

He thought about his mother.

He refused to think about Rodriguez.

He thought about different plans. He thought about the Plan. Most of all: He was working out more than anyone else.

Every day he ran twenty laps around the compound, along the inside of the walls. The total distance: five miles. Every other day: a session in the prison gym. Leg muscles were top priority. Front, back of thighs, and calves. He used the machines. Meticulously. Stretched like crazy after. People thought he'd lost it. The goal: 440 yards in less than fifty seconds, two miles in less than eleven minutes. Could work, now that he'd cut back on smokes.

The area was well groomed. The grass well cut. The bushes low. No tall trees—the risk was too obvious. Gravel paths around the buildings. Good to train on. Big open lawns. Two soccer goals. A small basketball court. A couple of outdoor bench presses. Could've been a nice college campus. What sabotaged the collegiate snapshot: a twenty-three-foot wall.

Running: Jorge's thing. His build was sinewy, like a guerrilla soldier's. Not yolked, no extra fat. Veins protruding on his forearms. A nurse in junior high once said he was every blood bank's dream. Jorge, young and stupid, told her to dream of someone else 'cause she was such a fucking dog. No checkup for him that time.

His hair was straight, dark brown, combed back. Eyes: light brown. Despite everything he'd been through in the asphalt jungle, there was an innocent look in his eye. Made it easier to sell snow when it came to that.

They slaved in the workshops during the weeks. Were allowed out twice a day: one hour for lunch and again between five o'clock and dinnertime at seven. After that: lockdown. Just you and your cell. They got more time on the weekends. Played ball. Hit the weights. The gangs shot the shit. Smoked, chatted, sneaked a roach when the COs weren't watching. Jorge worked out.

He'd started studying for his GED. It was appreciated by the prison administration. Gave him believable reasons to be by himself. He would sit with the cell door open and read between five o'clock and dinnertime every night. The show worked. The screws nodded approvingly. *Putos.*

The cell was small: sixty-five square feet painted light brown. The five-square-foot window had three steel bars across it to prevent escape. They were painted white, with nine inches between them. But the king, Ioan Ursut, had done it. Dieted for three months and smeared himself with butter. Jorge thought about what would've been the hardest to get through, the head or the shoulders.

Spartan decoration. A cot with a thin foam mattress, a desk with two shelves above it and a wooden chair, a closet and another shelf for storage. Nowhere to hide anything. A wooden strip intended for posters ran around the length of the room. No tape was allowed directly on the wall—there was a risk that drugs or other stuff could be hidden behind whatever was put up. Jorge'd tacked up the photo of his sister and one poster. A black-and-white classic: Che with a tangled beard and beret.

The screws searched the cell at least twice a week. Looked for drugs, pruno, or larger metal objects. Man, they were pissing in the wind. The place was crawling with weed, hooch, and Subutex pills.

The environment made him claustrophobic. Other days, he was riding high—thoughts of the escape were like a supertrip. At times, he acted like a fucking tweak fiend. Avoided everything and everyone. Dangerous/unnecessary. Just one tiny suspicion and his plan could be shot to hell—snitching fags sucked CO cock.

He thought about his background. Slyly racist teachers in Sollentuna. Welfare whities, pussy profs, cocky cops. All the right circumstances for a kid from the projects to make all the predictable mistakes. They didn't know shit about Life. Justice relegated to the rules of the streets. But Jorge never whined. Especially not now. Soon, he'd be out. He thought about trafficking blow. Collected ideas. Analyzed. Spun schemes. Learned from Rolando and the other guys.

Had strange dreams. Slept poorly. Tried to read. Jacked off. Listened to Eminem, the Latin Kings, and Santana. Thought about his training. Jacked off again.

Time cr*aaaaawled*.

Jorge waited. Anticipated. Contemplated. Fluctuated between rushes of joy and regret. Took himself more seriously than ever. Had never thought this much about any one thing in his entire life. It had to work.

Jorge had no one on the outside ready to take big risks. The consequence: He had to be his own fixer. But he didn't have to do everything.

Rolando'd never returned to their conversation about flight in the chow hall. The dude seemed trustworthy. If he was gonna sing, word should've spread by now. But Jorge had to test him more. Double-check that it was time to reveal parts of his plan. The fact was, he needed Rolando's help.

The first real problem: He needed to speak to certain people and he had to prepare stuff. Needed hours outside the prison. Österåker didn't grant regular parole anymore. But prisoners could get guarded parole if they had specific reasons. Jorge'd applied two months ago. Had to fill out form 426A. Specified "study and see family" as his reasons. Sounded okay. Anyway, it was true.

They approved of his studies. Liked that he didn't belong to a gang. He was perceived as orderly. Didn't mess around. Never high. Never cocky. Obedient without being a pussy.

They granted him one day, August 21, for studies and family relations. He even got permission to shop and see friends. First day on the outside since he'd been locked up. They made a schedule. Would be a hectic day. Fantastic. Maybe he'd pull the whole thing off; he had to do a good job. Not a chance that J-boy was gonna rot in Österåker for the rest of his life.

The one problem: This kind of parole always came with three screws.

D-day arrived: twelve hours of well-planned hysteria.

Jorge and the COs took the prison minivan into Stockholm at 9:00 a.m. Straight to the Stockholm Public Library.

Jorge'd joked with the COs on the ride in. "Am I going to see some Nazi or something?"

They didn't get it. "What do you mean?"

"A libr-ARIAN."

They howled.

Spirits were high in the minivan.

The day was off to a good start.

Fifty minutes later, they parked in the city.

On Odengatan.

Got out.

Walked up the stairs to the public library. Inside: the rotunda. Jorge dug the high ceiling. The COs eyed him. Was he into architecture, or what?

He asked to see Riitta Lundberg. The super librarian. He'd told her his story over the phone already: He was in a penitentiary, studying to get his GED at a distance. Needed a proper high school transcript to start a new life on the outside. Wah, wah. Now he was doing an independent study about the history of Österåker and the surrounding area in general. Was gonna study the cultural development of the place.

Riitta showed up. Looked like Jorge thought she would: Communist-academic in a knit sweater. A necklace that looked like a glazed pinecone. Straight from central casting.

The screws spread out in the rotunda. Sat by the exits. Kept an eye on him.

Jorge used his velvety voice. Toned down his ghetto accent. "Hi, are you Riitta Lundberg? I'm Jorge. We spoke on the phone earlier."

"Of course. You're the one writing about the cultural history of Österåker."

"Right. I think it's a really interesting area. It's been inhabited for thousands of years." Jorge'd done his homework. There were brochures at the prison. Certain books could be checked out from the prison library. He felt like the master of cheap tricks.

As long as the screws didn't hear.

She bought it. Had prepared what he needed after their phone conversation. A few books about the area. But, above all, maps and aerial photographs.

Sweet, sweet Riitta.

The screws checked that the windows in the reading room were high enough off the ground. Then they waited in the great hall, by the exits.

All clear. They were clocking *nada*.

Three hours of intellectual quibbling with maps and photos. Wasn't used to this kind of stuff. But he wasn't an idiot. Had checked the maps in the phone book and the map books in the prison library weeks before to learn how they were drawn. Regretted cutting geography class in school.

Spread the papers out in front of him. Asked to borrow a ruler. Went through them all, map by map. Aerial photo by aerial photo. Picked out the maps that showed the terrain and the roads best. Picked out the most detailed photos. Looked for nearby roads, the closest wooded areas, clear paths. Studied the guard towers he knew of, their placement and relation to one another. Checked out the connecting highway. Possible alternative routes. Learned the signs for marsh, hill, forest. Saw where the ground was okay. Visualized. Memorized. Measured. Marked. Mused.

What's the best way out?

The inside: two one-story main buildings with the inmate cells and a two-story building with workshops and the chow hall. Then there was an infirmary, a several-story building for the screws, a chow hall for the screws, and visitation areas. Between the first- and the last-named buildings was an additional wall.

The outside of the facility: around a hundred feet of clear-cut area, with the exception of a few bushes, brush, and smaller trees. Then miles and miles of forest. But there were small back roads.

He closed his eyes. Committed everything to memory. Studied the pictures and maps again. Went through the pile. Made sure he understood which lines indicated difference in height level. Which were roads. Which were watercourses. Checked the scales. Different for different maps. One inch was fifty feet, one inch was three hundred feet, and so on. Jorge: more meticulous than he'd ever thought he could be. Created an overview of the area.

Finally, he had three alternative spots for the escape and three for a waiting car. He made a copy of a map. Marked the spots on the map. Numbered them. Spots A, B, and C. Spots one, two, and three. Memorized them.

Double-checked everything.

Walked out.

The COs'd been bored. Jorge apologized. Had to stay on good terms with them today. They looked pleased that he was done.

Next stop, the most important of the day: Jorge's cousin, Sergio. Brother in arms from his time in Sollentuna. The key to the Plan.

Jorge plus screws stepped into the McDonald's by the public library. The burger smell brought back memories.

They were met by a broad grin.

"¡*Primo!* Good to see you, man."

Sergio: tricked out in a black tracksuit. Hairnet like some kinda cook. Dapped knuckles in greeting. Ghetto classic. Unnecessary of his cuz to roll in all gangsta in front of the screws.

They sat down. Chatted. Kept to Spanish. Sergio treated all four of them to burgers. Heavenly. The screws sat at another table. Ate like real pigs.

McDonald's seemed more modern since Jorge'd been there last. New interior. Chairs in light wood. The pictures of the burgers were sexed up. The chicks working the registers looked sexed up, too. More salads and greens. In Jorge's opinion: rabbit food. And still it was the sign of freedom. Sure, it sounded soft, cheesy, but McDonald's was special to J-boy. His favorite restaurant. A meeting spot. Ghetto base feed. Soon he'd be able to hang there whenever he wanted.

He felt stressed. Had to get to the point.

Briefly described his escape plan to Sergio. "Six different spots are marked on a map. The car should be parked at a spot marked with a number. On one of the spots marked with a letter, you're gonna do the rest of what I wrote in the instructions. I don't know what spots are best yet. I have to go back and think about it. I'll write you a letter telling you. I'll put the letter and the number of the spots in the third line from the bottom. A copy of the map and the instructions are folded inside page forty-five in a book called *Legal Philosophies*. The writer's name is Harris. At the public library, over there. You with me?" Jorge pointed.

Sergio: not the sharpest tool in the shed, but he understood this kinda shit. Jorge would be indebted to him forever, even though he had to take care of the planning himself. Sergio would do the best he could to deliver.

Jorge asked about his sister. The smell of McDonald's in combination with memories of Paola. Junk food equaled nostalgia.

The rest of their conversation was nonsense. They talked about their family, old friends from Sollentuna, and chicks. Put on a show for the screws.

It was time to roll.

Jorge kissed Sergio four times on each cheek when they parted ways. Exchanged Chilean pleasantries.

It was already four o'clock. At seven o'clock, he and the screws had to go back.

Next stop: He was gonna buy shoes. Had ordered catalogs. Read up. Called the stores. Researched the hell out of it. Gel, Air, Torsion, and the rest of the techniques for comfy kicks. God knows how much crap/fake technology there was. You had to see through the bull. Really buy good stuff. The two desired features: good running shoes—important; best shock resistance ability on the market—even more important. The screws thought it'd be fun to check out lame sporting goods stores. Jorge in the know. Stadium on Kungsgatan had the biggest inventory.

They drove the minivan into a parking garage on Norrlandsgatan. Jorge asked to drive the last short bit. The screws said no.

They got out of the car. One of the screws asked a guy who'd just parked if he had change for a twenty. Needed coins for the meter. The screw bought a parking pass.

They went out into the street.

Sweet feeling. Downtown. Kungsgatan. The pulse. August heat. Jorge remembered. He'd rolled down K-street in a BMW 530i, also known as a cocaine sled. That was two days before he'd been picked up. Sure, the car'd been on a long-term loan from a friend, but still. He'd been stylin'. Livin' life. Livin' cash. Livin' booty. Livin' his reputation.

And now: Jorge was back in town.

What'd he learned since then? At least he knew this: The next gig he did would be well planned. That's when he realized what made him different from so many others. He felt biggest/best/ballin'. But that's exactly what everybody else in his hood thought about themselves, too. The difference was that Jorge, deep inside, felt that maybe it wasn't so—and that was his strength. That would always make him think twice in the future. Always plan, prepare—make the impossible possible.

He kept dreaming.

Looked around. The screws were positioned around him.

The crowd was moving on the street. To the rhythm of free life. He stared. Hot *chicas*. He'd almost forgotten—the bitches were so much more *caliente* in the summer than in the winter. But they were the same chicks. How was that possible? A mystery.

And soon Jorge'd be out. Would roll down Kungsgatan. Grab a lot a boot*ay*. Fix all the chicks. Be Jorge again.

Joder, he longed to be out. He'd been given parole. Just that was superfly. Alone with three COs on Kungsgatan. What an opportunity. All you had to do was book it. He was fit. Strong. Knew the city like the back of his hand. He was a naughty, naughty little boy. On the other hand, the risk was too great. The screws were being nice today, but they knew their job. They were tense, hyperaware. Kept careful watch over him. Were in total control. Could lose it over nothing. Would have free rein. Cancel the parole. Make it impossible for him to complete his actual plan.

He wasn't prepared. Couldn't escape now. The fuckup risk was too big.

The salesclerk was hot. Jorge: horny. But the shoes were more important than pussy. They had the model he wanted. He already knew that. Asics 2080 DuoMax with gel in the heel. Still, he wandered around the store for a while. It was big. Him and his bros used to lift shit here when they were thirteen and Sollentuna grew too small for them. Again: flashbacks from his teenage years. First at McDonald's and now in the sports store. What the hell was going on?

He looked around the other departments for show. Bought a pair of track pants and a basketball jersey in addition to the shoes.

Five o'clock rolled around. Cool on time. Just one more thing. He was meeting a friend, a former screw from the prison, Walter Bjurfalk. The dude'd resigned of his own accord a year ago. The COs thought it was gonna be nice. Didn't think it was strange that Jorge and the ex-screw were meeting up. Some screws become friends with inmates; that's just how it goes. The surveillance COs had no idea why Walter'd really quit.

They were sitting in Galway's on Kungsgatan: Sven hangout. Swedeville. The place was decorated like a typical Irish pub. Signs on the wall: HIGHGATE & WALSALL BREWING CO LTD. Trying to be clever: IN GOD WE TRUST. ALL THE REST, CASH OR PLASTIC. It reeked of beer. Felt homey.

The screws sat down a few tables away and ordered coffee. Jorge ordered a seltzer, light on the bubbles. Beer wasn't allowed on guarded parole. Walter ordered a Guinness. It took ten minutes for the bartender to pour it.

They chatted. Memories from last summer, when there'd been mini riots at Österåker. How the guys who'd gated out were doing. How the ones who'd gone straight back in were doing. Finally, after a half an hour, Jorge lowered his voice, asked what he'd come here to ask.

"Walter, I've something serious to discuss with you."

Walter looked up from his beer. Looked intrigued. "Shoot."

"I'm gonna fly. No way I'm gonna rot three more years in prison. I've got an idea that might work. I trust you, Walter. You were always a good CO. I know why you asked to resign. We all know. You were good to us. You helped us. Would you help me now? I'll make it worth your while, *claro*."

Jorge was 99 percent about Walter. The last percent: Walter could double-game him. In that case, J-boy was a goner.

Walter leapt right in: "Breaking out of Österåker is hard. Only three guys've done it in the past ten years. Each one of them's been picked up within a year of the escape. 'Cause that's the hardest part, to lay low *after* the escape. Just see what happened to Tony Olsson and those other guys. Your plan's got to be damn solid. Or else you're fucked. You know, those guys were lying doggo under some bridge when the military forces plucked 'em. They didn't have a chance in hell. On the other hand, they were violent sons of bitches, so whatever. Fuck 'em. I'm not in that field anymore, so to speak, so I don't know if I can help you. But I'll give it a try for some jingle. Tell me what you need. I never snitch; you know that."

Jorge'd made up his mind. He was gonna put his chips on Walter.

"I need to know a couple of things from you. Five large if you can help."

"Like I said, I'll try."

Weird feeling. Sitting in a pub—with the screws only a few feet away—talking escape plans with an ex-screw. Had to strain his face. Control his body movements. Make sure you couldn't tell how stressed he was by looking at him. Jorge put his hands in his lap under the table. Crossed his legs. Picked at a napkin. Tore it to shreds. Tried to focus.

"Two questions. First, I want to know what routines the COs have to check on us when we're in the rec yard. Second, I need to know how fast the COs could pick up a chase if someone skipped over one of the walls, probably one on the south side, by D Block."

Walter sipped his beer. Got foam on his upper lip.

Started talking about what he'd done last summer. Uninteresting chatter.

Jorge looked at him. Walter was thinking, calculating, but he wanted his mouth to run in case the screws looked over.

Jorge glanced at them. The screws were talking. Chilling.

It was cool.

He calmed down.

Walter knew a lot. Went over it. Good info. Useful. For example: the placement of the guard towers, escape preparation plans, communications codes, established routines. Times for guard change, schedules for frisking, alarm systems. Plans A and B, where A was in case of an individual inmate's escape attempt, and B in the case of several inmates' escape attempts. Skipped C: plan in case of riot. Walter's knowledge was golden.

Jorge, eternally grateful. Promised to get Walter his five grand within a few weeks.

The screws waved.

Time to go back.

J-boy to himself: Rubber's rolled on and I'm ready to dip.

5

No one in the posh parts of Stockholm knew the following about Johan Westlund, alias JW, the brats' brattiest brat: He was an ordinary citizen, a loser, a tragic Sven. He was a bluff, a fake who was playing a high-stakes double game. He lived the high life with the boyz two to three nights a week and scraped by the rest of the time to make ends meet.

JW pretended to be an ultrabrat. Really he was the world's biggest penny-pinching pauper.

He ate pasta with ketchup five days a week, never went to the movies, jumped turnstiles, stole toilet paper from the university bathrooms, lifted food from the grocery store and Burlington socks from high-end department stores, cut his own hair, bought his designer clothes secondhand, and sneaked in for free at the gym when the receptionist wasn't looking. He rented a room from a certain Mrs. Reuterskiöld—well, Putte, Fredrik, Nippe, and the other guys did know about that. Being a boarder was the only thing about his real situation that he hadn't been able to hide. It was acccpted somehow.

JW became a pro at being cheap. He wore contacts only on the days he had to and used the one-month disposable kind much longer than recommended, until his eyes itched like hell. He always brought his own bags when he went grocery shopping to avoid the tiny bag fee, bought Euroshopper-brand food, poured budget vodka from Germany into Absolut bottles—miraculously, no one ever seemed to notice.

JW lived like a rat when no one was watching. Big-time.

He just barely earned enough to make it work. He got money courtesy of the welfare state: a student allowance, student loans, and housing assistance. But that didn't go far with his habits. He found salvation in a part-time job—as a gypsy cabbie.

Balancing the checkbook was hard. He easily dropped two thousand kronor on a night out with the boyz. With luck, he could pull in the same amount on a good night in the cab. His strengths as a driver: He was young, looked nice, and wasn't an immigrant. Everybody would brave a ride with JW.

The challenge of the game was becoming one of them, truly. He read etiquette books, learned the jargon, the rules, and the unwritten codes. Listened to the way they talked, the nasal sound of it, worked hard to eliminate his northern accent. He learned what slang to use and in which contexts, understood what clothes were *correct*, what ski resorts in the Alps were *in*, which vacation destinations in Sweden were *it*. The list wasn't long: Torekov, Falsterbo, Smådalarö, et cetera. He knew the trick was always to spend with class. Buy a Rolex watch, buy a pair of Tod's shoes, buy a Prada jacket, buy a Gucci folder in alligator skin for your lecture notes. He looked forward to the next step, buying a BMW cab in order to realize the last of the three *b*'s: backslick, beach tan, BMW.

JW was good; it worked. High society took him in. He counted. He was considered fun, hot, and generous. But he knew they still noticed something. There were gaps in his story; they weren't familiar with his parents, hadn't heard of the place he went to school. And it was hard to keep the lies straight. Sometimes they wondered if he'd really been on a spring break trip to Saint Moritz. No one who'd been there at the time remembered having seen him. Had he really lived in Paris, pretty close to the Marais? His French wasn't exactly super. They could feel it: Something was off, but they didn't know what. JW recognized what his challenges were: to create effective camouflage, to fit in and seem genuine to the core. To be accepted.

And why? He didn't even know the answer. Not because he didn't think about it—he knew he was driven by a desire for validation, to feel special. But he didn't get why he'd chosen this particular way of doing it, which was the easiest route to humiliation. If he was found out, he might as well leave the city. Sometimes he thought maybe that's exactly why he kept pushing it, because of some self-destructive desire to see how far he could take it. To be forced to deal with the shame of being found out. Deep down, he probably couldn't have cared less about Stockholm. He wasn't from there. Didn't feel as though the city had anything profound to offer—other than attention, parties, chicks, the glamorous life, and money. Superficialities. It could be any city, really. But right now, the capital was where it was at.

JW had a real story. He came from Robertsfors, a small town above

Umeå, in the rural north, and moved to Stockholm when he was a junior in high school. He took the train down without his parents, with only two suitcases and the address to his dad's cousin in hand. He stayed there three days, then found the room with Mrs. Reuterskiöld. Flung himself out into the world he now inhabited. Changed style, clothes, and haircut. Enrolled in Östra Real, a premier brat high school. Hung out with the right crowd. His mom and dad were worried at first, but there wasn't much they could do once he'd made up his mind. After a while they calmed down—they were happy if he was happy.

JW rarely thought about his parents. For long stretches of time, it was like they didn't even exist. His old man was a foreman at a lumber factory, pretty much as far from JW's life plan as you could get. His mom worked at a job-placement agency. She was so proud that he was going to college.

What he did think about, a lot, was the family's own tale. An unusual, unsolved tragedy. An incident that all of Robertsfors knew about but never mentioned.

JW's sister, Camilla, had been missing for four years and no one knew what'd happened to her. It took weeks before anyone even knew she was missing. Her apartment in Stockholm revealed no leads. Her phone conversations with Mom and Dad didn't give any clues, either. No one knew anything. Maybe it was just a mistake. Maybe she's grown tired of it all and moved abroad. Maybe she was a movie star in Bollywood, living it up. JW couldn't deal with home after it happened. His dad, Bengt, had buried himself in drink, self-pity, and silence. His mom, Margareta, had tried to keep it all together. Believed it was an accident. Thought it would help to get involved in the local Amnesty chapter, work longer hours, go to a therapist and talk about her nightmares, so that she, since she was reminded of them twice a week by the damn shrink, dreamed them over and over again. But JW knew what he believed: no fucking way Camilla would just up and leave somewhere without being in touch for four years. She was really gone. And deep down, everyone probably knew it.

It kept eating at him. Someone was responsible and hadn't paid the price.

The mood at home risked crushing him. He had to move. At the same time, he was forced to retrace his sister's footsteps. Camilla, who was three years older, had also left Robertsfors early, when she was seventeen. She wanted bigger things than to waste her life away behind some painted picket fence. Mom claimed that when they were little, Camilla and JW'd fought more than other kids. They had zero positive connection. But after she'd been in the city for two years, a relationship began to develop. He started getting texts, sometimes short phone calls, occasional e-mails. They reached a kind of understanding, that the two of them wanted the same thing. JW could see it now, they'd been a lot alike. Camilla in JW's imagination: the queen of Stureplan. The party's hottest *it* girl. Elevated. Well known. Exactly where he wanted to be.

The gypsy cab gig was easy. He borrowed a car from Abdulkarim Haij, an Arab he'd met at a bar over a year ago. He picked it up with a full tank and returned it with a full tank. The other city drivers accepted him—they knew he was driving for the Arab. The price was set ad hoc at each pickup. JW would write the info down on a pad: time of pickup, destination, price. Forty percent went straight to Abdulkarim.

The Arab would occasionally do tests. Like, one of his men would pretend to be a customer and take a ride with JW. Afterward, the Arab would compare what his controller'd paid with what JW wrote in his log. JW was honest. He didn't want to lose the extra cash he made on the job. It was his lifeline, his salvation in the race to score points with the boyz. JW only had one road rule. He didn't do any pickups at Stureplan. The risk of exposure was too evident on his own turf.

JW was driving off the books tonight. He picked the car up in Huddinge with Abdulkarim, a Ford Escort from 1994 that'd once been painted a pure white. The interior was crappy. There was no CD player and the seats were frayed. He smiled at the Arab's attempts to spruce it up—Abdul'd hung three Wunder-Baum air fresheners in the rearview mirror.

JW drove home. A cool August night—perfect for the taxi business. As usual, finding a parking spot in Ö-malm was tough. The SUVs hogged the streets. Driving by the latest beauty from Porsche made him drool: Cayman S. A 911 combined with a Boxter—hotness incarnate. He finally found a spot—the Ford wasn't exactly a big machine.

He went up to his room at Mrs. Reuterskiöld's. It was nine o'clock. No point in driving the cab before midnight. He settled down with his schoolbooks. Had a midterm in four days.

The apartment was located near Tessin Park. Lower Gärdet was okay for JW. Upper Gärdet wouldn't cut it—too far off the grid, too bitter. The room was 216 square feet, with a separate entrance, toilet, and a big window overlooking the park. Peaceful and calm, just like the old lady wanted it. The problem was that he had to be so damn quiet when he managed to get a girl home.

The room was furnished with a full bed, a red armchair, and a desk from IKEA, where he put his laptop. He'd swiped it from some oblivious sucker at school. Piece of cake. He'd waited till the owner went to the bathroom. Most people took their computers along with them, but others chanced it. JW'd seen the opportunity—just slid it into his shoulder bag and walked out.

The lamp from his childhood room was screwed into the desk. It still had glue marks from old cartoon stickers. Embarrassing, like whoa. Important to turn it off when he had a girl over—home game.

Clothes were strewn everywhere. There was one poster on the wall: Schumacher in a Formula 1 uniform, spraying champagne from the prize podium.

There really wasn't much to the room. Sparse. He preferred to go home with the chicks to their places instead—away game.

JW didn't mind studying. He liked writing his own papers instead of copying stuff off the Internet. He participated actively in class discussions when he was prepared. Always tried to make time to do the practice sets after. Tried his best to be ambitious.

He cracked the books. The Financial Analysis course had the hardest exam. He needed more time.

Turned the sets over in his mind, counted, fed numbers into the calculator. His thoughts returned to the discussion he'd had with the boyz the night before. How much did the *blatte* really make selling coke? How much did he pull in a month? What were his margins? Risk versus possible income. He should be able to calculate that.

JW went through the list of his life goals. One: to not reveal his double life. Two: to buy a car. Three: to become loaded. Finally: to find out what happened to Camilla. A step toward getting over it—if that was possible.

Principles of Corporate Finance—he got through seven pages. The difference between financing a company through stocks or through loans. How does the value of the company change? Preference shares, beta value, rates of return, obligations, et cetera. He took notes on a pad of paper and underlined in the textbook with a neon yellow highlighter. Almost fell asleep over the pages covered in graphs and equations.

When he nodded off for a second, he dropped his pen. That woke him. He thought, No point to keep going at this hour.

Time to drive home the money.

He was on his way to Medborgarplatsen, on the south side of the city. It was quarter past eleven. He was driving Sibyllegatan down to Strandvägen, past Berzelii Park. Dangerous area, way too close to the boyz' stomping grounds.

JW kept mulling over his thoughts. What did he really know about his sister's life in Stockholm anyway? The texts, calls, and e-mails he'd gotten were often without substance. Camilla'd had a part-time job at Café Ogo on Odengatan and gone to continuing-education classes at Komvux to get better high school grades in literary arts, math, and English. She'd had a boyfriend. JW didn't even know his name. He knew only one point of interest: The guy'd driven a yellow Ferrari. There were photos of Camilla in the car at home in Robertsfors. In them, she was glowing, smiling and waving through a rolled-down window. You couldn't make out the guy's face in the pictures. Who was he?

JW drove past the Foreign Ministry at Gustav Adolf's Square. There were a lot of people out and about. Everyone was back from vacation and wanted to make up for what they'd missed by vegging out at country houses and on sailboats. He drove through the tunnel at Slussen toward Medborgarplatsen.

He parked the car outside the Scandic Hotel and got out. Positioned himself outside Snaps. There was always someone there who needed a ride home or downtown.

Three chicks stumbled out. Possible good pickup. He cocked his head to the side, pulled an irresistible JW. "Hey, ladies. Need a ride?"

One of the girls, a blonde, looked at her friends. They knew what was up, nodded. She said, "Sure. How much to Stureplan?"

Damn it. Gotta play this. Coax, smile. He said, "There's so much traffic there. I know it sounds like a drag, but would it be okay if I drop you off by Norrmalmstorg?" Charm attack. Added, in a fake *blatte* accent, *"Special price for you only."*

Giggles. The blond girl said, "Only 'cause you're cute. But then you have to give us a good deal."

It was settled: 150 kronor.

JW drove toward Norrmalmstorg. The chicks chirped in the back. They were going to Kharma. It had been *so* nice at Caroline's. Amazing food, crazy atmosphere, sweet drinks. They were *soooooo* drunk. JW shut them out. Couldn't get interested in anything but driving tonight. He smiled, looked mysterious.

The girls babbled. Did he wanna come? JW felt the vibe, it would be so easy to score. But there was a major hurdle: These weren't the kind of girls he wanted to meet. Svens.

Before he dropped them off, he said, "Ladies, I have to ask you something."

They thought he was going to make a move.

"Have you ever met a girl out named Camilla Westlund? Tall, pretty, from the north. Like, four years ago?"

The babblebrauds looked like they were thinking, hard.

"I'm not too great with names, but none of us recognize Camilla Westlund," one said.

JW thought, Maybe they are too young. Maybe they weren't partying at the right places back then.

They got out by the bus stops at Norrmalmstorg. He gave the chicks his cell phone number. "Call whenever you need a ride."

Time for more driving.

He parked by Kungsträdgården Park. Couldn't stop thinking. It was the first time he'd asked anyone about Camilla. Why not, anyway? Maybe someone would remember.

Seven minutes passed before the next passenger was seated in the Ford.

It was a calm night. Everything went off smoothly. The clubbers were into it, wanted to get home. JW delivered.

Later. The night was a success; he'd made two thousand kronor so far. Mental arithmetic. That meant twelve hundred in his pocket.

He was waiting outside Kvarnen on Tjärhovsgatan. Mostly jailbait and soccer fans. The line was long, more orderly than the one outside Kharma. Lamer people than at Kharma. Cheaper than Kharma. No one was being let in just then—something'd happened inside. Two police vans were parked outside. Their flashing lights illuminated the walls. JW wanted to get out of there fast; it was needless to take risks with the car.

As he was walking back to the Ford, a familiar figure came toward him. One who walked with rhythm, dressed in a well-tailored suit with billowing pants. High hairline and short, curly hair. Without really being able to make out the figure's face, JW knew who it was: Abdulkarim. He had his big friend in tow, his very own gorilla: Fahdi.

JW looked at him, hoped nothing was up.

Abdulkarim said hi, opened the car door, and got into the passenger seat. The gorilla folded himself into the back.

JW jumped in behind the wheel. "Nice to see you out and about. Anything in particular you want to check?"

"No, no. No worry, man. Just drive us to Spy."

Spy Bar. Stureplan. What was he going to say?

JW started the car. Held off answering. Made a decision—he couldn't stir shit up with the Arab.

"Spy Bar it is."

"There a problem?"

"Absolutely not. It's all good. It's a pleasure to drive you, Abdul."

"Don't call me Abdul. It means 'slave' in Arabic."

"Okay, boss."

"Me, I know you donwanna drive to Stureplan, JW. Know you donwanna be seen there. Got fancy buddies there. You're ashamed, man. Never be ashamed."

The Arab fucker knew. How? Maybe not so strange, if you thought about it. Abdulkarim was out a lot. He'd seen JW with his friends around Stureplan. Connected the dots. Understood why he didn't tend to make pickups there. The rest was just simple math.

He had to do damage control.

"It's not that bad, Abdulkarim. Come on, it's no big deal. I just have to make some money. Want to be able to party and stuff. This isn't the kind of thing you tell everybody."

The Arab nodded. The Arab laughed. The Arab controlled the convo. Small talk.

Then it happened. The offer.

"Me? I know you need the big cheese. I got a suggestion. Pay atten-tion. Could be up your alley."

JW nodded. Wondered what was coming. Damn, did Abdulkarim like the sound of his own voice.

"I have some other business, other than the cabs. Sell C. I know, you've bought candy from me. Through Gurhan, you know, the Turk you and your buddies get it from. But Gurhan won't work. Big Jew. Tryin' to rip me off. Skims the top. Sells too high. Doesn't keep good books. And, worst thing, he buys from some other guy, too. Tryin' to be clever. Play us against each other. Pressure me. He says, 'If I can't get it for four hundred a gram I don't wanany this week.' Messy. No good. That's where you come in, JW."

JW was listening but didn't catch on. "Pardon me, but I don't think I'm following."

"I'm wondering, you wanna sell instead of Gurhan? You run this taxi thing real good. You hang at the right bars. Believe me, I know. Bars where people's drills are as full of sugar as sugar drills. You'd do good."

"What's a sugar drill?"

"Forget it. You in or what?"

"Shit, Abdul. I have to think about it. I was actually thinking about that the other day. Wondering how well the Turk makes out."

"Don't call me Abdul. And sure, go ahead. Think about it, big man. But remember, you could be like Uncle Scrooge. Swimming in it. You want in. I can feel it. Call before next Friday."

JW focused on the road. They drove down Birger Jarlsgatan. He was nervous. Kept a lookout for the boyz while trying to hunch as low in the seat as possible.

Abdulkarim rattled on in Arabic with the meathead in the back. Laughed. JW grinned without knowing why. Abdul grinned back, continued to jabber in Arabic to Fahdi. They were approaching their final destination.

Stureplan. Huge lines outside the nightclubs and bars: Kharma, Laroy, Sturecompagniet, Clara's, Köket, East, The Lab, and the rest. More people out than ever in the daytime. A gold mine for gypsy cabs.

JW stopped the car. Abdulkarim opened the door. "You know the deal. Before Friday."

JW nodded.

He stepped on it.

JW's last pickup of the night was a hammered middle-aged man who mumbled something about Kärrtorp. JW said he'd take him there for three hundred kronor.

He drove in silence. Needed to think. The man fell asleep.

The road was dark. Hardly any cars out except a few taxis. JW felt the anxiety of decision making wash over him.

On one hand: fantastic luck, a chance, a real opportunity. Probably nothing else offered the kinds of margins that coke did. How would it work? Buy a gram for five hundred, sell for one thousand? Calculate. The boyz alone could easily do four grams a night. He should be able to turn twenty thousand kronor. At least. He multiplied. Gains from one night: ten thousand. Holy shit.

On the other hand: mad dangerous, really fucking illegal, scary. One mistake and he could screw it all up, his whole life. Was it his kind of gig? It was one thing to use now and then. Dealing was a totally different ball game. Be a part of the drug industry, make money on other people's fried sinuses, their wrecked lives. Didn't feel right.

On the other hand: No one ruined their life on coke, as far as he knew. Mostly, it was better people who did it anyway. Like the boyz, for instance, who snorted to have a good time, not to escape some bottom-feeder existence. They studied, had money and good families. No problem for them. No risk of tweaky junkies. No risk JW had to suffer a bad conscience.

On the other hand: Abdulkarim and his crowd were probably not the nicest boys in town. Just take the backseat gorilla. Didn't take much to see that Fahdi was lethal. What would happen if JW couldn't pay, got in trouble? Messed up sales? Was robbed of merch? Maybe it was too dangerous.

On the other hand: the money. A sure way. An easy way. Learn from Gekko: "I don't throw darts at a board. I bet on sure things." The returns in this industry were guaranteed. JW had the need—and he wouldn't stay a tragic Sven. There'd be an end to the secondhand clothes, the home-cut hair, and the boarding. An end to being cheap. The dream of being able to live normally could come true. The dream of a car, an apartment, a fortune, could come true. He'd be included in the business plans the boyz had.

HE'D BE INCLUDED.

Successful C entrepreneur versus loser.

Crime versus safety.

What to do?

6

Saturday night in Stockholm: clubs, chicks, credit cards. Trashed seventeen-year-olds. Trashed twenty-five-year-olds. Trashed forty-three-year-olds. Trashed all ages.

Bouncers with leather jackets and cocky attitudes: denied, denied, denied. Some didn't get it—find your kind of place or be denied entrance. Don't try to get in where you don't belong.

Along Kungsgatan, the Svens caravanned. Along Birger Jarlsgatan, the brats were on parade. Business as usual.

Mrado, Patrik, and Ratko were going on a raid. They grabbed a beer at the blingy hub Sturehof before starting out. Tonight they were doing the south side, Södermalm.

Coat checks equaled gold mines. Calculation of a midtier place: Force everyone with some sort of jacket or other personal item to check it. Twenty kronor a head. Extra for bags. Four hundred people passing through on average. Sum: at least eight thousand kronor per night. Ninety percent off the books. All money in cash. Impossible for Big Brother Tax Collector to control the revenue. And the only cost was a pretty girl to stand there and run the show.

The scheme was advantageous: The Yugos collected a fixed rate of three thousand per weekend night. Nothing on weekdays. The place and the coat-check personnel had their own agreements about how the rest was distributed. Win-win: good business for everyone.

Strategy of the night: Mrado and Ratko stood in the background. Patrik fronted, did the talking.

It had to go off smoothly. If shit went down, Mrado would have to take the consequences. The fight for Radovan's favor was getting heated. Mrado was competing with the other men directly under R.: Goran, Nenad, Stefanovic. It'd been different under Jokso: Then they played like a team. Serbs together. Three types of coat checks in Stockholm: the ones Radovan controlled, the ones someone else controlled, like the Hells Angels or the club king Göran Boman, and finally, the ones that were independent. The latter: no good. Proceeded at their own risk.

They started at Tivoli on Hornsgatan. The place: Radovan-controlled. Patrik went up to the girl working the coat check. Mrado nodded. Recognized her. They went way back. He put his hand on Patrik's shoulder. "I got this. I know her."

Everything was cool. She was on ticket number 162. The night was young. He took a look in the cash box. Seemed straight. No funny stuff.

They moved on. The place across the street, Marie Laveau, was controlled by Göran Boman. His time would come one day, but they let it go for now.

They continued toward Slussen. The night was cool. Ratko talked about how he was gonna build his upper body. Chow on lean protein: tuna and chicken. Pop Dbols. Do double sessions at the gym. New ideas for how to plan his training.

Mrado looked at him. Ratko was built but needed many hours at the gym before he'd play in Mrado's league.

Patrik revealed that he'd eaten ice cream only twice in the past year. The single unhealthy thing he put into his body was beer.

Mrado got lost in thought. The guys were obsessed with the wrong stuff. He thought about Lovisa, his daugher. His ex, Annika, lived with her. Mrado had visitation rights, every other Wednesday night to Thursday night. It wasn't enough, but they were still the best days in the month. His schedule as a collector/dealer/hit man was perfect. Had the whole day free for museums, children's theaters, the latest Disney flicks. They ate pizza, watched movies, and read Serbian children's books. Mrado could honestly say to those around him, "I am a good father." Family court, Annika, society, everyone—they didn't think that a Serbian man could take care of kids. Bullshit.

He should retire. Get more visitation. Be more with Lovisa. Stop being hard-boiled.

They walked up to Götgatan. Checked spots off the list. Most were already controlled, but there were some wild cards. Patrik did good work. Stepped up. Mrado and Ratko stood in the background, clearly visible. Arms crossed. Patrik asked to speak to the person in charge of the coat check. Patrik explained the advantages. Patrik: in tight jeans, T-shirt, thin green military jacket, shaved skull covered in scars, tattoos protruding on his neck.

Be afraid.

"We make sure you don't have any trouble with mobs or gangs. You wouldn't want your coat-check cash robbed all the time, would you? Our insurance covers that kind of thing. We can help you get more paying customers. We have lots of good ideas about how to increase coat-check efficiency." Yada, Yada, Yada.

Most people bought the bull. Some'd been visited before. No problems. People didn't want to get the Yugos on their backs. Some refused. Patrik didn't make a scene. Just asked to come back later. They knew they were being fucked—smile and take it or have to take it from someone else.

They walked along Götgatan. Down to Medborgarplatsen. It was 1:00 a.m. A lot of places were starting to close. Down by Medborgarplatsen, Snaps, 5ifty4our, Kvarnen, Gröne Jägaren, Mondo, Göta Källare, and farther down, Metro and East 100, still open.

Snaps belonged to Göran Boman. Gröne Jägaren belonged to HA.

They went into Mondo, in Medborgarhuset. A youth center. Lots of people. Patrik did his thing. The place got the drift. Wanted to make a deal. Most restaurant and bar owners counted the coat-check revenue in their own balance sheets. Mrado thought the ex-skin did good. Over the year they'd been working together, Patrik'd toned down his hotheaded tendencies, picked up the right style: calm, assured, commanding respect.

They left at quarter past one. Gypsy cabs swarmed outside Medborgarplatsen.

On to one of the biggest bars and clubs on the south side: Kvarnen. An old boozehound and soccer hooligan hub. Place'd gone wild when Bajen, the area's team of choice, won the national championship in 2001. The old room had once been a beer hall. High ceilings. Columns, wooden tables, turn-of-the-century wood paneling. The new room was decorated in an aquatic theme. Aquariums and blue stylized water drops on the walls. The basement had a fire theme. Orange walls, no big tables, only bar stools and little tables screwed into the walls serving as parking spots for beers.

The line stretched all the way out to Götgatan. Nearly forty yards long. Pretty orderly. No drama at the door. Hipsters with complex hairstyles and accessories. Alternative types with tightly laced boots and Palestinian scarves. Popfuckers: dyed black hair with bangs. Bajen soccer fans: no frills.

Kvarnen drew quite a crowd.

Mrado, Patrik, and Ratko cut the line. People glared, pissed. But still—no protests. They got it. Unmistakably registered the aura of respect.

The bouncer said no. "No first-class boarding." This is the democratic south side. Jackass. Patrik kept cool. Explained that they just wanted to have a chat with the coat-check attendant. The bouncer was clueless. Refused to let them in. Mrado wondered who the loser was. Stared. Patrik tried again. Explained that they didn't want to cut the line, just had some business with the coat-check attendant. The bouncer turned his head. Saw Mrado. Seemed to get it. Let them in.

The coat check was run by the bouncers themselves. Unusual. Meant trouble.

The coat-check bouncers: three big guys. Their shirts bulged, the panels of their bulletproof vests visible beneath the fabric. Controlled the crowd with a rough attitude. Take no prisoners. Real southies. Wouldn't budge on the fee, didn't matter that tons of people only had thin jackets. Even the pretty girls had to pay. These boys worked for SWEA Security—a Sven company for real Sven boys.

The head bouncer, their front man, knew right away whom he was dealing with. Maybe he'd heard the outside discussion in his earpiece. "Hey, hey. Welcome to Kvarnen. Unfortunately, we're not interested in your business, but feel free to come in and have a drink."

Patrik, who'd already gotten fired up from the provocation at the door, was getting his edge back. "You in charge of the coat check here tonight? Why don't we go have a chat. I've got a proposition."

Mrado and Ratko stayed put in the background. Mrado, laser-focused. Tried to listen.

The bouncer said, "I'm in charge here. But I don't have time to talk right now. You either go in or out. Sorry."

"We weren't treated very well at the door. I want to talk to you now. You follow? Your other two guys'll be just fine here by themselves for ten minutes."

Attitude. The two other bouncers glanced over. Saw there was trouble. The front man said, "Excuse me. Perhaps I wasn't clear? We're not interested in your services. We play our own game. I don't want to be impolite, but you have to understand that we're fine. Without you."

Patrik's body language screamed, I want to take this fucker down.

His fists were balled, knuckles whitening. His tattoos seemed to spark.

Mrado stepped up, laid his hand on Patrik's shoulder. Calmed him. Turned to the front man, "Okay, we'll go in. We'll have a seat and wait for you. Come in when you have time to talk."

Shit was tense.

Mrado tugged at Patrik. Ratko did the same.

Patrik caved. Went in.

Anticlimax.

The bouncers won.

Mrado ordered beer. They sat down at a table.

The volume in the beer hall was on high.

Patrik leaned toward Mrado, "What the fuck was that? We can't tolerate that kind of shit. Why'd you pull me away?"

"Patrik, chill out. I'm with you. We'll talk to him, but not in front of all the guests. Not in front of the other bouncers. That'd be trouble. Listen. We'll sit here, relax. Maybe he'll come to us. Maybe not. But we don't forget, we wait, and when that cunt has to go to the bathroom or is on his way home or whatever, then we'll have a little chat with him. Tell him what's up."

Patrik calmed down. Looked more relaxed. Ratko cracked his knuckles.

They chilled. Mrado drank light beer. Checked out the chicks. Checked out the place. Checked out the bouncers on the sly. He was sitting so he could see straight into the coat check. But he didn't make any obvious eyes in that direction. Easy does it.

They talked about Ratko's upper body again. Went over different steroids. Mrado told a few Radovan secrets even though he shouldn't. Patrik told them how he'd shot a Magnum last weekend: the recoil, the pressure, the bullet holes.

Patrik got personal. Asked Mrado, "How many've you killed?"

Mrado, dead serious: "I was down in Yugoslavia in 1995. Draw your own conclusions."

"Right, but what about here in Sweden?"

"I don't talk about that. I do what needs to be done for business to run smoothly. That's one thing I can teach you, Patrik. Loyalty to R. and business is everything. Sometimes you just gotta roll with the punches. Can't sit and think about and regret the shit you've done. I'm not proud of everything."

Patrik pushed him, "Like what?"

"Learn one more thing: We do more than we talk. Sometimes you've got to do stuff that ain't pretty. What can I say? Like, for example, I've had to take care of friends who weren't reliable, or women, hookers, who messed around. That kind of thing, I wouldn't say it's what I'd put at the top of my résumé."

Patrik fell silent. Understood. There are some things you just don't discuss.

They jabbered on about other things.

An hour went by.

The general party mood in the beer hall was on the rise.

The bouncer guy was still standing in his spot. It was quarter past two. The place closed at four. They waited. The party people were shit-faced. Mrado drank a seltzer. Patrik ordered his sixth beer. Was getting really tanked. Ratko drank coffee. Patrik returned to their treatment at the door. Stoked the fire. The bouncer fags would be schooled. The bouncer fags would cry. Crawl. Beg. Groan. Concuss.

Mrado calmed him down. Glanced at the coat check. The bouncers couldn't have cared less about them. Were they stupid? Didn't they get who they were dealing with?

Another hour went by.

They waited. Jabbered on.

At one point, the head bouncer left his position.

Patrik drained his glass. Got up. Mrado saw he was okay, not too trashed. Mrado got up, right by Patrik. Face-to-face.

Patrik was wide-eyed. His breath reeked. Put a lighter in front of his mouth and the place would explode worse than a gas station.

Mrado took his face in his hands. The noise in the hall was deafening. He yelled, "You okay?"

Patrik nodded. Pointed toward the bathrooms. Probably had to piss after all that beer.

He walked in that direction.

Mrado sat back down. Ratko looked at him, leaned across the table. Asked, "Where he goin'?"

"Bathroom."

Like a bolt of lightning through Mrado's head. Fuck, how could he be so dense. The bouncer'd probably gone to the bathroom and Patrik was following him there—without Mrado or Ratko.

Mrado got up. Waved at Ratko. "Follow me. Now."

They hurried after Patrik.

Stepped into the bathroom.

White tiles and large metal sinks. One wall covered by a mirror. Five urinals on the opposite wall. Stalls farther in. Leaking toilets. Piss on the floor.

Contact.

The head bouncer was standing at one of the urinals. At the sinks, three guys were talking. Looked like losers: unbuttoned shirts over T-shirts. Farther in, two kids were queuing at the toilet stalls.

Patrik on his way to the guy.

The bouncer turned around, cock still in hand.

Patrik stood only inches away from him. "Remember me? You dissed me, straight out. Totally wrote off our services. You think I'd let that go unpunished?"

The bouncer understood. Mumbled something. Tried to calm Patrik down. The guy'd been around the block. Started fumbling for his earpiece with his free hand.

Patrik took another step, unclear if he'd registered that Mrado and Ratko'd followed him into the bathroom.

He head-butted the bouncer guy on the nose. The blood appeared even redder against the white tiles as it sprayed the wall. The bouncer yelled for his colleagues. Tried to shove Patrik aside. The bouncer, strong. Big. But Patrick, amped. The losers at the sink started hollering. The boys by the stalls ran forward to break it up. Mrado stepped between them. Pushed them away. Not exactly tough guys. Ratko positioned himself by the exit. Blocked. Patrik grabbed hold of the bouncer's short hair. Pounded his head against the urinal. Teeth went flying. Pounded again. More teeth. His nose broke in x number of places. The urinal looked like a butcher's sink. Patrik pounded the bouncer's head again. It sounded hollow. He let go. The bouncer guy collapsed on the floor. Unconscious. His face, unrecognizable. The losers by the sinks were crying. The kids by the toilet stalls were screaming.

Two bouncer colleagues rushed past Ratko. Patrik shoved one of them aside. Ratko got out of there. Mrado reached for one of the bouncer's knees. Grabbed hold. Did a lock. Twisted. The guy crumpled like a marionette with cut strings. Mrado grabbed the guy's foot in another lock. Twisted. Patrik ran amuck, yelled, swore. Mrado said in a measured voice, "Leave, Patrik. Now."

The ex-skin walked out. Mrado was the only one left. Saw Ratko and Patrik outside the bathroom. Twisted the foot in his grip a little more. The bloody bouncer under the urinal shook. The bouncer in Mrado's grip whimpered. One bouncer left standing. Hesitated. Looked like he was calculating the odds. Two bouncers on the floor. Immediate knockout. Left in the ring: him, alone, against a huge Yugo. And two more guys out there. Where was backup?

Tumult outside.

Quiet inside.

Mrado said, "Guys. You made a little mistake tonight. You messed with the wrong people. We'll be in touch regarding our business with you. One more thing, don't make a big deal outta this. I think you can figure out why."

Mrado released his grip and walked out of the bathroom. Three bouncers left in there. Like fools.

Mrado, Ratko, and Patrik pushed their way through the crowd. Outside Kvarnen, the cop cars' blue lights lit up the night. They jumped into a taxi. Patrik with blood on his jacket and T-shirt. Bad.

The place was crawling with cops.

7

It was almost time.

Jorge sat still in the chow hall. Concentrated. He didn't give a damn about the clatter, the crunching and munching. Today was the day.

Rolando called after him when he stood up. "Jorge, you gonna come blaze later?" Rolando was being ironic. The only one who knew.

Jorge said, "Don't holler like that. The screw over there can hear you."

Rolando grinned. "He don't know words like that. He just a small-town guy."

Jorge put his hand on Rolando's shoulder. "I'm gonna miss you, *hombre*."

Rolando looked serious. "Damn, Jorge, you doin' the right thing, you know it. Come on, wontcha tell old gangsta Rolando how you gonna do it? Who wanna be caged for the rest o' his life?"

"*Loco*, I can't tell you today. You'll see for yourself. Just watch and enjoy. As long as you do your thing." Jorge got up. He honestly felt like he would miss Rolando, his bullshit about cocaine paste, long lectures on the OG community and armored-car heists.

He'd tested Rolando several times. Revealed a few things to see what would happen. For example, that he exercised the way he did to prep an escape. If Rolando was gonna snitch, Jorge could've laughed it off as a joke. But it was cool. Rolando'd kept his mouth shut. No leaks. The Latino was trustworthy. Jorge'd made up his mind: Rolando would play an important part in the actual Plan. He would do his thing today.

But everything hinged on Sergio, who Jorge'd met on his jam roll. That he could fix what needed fixing on the outside. Thirty-odd yards beyond the walls: cleared land—would be hard to do anything that took too long without being spotted. If things worked out today, Jorge would be forever indebted to him. Jorge knew enough to fix this thing. The COs' routines. Where Sergio'd come from. Where the car would be parked. The best way to drive. The forks in the roads. Jorge knew he could run 440 in less than fifty seconds, two miles in less than eleven minutes. Knew people'd have to pick their jaws up off the ground. Jorge had the know. Jorge had the skill. He got this—without violence and without Sergio's ass too much on the line. Man, he was *el rey*.

After lunch they had an hour break from work. Everything ready to go. Now was the time. The plan was simple and genius. Jorge, surprisingly calm. If the shit hit the fan, so be it.

Jorge went back to his cell. Closed the door. Removed the Che Guevara poster from the wall. Unscrewed the wooden panel with his fingernails. It came off easily. He'd done it many times before.

Took out the rope that lay coiled like a thin snake in the space he'd carved into the concrete. The only place the screws didn't check when they searched the cell. A shallow but long hole. Perfect for a cable.

They thought that panel was smart. Jorge—the Salsa Breaker—was smarter. Honestly: He thought even his sister would be proud. No matter how college-educated she was, she could still recognize finesse when she saw it.

The rope: twined out of long strips of bedsheet. The ritual before turning his sheets into the laundry once a week: tearing off a strip, about half an inch wide. The dude who picked up the sheets was Colombian. Their deal: *Hombre* didn't say anything about Jorge's sheets looking funny in exchange for one pack of smokes a week.

The rope would hold. He'd tested every segment after every new foot he twisted into shape.

He walked out.

It was sunny outside. Sweet. Swedish summertime.

The rec yard was full of people. The screw on duty was playing soccer with the guys. Rolando was on the screw's opposing team. Beautiful.

Jorge checked the time.

Showtime in exactly thirty seconds.

Rolando glanced at him. After ten seconds, he made the sign they'd agreed on. Rolando braced himself. Ran toward the screw. Full-on slide tackle à la Vieira. The screw went flying. Screamed like a pig. Writhed in pain. Attention: zero.

Jorge ran to the wall. Got in position.

Waited.

Saw what he'd planned now for so long: The top of an aluminum ladder appeared above the wall, on the other side.

Sergio, the savior, had followed instructions. Driven as close as he could, parked the car at the edge of the woods, where the cleared land was at its narrowest. Ran the last yards, placed the ladder, leaning, against the outside of the wall at the point they'd agreed upon. At the right place. At the right time. At the right second. Incredible.

Jorge got out the rope. Had kept it coiled in his pocket. Clasped the hook onto the end. It'd been crafted out of one of the rings on the basketball hoops, which he'd paid a pretty sum to have removed. Bent it into shape with Rolando's help an hour ago.

Positioned himself opposite the top of the ladder. Looked up. He'd calculated this.

Felt the mass of the hook in his hand. Weighed it. This was the only part he hadn't been able to practice. Everything depended on his succeeding in hooking the rope onto the top of the ladder and pulling it over the wall, to his side.

He pitched it. The white rope arched in the sky. Settled over the rounded edge of the wall. Didn't connect with the top of the ladder. He pulled the rope to the side. Hoped to make the hook catch somewhere lower down on the ladder. Didn't feel any resistance. Shit. Tugged again. Nothing. No resistance. He pulled at the rope. The hook fell down on his side of the wall. Fucking cock. He ran to it. Picked it up again and got into position. The ladder remained on the other side of the wall; he could see the top of it plainly. The way out. He had to get it right this time. Pitched it again. Come on. The clank of metal. Had he gotten it? He pulled the rope. There. Resistance. The hook had caught onto something—it was the ladder. He made a test tug. It worked. Started to pull. Pulled harder. The ladder scraped. More than half was visible over the wall. He tugged. Even though it was aluminum, it was heavy. Finally: It fell down on his side. He heard yelling in the background. He turned around. Saw the screw get up.

Fumble for his walkie-talkie. Jorge moved quickly. Leaned the ladder up against the wall. Glanced over his shoulder. The screw was running toward him. Jorge climbed up as fast as he could. Good grip. Didn't weigh too much. Strong arms. Up at the top. Looked down, then back: more screws in action. He kicked the ladder aside. It fell into the grass. He heaved himself down, dangling on the outside of the wall. Let go. Jumped. Sixteen feet down. Rough landing. Asics 2080 DuoMax with gel in the heel—his foot still suffered the impact. *Mierda*.

He ran. Felt good to weigh 147 pounds today. The adrenaline pumped. The clearing like a mirage.

The map in his mind. His foot hurt. Sight set on point number two. Felt the sweat on his back. Heard himself pant. Heavily. Fuck, wasn't he in better shape? Relax. Lower your shoulders. Enter the zone. Think about your breathing.

Remember: guaranteed the best shape you've ever been in. Guaranteed the best shape of any of the inmates. Guaranteed the smartest slumdog. For real. Fuck the fucked-up foot.

Run.

Through the woods. Along the small gravel road.

Sergio should've peaced long ago.

His back, completely drenched. In the middle of his mad rush, a thought about his sweat. His smell now: sharp, strong, stressed.

Keep going down the gravel road.

Never slow down.

And there was the car. Sergio'd parked it exactly where they'd agreed. Point number two. Oh, you beautiful new world. Jorge heard the sirens in the distance. Jumped in. The key was in the ignition. He gunned it.

There was a God.

The sirens in the distance came closer.

8

The line could be seen all the way from Sturecompagniet. JW walked up Sturegatan with the boyz. They were pumped, amped, ready to roll. JW felt the energy like currents of electricity through his body—they were riding high.

Earlier that night, they'd eaten at Nox. Ordered fine wine with dinner. It'd been two weeks since the last time they'd gone out. The boyz' needs were making themselves known: Putte wanted to hook up, Fredrik to booze, Nippe to chase tail. JW was speeded; he wanted to test his new job, mark his territory.

Thirty grams of his own ice, on credit from the Arab, were packaged in ten mini zip baggies—Red Line brand. He had six grams in his pockets right now. The rest was stashed behind a radiator in Mrs. Reuterskiöld's foyer.

The boyz strutted down the street. JW kicked his feet widely with each step. Thought about the *Men in Black* sound track.

The line wasn't a line—it was an organism made up of human bodies. People screamed, waved, jammed, pushed, hurled, cried, flirted. The bouncers tried to keep things under wraps. Drove people like cattle into a number of lines behind the roped-off area. The line for you with Kharma Cards. The line for you with VIP Kharma Cards. The line for you with VIP VIP cards. The rest needn't bother. We're at capacity. Only regulars tonight. Don't you get it? We're AT CAPACITY.

Oversized ghetto kids threatened to beat them up. Banker boys pressed crumpled bills into their hands. Girls offered blow jobs. They were denied, one bouncer at a time. The air was thick with one word that no one said but everyone who wasn't ushered in through the velvet rope felt: *humiliation*.

It took five minutes just to push through the crowd and up to the bouncers. Some got the drift and let the boyz through. Others thought the world was a fair place, tried to keep them back. Sharpened their elbows and jabbed.

Nippe nodded to one of the bouncers.

The never-flagging confidence that JW was doing his utmost to copy worked its magic. They floated past the crowd. Humiliation was reserved for other people. The feeling: better than sex.

At the cash register, they were welcomed by a tall blond guy with clean features: Carl. The guy was 100 percent jet set. Hence his nickname: "Jet Set Carl." He and a partner owned the place. Kharma: premier hub of the *riches-royales*. Brat central. Backslick bay.

Nippe threw open his arms. "What's up, Calle? Things going well, as usual, I see. Incredible amount of people out tonight. Awesome."

"Yes, we're pleased. Af Drangler is running the club tonight, really sweet crowd. You guys have a table?"

"Of course, always."

"Great. We'll have to chat more later. Have a good night, boys." Jet Set Carl turned and walked in toward the venue.

For a brief moment, Nippe looked like he was fumbling. Cut off with his mouth full of brownnosing shit. JW thought, It worked, so who cares?

The girl at the register recognized Nippe. She waved them past without asking them to pay.

Inside, the place was half-empty.

Nippe and JW looked at each other. Laughed. They could hear the bouncers yelling outside: "We're at capacity. Only regulars with cards tonight."

An hour later, Nippe was on his knees in the bathroom, bent over the toilet seat, with paper napkins spread out on the floor.

Putte took the opportunity to sneak a Marlboro Light. Hummed along to the Eurotechno streaming in from the dance floor. "Why is this kind of music so popular at Kharma? Why not music with some more *song* to it, like R 'n' B or hip-hop. Or why not some honest-to-goodness pop, like Melody Club. But *no*, they basically just play really fucking boring, watered-down, mainstream, party Eurotechno. A load of crap."

JW sometimes tired of Putte's know-it-all attitude when it came to music. The guy had over eight thousand MP3s at home in his hard drive and was always complaining about other people's taste.

JW said, "Come on, do you have to whine? This place has amazing fuckin' pull tonight."

Nippe put a mirror down on the closed toilet seat lid. The place wasn't exactly spick-and-span. There were brown burn marks on the lid and the top of the toilet from people sneaking cigarettes and putting them down while doing other stuff. Such as cutting lines, the way the guys were doing now, talking on cell phones, pissing, being sucked off. If JW squinted, it looked as though there were raisins spread out on the lid.

JW pulled out a baggie and carefully poured out about one-third of the contents in three piles on the mirror.

Nippe looked surprised. "You bought again this week?"

"Sure. But from another guy."

"Okay. Better price than the towelhead?"

JW lied. "Not much, but nicer guy. I didn't like that *blatte*. Thought he was trouble. I brought a lot tonight. If you know anyone who wants any, let me know." He grinned, "Preferably ladies, of course."

Nippe shaped the powder into three lines. "This is so ill. I'm getting horny just looking at these lines. I'm gonna fucking beat my own record tonight. At least three girls."

JW looked at him. "Dude, no way. You're insane. I thought it was pretty good when you got blown by two girls in the same night."

"Sure, but tonight I'm *on it*. I can feel it in my cock. After this little dose of mirror magic, I'll be scoring a hat trick. At least three girls are gonna taste the pinecone."

"You're ridiculous, man. Where do you go? In here?" Putte stubbed his cigarette against the toilet. Another raisin.

"Yes, my love. Here, or the ladies' room. And now that it's almost summertime, Humlegården Park is prime real estate."

JW wanted to be like him, Nippe, Stureplan's uncrowned prince of BJs. With a profound self-assurance that always showed—no matter the situation, he radiated confidence. But sometimes JW wondered how deep it really ran. Like, did Nippe really think he was God's gift to women, or was he just such a damn good actor that he even convinced himself? Whichever it was, it made him someone with edge, the guy everyone talked about. Someone JW wanted to be. And still, he didn't want to be him—the guy could be such a tool.

Nippe pulled a bill out of his back pocket. Rolled it Hollywood-style, leaned over, and vacuumed the mirror.

JW and Putte followed suit.

The powder hit right away. White dynamite.

Life glowed.

He lost the boyz out on the dance floor. The music pounded. Bob Sinclair in autotune: "Love Generation." A smoke machine hummed in the corner. Strobe lights flashed. The world in movie snippets. Scene one: the chicks, top of the line. Cut: A chick swings her arm over her head. Cut: The same chick's cleavage is pressed up against JW's face.

Kharma was a class-A meat market—for the crème de la crème.

He got lit, hot. Felt like he was running on 98-octane gas. JW wanted to dance, touch, grope, hump. Most of all, he wanted to explode. He got an erection so rock-hard, a cat could've sharpened its claws on him.

He kicked ten times more than usual with his legs. Strutted.

The feeling was so crisp: He was the best, horniest, smartest. Coolest. They'd see.

Another girl came toward him. Kissed him on the cheek. Yelled in his ear, "Hey, JW! What's up? Did you guys have a good time the other weekend?"

JW pulled his head back. Clicked into focus. "Sophie. You look so pretty tonight. Are you here with the rest of the girls?"

"Yes, everyone except Louise. She's in Denmark. Come to our table and say hi."

They held hands. He was pulled along.

His gaze swept over the people at the table. Four insanely hot girls were seated in a row, dressed in tops that revealed more than they covered. The dominating colors: pink, purple, turquoise. All with push-up bras or boob jobs, tight blue jeans or short skirts.

Straighten up now, JW—fucking focus.

Nippe was already sitting at the table, had his arm around one of the girls. Buttering her up, joking, gazing deep into her eyes. JW thought, Which number was she in line? Damn it, could he have scored one *already*?

JW sat down. On the table was a "banker tray": an ice bucket with a handle of vodka and smaller bottles of Schweppes tonic, ginger ale, soda water. JW got one of the basic rules confirmed: You drink hard stuff or bubbles. No beer.

It was hard to talk over the music. Sophie poured him a vodka tonic. JW sipped, stirred, picked up an ice cube with his fingers and popped it in his mouth. Sucked on it, hard. Sophie looked at him and sipped her drink.

He went over Abdulkarim's advice silently to himself. Start by handing out freebies. Make friends by being generous, friends who like coke. Friends with cash or other friends with cash. Try to make sure people take as little as possible at the club—it's an unsafe environment. Go to after parties instead. Organize after parties. Deliver to B-list celebs at after parties. Use at home. Don't sell too-large quantities in the beginning—you don't want to create a secondhand market.

Nippe leaned over and started talking to Sophie. JW couldn't hear what they were saying. He dug the rush instead, unbuttoned another button on his shirt and gulped his drink. Felt how sharp his thoughts were—like a Mach3 razor blade.

JW had his own ideas. He wouldn't carry too much at a time. If he was picked up, he wanted to be able to claim it was for his own use. He hid the rest in smart places. When he sold out: home for more. No problem, Stureplan was close enough to Tessin Park. Even more important: keep his buds well heeled so they didn't question too much why he'd always be the one delivering from now on.

Sophie leaned over and brushed JW's ear with her lips. He shuddered.

She said straight out, "Nippe says you've got Charlie. Can I taste some?"

Silently, JW thanked Nippe. This was an opening. Play your cards right now. Don't make a big deal about it.

"Sure," he said. "I have some left over. Bring your friend Anna and we'll go to Humlegården."

They held hands again, pushed through the crowd. Past the golden boys, the silicone babes, the Yugo Mafia dudes, and the corporate schmucks.

The Eurodisco beats kept pumping.

They walked toward the exit. It was packed by the cash registers. Jet Set Carl was there, keeping watch over the cash flow. But his real, more important job was to hug, smile, introduce, make small talk, laugh, flirt. Jet Set Carl had control. Jet Set Carl had style. The money poured in. JW took note: He's a good contact for the future.

He walked up. Positioned himself with Sophie and her friend Anna on either side and extended his hand. Jet Set Carl raised his eyebrows. "And you are . . ." JW was prepared. Replied, "Nippe Creutz's friend, you know."

JW saw a flicker of recognition in his eyes. But maybe it wasn't genuine recognition. One of Jet Set Carl's most valuable skills was making people feel welcome and well treated, even though he didn't remember them or have any idea who they were. Some called it two-faced. JW called it business-minded.

JW pulled some quick, prepared one-liners. Followed by mutual laughter. Carl checked out JW's entourage: two hot chicks—he'd made the right move. He explained that they were only getting some air but would be coming back in. Carl nodded. JW fired off a couple more jokes. They connected. Good vibes. Jet Set Carl looked happy.

JW to himself: Nice work, JW.

They stepped out. It was 2:00 a.m. The line was gigantic, hysteric, chaotic. He made a deal with a bouncer that they'd be back soon. Humlegården Park stretched out in front of them, still dark green even though the sky was beginning to brighten. The sounds from the line could be heard *en baisse*. The girls were ready to go. They sat down on a park bench. Made some lame jokes. The air was cool; the sweat dried on their bodies. JW jabbered on, showered them with compliments, put in the highest charm gear possible. He played confidant, on their side. "Damn, you two look good tonight. Have you seen any sweet guys? Nippe's pretty hot, isn't he? I can set you up, Sophie." And so on, and so on. Sophie was brutally beautiful. He wanted her.

He knew them, but still not really. The girls belonged to the clique from Lundsberg, an elite boarding school. A school with the motto Knowledge, Tradition, Community. They all had the same first names as their parents and their parents before them. JW was used to most things from hanging with the boyz. Knew the jargon and the etiquette. He ought to have a chance.

Anna giggled. "Didn't you have something for us to taste?"

JW said, "Absolutely. I almost forgot." He hadn't wanted to be too pushy. Waited for them to ask.

He brought out an etui with a mirror, the flip kind. The baggie was ready in his jacket pocket. He poured out a pile and cut it with a razor blade—three thin lines. Presented the girls with a polished-steel snort straw. He glanced around, then handed over the straw.

"Help yourselves."

Fifteen minutes later, the girls went inside. The bouncer remembered them. Girls like Sophie and Anna would've gotten in no matter what—they glided through the line like Moses through the Red Sea.

JW stayed in the park, wanted more nose candy by himself.

Everything was going so damn well. The girls seemed pleased. High, bouncy, and filled with spontaneity. It was a good start. JW's first step into the C world. *C* as in cash.

It could only get better.

The sky was pale gray.

The glass-covered ramp connecting two sections of the Royal Library in the park seemed to glisten. JW usually studied there when he wasn't studying at home. He'd seen Sophie there many times. Had learned to recognize the click of her heels on the floor when she walked between different reading rooms, had checked out her girlfriends, seen which guys she said hi to. And after a time, it turned out that he actually already knew some of the people in her group. The circles were smaller than he'd thought.

He brought out the etui and held the straw in his hand.

That's when he saw it.

The motor sounded like a nuclear power plant as it blew past down Sturegatan, a tear through the Stockholm night.

A yellow Ferrari.

His first thought: The model looks the same as the one in Camilla's pictures.

His second thought: There can hardly be more than one car like that in all of Stockholm.

The memory of his sister washed over him.

He had to know.

Who owned that car?

EASY MONEY

* * *

DISTRICT COURT OF STOCKHOLM

SENTENCE

PARTIES

PROSECUTION
District Attorney Markus Sjöberg
Stockholm District Attorney's Office

PLAINTIFFS
1. Joakim Berggren, 740816-0939
   Vapengatan 5
   126 52 HÄGERSTEN
2. Daniel Lappalainen, 801205-2175
   Lundagatan 55
   117 27 STOCKHOLM

DEFENDANTS
1. Patrik Sjöquist, 760417-0351
   Rosenlundsgatan 28
   118 53 STOCKHOLM
2. Mrado Slovovic, 670203-9115
   Katarina Bangata 37
   116 39 STOCKHOLM

PUBLIC DEFENDER
Martin Thomasson, Esq.
Box 5467
112 31 STOCKHOLM

CRIMES COMMITTED
Aggravated Assault

PARAGRAPH
Subsection 3, Paragraph 6

SENTENCE
Prison, 3 years.

CHARGE ON APPEAL
Count 2 (Mrado Slovovic, regarding assault)

GROUNDS FOR THE DECISION

COUNT 1 (PATRIK SJÖQUIST, THIRD-DEGREE ASSAULT)

Evidence

The prosecutor has as *written evidence,* referred to a medical report regarding injuries incurred by Joakim Berggren. The report is in reference to, among other things, a fracture in the nasal bone, a crushing of the jawbone in two places, a fracture in the right cheekbone, torn skin in five places, bruises and swelling on cheeks and forehead, bruising around the right eye, swelling and tearing of the lips, four severed teeth in the upper front row, as well as bleeding in the brain, severe swelling of the brain, and brain contusion.

As *verbal evidence,* the prosecutor has referred to the statement of the witness Joakim Berggren, the statement of the witness Peter Hallén, security guard at restaurant Kvarnen, as well as the statement of the witness Christer Thräff, guest at the previously named restaurant at the time of the incident.

The plaintiff Joakim Berggren has, among other things, said the following: The three men, Patrik Sjöquist, Mrado Slovovic, and Ratko Markewitsch, came to restaurant Kvarnen at around 0120 on August 23 of this year. The security guard who was working the line at the door, Jimmy Andersson, informed Berggren through the internal communication system that the three men had acted in a hostile manner and had demanded to speak with the person in charge of the coat check. Jimmy Andersson chose to let them in. Berggren understood that the three men belonged to the so-called Coat Check Mob, a segment of Stockholm's organized-crime world that seeks to make money on different restaurants' and bars' coat-check business. He therefore informed them that Kvarnen was not interested. Despite this, he welcomed them into the restaurant. The three men acted aggressively. Among other things, Patrik Sjöquist said that

they refused to leave the venue if they were not permitted to speak to the person in charge of the coat check.
After approximately two minutes, the men entered the venue
without having spoken to anyone regarding the coat check.
Berggren continued to work the coat check and the door. At
around 0300, he went to the rest room to urinate. Patrik
Sjöquist entered the rest room. Shortly thereafter, the
other two men also came in. Berggren was standing at one
of the urinals. Patrik Sjöquist went up to him and head-
butted him across the nasal bone. He believes the nose was
broken. After that, Patrik Sjöquist grabbed hold of Berggren's hair and hit his head against the side of the urinal. Thereafter, Patrik Sjöquist pounded Berggren's head
against the edge of the urinal at least three times. He
remembers that Patrik Sjöquist yelled, "You fucking fag"
and "This is what happens to people like you." Shortly
thereafter, Berggren lost consciousness.

In response to the charges, the defendant Patrik Sjöquist
has made the following claims. He was threatened by Joakim Berggren, who said that "he would grind him to a pulp
if he ever set foot in Kvarnen again." The reason for
this was that Patrik Sjöquist had refused to check his
coat. He believes that is the reason that Joakim Berggren believes that he belongs to some so-called Coat Check
Mob. Later, he went to the bathroom to urinate. Inside the
bathroom, he was shoved in the chest by Joakim Berggren.
He tried to defend himself and there was a scuffle. He is
not able to remember exactly what happened, but he knows
that he received several punches and, in turn, hit Joakim Berggren. He is claiming self-defense against Joakim
Berggren's assault. However, he admits that he hit Joakim
Berggren in the face with at most three blows. The reason
for this is that he was protecting himself and acted in
self-defense. He does not believe that he pounded Joakim
Berggren's head on the urinal. He would not do something
like that. After that, the two other persons ran into the
bathroom. Sjöquist did not know that they were security

guards. One of them began to fight with Mrado Slovovic. Sjöquist does not know why. He was inebriated at the time.

DISTRICT COURT'S JUDGMENT

The security guard Peter Hallén has recounted, among other things, that he saw Patrik Sjöquist holding Joakim Berggren by the neck when he entered the bathroom. He also saw how Mrado Slovovic "wrestled" one of the other security guards, Daniel Lappalainen, to the floor and put his leg in a lock. The restaurant guest Christer Thräff has recounted how he heard Patrik Sjöquist yell to Joakim Berggren that he would "teach him a lesson," as well as that he saw how Patrik Sjöquist head-butted Joakim Berggren. The witnesses' testimonies appear to be reliable. The District Court further believes that Joakim Berggren's testimony is reliable. For example, he has described details regarding what Patrik Sjöquist yelled. His testimony is supported by the medical reports and by the testimonies of witnesses Peter Hallén and Christer Thräff.

Patrik Sjöquist sustained no reported injuries and also did not consult a doctor after the incident in question. The witness Christer Thräff has recounted that it was Patrik Sjöquist who, unprovoked, head-butted Joakim Berggren. This leads the District Court to believe that Patrik Sjöquist's testimony is unreliable.

In summation, the District Court finds Patrik Sjöquist guilty of assaulting Joakim Berggren, consistent with the prosecution's allegations. Patrik Sjöquist did not act in self-defense. The assault was of an unusually ruthless nature and shall be judged as aggravated assault, since it included repeated blows to the head, with severe injuries as a result. The charges are supported and will therefore be accepted. The crime shall be labeled aggravated assault.

Patrik Sjöquist has seven previous convictions on his criminal record. Most recently, he was convicted for assault by Nacka District Court and sentenced to four months in prison. His record also includes a previous conviction for assault as well as unlawful threats, hate crime, illegal possession of arms, illegal doping, and various traffic infractions. Based on medical records by court-appointed doctors, it is clear that Patrik Sjöquist lives in an orderly way. He is employed as a construction worker and spends a great deal of his free time on so-called body-building. He has a yearly income of around 200,000 kronor. There is no present need for surveillance. Patrik Sjöquist has agreed to community service.

Considering the severity of the crime and the aggravating factors discussed supra, no alternative sentence to imprisonment is available. The sentence shall therefore be set at three years in prison.

COUNT 2 (MRADO SLOVOVIC; ASSAULT)

Evidence

The prosecutor has, *as verbal evidence*, referred to the statements/questioning of the plaintiff, security guard Daniel Lappalainen, as well as to the questioning of the witness, security guard Peter Hallén.

Daniel Lappalainen has, among other things, recounted the following. He does not know if he was wearing his security guard's badge at the time of the incident. He understood that there was something "going on" in the men's bathroom. When he entered it, he saw Joakim Berggren lying on the floor. There was blood on the wall and on Joakim Berggren's face. There were a number of people in the bathroom. He yelled at everyone to stay in the bathroom. One man ran past him out the door. Another man, Mrado Slovovic, grabbed hold of his leg, so that he lost his balance. Mrado Slovovic then put his foot in a lock. It hurt a great deal. He thought that Mrado Slovovic would break off his foot. Then Mrado Slovovic told him that "Kvarnen would be visited again" and that "Joakim Berggren had messed with the wrong guys." After that, Mrado Slovovic and Patrick Sjöquist left the venue.

The security guard Peter Hallén's version of events is the same as under Count 1.

In response to the charges, the defendant, Mrado Slovovic, has made the following statement. The security guard Joakim Berggren had been very unpleasant to his friend Patrik Sjöquist earlier during the night. When Mrado Slovovic came into the men's bathroom, he saw that the situation was generally tumultuous and that a fight was going on between Joakim Berggren and Patrik Sjöquist. He was on his way to break up the scuffle when two men entered the bathroom. Mrado Slovovic did not realize that they were security guards. One of the men, Daniel Lappalainen, must have thought that Mrado Slovovic was involved in the fight, because he tried to "wrestle" him to the floor. At that point, Mrado Slovovic became very frightened. Mrado Slovovic succeeded in freeing himself from Daniel Lappalainen's grasp. He may have grabbed Daniel Lappalainen's foot in order to tear himself away, but it was not hard. Daniel Lappalainen was not wearing a security guard's badge and Mrado did not realize that he was a security guard.

DISTRICT COURT'S JUDGMENT

Daniel Lappalainen and Mrado Slovovic's versions of events differ when it comes to who attacked whom and whether or not Mrado Slovovic injured Daniel Lappalainen's foot in self-defense. Both have given believable accounts. Daniel Lappalainen's version is supported by the security guard Peter Hallén's testimony regarding the fact that it was Mrado Slovovic who "wrestled" Daniel Lappalainen to the ground. Mrado Slovovic's version is supported by Patrik Sjöquist's account that it was the security guard who began to fight with Mrado Slovovic.

According to Swedish law, the defendant's claims shall form the basis of the Court's judgment unless they are refuted by the prosecutor. In instant case, this is a situation of one man's word against another's, and both versions have certain support in the observations of others.

It should also be noted that there is no medical record that supports the claim that Daniel Lappalainen's leg was injured. However, it shall be regarded as irrefutable that the general conditions in the bathroom at Kvarnen were tumultuous. A scuffle had arisen in this situation, and it is possible that it was unclear who attacked whom. It will be considered confirmed that Mrado Slovovic entered the bathroom at a later point than Patrik Sjöquist and therefore may have interpreted the situation differently. Even if Mrado Slovovic did, in fact, injure Daniel Lappalainen's leg in the alleged way, this may have been defensible if Mrado Slovovic did indeed perceive that he was attacked and therefore acted in so-called putative self-defense; in other words, he believed he was in danger of becoming the victim of a criminal act. It is also not clear whether or not Daniel Lappalainen was wearing his security guard's badge. Mrado Slovovic's claim that he did not realize that Daniel Lappalainen was a security guard should therefore be given due consideration. In conclusion, the District Court finds that the prosecution was unable to prove the alleged act. The charges will therefore be dropped.

TO APPEAL, see attached information (DV 400).
An appeal should be made to Svea Court of Appeals and be submitted to the District Court no later than three weeks from today.

On behalf of the District Court
Tor Hjalmarsson

9

Mrado in the serene suburb—like a penguin in the jungle. Didn't fit in. Wrong habitat. Wrong climate. Wrong size. Attracted stares. A relief that Radovan invited him over to his house relatively seldom.

He couldn't find a parking spot. The risk of not making it on time was increasing. He drove in circles. Kept his eyes peeled. Maybe someone was on their way to their car to drive off. Improvised with streets. Like a rookie. No structure. No success.

He was busy worrying about other stuff.

No open legal spot to park his Mercedes SL 500. Finally, he parked the car too close to a pedestrian crossing. Ticket bait. Whatever. It was leased. Parking tickets would go to the leasing company.

Mrado walked up to Radovan's house.

The house: a long one-story, almost four thousand square feet. White walls and a flat roof with black panels. Door and window frames in dark wood. Well-groomed garden during the summer. Fuchsias, perennials, rhododendrons. Now on their way to the inevitable fall brown. The property was surrounded by a wooden fence about five feet tall. Roses grew along the inner periphery. It looked peaceful, boring, and harmless from the outside. Mrado knew that it was heavily guarded from the inside.

"*Dobre dosao*, come on in, Mrado."

Stefanovic, Rado's jack-of-all-trades, opened the door. Led Mrado through the house.

Radovan was seated in a leather armchair in the library. Dapper as always. Dark blue blazer. Light-colored corduroys. Well coiffed. The furrows/scars on his face spelled out the word *respect*.

Dark wallpaper. Tall as well as short bookcases along the walls. On the walls, above the shelves: framed maps, paintings, and religious icons. Europe and the Balkans. Lovely Donau. The Battle of Kosovo Polje. The Federal Republic of Yugoslavia. History's heroes. Portraits of Karayoryc. The Holy Sava. Most of all—maps of Serbia-Montenegro.

Stefanovic left them alone.

Radovan, in Serbian: "Welcome."

"The pleasure is all mine. We don't see each other that often." Mrado remained standing.

"Have a seat, for Christ's sake. No, we don't see each other that often. I guess that's for the best. But we talk on the phone."

"Of course. As often as you like."

"Mrado, let's skip the pleasantries. You know me—I express myself plainly. No frills. That doesn't mean it's personal. I think you know how I feel about what happened at Kvarnen."

"I think I do."

"A total clusterfuck. Shit like that just can't happen. I trust you, and you've made a fool of yourself. Now the whole situation's hysterical. Do you understand what the hell you've done? The blowback could be war."

"I'm incredibly sorry, Rado. I misjudged the situation. I take full responsibility for what happened."

In Mrado's head: The whole shit show was really Patrik's fault. But there's no point in blaming others. If you're in charge, you're responsible.

Radovan said, "Well, you fuckin' better. Anything else would be crazy. You know our situation. That skinhead you used, Patrik, was convicted of aggravated assault. He can't call or write when he wants. No information goes in or out. We don't know shit about what he's saying about us in there. You can't trust just anyone. For your sake, you better hope the fucker's no canary. For our sake, too."

"I think it's cool."

"You've done good all these years. And now this? Why didn't you stop that unprofessional skin faggot? The police can crack that guy easier than an egg in a frying pan. What's more? Hells Angels, Bandidos, Boman, or someone else can flip their shit. The relations between the factions in this city are tense enough as is. Things can't get worse."

Mrado was usually Mr. Hard Ass. But Rado was the kind of man that people, even the Yugo Mafia, lowered their voices around and avoided eye contact with. Mrado felt the worry grow in the pit of his stomach. Radovan was really angry. Pulsating thought: Can't fuck up my relationship with Radovan. Repeat: Can't fuck up my relationship with Radovan.

On the other hand, Mrado more than pulled his weight. Worked the coat checks, racketeering, and more. Remembered the time under Dragan Joksovic, when he and Rado'd been equals. Colleagues in Jokso's monopoly of violence. Now Radovan was sitting there saying that he'd "done good all these years." What bullshit. Radovan was the one who'd done good under Jokso. It was repulsive: Radovan was playing God.

What's more: Mrado's cut these days wasn't big enough. Rado let him in on too little. Most important, too little of the profits. As if they didn't have a past. As if R.'d always been at the top of the ladder.

But now he had to grovel pretty. Think constructively. Come up with solutions. Subtle mood fixers.

"Rado, Patrik's good. On my honor. Yeah, he's a hothead, still too impulsive, but he's no rat. He's cool. He knows the rules. I'm not worried about that."

"That's good news. But we could be in shit up to our knees all the same. Patrik's dumb. The guy needs Google Maps to find his own dick. There're a couple possible scenarios. The first is that the pigs press the skinhead till he serves our asses on a plate. Then they're gonna start the world's biggest fucking investigation, cops swarming every bar we've got stakes in. Maybe we'll have to shut down a whole lot of our businesses, pull out. Another scenario is that HA, Göran Boman, or someone else flips 'cause the strategy we've been pushing on the coat-check front's too heavy on the artillery. We don't want to make the situation any worse than it is, Mrado, and you, of all people, know that. Four of our guys went down in the last round. And let's not even get into what happened to you. I know war. All of me's a fucking war. You know the balance—after Jokso, no one's allowed to be king. Between us, Mrado, they can forget about it. But this is no time to rock the boat."

"A good analysis, Rado. As always. Allow me to offer some additional ideas. Want to hear them?"

"Absolutely. That's also why we're getting together now. What're you thinking?"

"Patrik knows the drill. Knows our code. Rats catch cold. Only a couple days ago, he saw what happened to a dude at the gym who was acting up. And that was no little guy, either. The skinhead gets it. If he snitches, he won't live long enough to make it to the joint's unguarded urinals and back. Trust me, I know a lot of people who've been taken down in the Tidaholm pen. But that won't happen, him snitching."

Mrado'd been thinking. Loaded up on ideas. Helicopter perspective. Big-picture perspective. Future perspective. Possibility. Expansion flexibility. Radovan wanted to be king. He had potential. At the same time—Mrado wanted to bring up his cut of the coat-check business.

"We can't lose the coat checks. Since we put it in high gear last year, that business has yielded around three hundred thousand per month in the winter season and just under one hundred fifty thousand per month in the summer. We've got about twenty places. The more places we can control, the more people'll get used to paying a fee. Finally, every little shit pub in this city'll be able to charge people something to check their stuff. The crux is what we do with the gold. The coat checks are perfect. We operate cash only. Big Brother doesn't have a chance in hell to calculate our revenue. All salaries are under the table. The places themselves don't declare a cent anyway."

Radovan smiled. He loved cash talk. Squinted. Brought out paper and pen. Calculator. He already knew the numbers. He already knew the advantages. He already knew the money had to be laundered. But Mrado knew that Radovan liked to hear what Radovan already knew.

"It works well, Mrado. I agree, we've got laundry issues right now. We need to get rid of the money somewhere. Clara's and Diamond can't swallow the kind of sums the coat-check business brings in. We need more companies. In a way, it's a luxury problem. Sign that business is booming."

Mrado replied, "Video-rental stores would work, I think. Big Brother can never find out how many movies we actually rent out. We'll inflate the returns as much as we want. I can do it. I've done it before. If it gets messy after all and the state starts getting suspicious, someone else's head'll fall. A straw man."

"Right on. Who?"

"Someone with no folding history. Not a total tool, but someone who doesn't have a lot to lose, either. I'll get on it. But the fall guy doesn't really protect if Big Bro wants the laundry money back. Mostly protects against bankruptcy if we get hit with fat tax debt or something. But you don't want to get your name dirty with suspicious bankruptcies that'll nix your trade license. This'll be perfect."

"You know this. Start tomorrow."

Stefanovic knocked. Brought in chai tea and biscotti. Radovan leaned back. Dipped the biscotti in his tea. Like a Sven. Smacked his lips. They made some small talk about Radovan's daughter. She was starting school. Private school, inner-city school, the suburban school—what was best? Mrado vented his own shit. That he saw Lovisa too seldom. The custody battle with the mother. Rado-style: asked if there was anything he could do. Mrado thought, Hell no. If Social Services finds out you're in the picture, my custody battle is shot.

Two real Persian carpets on the floor. Radovan'd decorated this as his classicist room. The books on the shelves were mostly for show. On the shelves: encyclopedias and map books. Collected works by Serbian writers. Mrado didn't even recognize the names: Jovan Jovanović Zmaj, Sima Milutinović Sarajlija, Kraljević Marko. Only one was familiar: the Nobel laureate Ivo Andrić.

Mrado thought about his teacher in Native Language Studies class, who'd gotten him to read Ivo Andrić. A year later, he was Södertälje's toughest fist.

Radovan set down his glass of chai.

"The smokes business is going well. Goran's good. But in the long run, we can't rely on it. Society at large is against smoking these days. The ban on cigarettes at restaurants is catastrophic, the new pictures of black lungs are repulsive, and increased customs control with non-EU countries is devastating."

"You're right, but it's important that we maintain our contacts with the teamsters. The logistics wouldn't be easy to build back up from scratch. Soon all of the Balkans will open up with EU membership. Heroin is eight times cheaper there. Even if it rises somewhat, we've got to be prepared. The same truckers who drive smokes today can drive brown sugar tomorrow."

They kept the discussion going. Went through all of Radovan's businesses and projects: cigarette and booze smuggling, the debt collectors, drugs, the Jack Vegas gambling machine fakes, the apartment brothel, the call-service hookers.

And then the semilegal ones: Clara's, the bar, and the Diamond, a nightclub. Laundromats.

The abstract read cash flow, rising dough, money that had to be taxed to come back clean. The bar and nightclub didn't cut it. Radovan had to appear like a law-abiding, respectable citizen.

The conclusion: They definitely needed two video-rental stores. Maybe more.

All along, Mrado had wanted to get to the question of his cut of the coat checks.

Finally, he raised the tea glass to his lips and tried to drink from it, even though it was obviously empty. Hoped he'd softened Radovan up enough.

"Rado, I also want to talk about the economics of the coat checks."

Radovan looked up from the number-covered papers that were spread out in front of him. "And what exactly do you mean by that?"

"Maybe I didn't handle this whole Patrik thing too well. But I'm taking responsibility for it and I do a good job. We just went over the numbers. They point straight up. What'll my cut be?"

Silence.

Mrado tried to push it. "Did you hear what I said?"

Concrete wall.

"Mrado, let me make one thing clear. You don't make the rules here. No matter how fucking brilliant your business ideas are, they're all mine. No matter how well you do your business, in the end it's my cash. We'll have a discussion about your piece of the pie when I feel like it. Let's not ruin a good night with that kind of thing. I'm going to forget what you just asked me, okay?"

Mrado, speechless. How could he have made such a miscalculation? And he'd groveled like a fucking faggot begging to be reamed just to ask the question about his cut. Another thought took hold: One day, someone else will be king of the hill.

It was eight o'clock. They moved to the dining room. Radovan's wife came home. Made small talk with Radovan and Mrado for half an hour. She was thin. Mrado thought she was the most beautiful Serbian woman he'd ever seen.

She ate in the kitchen with the daughter.

Radovan acted irreproachably. As though Mrado's question'd never been asked.

The mood went back to normal.

They uncorked a Burgundy from 1994. Radovan tasted it. "I'm assuming you already know this, but Jorge Salinas Barrio fled the coop."

"Ratko told me. I think some rag had a story on it last week, too. It didn't say much, but apparently he hopped over the wall. Impressive."

"It's a bad thing he's out. We wrapped him at the trial. He might be sitting on a whole mess of shit about our blow business. From what I've gathered, he's pissed at us, and his life is pretty shitty right now. On the run, not a lot of friends. He might decide to do something stupid. I honestly don't know how much he knows. Do you?"

"Not really. But I know what you mean. What should we do?"

"Nothing yet. But if he tries anything, we gotta stop him. Remind him who's boss. Rough him up. Right, Mrado, the way we deal with troublemakers?"

Mrado stared down at his wineglass. Was that last statement referring to how Rado was going to treat him if he kept making demands? Either way, the Jorge thug should get it right now. The Latino was a threat to the Yugos.

Mrado had other things to think about. Deal with the coat checks after the Kvarnen fiasco, find a front man to build up the money-laundering biz, fight for his daughter. The Latino'd have to wait.

What's more: no point in overstepping Radovan's bounds, taking things into his own hands. Their relationship already felt strained enough.

He'd wait for a green light before he went after that Jorge fucker.

And their strained relationship—he had to think about that.

10

Jorge the man, *rey de los bandidos*, blew the popo outta the water. The 5-o could drag their bloodhounds around. Forget it—they weren't finding Jorge-boy.

He was out. He was loose. He was the city's slickest slumdog.

He thought about how the gab must be rolling. The man who ran faster than Ben Johnson. The man who screwed the screws up the ass with his smarts. The man who caged out of Österåker with the help of a couple of bedsheets and a hook from a basketball hoop. Slam dunk. *Gracias y adiós*.

The man. The myth. The legend.

And they didn't have a fuckin' clue.

Jorge's plans before the break had been well oiled. His plan now: stay alive, and stay free. Get cash. Bust the border. In other words: not much of a plan.

Santo Sergio'd delivered the ladder at the right place. Hauled ass to his car and driven outta the woods before Jorge'd even gotten halfway over the clearing. He'd parked the other car perfectly.

Fugitivo fantástico. A Latino with balls.

Jorge'd driven like a maniac down the forest road. Like a back-road racer. The COs missed his curveball, didn't see him get in the car. Thought he was still booking it on foot. He'd planned it that way. The road forked three times. By the time the screws realized he was on wheels, it'd probably take them an hour to figure out which road he'd taken. Out on the highway. Past Åkersberga. Exit. Into the woods. That's where he'd met Sergio. Sergio'd jacked the car that he'd left waiting for Jorge three days earlier. They dumped it. A tank of gas in the trunk. Torched it. Not worth waiting around to watch the flames.

That's where the trail ended: deep in Hansel and Gretel land.

If the 5-o even got that far.

———

He'd arrived at the apartment at two-thirty in the morning. They'd waited all night in the car until the coast was clear—wanted to avoid neighbors seeing Jorge go in. They ate falafel, drank Coke and coffee. Listened to Hit FM. Chatted. Stayed awake. Jorge chillin', coming down off the adrenaline high.

The following days: Jorge could live in the empty apartment. It belonged to Sergio's aunt. The old lady'd been in a retirement home since seven weeks back.

The deal: Jorge could stay for ten days tops. Jorge couldn't so much as wiggle a foot out the door. Jorge had to lay subterranean low. After that, he could do what he liked, but he had to pay Sergio back for everything—he'd sworn his life on it.

Jorge was grateful. Sergio was an angel. Had already done more than anyone. Sacrificed. Gambled. Taken risks. Like family oughta do for one other, but what no one'd ever done for him. He was planning on staying no more than a week.

Shut in the apartment. Heavy—he was supposed to be free. Now this, caged again. The only difference between this and the cell at Österåker was a few additional square feet. He had to prepare for his new life on the run.

Jorge let his beard grow. Cut his hair. Dyed it blacker.

He asked Sergio to buy small curlers and perm solution: thio balance perm. Read the instructions over and over, all the fine print. Stood over the bathtub. Rinsed his hair under the water. Carefully rolled his hair on the curlers. Good thing no one was watching. Felt like a real fairy.

Practiced a new walk. Tried to disguise his voice as much as possible.

Jorge knew: People instinctively recognize you by your body language, the way you walk, talk, run your hand through your hair, and smile. Your unconscious tics. The way you use certain expressions. Rodriguez's only good deed, according to Jorge: The dude'd recorded home videos of him and Paola when they were kids. Two completely different people: a boy and a girl, sinewy and graceful, angular and round. And still, their body language was almost identical. Jorge remembered. Codes of character more dangerous than looks.

Change that kind of stuff, Jorge-boy—fast as fuck.

The apartment was rough. He wanted out. Took down the mirror from the hall and propped it up against the wall in the living room. Walked around from 10:00 a.m. to 7:00 p.m. that first day with Marge Simpson hair and rehearsed new moves. Practiced new tics. Practiced new lingo.

After twelve hours, his new hair—curly. It wasn't as kinky as he'd hoped, even though he'd kept the rollers in double the instructed time.

He smeared himself with self-tanner: Piz Buin, the darkest kind. According to the directions on the back of the tube, the color would last for three days. Should work.

Finally, the total effect: he looked like a *zambo*—*el zambo macanudo*. A lip and nose job and his own mother wouldn't even know him.

Amazing.

Blinds shut. A constant pale gray light in the room.

The apartment was small—two rooms and a kitchen. There was a narrow bed with no sheets in the bedroom. Jorge thought they'd have that kind of stuff in the retirement home, but they seemed to have emptied every drawer when they picked up the old lady. The living room had a couch, a TV, a rug, and a dark wood coffee table in it. There was a yellow glass lamp suspended from the ceiling. The bookshelves were filled with family photos, postcards from Chile, and books. Mostly in Spanish. He caught himself wondering if she'd had a family. Tried to check out the postcards. Read a few. Got bored after a while. The Asics shoes hadn't cut it. His foot still hurt. It might be sprained.

Midday, he rang the doorbells of the neighbors over, under, and next to him. Hid in the stairwell in case they opened. No one was home. He could watch TV.

Lowered the volume anyway. There was no cable. Listened to the news. Nothing about him. He watched reruns, matinee movies, and shopping shows. Got nervous.

Kept practicing his new walk. Nail the rhythm. Swing your arms. His right leg made an extra little swerve with each step. Nigga with attitude. Walk with soul. Movements with flow. Don't overdo it; make it seem real. Felt as if he'd moved like this all his life. Had it in his blood. From birth.

He read the evening papers that Sergio'd brought with him. They hadn't written much about the escape. Just a short article in *Expressen* on the first day after and a small notice in *Aftonbladet*.

According to *Expressen*:

A man convicted of possession with intent escaped from the Österåker Penitentiary on Thursday afternoon under spectacular circumstances. One of the correctional officers told Expressen *that the fugitive, Jorge Salinas Barrio, was not a troublemaker and that the staff did not suspect that he was planning an escape. According to a source at the facility, Jorge Salinas Barrio climbed over the exterior wall with help from the outside. Then he is said to have run toward the woods, where it is probable that a car was waiting for him. The same source stated that the fugitive had been training long-distance running in what is described as a "manic" way for months before the incident. The prison administration has expressed self-criticism over what has happened, though they are pleased that the incident involved very little violence.*

After the wave of escapes in 2004 when, among others, Tony Olsson, convicted of the murder of a police officer in Malexander, succeeded in escaping on two separate occasions during the same year, the control and security at the country's penitentiaries have been improved. After yesterday's incident, the Criminal Investigation Department has given word that an eventual investigation will be implemented to further heighten the level of security at penitentiaries of this kind.

Jorge smiled. So, they'd thought his training was exaggerated. Wonder what they'd thought about his studies at the city library? Had they even connected the dots?

There was nothing in the papers on day two. He was disappointed. At the same time, relieved—the less attention the better.

He missed running. Disliked the silence. Was scared his endurance and his fit body would break down.

Time slower than a Prius without a plug-in. He tried to plan. Jacked off. Peered between the blinds. Got nervous. Practiced the new Jorge over and over again. Listened for suspicious sounds on the street or in the stairwell. Fantasized about his success abroad.

Boredom: ten times worse than in the slammer.

He slept poorly. Woke up. Listened. Raised the blinds. Stared through the peephole in the door.

Paced. Looked himself in the mirror. Who would he become?

Jorge's dilemma: The blow biz was all he knew. But how could he get back into it without disclosing his identity? As Jorge, he was respected. Not as whatever his name would be now. It was a tough scene to break into solo. Impossible without support.

He needed a personal identification number and an address in order to hide behind a temporary identity. Besides, he wanted to jump stiles. If you got collared, you could always give someone else's digits and address to placate the subway controllers.

What's more, he had to find a tanning bed so he could cut the self-tanner. Needed contacts with a darker brown tint than his natural eye color. Needed more threads than the dingy tracksuit Sergio'd given him. Needed a cell phone. Needed to get in touch with certain people. Most of all, J-boy needed cash. He missed Paola. Wanted to call but knew he shouldn't. It'd have to wait. After five days, he started wigging out. Thought every single car that stopped on the street was the 5-o. Sergio came that night; they talked the situation over. The cops hadn't visited Sergio yet. Everything seemed cool. Jorge, still buggin'. Wanted out.

Sergio picked him up at 6:00 a.m. the next day. Jorge was totally spent. Hadn't slept a wink. Had crawled around the apartment with a sponge, wiping every piece of hair and other possible traces of himself off the floor.

They drove to Kallhäll. Jorge asked Sergio to make a few extra loops to lose any eventual tails.

Sergio shook his head, "You tweakin' out, *primo*."

The next place for Jorge to sleep: a room at Sergio's best bud's place, Eddie's. The advantage: If the cops were on his heels, they'd definitely lose the trail now. The downside: The circle of trust widened.

Really, the optimal thing would be to stay with people who didn't know who he was, or who wouldn't recognize him. You couldn't fool Eddie. Laughed when he saw Jorge. *El negrito.* He was introduced to Eddie's wife and two kids. Didn't know squat about Jorge's story. Not perfect, but okay.

Jorge lay on a bed for days on end. Listened to the kids crying. Studied the patterns on the ceiling. Thought about what it must've been like when his mom came to Sweden big with him. From the dictatorship. Alone with the memories. He was ashamed that he knew so little. Hadn't asked enough.

The room was small. Belonged to one of the kids. Legos all over the floor. Kid posters on the walls. Some teen idols Jorge didn't even recognize. Flowery curtains over the windows. He read comics. Wished he could play Eddie's Xbox but didn't dare leave the room. Yearned to be back in the old lady's crib, but still knew he was safer where he was. Yearned for real freedom. Yearned to be out.

A few days later. Eddie knocked on the door at around 2:00 p.m. He should have been at work. Jorge knew right away: Something was wrong. Eddie was sweaty. His shoes were still on. His kids were screaming in the background.

"Jorge, you gotta go. They've picked Sergio up for questioning."

"When? How do you know?"

"They called this morning and told him he had to show up before one p.m. He called me right away and said I had to tell you but that I couldn't call."

"Good. I'm the one that told him no calls. They can tap 'em, and God knows what else they can do. You weren't followed?"

Eddie: not the world's sharpest Latino. But he'd been around the block. Knew to keep a lookout.

Jorge started getting dressed. Besides the tracksuit, he'd borrowed a jacket from Sergio. Not much to pack: a tube of Piz Buin, the curlers, a toothbrush, two pairs of boxers, and an extra pair of socks. It'd all come from Sergio, along with five grand he'd borrowed.

Shoved the stuff into a plastic bag. Kissed Eddie on the cheeks. Waved to the screaming kids. Thanked the oldest *niño* for the use of his room. Hoped Eddie hadn't told his wife his name or who he was.

He'd been on the run for ten days. Was it already going to hell?

Wrote a note in Spanish for Sergio, coded according to their agreement. Gave it to Eddie.

Stepped out of the apartment. Thought he heard a siren outside.

Opened the door to the street.

Looked around. No cars on the street. No people. Coast clear. Paranoid Latino on the run.

What the fuck was he gonna do now?

The air was getting chillier. September ninth. Jorge walked around the city all day. Downtown: Drottninggatan, Gamla Brogatan, Hötorget, Kungsgatan, Stureplan. Ate at McDonald's. Window-shopped. Tried to check out *chicas*.

Couldn't enjoy. Only stress. Whichever it was—OCD or rational security measures—he kept looking around like every *hombre* on the street was an undercover on the LO.

Get to know broken Jorge: *El Jorgelito*—a scared little shit. He wanted to call his sister. He wanted to talk to his mama. He almost wanted to go back to prison.

This wouldn't fly; he had to wise up. Stop thinking about his mama and sister all the time. What the fuck was wrong with him anyway? Family's everything, sure. That was rule *número uno*. But if you didn't have a real family, if you had to take care of yourself, then other rules applied. He focused on the important stuff.

Nowhere to sleep and no bros/co-dees he could trust right now.

Five grand in his pocket. He could pay some old blow buddy to put him up for a few nights. But the risk was too big; they'd rat for anything, just show them the cheese.

He couldn't stay at a motel. Probably too expensive. Besides, they'd want to see some kind of ID.

He could get in touch with his mama or his sister, but they were probably under surveillance by the cops and it was unnecessary to put them through that kind of crap.

Mierda.

During the days on the bed in the kid's room, an idea had started to take shape: Go to a homeless shelter. Would solve the problem of needing a bed, but his need for cash remained. There was another, bigger idea, too. Dangerous. Dicey. He tried to push it away, since it involved Radovan.

Jorge asked some junkies downtown where he could sleep. They told him about two places: Stadsmissionen's place by Slussen, Night Owl, and KarismaCare by Fridhemsplan.

He walked down to the Hötorget subway stop. It was eight o'clock at night. The turnstiles didn't look like how he remembered them before he was locked up. Harder to jump. High Plexiglas barriers that slid open and closed like doors when you swiped your pass at the front of the turnstile. He didn't want to waste money. He didn't want to walk to Slussen. Risk analysis. The turnstiles were too high to jump. He glanced toward the guard in his booth: He was reading the paper. Seemed to care less about his job. He watched the flow of the crowd. Not a lot of people. He made loops. Navigated. Speculated. Calculated. Finally, a group of youngsters approached. He walked into their group. Slid along. Close behind a guy in his early twenties. There was a beep from the turnstile when it sensed that he'd slipped through behind someone. The guard didn't give a fuck.

Rode to Slussen. Checked the address on a map in the subway station.

He was tired. Longed for a bed.

Rang the doorbell. Was let in.

It looked cozy. The reception desk was right by the entrance. Farther in: a group of tables and chairs, a sink and an oven against one wall. A TV stood in a corner. People sat and played cards. Chowed. Watched TV. Talked. No one so much as glanced at him. There was no one there that he recognized. No one there seemed to recognize him. Super.

The receptionist looked like the librarian at the city lib. Same style, same dowdy threads.

"Hi, can I help you?" she said, looking up from a crossword puzzle.

Jorge said, "Yeah, I've had some trouble finding a place to stay lately. Heard this is a good place."

Put on that saccharine-sweet pity-me voice. He didn't have to fake it. He was broken, for real. The woman seemed to get it. Social Services ladies/welfare officers/shrinks were always understanding. Jorge knew their kind.

"We've got some beds open, so it should be fine. Have you been without a residence for long?"

Converse. Be nice. Say something believable. "Not too long. About two weeks. It's been rough. My girlfriend kicked me out."

"That sounds difficult. But at least you can stay here for a few nights. Maybe things will work out with your girlfriend. In order for you to stay here, all I need is your name and personal identification number."

Fuck.

"Do you really need that info? Why?" He thought, I do have a personal identification number. Can I give it out?

"I know that a lot of people may not want to disclose that kind of information, but even a place like this costs money. We'll send an invoice directly to your social welfare officer, if you have one. Two hundred kronor per night. So, unfortunately, I'm going to need your personal identification number."

Cunt. He couldn't give her fake digits. No way it'd work.

"I can't do that. I'd be happy to pay cash."

"I'm sorry, but we don't take any cash payments anymore. We stopped doing that two years ago. Maybe you should be in touch with your social welfare office?"

Fucking cunt fuck.

Jorge gave up. Said his thanks. Stepped back out on the street.

Regretted trying. Hoped he hadn't raised any red flags.

Wondered if anyone'd recognized him. Looked at his reflection in a shop window. Black hair. Curly. His beard was getting longer. His skin darker than it really was. It should be enough.

A thermometer pointed to fourteen degrees Celsius.

Where would he sleep?

He thought about his other plan—his cash idea. Did he dare? Challenge Radovan.

11

JW counted the money again. Twenty-two thousand clean, and then he'd still partied like Paris Hilton four weekends in a row, and on top of that been able to buy a Canali blazer.

He weighed the forty-four five-hundred-kronor bills wrapped with a rubber band in the palm of his hand. Usually, he kept them hidden in a pair of socks in the closet. Selling coke paid well. He'd made the money in a month. Paid back his debt to Abdulkarim and passed his Financial Analysis exam, too.

Abdulkarim praised him, wanted him to work with coke full-time. The flattery warmed. The flattery fed him confidence and sweet dreams for the future. But JW declined—he was planning on doing it all: partying, dealing, studying.

The boyz'd accepted that he provided the goods. They were polished boys. It suited them, having the goods delivered without needing to get their delicate hands dirty. The only one who reacted was Nippe, who dissed him as a joke, "Are you low on cash, or what? Kinda seems like it, since you're, like, a runner all the time now. Just say the word and my old man will lend you some." JW ignored him. Thought, Soon I'll be able to buy Nippe's old man and shut him up for good.

JW checked himself in the mirror. His lion mane was well groomed with the generous amount of Dax wax he'd just smeared into it, on top of all the wax that never completely washed out. He used to cut his own hair. Now he had other opportunities. Maybe he'd go to the same hairdressers as the boyz: Sachajuan, Toni & Guy, only the best. Fine thought.

All his clothes were secondhand: the Gucci jeans, the Paul Smith shirt, and the Tod's loafers with the characteristic cleat-like rubber soles. That's why it felt so good to put on the Canali blazer. No wrinkles, nice structure, crisp feeling. Even the smell was new.

He was nearly six feet tall, fair and with a slim face. Slim wrists. Slim neck. Everything slim. Piano fingers. Defined jaw. JW changed his pose in front of the mirror. I look good, but maybe I'd look better if I bulked up a little. Gym membership, here I come.

It was a Saturday. He was going with Nippe to one of his friend's parents' place, an estate in Sörmland. JW had met the guy, Gustaf, a couple of times before at the nightclub Laroy. The plan: dinner followed by a party. Everyone was staying the night. Sophie and Anna were going. Some people he didn't know were going. Best of all, Jet Set Carl was going.

With some luck, maybe he'd be able to get with Sophie. With even better luck, he'd make a good impression on Jet Set Carl. Definitely an opening to C channels.

It was 3:00 p.m. JW felt sluggish, tired for no reason. He hadn't even partied the night before. He sat down on the bed, pulled up his legs, and counted the money again. Relished the rustle of paper. Waited for Nippe to honk down on the street.

The sales curve pointed straight up. The weekend after he'd treated Sophie and Anna in the park, he'd made his first deal. It started with him treating a second time. But never in Humlegården again—he'd decided that was a one-time thing. Too lame.

They'd been hanging out at Putte's, as usual. The whole gang: JW, Putte, Nippe, and Fredrik. Sophie, Anna, and two other prep school broads'd been there, as well. The boyz were in on the deal: JW scored the ice and they all split the bill. This time, the girls wanted in. JW played pasha, all generous and munificent, treating them each to a nose. The two new girls, Charlotte and Lollo, had never tried before. The mood got high, not just metaphorically. They felt molten-hot, impulsive—Autobahn-speeded. Everyone appreciated JW, the guy who brought the party. After three hours, they jumped in cabs and rode down to Stureplan. JW packed four grams. They went into Köket. Business as usual: danced, boozed, flirted. Nippe managed to get blown by two birds. After half an hour, one of the new girls, Lollo, came up to JW and said she thought the whole thing was so wonderful. Asked if he had any more and insisted on paying. JW looked concerned. Said she shouldn't have to pay but that he'd promised another friend some. She said, "Come on, you just gotta give me a few noses. You gotta let me pay." He said, "Sure, I'll see what I can do." He thought, Daddy's paying anyway. He unloaded the whole stash for twelve hundred a gram. Wholesale price was six hundred. Profit: 3,400 kronor. Compared to the gypsy-cab gig, it was mind-blowing—a whole night's work in the Ford equaled three minutes of ingratiating talk at a club, and he'd had a drink in his hand and a pretty girl to look at the whole time. Not bad.

Same deal the next weekend, but with different people. Pregame in a different apartment, party at a different club, after party in a different pad. He'd raked in seven thousand kronor net, even though he'd handed out a total of five grams for free.

The week after, he'd met Sophie for a coffee in Sturegallerian, by Stureplan. They talked about sweet clubs, stylish clothes, shared acquaintances. Talked about serious stuff, too. What they wanted to do when they graduated. Sophie was studying economics at Stockholm University but wanted to try to transfer into the Stockholm School of Economics for her junior year. Had to get top grades on all her exams, study hard, be disciplined. Then she was going to London to do right for herself, to work. JW wanted to work with stocks; he had a head for numbers. She got personal, asked about his parents and background. JW was evasive, said they'd lived abroad most of his childhood, that they lived on an estate in Dalarna now, and that she probably didn't know them. She wondered why they didn't live in Sörmland, or somewhere else closer to the city. JW changed the subject. He was an old hand, had a store of conversation topics up his sleeve. They talked about her family. That worked; Sophie let his background go and talked about her own instead.

She came from the countryside, from an estate, and had enrolled in a regular school in first grade. Hadn't worked. Her classmates weren't nice to her. Called her a snob, didn't pick her for teams in gym class, thought it was totally fine to swipe her stuff. It almost sounded silly, but JW understood, for real. After sixth grade, she'd switched to the prep school Lundsberg. To her own kind. She loved the place.

JW couldn't stop thinking about her. She was his best source of sales and she was so foxy, but she seemed genuinely nice, too. A good girl. His goal was clear: He would work on her, doubly.

The next weekend, JW'd hung out with Sophie and her group of girlfriends at a private party. Lollo loved snow, shouted at JW, "This stuff totally gets me off! My sex life is, like, amazing!" Sophie loved snow. Anna loved snow. Charlotte loved snow. Everyone at the party loved JW. He made eight grand.

The weekend after that—last weekend—they'd pregamed at Nippe's on Friday, then went to Kharma, where a table waited for them, and then on to an after party at Lollo's. Saturday started with dinner at Putte's, followed by a reserved table at Café Opera. The evening ended with an after party at Lollo's again—crammed with new faces.

A new record: He'd cashed in eleven grand net.

Weekdays he tried to study. He felt like a new person. C sales did wonders for his finances, his confidence, and his wardrobe. Still, he got no peace. Thoughts of the yellow Ferrari kept bothering him. The night the Arab'd suggested he sell coke was the first time he'd ever asked about Camilla. He'd hoped that maybe someone knew something, but deep inside he didn't think it would lead anywhere. But now there was the Ferrari tearing down Sturegatan at a furious speed as a constant image in his mind. He had to know more.

He'd called the National Road Administration. Unfortunately, JW didn't remember the car's license plate number, but it worked anyway— vehicle registration was a wonderful state institution. Anyone could find out who the owner of any Swedish registered car was. If the car was unusual, you could get information even without the license plate number. According to the guy at the Road Administration, there were two yellow Ferraris in Sweden the year Camilla went missing. One was owned by the IT millionaire Peter Holbeck, and the other was owned by a leasing company, Dolphin Finance, Ltd. The company specialized in sports cars and yachts.

JW began by looking up Peter Holbeck. The man'd made his money on Web consulting. Now, in retrospect, JW thought the whole thing seemed so obvious. How the hell could they think that consultants should make five million a head for building websites that any fifteen-year-old computer geek could handle? But that hadn't bothered the entrepreneur and fake visionary Peter Holbeck. He sold out in time. The Web agency had 150 employees. Six months after the sale, the agency was shut down. One hundred and twenty of the employees lost their jobs. Peter Holbeck made 360 million. Now he went skiing eighty days out of the year and spent the rest of the time in Thailand or other warm places with his kids.

JW's question: What had the IT millionaire been doing the spring Camilla went missing?

He took a chance on easy answers, tried to call Holbeck. It took three days to track him down. Finally, he got hold of him. Holbeck sounded short of breath when he answered the phone. "This is Peter."

"Hi, my name is Johan." It wasn't often that JW introduced himself with his real first name. "I have some questions for you. I hope I'm not calling at a bad time."

"Are you a journalist? I don't have the energy to speak to you people."

"No, actually not. It's regarding a private thing."

Holbeck sounded surprised. "Shoot."

"I'm looking for a woman, Camilla Westlund. She disappeared about four years ago. No one knows where she is. We know that she was sometimes seen in a yellow Ferrari before she disappeared. You owned one of those during the year in question. Thought maybe you know something. Maybe you lent out the car, or something?"

"Are you calling from the police, or are you a journalist?"

"Not a journalist. Didn't I already say that? Not from the police, either. I'm a private person, calling about a personal matter."

"Either way. I don't know what the hell you're talking about. Are you insinuating something?"

"Sorry if this sounds strange. I just wanted to know if you remember anything."

"Whatever. I was in the Rockies half of that year. On skis. The rest of the time I was in the south of Sweden or in Florida. With my kids. The car was parked in a garage in Stockholm."

JW realized: no point in pushing it any further. Holbeck'd said enough. He ended the conversation.

The next day, he Googled Holbeck for hours. Finally ended up in the archives of *Aftonbladet*. Holbeck was mentioned in articles about luxury vacationers. It was true: He had a house in the south of Sweden and one in Florida, and he'd been skiing in the States the same year that Camilla disappeared. Maybe the IT millionaire wasn't involved.

There was one more yellow Ferrari, after all. JW looked up the leasing company, Dolphin Finance, Ltd. Just the name gave off sketchy vibes. He got in touch with the National Registry of Incorporated

Companies. The administrator on the other end of the line was helpful, told him that the company'd gone bankrupt a year ago. All the assets—the cars and boats—had been bought by a German company. There wasn't much more JW could do. It was almost a relief. He could let the Ferrari go. Or could he?

A honk from the street. JW looked out and saw Nippe in the Golf that'd been a twenty-first-birthday present from his mom and dad.

They headed south on the freeway—on the road to peeps, parties, possibilities.

A classic Swedish hip-hop song on the radio. JW wasn't a big fan of hip-hop, but he couldn't help but dig Petter's lyrics: "The tide has turned."

It applied to him. Big-time. His time had come—to stop living a double life, to become like them, for real. To get even deeper in the clover. Eat them for breakfast.

They chatted. JW listened. Nippe had the hots for Lollo. Nippe thought Jet Set Carl'd had attitude last weekend—who did he think he was? Nippe complimented JW's Canali blazer. Nippe discussed the latest reality-TV show. Nippe had verbal diarrhea.

"I might quit the finance focus. Thinking about marketing instead."

JW's interest, lukewarm. "Really."

"Marketing's where it's at, especially branding. Sell any product at any price, no matter how cheaply it's made. As long as it's branded and marketed correctly. There's such fucking potential."

"Sure, but in the end it's your core business that matters, the leverage of capital employed, the financing. If your marketing costs too much, and you never really make a profit, you die."

"Sure, but you make money. Just look at Gucci and Louis Vuitton. The clothes, the boutiques in Stockholm, the fashion collections, all of that is just an excuse. What really makes it rain are branded accessories. Shades, perfume, belts, purses. China-made crap, little stuff. Branding, that's, like, all it is."

In JW's opinion, Nippe wasn't the sharpest brat in the pack, and today he'd apparently gotten hung up on one word. Like a broken record.

They chatted on.

JW dug life. Next month, he'd triple sales. He did some mental arithmetic: added, subtracted, multiplied. He saw sales curves, credit, cash. He saw a bull market in himself.

It took an hour to get there. Nippe told him it was an old manor where Gustaf's parents lived. The parents—good friends with His Majesty King Carl XVI Gustaf.

Gustaf welcomed them. JW made the same analysis of the guy as the last time they'd met: He was the essence of a backslick brat. Dressed in a tweed jacket, white chinos, red cravat, checked shirt with double cuffs, and Marc Jacobs loafers. Slicked hair stiff as a helmet—lion mane of lion manes.

The main house was over 21,000 square feet. Two massive crystal chandeliers dangled between the pillars in the hall, and paintings of snow-covered landscapes hung on the walls. A curved staircase led upstairs. Gustaf introduced them to Gunn, "the housemother," as he put it.

"She's the one who looks after me when Mom and Dad are gone."

JW retorted, "I guess that'll be needed tonight."

Gunn laughed. JW chortled. Nippe giggled. Gustaf guffawed, loudest of them all.

Definite good vibes. Gustaf seemed to like him.

Nippe and JW were led away by Gunn, who got them settled in a guest room in one of the wings of the house.

JW fingered the manila envelope in his pocket. Fourteen grams, just to be on the safe side.

Dinner was served at seven-thirty. Beforehand, Sophie and JW played tennis doubles against Nippe and Anna. Seven-five. Six-four. Four-six. Seven-five. Spirits soared among the winners. Nippe was a bad loser, threw his racket on the ground. Anna stayed calm. JW hadn't really played tennis while growing up and thanked his natural athleticism for his ability to impress—made it look like he'd been playing all his life.

They showered. JW napped for half an hour. Nippe took a shit.

They changed into tuxes. JW had a secondhand Cerruti that he said had cost twelve grand. The actual damage was 2,500. Nippe wondered if JW'd brought some gear. "Seems like you're reliable these days."

JW didn't know if the comment was good or bad. Had he moved too quickly?

He laughed. "Sure, I've got some. You want a taste?"

They split thirty milligrams, enough for a mild rush.

The coke hit right away.

They were slammed unexpectedly fast with a fit of giggles.

They walked down the stairs to the cocktail party in the salon. JW felt like the world's most intelligent human being.

The fourteen other guests waited with champagne glasses in hand. JW scanned the crowd.

The guys: JW, Fredrik, Nippe, Jet Set Carl, Gustaf, and three other dudes.

The girls: Sophie, Anna, Lollo, and five chicks JW hadn't met before. They were all upper-crust creamers. Girls with good genes. Rich dads equaled hot moms, or the other way around. They knew how to make themselves up. How to apply the right rouge, the best eye shadow, smooth foundation. Above all, they knew how to rock self-tanner for a sun-kissed look. They knew how to dress themselves, how to cover up the flaws: a somewhat saggy belly, a thick waist, too-small breasts, too-flat back. They highlighted their strengths: nice neck, full lips, long legs. Fit, slim girls. Odds were, they all had luxury gym memberships.

Gustaf was selective with his invites. It was an honor to be invited, especially since he'd met the evening's host only three times before.

Everyone sipped, made small talk, chilled. JW had to try to contain himself; he was soaring. Felt like every word coming out of his mouth was brilliant, like he was the life of this party. Nippe winked at him— you and me, JW, flyin' in the C sky.

They sat down for dinner.

JW was seated between Anna, whom he often sold to these days, and a girl named Carro. Worked well; both were easy to chat up.

The appetizer was already on the table. JW could see right away that it was not of this world. A piece of toasted bread topped with Kalix roe, sour cream, and finely chopped red onion. The basic idea wasn't too original, but it was the large glass bowl in the middle of the table that made it so ridiculous—at least eleven pounds of extra roe. An orgy of excess. JW piled at least four hundred kronor's worth on his plate.

Gunn brought the main course: venison with a sauce of wild chanterelles, and oven-roasted potatoes. JW loved game. They drank a Bordeaux. Anna told him about her parents' wine cellar. Sorbet with blackberries and raspberries for dessert. JW promised himself: Within ten years, he'd have his own Gunn. Gorgeously good gastronomical miracles.

The mood grew lighter in time with the bottles of wine that Gunn kept bringing. After dessert, Gustaf walked around with a frosty bottle of Grey Goose and poured out brimming shots. The heat intensified.

The girls eyed Jet Set Carl and Nippe. Always Nippe.

JW checked out Sophie.

She didn't give him the time of day.

The room wasn't a room. The right word would probably be *salon*. Or maybe *hall*. Huge, incredibly high ceilings, tremendously grand decorating job. Two chandeliers with real candles burning in them were suspended from the ceiling. Two-toned dark red wallpaper with wide stripes. Modernist art on the walls. A few were possibly very valuable.

JW'd gone to the Museum of Modern Art with Sophie that week. He wasn't exactly a fine-art kind of guy, but Sophie said she liked powerful color combinations and therefore was more a fan of modern art. JW'd read up on what was on display in the museum a couple of days beforehand. He wanted to make an impression. Without realizing it, he'd gotten a feel for a couple of artists. Maybe one of the paintings here was a Kandinsky. An enormous one with three muted fields of color that matched the wallpaper might be a Mark Rothko.

The table was set with style and panache. White linen tablecloth, pressed green linen napkins, and silver napkin holders. Antique coasters for the wine bottles. Gleaming silver cutlery and crystal stemware—only appropriate.

JW ate it all up.

They kept chatting. The guys liked the sound of their own voices. Jet Set Carl bragged, Nippe made lame jokes, and Fredrik spewed business plans. Same old.

Anna told him about her latest trip to Saint Moritz. Reapplied lip gloss between every other sentence. She and a girlfriend'd become friendly with a polo team that traveled down every year to play on the frozen alpine lake. Normally, they were bankers in London; polo was just a little weekend fancy. JW dove right in, told her about his trip to Chamonix last year. Made up most of it, added and exaggerated. The only time he'd been to the Alps for real was on a budget trip during spring break five years ago, when fifteen guys from up north, from Umeå and Robertsfors, had crowded, slept, and farted on a bus for twenty-six hours.

Anna was pretty and nice. But boring. No spark. He listened to her, laughed at her jokes, and asked follow-up questions. She kept talking, seemed to like his company. JW only had thoughts for Sophie.

The dinner rolled on. People were lit but still mellow. Gunn kept serving and clearing the table. Everyone seemed expectant.

Fredrik gave a speech of thanks to the host.

They rose from the table and went into a kind of barroom. Wide couches piled with pillows stood along two walls. A long table was placed in front of each couch. Gunn had put iittala glass candlesticks in four different colors on the table. In one of the corners of the room was a bar, built with classical wood paneling. Behind the bar: martini glasses, highball glasses, tumblers, beer steins, and wineglasses in a built-in glass display case. An insane number of bottles lined up on shelves.

Gustaf positioned himself behind the bar. Hollered that he was the bartender for the night and that it was time to place their orders. Someone put on music. Beyoncé. Badonkadonk beats.

They boozed. Drank apple martinis, G and Ts, beer. Gustaf's dad had a blender. They made fruity drinks: strawberry daiquiris, piña coladas.

JW drank a beer. Eyed his friends.

Nippe hit on Carro. Jet Set Carl was at the bar, talking to Gustaf. The rest of the guests sat on the couches, chatting.

Music played in the background. JW heard clatter from the dining room as Gunn cleaned up.

He got the feeling that something was off.

Gunn's sounds were distracting, too audible.

JW understood what was wrong. The barroom lacked volume—no one was dancing, no one laughing, no one hollering. Simple conclusion: It wasn't much of a party.

He got behind the bar and walked up to Gustaf. Took a sec to listen to what Jet Set Carl was saying before he excused himself. Asked to speak with Gustaf privately. Suggested they talk in another room.

They went back into the dining room, where the table was completely cleared. Gunn was efficient. JW pulled out a chair for Gustaf.

"Gustaf, it's so damn nice to be invited here tonight. What a fantastic dinner." JW knew the linguistic ground rules: Swearwords were permitted only in positive contexts. He started his pitch. "I've got a totally sick idea. I happened to bring a couple grams of Charlie. I know you've tried before. How about taking some? That'll rev up the party for sure."

"Yeah, you're totally right. You got coke? That's fuckin' sweet. We've gotta have some. What do you want for it?"

Best-possible question. Saved JW the tricky business of asking for money. Gustaf wanted his party to be a rager. Who didn't? JW could deliver.

"I don't usually, like, sell and stuff, but right now I've got some left over. You want six grams? You can have it for twelve hundred a gram. That'll last all night, for everyone. The chicks go wild, too; you know that."

Gustaf bit the bait straight off. He didn't have cash but promised to pay JW the following week—no problem for JW.

Gustaf positioned himself behind the bar once again. Blazoned out, "There's a fuckin' blizzard over here!" JW'd already lent him a snort straw and two mirrors.

Everyone but two guys took a hit, twenty milligrams each.

The party exploded.

The music was jacked up. The girls climbed up on the coffee tables and danced, rolled their hips. Fredrik shouted along to Eric Prydz's "Call on Me." Sophie rocked back and forth, Nippe sucked Carro's face on one of the couches, Gustaf tore his shirt off and jumped to the beat on the other couch, Jet Set Carl dug it all hard. He did the brat dance—pumped one fist in the air in time with the music.

The success of the party was sealed. Their transformation into party animals, total. The two guys who hadn't snorted the first time tried now. It gave the desired effect. Everyone got down, dug, danced. The music blared. The party spun. Everyone poured stiff drinks. Shouted along to the music, laughed at nothing, danced, bounced without stopping like Energizer bunnies. Felt hot like hell. Superfly. Jet set. Coursing through everyone's veins: energy, intelligence, hard-ons. Gustaf's party was the sickest rager. Rock on.

Five hours later, the cocaine ran out. JW was still wrapped up in the rush. He'd been checking Sophie out all night. She couldn't have cared less about him. He felt deceived.

But Anna came up to him. Said she thought he was really nice, thanked him for their conversation at dinner, and started dancing with him. They got more and more entwined. Half the party'd passed out. The rest'd crashed on the couches, talking or making out.

JW and Anna went up to her room.

It was five-thirty in the morning. JW felt like he could go forever.

They locked the door and sat down on the bed.

Anna giggled. They looked at each other. Got turned on. JW caressed her breasts through her top. She unzipped his fly, pulled out his cock, bent down, and started sucking. Lip gloss on his cock. Groaned. Really tried to hold it, didn't want to come yet. He pushed himself away and sat up, undressed her instead. Licked her tits. She grabbed hold of his cock again and guided him inside her.

They fucked furiously.

It was way too quick.

He pulled out, came in his hand.

Wiped himself on the sheets.

They lay still, chilled for a moment.

Anna kept talking; wanted to go over the events of the night.

JW didn't want to talk. Cocaine better than Viagra—after fifteen minutes, he was fit for fight.

Cut the foreplay—just fucked right away.

He came after two minutes, max. Embarrassing.

He felt empty.

Slept like shit.

12

Mrado's areas of responsibility within Radovan's sphere: the coat checks, general racketeering, keeping the lackeys in line. He sometimes helped to set dealers or pimps straight who thought they were Dragan Joksovic, or took care of whores who thought they could make their own decisions. Mostly used Ratko or other guys from the gym as backup.

Mrado had his own business on the side. Import firm. Bought wood from Thailand: teak, ebony, balsa. Sold to fine carpenters, interior designers, and contractors. Smooth sailing. Above all, he needed clean, taxable income.

Mrado's headaches: Patrik convicted. The ex-skin probably wouldn't hang anyone, but there was always a risk. Fucking shit luck that the skinhead'd been such a hothead. Even worse: that Mrado'd been stupid enough to bring up his demand for a bigger cut when Rado'd already been pissed. Was a crisis of trust between him and Radovan on the horizon? What's more: Mrado should find that coke monkey, Jorge. Even more: Mrado'd been given the order from Rado to deal with the so-called Nova Project, the cops and the courts in cahoots on a big-budget crackdown to bring the city's organized-crime scene to its knees. Finally: Mrado had to see Lovisa, or else he'd explode. Annika, that cunt, was battling him in court. He was preparing to fight for his daughter. Felt like all of society was against him. He had a fucking right to have a good relationship with his kid, just like anyone else.

He was having trouble sleeping. It wasn't what he had to do or the sheer number of things he had to take care of that made him wake up in the middle of the night; it was thoughts of Lovisa and of a different kind of life that did it. The risk of not being permitted to see her. Thoughts about what he'd do if he stopped doing what he was doing now. Maybe there was another way to live, other businesses where he'd fit in. And still, no. Mrado was who he was. This city needed men like him. The smallest of his current problems was finding a straw man for the video-rental companies. That's where he'd begin.

He made the rounds at the gym. No one wanted to be a part of it. Not because they had fortunes to lose—at least not any that Big Brother knew of—but because they didn't want to fold. The boys had big biz dreams. In the end, everyone had to play somewhat by the legal rules. Conclusion: Don't dirty your record unnecessarily.

Mrado didn't want to fuck things up. At the same time—if things got messy, someone else'd have to take the hit.

He could call one of his peers: Goran, Nenad, or Stefanovic. All were underlings of the Yugo king, on the same level as Mrado in the hierarchy. Guys with their ears to the ground. But also competitors in the race for Radovan's favor.

He called Goran.

The guy was Radovan's smokes and booze importer. A greasy prick. A brownie. If Rado chewed Goran out, he'd lie on his back and wag his legs in the air. Like a bitch. Despite that, the dude was disgustingly good with his gear. Big profits, a turnaround of seventeen million a year.

Smokes and booze import: complicated logistics, administrative mathematics, well-developed transportation and freight methodology. A global enterprise based in Stockholm's criminal underworld. Cheap booze and chic booze. Via Finland from Russia, the Baltic countries, Poland, and Germany. Repackaged, with the country of origin and mode of production blacked out. Goran knew the business. Had solid connections within the Swedish Transportation Union. Had his eye on the teamsters. Was friendly with the bosses. Knew which ones to bribe. Knew what European smuggle routes to use. Faked freight passes, rigged credible chains of transport, recipients and senders. Stuck with the tough guys. The ones who wanted to make easy money. Who set the bar low. Old-timers who worked full-time without giving a cent to the Man.

Mrado wanted to get at the latter group. A different type from the guys at the gym. Older. Prestige-free. Saw the world through the bottom of a bottle. Were done striving. Had seen better days.

Mrado on the line with Goran. Even made himself believe he liked the guy. In Serbian: "Goran, my friend. It's me."

"Mrado, I hear. Since when did we become friends?"

Goran: a dick to everyone and anyone except il Padre, Mr. R. Mrado bit his lip. Let it slide—his mission was more important.

"We work for the same man. We're countrymen. We've gotten shit-faced together. Aren't we friends? We're more than friends."

"You'd do best to remember that we're not friends, and we're not family. I'm a businessman. I've never really understood what the hell it is you do. Beat the crap out of poor coat-check people. Do you steal their jackets, too?"

"What're you talkin' about?"

"Last weekend, I lost my jacket at Café Opera. The faggots in the coat check didn't have a clue. Someone pointed to it and claimed he'd lost his tag."

"Shit happens."

"Is that the kind of shit that happens at your coat checks?"

"No idea."

"You should check up on that."

"Goran, it's not often that I ask for help. And that's not what I'm doing now, either. I'm going to reward you; that's not what I call help."

"Stop speaking in riddles. Something good can come of this talk. I can feel it. My only question is, What? You started this off so nicely. Calling me a friend."

If it'd been anyone else, Mrado would've hung up. Hunted the person down. Ended said person. But first, preferably, snipped off one finger at a time with a ratchet lopper.

"Witty as usual, Goran. I need someone who's got the DL on the teamsters. A trusty old-timer. If you hook me up with a good contact, I'll let you in on five percent of the profits."

"What'll that be for me per month?"

"Honestly, I don't really know yet, but it's a supertight Rado gig I've got going. I'm supposed to set up two companies for him. I'd guess we're talking at least five grand a month and up. Clean."

"Five thousand and up, for a name? Per month? What hole are you fucking me in, exactly?"

"I'm not fucking you. It's just really important to me that this works out. That's why I'm ready to pay."

"What the hell. Shoot. What can I lose? What exactly do you need?"

Mrado explained without saying too much.

Goran said, "I've got a guy. Christer Lindberg. I'll text you his number. That cool?"

"Sure. Thanks. I'll call you this week to let you know how it goes. Maybe you're a good guy after all."

"'Good'? Good is just my middle name. Remember that."

Mrado hung up. Wondered if he'd been smart or a total dipshit.

13

Fall was coming. Jorge'd managed to get a bed at a homeless shelter fourteen out of the past twenty-four nights. Bought personal identification digits from a junkie in the Sollentuna Mall for three grand. Good till the end of the month. The shelters sent their invoices to the junkie's social welfare officer. The mainliner lost his welfare check—he wanted cash for heroine/amphetamine instead.

Jorge didn't get why there were mostly Svens at the shelters, when he knew immigrants were the real dirt-poor suckers—*blattes* with *nada*. Did the blizzardheads have no pride?

Life in the shelter was sweet. Well-cooked meals were included for breakfast and dinner. Jorge watched TV. Read newspapers. They weren't writing shit about his escape.

Chatted a little with the others. Kept it bare bones.

He tried to do push-ups, sit-ups, or jump rope when no one was around. He couldn't run; his foot was still busted from the jump off the wall.

It wasn't working in the long run. Couldn't keep his hair curly without people wondering. Couldn't smear himself with self-tanner without them looking. There was the risk that one of the bums would recognize him. What's more: After fourteen days, the shelter started charging five hundred kronor a night instead of two hundred. There was no fairness in this world. The junkie's money could run out. The Social Service rep could get suspicious.

He hadn't been able to pay his cousin, Sergio, or his screw fixer, Walter, back. Shameful.

Everything sucked.

Gray, frightened thoughts. Psychological low point.

Zero ability to run. Shitty stamina. Physical low point.

This wasn't what he'd gone AWOL for.

He had to score money.

Out one month. Not bad, if you thought about it. Better than many others. But no big success. What'd he been expecting? That plastic surgery, a passport, and a field of clover'd just materialize, for free? That he'd find a few pounds of blow under his pillow at the Night Owl homeless shelter? That his sister'd call and tell him she'd bought tickets to Barcelona and borrowed her BF's passport? Fat chance.

Sergio'd taken a lot of risks. Jorge hadn't heard from him since the day before he left Eddie's. Didn't dare get in touch with him. His bad conscience burned. He should pay Sergio back. But what could he do?

What the FUCK could he do?

He didn't think the cops had a red alert out on him. In their eyes, he was a harmless small-time druggie. Armored-car robbers, rapists, and other violent criminals were much higher up on their list. That was his luck: He hadn't used any violence during the break. Still: Life on the lam was no cakewalk. Cash was the solution.

The thought of Radovan. The ace up his sleeve.

He didn't want to use it. Had been lying at night in the shelters, thinking. Tossed. Turned. Sweated. Reminded him of the nights before the break. But worse, somehow. Then, it could either fly or not fly at all. Now, it could either get fucked up or even more fucked up. Still, he had hope. Maybe it'd work.

The idea: Jorge'd worked for Radovan's organization. Knew stuff they didn't want leaked. Above all, they didn't know exactly how much he knew. He could scare them. Had learned the game on the inside; snitches are bitches and silence is golden. The Yugos should be willing to cough it up.

R. was difficult to get in touch with. No one could or wanted to disclose his home or cell number.

Impossible to reach the Yugo boss.

Radovan's underling, the rat who'd wrapped him in his witness testimony, Mrado, would work fine. Jorge tracked him down instead.

He finally got Mrado's cell phone number from an old dealer in Märsta. Mrado wasn't Radovan, but he was as close as Jorge was gonna get. It'd have to do.

He made the call from a pay phone near Östermalmstorg's subway station.

His fingers shook as he dialed.

He immediately recognized Mrado's voice. Deep. Dangerous. Damning.

Almost shat a brick. Straightened up. "Yo, Mrado. It's Jorge. Jorge Salinas Barrio."

Silence for a short moment. Mrado cleared his throat. "Jorge. Nice to hear your voice. How's life on the outside?"

"Cut the crap. You guys fucked me two years ago. The game you pulled at the trial was bullshit. Still, I'm willing to make a deal now."

"Wow, talk about cutting to the chase. What's this deal about?"

Jorge didn't let himself get provoked. "You know what it's about, Mrado. I had your back, yours and Radovan's both. And you let me sink. Fucking deep. You owe me."

"Ah, I see." Mrado sounded sarcastic. "I guess we'd better see to it that you're happy right away."

"Sure, you can choose to fuck me. But I'll talk, fast. You know I know too much about Radovan's business. I got slammed with three fuckin' years for your sake."

"Easy, Jorge. If you hurt us, we'll make sure you're sent right back to where you came from. But a little deal isn't a bad idea. What'd you have in mind?"

"Simple. Radovan gets me a passport and a hundred G's, cash. I'll jump ship and you'll never hear from me again."

"I'll convey your request to Radovan. But I don't think he's gonna like it. Blackmail isn't his thing. Nothing he lets himself get subjected to. How can I reach you?"

"You think I'm a fuckin' idiot? I'll call you on this number in ten days. If he's not in on my deal by then, I'll fuck him up."

"It's lucky for you Radovan didn't hear that. Call me in two weeks. Good passports can't just be bought on the street."

"No, ten days. Can't you fuckin' order passports from Thailand, or somethin'? And yo, one more thing. If anythin' happens to me, some accident or somethin', you catch my drift, what I know'll leak on the spot."

"I follow. Make it two weeks."

Mrado hung up. Fucking chesty Yugo fuck. Jorge was the one setting the rules, wasn't he? But now all he could do was accept. Two weeks. That was still better than expected—could be kale at the end of this. Was he back on track?

Jorge kept standing where he was. People kept streaming past.
Jorge-boy: the world's loneliest homeboy. *Solo y abandonado.*

Jorge'd been thinking about a possibility—seemed served on a plate.
Svens shut up their summer homes during the off-season. New housing market for him. Maybe that would at least solve one problem.

He was screwed when it came to cash. Had one G left of the five
Sergio'd given him.

His expenses had been too big so far. A total of three thousand kronor for the shelter. Every session at the tanning booth: sixty-five kronor. Vending machine grub for lunch. A new pair of pants, gloves, two
T-shirts, a knit sweater, underwear, socks, and a winter jacket from a
thrift store: 450 kronor. In preparation for a cold autumn.

He took a last trip to the tanning bed. He was dark now. Had nailed
the walk. The right rhythm. Now he wanted to get away for a while.
Wait for Radovan's answer.

He took the subway to the Royal Technical Academy station. Didn't
really know where he was going. Just that he wanted to head north.
Somewhere deserted. He nixed the express bus to Norrtälje. Got on
bus number 620 instead, also headed north to Norrtälje, but with a
more roundabout route.

He dozed.

The bus drove past Åkersberga. There were hicks on the bus. A lady
with two wiener dogs stared at him.

He got off at a stop that looked nice, called Wira Bruk. The plastic bag
with his clothes in it was twisted around his wrist. He let it get tangled.

Not his kind of turf. Jorge'd been to the country once in his life,
on a school field trip when he was thirteen. Ended with his being sent
home. You weren't allowed to set the forest on fire.

To his right was a stone church. The clock tower stood separately,
built of gray wood. A couple of gravestones in the grass around the
main building. To the left, the land slanted upward. To the woods. One
road kept going straight, and one took off to the left. Fields farther up.
The crops had been harvested.

The sky was gray.

He started walking.

Toward the fork in the road. Looked down the road that veered to the left. A couple of houses and parked cars. He walked closer. Saw a sign: WIRA BRUK—OLD HOMESTEAD MUSEUM. He walked across the parking lot. Nine cars total. Toyed with the thought of boosting one, then scrapped it. Walked down toward the houses.

A stream to his left. Picturesque. A little bridge. Leafy trees. Gravel road. Red kiosk. Seemed boarded up for the fall, but they'd forgotten the ice-cream cardboard cutout outside. Farther down, three larger houses. A gravel square between them. Signs on the houses. An old school. An old parish hall. An old county sheriff's house. A middle-aged couple entered the school. He was seriously off. There were no vacation homes here. It was a fucking museum.

Out on the main road again.

He kept walking. For fifteen minutes. No houses in sight.

Fifteen more minutes.

Saw houses farther up between the trees.

Got closer.

The first seemed lived in. There was a Volvo V70 parked outside.

He went on to the next one. Woods all around.

Jorge wondered if it'd been the right move to come up here. Unknown territory. Away game. Simple fact about J-boy: He wasn't exactly the type who'd been raised a Boy Scout, field biologist, or explorer. Limited exposure to a world without asphalt and McDonald's.

The house was about three hundred yards farther up. Couldn't be seen from the first house. No car parked outside. It was big. Two glassed-in porches. Faded red paint. White trim. Green paint around the windows. The bottom porch was hardly visible behind all the wild trees and bushes. Jorge walked up the path. The gravel crunched. The door to the house faced the yard, at the back of the house if you stood on the road. Perfect. Looked in through all the windows. No one home. Knocked on the door. No answer. Yelled "Hello." No one came out. Walked back out on the road. No other people or houses in sight. Went back. Tried to locate an alarm system. *Nada*. Put his gloves on. Broke a window. Carefully reached his hand in. Didn't want to cut himself. Unhooked the window latch. No problem. Opened the window. Pulled himself up. Jumped in.

Listened. No alarm. He yelled again. No answer. *Qué lindo*.

After two days in the house, he felt right at home.

He made a room with a window facing the hedge his bedroom. Avoided the other windows. Cleaned all the grub out of the cupboards. Found pasta, rice, canned goods, beer, herring. Old condiments. No favorite foods, but it'd have to do.

During the day, he did push-ups and jumped rope on one foot. More training: sit-ups, back exercises, stretching. Wanted to stay in shape. Make up for what he'd missed during the time in the shelters.

Nervous. Ears perked. He listened for the sound of cars. Crunching on the gravel. Voices outside. He took an old beer can and put it on the handle of the front door—if someone came, it'd fall on the floor and make enough noise to wake him up.

It was peaceful. Tranquil. Quiet. Damn dull.

He was supposed to call Mrado in ten days.

He couldn't sleep that night, his thoughts distracted. What would he do if Radovan refused to give up? How would he make cash? Maybe he'd have to be in touch with someone in the C business after all. Flip a few grams. Deal for dosh. Back to the old routine.

What'd happened to Sergio? Eddie? His sister? His mama? He should really give them a call. Show he cared.

He thought about Sångvägen, the street where he'd grown up. His first pair of soccer cleats. The grass field down by Frihetsvägen. The hangout room in Tureberg's School. The basement of his house. His first joint.

Man, he wanted one.

Got up. Looked out the window. The sky was starting to glow. Fog rose off the ground. Sappy flick. Cue the music. Dig the paradox: him, Jorge, progeny of the asphalt jungle, sucking up the bumpkin paradise and enjoying it. It was so beautiful outside.

In that moment, he didn't give a shit if anyone saw him.

14

JW was soon a real hot ticket. The rings spread on the water after the party at Lövhälla Manor. The talk about the rager went on for weeks: how crazy Nippe'd been, how funny Jet Set Carl'd looked when he'd run riot, the killer jokes Lollo'd made, how randy Nippe was all the time. The gossip exaggerated the drinking, the dancing, the scandals, and the rush, to JW's advantage.

He made good money in the weeks that followed. Abdulkarim loved him. He painted their brilliant plans for the future, fantasized—they were going to own this town. JW didn't know if he should take Abdul seriously or if he was kidding around. The Arab talked so damn much.

JW stopped driving the gypsy cab, let another guy take over. Checked with Abdulkarim first. It was cool with the Arab.

JW saw himself with new eyes: business baron, blow bringer, bitch banger—got three girls home in two weeks. A personal record. He felt like a mini Nippe.

During the days, he went berserk in the boutiques. Two new pairs of shoes to call his own: Gucci loafers with the gold buckle, and Helmut Lang boots for the winter. He bought a suit, Acne design with visible seams at the cuffs. It was hip, possibly too hipster. Maybe not the correct, strict style. He gorged himself on new shirts with double cuffs: Stenströms, Hugo Boss, Pal Zileri. Bought new jeans, pants, socks, belts, tank tops, and cuff links. The best buy of all was a cashmere coat from Dior, for the winter. The price was twelve thousand kronor. Expensive, sure, but it costs to be on top. He hung it in front of his bed so it'd be the first thing he saw when he woke up in the morning. Coat for a king.

JW loved every minute. He didn't save a cent.

As for the Ferrari, he kept repeating to himself: There'd been two cars like it in Sweden that year. It shouldn't be impossible to find someone with a connection to them, someone who'd known Camilla or at least knew more than the police. Peter Holbeck, the owner of one of the cars, had hardly used his. Anyway, it didn't seem likely that Camilla would've had anything to do with the guy; the dude was never in Sweden. That left the leasing company, Dolphin Finance, Ltd. The company'd filed for bankruptcy a year ago—that was obviously shady.

JW looked up info about the company with the National Registry of Incorporated Companies. It was bought as a shelf company, Grundstenen, Ltd., but had immediately changed its name to Leasing Finance, Ltd. Six months later, it changed its name to the Finance ER of Stockholm, Ltd. A year later, it changed its name again, this time to Dolphin Finance, Ltd. Three name changes in less than three years. The fish stink was unmistakable. The same person'd been on the board ever since the storage company's buyout, a certain Lennart Nilsson, born March 14, 1954. JW looked the man up with the Civil Population Registry.

Lennart Nilsson was dead.

JW ordered a copy of the documents connected with the bankruptcy case.

Peculiar information: Lennart Nilsson was a known user from Nacka and had died of cirrhosis. According to the compulsory information the administrator of the bankrupt estate was obligated to supply in case of eventual falsifications, the man was probably a cover, a so-called front man.

JW'd reached a dead end. The Ferrari was leased by a company that'd gone under and whose only physical representative had passed away. How would he proceed now?

The only thing he could think of was to get in touch with the administrator of the bankrupt estate personally. He called, got a secretary on the line, and asked to speak with the lawyer. According to the secretary, there were tons of hurdles. Every time JW called, she said, "Can you call back? Unfortunately, he is in a meeting at the moment." JW asked her to tell the lawyer to call him. He thought that should be enough. The lawyer jerk never called back. JW had to keep at it. Took over a week to reach him.

Finally, they were able to talk. A real anticlimax for JW. The lawyer/administrator didn't have any more information than what was written in the documents he'd ordered. The company hadn't kept any books, had no employees, and there were very sparse annual financial reports.

The accountant wasn't in the country, and it wasn't clear who owned the stocks.

All the leads to the Ferrari ended in a bankruptcy that seemed Criminal with a capital *C*. It was blatantly obvious that something wasn't right, but JW'd stopped thinking about the car for a few days. There wasn't much more he could do.

He tried to let it go.

Didn't work. He couldn't escape his thoughts. His sister was missing and there had to be a way to learn more.

Four years ago, a policeman had told JW's family the odds: "Normally, the unfortunate fact is that if we don't find a missing person within a week, the person is most likely dead. The risk of that is nine out of ten." The police kept explaining, "Most often, the person hasn't been the victim of a violent crime. As a rule, there are accidents, like drowning, heart attacks, unfortunate falls. The body is usually found. On the other hand, if it isn't, it can be a sign that other circumstances brought about the death."

Memories of the conversation with the police gave JW ideas. He knew Camilla'd last been heard from on the night of April 21 of the year she went missing. At the time, she called a friend, Susanne Pettersson, who was also the only known acquaintance of Camilla's that the police'd been able to dig up in Stockholm. She'd told the police she didn't know anything. Her only connection to Camilla'd been that they studied together at Komvux, a continuing-education center. Maybe that's why he hadn't given her more thought before.

In JW's opinion, the police couldn't have done a particularly thorough job; they must've seen the pictures of Camilla in the Ferrari. Still, it wasn't mentioned in the reports JW's family'd been shown. They could've missed other things, too.

JW grasped desperately at the poor odds—one in ten missing people wasn't dead.

Maybe Camilla was still alive.

He had to know more; he felt he owed it to his sister. A week after he heard about the dead board member of Dolphin Finance, Ltd., he called Susanne Pettersson. They talked for a bit. She'd never completed her studies, never gotten her GED. Now she worked as a salesclerk at H&M in the Kista Mall. When he suggested they meet up, she asked if their phone conversation wasn't enough. It was obvious that she didn't have an interest in digging deeper into the Camilla story.

JW went out to Kista anyway. Wandered around the brightly lit mall until he found the H&M store and asked for Susanne. He introduced himself to her.

They stood in the middle of the shop floor. There were few customers in the store at that time of day. JW wondered how it could be worthwhile to keep the place open.

Susanne had bleached-blond hair, but dark roots were visible at the base of her scalp. She was dressed in skinny jeans tucked into a pair of high boots, and a pink top with print across the chest: *Cleveland Indians.* Her entire body language screamed, I don't want to talk to you. Arms crossed, gaze glued somewhere other than on JW.

JW tried to pressure her, gently. "What subjects did you study together?"

"I had to redo almost everything. Math, language arts, English, social science, history, French. But school was never my thing. I wanted to be a lawyer."

"It isn't too late."

"It is. I have two kids now."

JW sounded genuinely happy, "That's great! How old are they?"

"One and three, and it's not great. Their good-for-nothing dad left five months before the youngest was born. I'll stay in this store till the cellulite finishes me off."

"I'm sorry. Don't say that. Anything can happen."

"Sure."

"It can, I promise. Would you please tell me more about Camilla?"

"But why? The police asked all they needed to know four years ago. I don't know anything."

"Relax. I'm just curious. You know, I hardly even knew my own sister. I was just wondering what kind of classes you took together and stuff."

"I would've been a good lawyer—you know, I can really argue when I need to—and then Pierre came along and fucked it all up. Now I'm here. Know what a salesclerk makes?"

JW thought, The chick could never have been a lawyer. Totally lacks focus.

"You don't remember which classes you took with Camilla?"

"Hold on. I think we were in the same language arts and English classes. Used to do our homework together, study for the tests. She got good grades even though we cut a lotta class. I got shit grades. Never knew how the hell Camilla did it. But then, I didn't really know her that well."

"Do you know if she hung out with anyone else?"

Susanne was quiet for a beat too long.

"Not really."

JW looked her in the eyes. "Please, Susanne. I care about my sister. Don't I have a right to know what happened to her? Don't I have the right to ask you these questions? I just want to know more about Camilla's life. Please."

Susanne twisted uneasily, looked toward the empty registers, as if she had to go help some invisible customer. Obviously uncomfortable.

"I don't think she was friends with anyone else in her Komvux classes. Camilla sort of kept to herself. But ask the language arts teacher, Jan Brunéus. He might know."

"Thanks. Is he still at Komvux, do you know?"

"No clue. Some made it; some didn't. I never finished. Haven't set my foot in that place since and don't plan to, either. And I don't know anything about Jan. But there are a lot of salesclerks who've made a load of money. Won reality-TV shows and stuff like that. Camilla might've done something like that."

Susanne said she really had to get back to work. JW got the hint, went home. Wondered about Susanne's last comment. Reality TV and Camilla—what was the connection?

He thought that he had to concentrate on school and selling C, couldn't waste more time playing detective. The Susanne Pettersson trail didn't lead anywhere. The chick would've already said something if she knew something, wouldn't she?

JW was at home studying when Abdulkarim called his cell phone. The Arab wanted to meet up—preferably today. They decided to meet for lunch at the Hotel Anglais on Sturegatan, near Stureplan.

JW kept reading. He couldn't let his studies slip. He'd made a deal with himself: Go ahead and snort, deal, make millions and be happy—but don't flunk out of school. He saw that kind of thing among the boyz. There were two types of people for whom Daddy picked up the tab. The knowledge that they'd never have to worry about money made one type into lazy, disinterested, stupid freeloaders. They couldn't care less about their studies, failed their exams, made fun of people who were ambitious. They wanted to do their own thing, pretended to be entrepreneurs, visionaries. In the end, things worked out no matter what. The other type got anxious, knowing they'd never have to lift a finger for their own livelihood. They wanted to prove themselves, had to prove themselves, to create their own successes, to earn the right to the fortunes they were going to inherit anyway. You found them at the Stockholm School of Economics, in law school, or in London. They sat till one in the morning with group projects, before quizzes, tests, oral exams. If they could fit it in, they had part-time jobs, at law firms, banks, or with Dad. They strove and achieved—got somewhere on their own merit.

JW wasn't the kind of guy to take shortcuts, not really. Sure, he could probably live on C for a few years, but he still wanted the safety. Study a lot, never flunk out.

He packed up his books. Undressed and got into the shower.

With practiced technique, he held the showerhead in his hand with the stream of water angled away from him, as he tried to set the right temperature. Why was it that no matter how you turned the dial, it was impossible to get it right? Too hot. A nanotwist to the left—too cold.

He began by running the water over his legs. The blond hairs flattened downward when the stream of water washed over them. He put the showerhead back in its holder, let the water pour over his hair, head, and torso. Turned up the heat.

Tried to forget about Camilla. Thought about Sophie instead. What was he doing wrong? He'd thought he was going to score with her at the Lövhälla Manor party. Instead, he'd ended up with Anna, her best friend. Anna was nice and all, but she didn't have that extra something. How retarded was it to fuck Anna? Gossip about the party'd spread so widely, it might as well have been in the tabloids. Sophie could've found out. Maybe she was pissed.

Sophie in JW's eyes: pretty as hell, body like a bikini model, sexy like a Playboy Bunny, charming like an intelligent talk-show host. And she had brains, too. Wrestled him to the ground verbally every time they had a discussion. Radiated smarts every time she opened her mouth. One-upped his jokes with a twinkle in her eye. But that wasn't all—she seemed nice, too, even though she'd dissed him like a typical Lundsberg prep school chick. She got top grades, ten out of ten. He had to see her more, but without the boyz. Alone.

JW turned up the heat even more. Thought about peeing in the shower but didn't. Wasn't his style.

Maybe he didn't have enough game. Maybe he should ignore Sophie. Not be so obviously into her. Not seem so happy to see her. Talk to her less and hit on her friends more. JW hated the tail game. And yet he was an expert at playing his own game in front of the boyz. But when it came to Sophie, he just wanted to hold her every time she was near. Hug her, kiss her, and all that. How the hell would he be able to act ice-cold? Sure, he could pick up girls at bars. Pull some one-liners. Get 'em in bed. Bag 'em. Brag in front of the boyz. But the serious stuff was trickier. The real game was wily.

He turned the heat up again. That's what he always did; began with a temperature that was hard to perfect and felt good at first but got too cold after a couple of minutes. Made hot even hotter. In the end, the water was almost scalding. The mirror fogged up; the bathroom turned into a steam room.

Time to have lunch with Abdulkarim. JW got out of the shower and readied himself in the bathroom. Put on Clinique Happy under his arms and Biotherm moisturizer on his face. Putting wax in his hair was the last thing he did—the goo was so difficult to get off his fingers. He looked at himself in the mirror and thought: I look good.

He stepped out of the bathroom. Shivered. Got dressed. Put on the cashmere coat—a boy with class. Put his new MP3 player, a tiny Sony, in his pocket and put the earbuds in. They didn't stay very well, tended to fall out. He tried to wedge them in at an angle. Put on a Coldplay song and walked down toward Sturegatan. It was a bright day. It was already twenty past three.

The Hotel Anglais was half-empty. Two waitresses sat at a table, folding napkins in prep for the night. Behind the bar, a guy in jeans and a T-shirt was sorting bottles of booze. Sly and the Family Stone was playing from the hidden speakers. Only two guests sat at a table. Abdulkarim didn't appear to have arrived yet.

One of the napkin-folding chicks walked up to him. Led him to a table by the windows, far from the other guests. He ordered a coffee. Looked out through the floor-to-ceiling windows. Out toward Sturegatan. Humlegården was right across the street. He thought about the first time he'd treated Sophie and Anna to a hit in the park. The gateway to the network. That was a little over five weeks ago now. He'd gotten to know more new people during that time than during his entire life. Cocaine-controlled chum cartels.

There weren't a lot of people on the streets at three-thirty in the afternoon on a weekday. A couple of stressed-looking bankers in dark blue suits hurried past. Two moms, each pushing a baby carriage with one hand and holding a cell phone in the other, strolled up toward the park. One of them was pregnant again. JW thought about Susanne Pettersson. He'd be bitter, too, if he was in her situation. A lady walked by with a pug on a leash. JW leaned back in his chair and pulled out his cell phone. Fired off a text to Nippe, asking what the plan was for the night: *Drinks at Plaza, maybe?*

"*Salam aleikum.* How's school going?" Abdulkarim's shrill voice, almost unaccented. JW looked up from his texting.

Abdul stood by his table. At least as much wax in his hair as in JW's, but shaped differently. Some sort of pageboy look. Abdulkarim was always dressed in a suit, with the cuffs of his shirt peeking out of the jacket. As if he were some honest, hardworking banker or lawyer. What gave him away were the pants. They were three times baggier than the current fashion and had old-man pleats in the front. In 1996, the rest of the pants world had moved on and left Abdulkarim behind. The only thing he got right was a stylish silk handkerchief tucked into his breast pocket. Abdulkarim had a gait with attitude, a constant five o'clock shadow, and dark, glittering eyes. The heart of it: The Arab was the definition of a *blatte* playboy.

JW replied, "School's good."

"Isn't college a little gay? Buddy, when you gonna realize there are faster roads to success? I really thought you'd have understood that by now."

JW laughed. Abdulkarim took a seat. Waved his whole arm in order to get the attention of one of the waitresses. True Abdul the Arab. His gestures were too big. Un-Swedish, unreverent.

Abdulkarim ordered sesame-marinated, finely sliced filet of steer and noodles. Trendy. In the same breath, he managed to say that he wanted the waitress's number, that she ought to change the music, and that he wondered whether the steer'd been well hung. He laughed for five minutes at his own joke.

JW ordered a seafood soup with aioli.

"Very good to see you like this. Was getting tired of just buzzing on the phone all the time."

"You're right. We need to get together, to celebrate. These are glorious times, Abdulkarim. If you can get me more, I need more. You know that."

"Times are fattening you up. You switch that out, like I told you?" Abdulkarim pointed to JW's cell phone.

"Nope, not yet. Sorry. I'll buy a new one this week. Sony Ericsson's latest. Have you seen it? It's got a super-high-def camera. Really damn sweet."

Abdulkarim imitated him. "'Really damn sweet.' I know your story. Stop talkin' like you lived in Östermalm since the cradle. Plus, I want you to buy a new cell phone today. Damn it, you gotta watch yourself. We do good business, you and me. Too good to fuck up because of bad phones, if you know what I mean."

The Arab could seem silly sometimes, but JW knew the guy was a real pro. Cautious, never used words like *police*, *cops*, *risk*, *cocaine*, *coke*, or *drugs* in public. Knew that restaurant employees and customers could eavesdrop better than a gramps with his hearing aid turned up to max. Knew the police easily tapped cells, tracked contracts. Abdulkarim's rules were safe. Always call from a pay-as-you-go SIM card, exchange the card every week, preferably switch phones every other week.

"You know, I got two other guys selling. They do good. Not as good as you, no, but okay. We can talk numbers on the phone. Prices are going down. My boss's suppliers, they're not perfect. Think there're at least two middlemen between them and the wholesaler."

"Why don't you go straight to the wholesaler?"

"First of all, it's not really my call. I work for the boss and don't run my own fuckin' business. I thought you knew that. Second of all, I think the wholesaler's in England. Hard to read. Hassle to negotiate with. But we're not here to talk about purchasing prices today. Not at all. What I want to tell you is, we need salespeople. In the boroughs, the projects. Someone who knows that market. Someone who can sell to other retailers. Someone who knows the business and the tricks, if you know what I mean. The prices are going down. The product is getting popular in Stockholm's satellites. At the beginning of last year, the proportions were something like twenty borough, eighty inner city. At the end of last year, it was fifty-fifty. You with me, my man? The boroughs are waking up in winter, and loving the snow. It's not just inner-city people, your upper-class buddies, and the partyers doing this stuff anymore. Everyone is. Svens, niggers, teenagers. It's populist stuff. Folksy. Like IKEA, H&M. We're talking bigger volume. We're talking lower purchase prices. Growing margins. You follow, college boy?"

JW loved the Arab's parley. He spoke better Swedish than expected, like a real businessman—serious business. The only thing that put him off was the fact that Abdul seemed scared of his boss for some reason. JW wondered why.

"It sounds interesting. For sure. But you know, the boroughs aren't my turf. I can't sell there. I don't know anybody there. That's just not me."

"I know that's what you want people to think about you. That's fine with me. You got your market and you do good. But listen up." Abdulkarim leaned across the table. JW got his drift, pushed his plate to the side. Crossed his arms and leaned his chest in closer.

Abdul looked him in the eye and lowered his voice. "There's a guy, a Chilean or somethin', who just broke outta the joint. I remember him from a couple years back, a clocker without much of a clue. But now talk has it the guy knows the northern boroughs like you know the bathrooms at Kharma. Learned even more on the inside. The joint's a better school than all the projects combined. I know some of his buds from Österåker. They say he's smart as hell. The Chilean pulled off quite a show five or six weeks ago. Fucking Cirque du Soleil. Climbed over the wall and disappeared in the woods. A twenty-three-foot wall, you dig? The guards just stood there twisted up like question marks. He's a good guy. But right now he's a guy under a fuckload of pressure. I know he hasn't left the country yet. He's got what we need. Most important, he'll work for cheap in exchange for me taking him on."

"What am I supposed to say? I don't know about all that. Don't know why you'd want to get involved with some guy who's obviously gonna attract the cops like flies to shit."

"Right now, at this stage, I'm not gonna get involved with him. You are. I want you to find him. Flatter him. Pay him. Take care of him. Then he'll help us tighten our grip on the boroughs. But don't scare him; remember, he's on the run. But that's the whole point. You dig, my man? Since he's on the run, he'll get dependent on us providing for him, giving him a safe place to stay, keeping him undercover."

JW didn't like what he was hearing. At the same time, it was like he'd tasted blood, whet his appetite for the Arab's business. He'd been hesitant in the beginning, but now the sun just seemed to keep on shining. Maybe the Chilean runaway idea wasn't so bad after all.

"Why not? Let's try it. How and where do I find this Chilean?"

Abdulkarim laughed out loud. Praised JW. Praised Allah. JW thought, is Abdul getting religious, or what?

The Arab leaned in even closer and gave JW the info. The little he knew. The runaway's name: Jorge Salinas Barrio. The guy was from Sollentuna and his family consisted of a mom, a plastic papa, and a sister. Abdulkarim's best piece of advice: "Go to Sollentuna and talk up some of the right people. It should give you something, *inshallah*; just make it obvious you're not a narc."

He ended by tucking a bag in JW's jacket pocket. JW felt with his hand—bills. He looked at Abdul, who held up all ten fingers. "There are this many bills in there and a piece of paper with six names on it. That's the best help I can offer."

JW fished out the slip of paper. All the names except for one sounded Spanish. The money was, as the Arab put it, "for getting all the homeys in Sollis to dish about el runaway-o."

JW finished his soup. Abdulkarim settled the bill.

They walked out. It was chilly outside.

JW started thinking. This could be big. This could be a little conglomerate all on its own.

He was going to track down that Chilean.

He walked home. Had trouble studying. Couldn't concentrate. His mind kept wandering. He stretched out on the bed and tried to read the last issue of *GQ*.

His cell phone rang. JW realized he'd forgotten to keep his promise to Abdulkarim about getting a new one.

Jet Set Carl's voice on the other end of the line.

What the hell? What could he want?

After saying hi, Carl said, "JW, Lövhälla Manor was such a great fucking time. Totally insane."

"Ridiculous. We've gotta do that again sometime."

"For sure. Really damn sweet that you could help bring the party. I really think everyone appreciated it."

"Nice to hear. I tend to be able to find a way to bring some fun, so to speak."

"Did you know I jumped the shit out of a couch? Totally busted it."

JW gauged his tone—no problem, okay to laugh.

Carl scoffed.

"It was a real piece, too. Designer."

"You're kidding? What'd Gunn say?"

More laughter. I mean, Gunn? Please.

They chatted about the awesome dinner, Nippe's game, that Jet Set Carl'd paid fifteen big ones to fix the couch, that Gunn must've wondered why everyone was sneezing up a storm the morning after.

In JW's mind, the same question kept coming back to him: Why is Jet Set Carl calling me?

He didn't have to wait long for an answer. "It's my birthday and I'm having a big party at my house. Think you could bring some fun?"

JW was used to the slang and the roundabout way of saying things. Even so, it took him a sec to catch on. "You mean C? Of course. How much do you need?"

"Hundred and fifty grams."

JW: brain freeze.

Jesus.

He tried to sound unperturbed, "That's a lot, but I think I can get it. Just have to check the amount first, make sure it's cool."

"I don't want to be a drag, but I have to know pretty soon. I'll call you back in an hour. If you don't know, I'll ask someone else. What's your price?"

JW did some rapid mental arithmetic. It was dizzying—if he could get a hold of the amount, that is. Maybe he'd be able to push the purchase price down to five hundred. Could charge Carl at least a thousand. Left for him: at least seventy-five grand.

Jesus Christ Superstar.

"I'll do my very best, Calle. I'll call you as soon as I know."

Jet Set Carl thanked him. He sounded like he was in a good mood.

They hung up.

JW sat on the bed—with the stiffest hard-on in northern Europe.

* * *

Dagens Nyheter, daily
October

TONIGHT, THE STOCKHOLM POLICE BEGAN A MAJOR OFFENSIVE AGAINST ORGANIZED crime. The goal is to eradicate at least one-third of the 150 specifically targeted persons from the criminal underworld—and to deter young people from taking up a life of violent crime.

The offensive, classified as "Nova," was actually supposed to begin over six months ago. The planned action had to be postponed because resources were allocated to a number of other recent highly publicized investigations.

But the first hit took place tonight. Hundreds of police officers from various divisions, including special operations from the gang unit, took part in a number of crackdowns in different parts of the city and the surrounding boroughs. The result of the work is not yet known and the district police have not answered any of *Dagens Nyheter's* questions.

Through Nova, the district police hope to combat the networks of more or less career criminals who are behind violent crime, protection racketeering, drug trafficking, human trafficking, prostitution, and cigarette smuggling. The project's action plan states that violent crime is on the rise in the Stockholm area and that the likelihood of criminals bearing arms has increased.

The strategy is to first and foremost strike out against the leaders of these criminal networks. In connection with the offensive, 150 known criminals across the region have been pinpointed as being of special interest. The goal is that at least fifty of these will, "by means of distraction or force of law," be "made to refrain from criminal activity in the long term." None of these persons is currently serving time or is charged with crimes that can lead to more than two years in prison.

The goal is to be reached within two years, at the latest.

15

On his way to Radovan. Serbian music on the stereo: Zdravko Colic. Mrado, pissed—that faggot Jorge'd been uppity. Threatened Radovan. Indirectly threatened Mrado. Tried to blackmail. Tried to be smart. Tried to play with fire.

Jorge had info on the cocaine business. Knew of storage spots, import routes, smuggling methods, dealers, buyers, labs, bulking techniques. Most of all, the *blatte* knew who ran the show. Mr. R. himself risked being in the danger zone. *Gospodin Bog*—the *blatte* fucker was the one should be in the danger zone.

That cocksucker. Mrado would find Jorge, tape him up, cut him to pieces. Eat him up. Shit him out. Lap up. Shit out again.

Mrado'd called Radovan right after he got off the phone with the *blatte*. Radovan sounded calmer than Mrado. But Mrado sensed the vibes under the surface: Radovan even more pissed than he was.

Jorge, prepare for revenge of the Yugos.

The good thing about the Latino's provocation: The incident diverted Radovan's irritation from Mrado. Last time they'd gotten together, the mood'd hit an all-time low. Radovan'd gone too far.

Twenty minutes later, he arrived in Näsbypark. The leafy suburb. Gaudy paradise of the straitlaced and square. Cunts. He parked his car and lit a cigarette. Held it between thumb and pointer finger— Slavic-style. Took deep drags. Had to calm down before his meeting with Radovan the Great. Phlegmy cough. Thought about Radovan's paintings. Total value? Couldn't be measured in money.

He stubbed out his cigarette. Walked up to the house.

Rang the doorbell.

ovic opened the door. Didn't say a word, just led Mrado to the adovan was seated in the same chair as last time. The leather on the armrests was worn and faded. A bottle of whiskey on the coffee table: sixteen-year-old Lagavulin.

"Have a seat, Mrado. Thanks for calling right away. We could've done this over the phone, but I wanted to look you in the eyes to see that you're not too rabid. You've got to take it easy. We've got to take it easy. Solve this one step at a time. It's not a huge deal. Others have tried. Only difference now is that he actually might know something. Tell me what he said. From the beginning, please. Full transcript."

Mrado told him everything. Tried to keep it short without leaving out the most important part—the *blatte*'s attitude.

"Jorge Salinas Barrio's on the run. You know more than me about that story; you were the one who informed me. According to what I've heard, the guy's some sort of hero at Österåker. Even the heavy hitters at federal joints like Kumla and Hall admire his style and finesse. Disappeared into thin air like some fucking magic trick. Broke out, Houdini-style. I should've dealt with him right away. That fuckin' fag."

"Houdini—I like the comparison. But don't tell me you should've taken him down right away. We don't know what could've happened then. Just keep talking."

Mrado told him about his conversation with Jorge. That Jorge'd sounded stressed-out, that the *blatte*'d probably called from a pay phone, that he wanted a passport and a hundred G's, that he'd said a lot of shit would be leaked if anything happened to him.

Radovan sat silently. Refilled his glass of Lagavulin. Took a sip.

"He knows a lot about us. But not *that* much. He can't make me dance like some kinda monkey with the shit he knows. This is his big chance to get me to help him. Of course I could get him a new passport. Cash. A new life in some warm country. The only problem is, he's gotten me all wrong. No one forces me to do anything. Anyway, what's to say he'll stop there? You know how the fucking Croats were back in the homeland. They wouldn't settle for ninety-nine percent of the coastline, they wanted it all. It's the same with this guy. One day I get him a new identity, and the next day he'll be back asking for money. Or asking for plane fare. Or asking for any fucking thing—stake in Radovan's empire."

Mrado laughed. Rado: the gangster king who talked about himself in the third person. Mrado relaxed. Better mood than last time he'd been here. Felt the whiskey warm his body. Soften his shoulders. Caress his insides.

"His trump card is what he knows, or maybe knows. I'm not really sure that he actually has enough info to hurt us, but he's a threat. Our trump card is that we can send him right back to jail, without passing Go. The disadvantage of our advantage is that there's a risk he'll lose hope if we send him back in. If he doesn't have anything to live for anymore besides building biceps at a supermax, that canary'll sing quicker than you can say blow. I can guarantee you that."

"Excuse me, Radovan. But why not just pop the fucker?"

"That's not how we do. Too dangerous. You heard him. It'll leak. We don't know who else he's told. Jorge Salinas Barrio's no idiot. If we rub him out, I promise he'll have made sure the info we don't want seeing the light'll be up and out with the fucking dawn. He's probably already leaked to someone who'll tell all if we so much as pluck a hair on his nappy head. But, you know, he could do anything. Lock papers in some safety deposit box. If he bites it, no one'll be there to keep paying the fee, the box'll be opened, someone'll see all the papers he put in there, including detailed accounts of our business. Or else he's written some e-mail that's programmed to be sent to the cops after a certain date unless he stops it. You know where this is going—point is, we can't off him. He's too smart for that. But there are ways. Classic methods, you know, Mrado. You find him, or get in touch with him in some other way. Do your thing. Explain to him that he can forget about his ugly blackmail attempts ever making Radovan quiver. And then, once you're sure he knows who sent the greeting, crush him. You ever stabbed someone in the stomach?"

"Yes, bayonet, Srebrenica, 1995."

"Then you know it bleeds like a bitch, will fold anyone. So many soft parts to hit and so much to injure. That's the way to approach Jorge—break him right away, fast and easy. Like stabbing with a knife."

"I'm following. Do I have carte blanche?"

"Yes and no. You can't finish him. No knife. That was just to paint the picture. Let me put it this way: You have to use soft brass knuckles."

Radovan laughed at his own joke.

"I understand. Do you know anything else about where I might find him?"

"Not really. But he's from the Sollentuna area. Ask Ratko or Ratko's brother. They're from there. One more thing. You can't fuck the *blatte* fag up so much he has to go to the hospital. Then he'll be sent back to prison, and we'll be back in the risky territory I just mentioned. In the slammer without hope, he'll screw everyone. Turn into a rodent in no time."

"Trust me. Not a single bone will be broken in the body of that little pussy. Still, he'll wish he was back in his mother's."

Mrado's vulgarity made Radovan smile. He whisked the whiskey around in his glass. Took a sip. Leaned back in the armchair. Mrado, pumped. Wanted out, on the street. Away from Radovan. To the gym. Talk to the guys. Find leads. Crack the code. Crush Jorge.

They talked about other stuff: horses and cars. No business. Nothing about Mrado's demanding a bigger cut of the coat checks last time. After fifteen minutes, Radovan excused himself. "I've got some things to attend to. And Mrado, considering the fiasco at Kvarnen, I want Jorge now. Know what? I want him yesterday already."

Mrado went to the gym. Talked to the guys working the desk. Interrupted their discussion about the latest muscle medicine. Asked questions. Did they know anyone doing time at Österåker? Did they know anyone working as a guard at Österåker? Did they know anything about that slick break that'd gone down five weeks ago?

One of them said, "You seem interested. Are you on your way in and want to know how to get out?" Grinned at his own joke.

Mrado, indulgent. Refrained from biting back. Joked along instead. "Preparation's a shortcut, right?"

The guy leaned over the desk: "That escape was totally SUPERior. I mean, honestly, the dude that stepped over the wall must've been Sergej Bubka himself. Twenty-three feet, Mrado. How the hell do you jump that without a pole? Is he Spider-Man, or what?"

"Do you know anyone doing time there?"

"I don't know anyone doing time there. I'm a refined person, don't you know. Don't know any guards, either. Ask Mahmud, maybe. You know, Arabs are always a little criminal. Half the race is, like, behind bars. Check the showers, I think he just did his morning sesh."

Mrado went downstairs. Into the locker room. Mahmud wasn't there. A couple other guys were getting dressed. Mrado said hi. Walked back up. Looked around the room on the right. The Eurotechno blared. No Mahmud. Looked around the room on the left. Saw Mahmud kneeling on a red mat. Stretching his back. Looked like a grotesque ballerina mid-pose.

Mrado knelt down next to him.

"Yo, twiggy. How's your sesh? What d'you do?"

Mahmud didn't look up. Kept stretching his back. "I don't know who you're calling twiggy, twiggy. The sesh was good. I've worked the crap out of my lower back and shoulders today. Is fine. They're far from each other. How're things with you?"

"Rollin'. I need help with something. That cool?"

"Course. Mahmud never leaves you hangin'; you know that."

"Cool. Do you know anyone doing time at Österåker?"

"Yeah. My sister's husband's there. She visits a lot. They get a room to themselves, have a little fun." Mahmud changed positions. Stood up. Arms between his legs. Hunched his back. The sound of joints cracking.

"When's the next time she's gonna visit?"

"Don't know. Want me to ask?"

"Yeah. Would you call when you're done here? I need to know as soon as possible."

Mahmud nodded. They were silent. The Arab did a few more stretches. Mrado waited. Chatted with two other guys in the room. They walked down to the locker room. Mahmud called his sister. Spoke in Arabic. His sis was going there on Thursday.

They met up at a place on the south side. Supercheap—greasy kabobs and falafel in pita bread for twenty kronor a pop. Mrado ordered three. Scoped out the place. Pictures of the Al-Aqsa Mosque in Jerusalem and Arabic texts on the walls. Genuine or for show? Who cared when the kabobs were so good, they'd melt in your mouth.

Mrado's take on Mahmud's sister: tacky *blatte*. Clothes a little too tight. Skirt a little too short. Makeup a little too much. The Louis Vuitton accessories? A little too fake. Much too much ghetto Swedish. Tone it down, *habibti*.

She was amenable. *Nema problema*. He instructed her on what to ask: If Jorge'd had an unusual amount of contact with another inmate the days before the escape. With a CO? How'd he gotten over the wall? Had he belonged to a gang? Did people know who'd helped him on the outside? Who were his friends on the inside?

She wrote the questions down and promised to memorize them before her next visit to the penitentiary. Wanted two thousand cash for her time.

Mrado knew Jorge's type; they never shut up. Bragged, showed off, said too much.

He felt certain: With a contact at Österåker, the Latino'd soon be found.

The hunt could begin.

16

Spanish dreams. "Jorgelito, I'll sit here till you fall asleep. Jorgelito, wait here and I'll get the storybook. Jorgelito, have I told you you're my prince? Paola's my princess. You're my own royal family."

Jorge woke up.

It was light outside. Hot in the room. Sweet dreams were over. He lay on a mattress that he'd pulled off a bed. Reduced the risk that someone would see him from the outside. Double safety measures—tall bushes outside the window blocked the view.

He'd spent a total of six days in the cottage. Bored. Soon time to call that Yugo. He thought about Rodriguez. One day, Jorge-boy'd be back. Redecorate his face. Make him crawl. Lick mom's feet. Beg. Creep. Cry.

Maybe he'd been stupid. Careless. For instance, he'd run out of food the day before. He'd walked out to the road. Followed it until he reached a bigger road. Kept going. Saw water. Boats that people were taking out of the water. Haloed autumn panorama. About an hour and a half later: a grocery store, ICA Nygrens. He went in.

Never felt as dark as there, in the Aryan Swedish national store. The *blatte* stood out, sharp contrast. No one said anything. No one seemed to care. But Jorge, *el negrito*, thought he was gonna be lynched, dipped in poisonous boat paint and rolled in granola.

He bought spaghetti, chips, bread, sandwich meat, eggs, butter, and beer. Laundry detergent and hair dye. Paid cash. Didn't say thank you to the lady working the cash register. Just nodded. Thought everyone was eyeing him. Hating him. Planning to turn him over to the cops.

Already on his way out of the store, he felt like an idiot. Tried to walk through the woods on his way home. Didn't fly. Kept hitting private property, houses. Got scared that people might be home. Get suspicious. Get pissed off. Report the nigger to the police. Walked back out to the main road. Hoped no one would take note of him, *el fugitivo*.

Jorge fried two eggs. Buttered five pieces of bread. Added sandwich meat. Drank water. A tower of plates and silverware balanced precariously in the sink. Why bother doing dishes? The house's rightful owner could take care of that later.

He sat down at the kitchen table. Ate the sandwiches quickly. Ran his fingers over the tabletop. It looked old. He wondered if poor people owned the cottage, or if they'd chosen an old table on purpose.

Then: a sound outside. Jorge's ears perked up.

A voice.

He hunched down.

Slid off the chair, onto the floor.

Lay flat on his stomach.

Crawled toward the window. If someone was on the way in, he could be cooked. If it was the cops outside, he was definitely cooked.

Goddamn it, why hadn't he prepared better? Nothing packed. His clothes, hair dye, food, toiletries—everything was spread out in the room where he slept. Fucking idiot. If he had to run now, he wouldn't manage to take a fucking thing.

He tried to look out the window. Didn't see anyone outside. Just the tranquil garden, surrounded by trimmed hawthorn bushes and two maple trees. Again: the voice. Sounded like it came from the little road leading up to the house. Folded in half, he slunk over to the other window. Through the hall. The broad wooden planks in the floor creaked. Fuck. Didn't dare look out the window. They might be able to see him from the outside. Listened first. Heard another voice, closer now, but not right outside. At least two people talking to each other. Was it the 5-0 or someone else?

Listened again. One of the voices had a slight foreign accent.

He peeked cautiously. No parked car. Couldn't see the people. Looked up the road that continued past the house toward a dark red barn behind the garden. There. Three people were walking toward the house.

Jorge fast-forwarded through his options. Weighed the advantages and the risks. The cottage was good. Warm, relatively shielded from view, far from the city and the cops' searching. He could bunker down here until all his money ran out. On the other hand, the people on the road from the barn. He couldn't really make out who they were.

They could be the owners of the house. Maybe it wasn't their house but they were just curious. Took a look-see through the windows. Saw the mountain of dishes, saw the mattress on the floor, saw the mess.

It could be the cops.

The risk was too big. Better to pack up his things and clear out before they got here. There were other houses. Other warm beds.

Jorge shoved his stuff into two bags, food in one and clothes and toiletries in the other. He went to the door. The upper half was made of painted glass. He looked out. Didn't see the people. Opened the door. Walked quickly to the left. Not the gravel path out to the little road. Pushed through an opening in the bushes instead. Got caught on thorns.

Thought the voices sounded closer.

Fuck.

He ran without looking back.

17

JW: on his way to the top. Jet Set Carl's offer—a golden opportunity. Abdulkarim: overjoyed. Babbled on about their expansion plans. "If you just find that Jorge dude," he reminded JW, "we'll own this city."

JW didn't break any unnecessary sweat looking for the Chilean. He'd put out some hooks here and there. Had dinner with peeps from the Sollentuna area and offered them money for information that could lead to zeroing in on the fugitive. It'd work out.

Today, he had another project.

JW'd called the Komvux teacher, Jan Brunéus, a couple of days ago. The teacher remembered Camilla well but really didn't want to talk about her. When JW'd insisted, he'd hung up on him.

JW hadn't been able to deal with his reaction at the time. Hadn't bothered to call him again. Tried not to think about the whole thing.

But today it was time. He had to.

He put on jeans, shirt, coat.

Walked toward Sveaplan Gymnasium, the high school below the Wenner-Gren Center where the continuing-education center, Komvux, was located. Wanted to meet Jan Brunéus face-to-face.

Valhallavägen was louder than usual, either due to the heavy traffic or due to his headache. Probably due to both.

He spotted the school building at the end of Sveavägen.

It was 11:30 a.m. Lunch break. JW suspected that the reception desk would close during lunch. He didn't want to have to wait till after, ignored the arrows and signs and just asked someone for directions. A woman with a Fjällräven Kånken backpack who seemed on her way out gave him a good explanation of how to get there: Take the main entrance, up the stairs, then to the right.

JW ran against the current. Mostly young people his own age on their way out to lunch. The washed-up middle class—didn't realize there were faster ways to Life.

He took the stairs three at a time. Got short of breath.

Reached the reception area.

A woman in a pleated skirt and an old-fashioned blouse was on her way out the door with purposeful movements that said, I'm closing now.

Typical.

He said, "Hello, ma'am. May I please ask a question before you close for lunch?"

JW'd become the prince of politesse—calling the receptionist "ma'am." He'd learned well from his Stockholm crowd.

The lady was mollified and let him in. She got back behind the counter.

"I need to speak with one of your teachers, Jan Brunéus. Does he have classes this week, and if so, where might I find him?"

The woman grimaced, looked uncomfortable. JW didn't like her style. Instead of using clear communication, some people grimaced their way through life.

She pulled out a schedule and ran her finger down the boxes. Finally, she said, "He has a class today that is letting out in ten minutes, at noon. Room four two two. That's one flight up."

JW thanked her kindly. Wanted to maintain a good relationship with the woman, for some reason. Sensed he might need it later.

He ran up the stairs. Found the right hallway.

Room 422. The door was closed, still five more minutes till lunchtime.

He waited outside. Put his ear up to the door, heard a chanting voice but couldn't recognize if it was Jan Brunéus's.

JW checked out the hallway. Beige walls, wide windows, simple white china light fixtures in the ceiling, graffiti on the radiators. Classic high school. He'd expected a different vibe at Komvux. More mature.

The door to the classroom opened.

A black guy with baggy clothes and jeans almost down to his knees stepped out. Twenty-odd students streamed out behind him.

JW popped his head into the classroom. A couple of girls were collecting their pens and notebooks by the desks.

A teacher stood at the whiteboard, erasing writing. He didn't see JW.

It had to be Jan Brunéus.

The teacher was dressed in a brown corduroy suit with leather patches at the elbows. He wore a green V-necked knit sweater under the jacket. Three days' worth of stubble made it more difficult to appreciate his age, but he was probably around forty. He had thin-framed glasses, maybe made by Silhoutte. JW thought he looked like a nice guy.

He walked up to Jan.

Jan turned around, studied JW.

JW thought, Does he see the resemblance between me and Camilla? Jan said, "How can I help you?"

"My name is Johan Westlund. We spoke on the phone a couple of days ago, as you might remember. I would like to speak to you about my sister, Camilla Westlund. If that's okay."

Brunéus sat down on the edge of the desk. Didn't say anything. Just sighed.

Did he want to seem like he was ready for a heart-to-heart, or what?

The girls who'd been in the classroom left.

Jan got up and closed the door behind them. Sat back down on the edge of the desk.

JW remained standing. No comment.

"I really want to apologize for my behavior. Thinking about her made me upset. The whole disappearance is just so tragic. I didn't mean to hang up on you like that."

JW listened without saying anything in return.

"I remember Camilla very well. She was one of my favorite students. She was talented and interested. Good attendance. I gave her an A in every subject."

JW thought, Teachers care about bullshit like attendance.

"What subjects did she have with you?"

"Language arts, English, and, if I'm remembering correctly, social studies. You know, around two hundred faces pass through my classes every year, but I remember Camilla. You look a lot alike."

"People say that. Can you tell me more about what you remember about her? I know that she hung out some with a girl named Susanne Pettersson. Did she have other friends here?"

"Susanne Pettersson? I don't remember her. But I honestly don't think Camilla had a lot of friends, which was strange. I thought she was very extroverted and nice-seeming. She looked nice, too."

Something was off. Susanne Pettersson'd said that she and Camilla used to cut class. Now Jan Brunéus was saying she'd had a good attendance record. And that she'd looked nice. Did teachers usually say stuff like that?

They talked for another two minutes or so. Jan spoke in generalities. "Komvux is an important social institution. High school doesn't suit everyone. Here, they can get a second chance."

JW wanted to get away from the classroom. Away from Jan Brunéus.

Jan shook his hand. "It's a sad story. Send my regards to your parents. Tell them that Camilla would've gone far."

Jan picked up a worn leather briefcase from the floor and disappeared out into the hall.

JW walked back to the reception desk. Took note of the hours. The administration offices were closed for the day. Typical, or what?

At home, he flipped through the phone book. City of Stockholm, Education Department. Called the number and asked to be connected to someone who could answer general questions about transcripts and official records. He was put through to the responsible administrator. They discussed JW's questions for fifteen minutes. That was enough. JW got all the answers he needed.

He would definitely go back to the reception at Komvux. Dig deep in the school's transcript archives. Something wasn't right with Jan Brunéus's story.

18

Mrado'd played crime thriller for two and a half days while he waited for Mahmud's sister to visit Österåker. Ordered passport photos of Jorge. Called his two cop contacts, Jonas and Rolf. Promised five grand to the one who'd dig up useful info on the Jorge fucker. Looked up the Latino's relatives with the Population Registry. No leads. Checked in with his colleague Nenad, Radovan's blow and whore page. Nenad didn't even remember Jorge, other than from the trial. Mrado had breakfast with Ratko and Ratko's brother Slobodan, alias "Bobban." They gave him the lowdown on Stockholm's northwest criminal map—which junkies to talk to, which employees to talk to at which bars, which dealers knew Jorge's crowd. He went out to Sollentuna and Märsta twice and talked to various cocaine contacts and Latinos. Bobban went with him. Good visual aid.

Most already knew who the fugitive was, and those who didn't got the passport pics shoved under their noses. A hero. A legend. Everyone wanted to buy the hero a drink. Celebrate the guy. Congratulate the guy. But no one'd seen him.

Jorge's mom lived with a new husband, and he had a sister, Paola. The mom lived outside Stockholm. The sister in Hägersten. He ordered passport photos of the sister and mom. Got two hits when he Googled the sister's name. She'd written an article in the Stockholm University newspaper, *Gaudeamus*, and taken part in the campus Literature Days. Good girl. Was apparently trying to make her own way from scratch. He figured maybe he should take a closer look at the university.

He called the Literature Department. The sis was taking the "level 3 course," whatever that was.

Mrado drove out to Frescati, university playground. Parked the car at the back of the blue high-rises. His Benz stuck out. The rest of the cars in the parking lot: dud cars.

The university for Mrado: a foreign country. Population: stick figures, four-eyed bookworms. Players who preferred parlance to performance. Pussies. To Mrado's surprise, however, there were hot chicks en masse.

He eyed some signs. Found the Lit Department. Rode up in the elevator. Asked a lady in the hall who was responsible for the level 3 course. Got the name of the teaching assistant. Eyed more signs. The TA's room was farther down the same hall. Tacked on the door was another sign: I LOVE MY WORK . . . DURING LUNCH AND COFFEE BREAKS. Mrado knocked. No answer. Asked a woman in the room next door. The TA was in a meeting in room C 119. Rode down again, all the way down. The halls felt half-finished. Pipes and ventilation systems hung from the ceiling. Some walls looked unpainted. White wood panels leaned up in a corner. He eyed the arrows. Found the room. Knocked. A guy in a blazer and frizzy bangs opened the door. Mrado asked to speak to the TA. The guy said they were in a meeting. Mrado cocked his head to the side. Put his foot in the door so it wouldn't close. Stared the guy down. Mr. Frizz stood his ground. After fifteen seconds, he looked away. Went to get the TA. A young girl—twenty-five tops. Mrado'd expected an older woman. She asked what he wanted. He pulled some bull. Said he was supposed to buy books from a girl who hadn't shown. Wondered if the TA had her number or knew where she had class today. She asked why he was in such a hurry. Mrado pulled some more bull, something about heading out of the country and needing the books today. An emergency. The TA: gullible and too nice, a cold trick. They went up to her office. She found Paola's telephone number and the schedule for the level 3 course. Said Mrado was in luck. "Paola is in a seminar today in room D three twenty-seven." Finally, a hot hand.

How she let herself be fooled by a six-foot Yugoslav, he couldn't even begin to imagine.

To D 327. Eyed signs again. Found the room.

Same deal as with the TA. Some dude opened. Mrado asked him to get Paola.

Mrado closed the door of the seminar room behind her. Paola understood immediately that something wasn't right. Jerked her head around. Took a step back, averted her face. Mrado had time to see her eyes. If unease had a face, it would look like hers.

Not what Mrado had expected from a lit major. She was wearing a light blue blouse with wide cuffs. Dark, tight blue jeans. Straitlaced style. Black hair, pulled back in a ponytail. It gleamed. Innocent look. Something sparked within Mrado.

He waved toward a bathroom. They walked in that direction. Paola: stiff movements. Mrado: focused. They stepped into the bathroom. Mrado closed the door.

The bathroom was covered in graffiti. Mostly written in pencil and ballpoint pen. Mrado, surprised. College students weren't supposed to do that kind of thing, were they?

He told Paola to sit down on the toilet. Her face flushed.

"Calm down. I don't want to hurt you, but there's no point in scream-ing. I prefer not to use violence on girls. I'm not that kinda guy. Just need to know a few things."

Paola spoke perfect Swedish. No trace of an accent. "It's about Jorge, isn't it? Is it about Jorge?" Near tears.

"You got it, babe. It's about your bro. You know where he is?"

"No. I don't have a clue. I don't know. He hasn't been in touch. Not with Mama, either. We've just read about him in the papers."

"Cut it. I'm sure he cares about you. Of course he's been in touch. Where is he?"

She sobbed. "I told you—I don't know. I really don't. He hasn't even called."

Mrado kept pushing it. "Don't lie. You seem like a good girl. I can make your life a living hell. I can make your bro's life good. Just tell me where he is."

She kept denying it, point-blank.

"Listen carefully, little lady. Stop pouting. This bathroom looks like shit, don't you agree? Walls totally scratched up. You're leaving this kind of shit behind. You want to get out with your fancy education. Up in life. Your brother can get a good life, too."

She stared straight into his eyes. Her pupils big, glossy. He saw his reflection in them. She'd stopped crying. The mascara painted black lines down her cheeks.

"I really don't know."

Mrado analyzed. There are people who can lie. Dupe. Fool anyone. Stand up against cops, prosecutors, and lawyers in interrogation after interrogation. Even stand up against guys like Mrado. Maybe they believe their own stories. Maybe they're just extremely good actors. Other people try to lie and it shows right away. Their eyes shoot up to the left, a sign that they're making things up. They blush. Sweat. Contradict themselves. Miss details. Or the opposite: try to be calm. Pretend it's raining. Speak slowly. But it shows. They're too confident. Their stories are too sweeping, too big picture. They sit abnormally still. Seem too secure in their statements.

He knew them all. Paola didn't belong to any of these. Mrado'd been in the protection-racket business long enough. Had squeezed juice out of people. Forced them to show him where the cash was stashed, how much blow they'd dealt, where they were delivering their moonshine, how many johns they'd had. Held his gun to people's temples, in their mouths, against their cocks. Asked for answers. Appraised their answers. Forced answers. He was an expert at answers.

Mrado checked her hands. Not her face. He knew people control their mugs, but not their bodies. Hands speak the truth.

Paola wasn't lying.

She really didn't know where the Jorge fucker was.

Damn it.

He left her sitting on the toilet. Paralyzed.

Jogged down to the parking lot. Jumped in the car. Pulled the door shut hard behind him. Drove off to meet Mahmud's sis.

Mrado felt stressed-out. He saw her right away. She was sitting with a Pepsi in front of her. The Arab joint was packed. Two veiled women with at least 140 ankle biters occupied the back half of the place. In the front were a couple of Svens lapping up multicultural Sweden. Mahmud's sister held out her hand. Meaning: I want my two thousand cash. The chick'd been compliant last time. Now: considerable attitude problem.

Mrado sighed. Thought something that surprised him: Too many people who are downright losers rock an attitude. He'd experienced it a lot. Unemployed Sven boozehounds, uneducated bouncers, and cocky project *blattes* played tough guy. Did that protect them? Did it keep them from feeling like the dregs they were? This chick was an obvious loser. Why did she even try?

He sat down.

"Okay, babe, let's hold off on the money. You'll get it soon. First, tell me what he said."

Before she'd even said a word, he knew the answer.

"My man, he know nothin'."

"What do you mean? He knew about Jorge, didn't he?"

"No, I mean, like, they hung never, or whatever."

Got irritated. The chick couldn't fucking speak straight. Someone should return her to the store. Reclaim the warranty.

"Come on. Of course he knew who Jorge was. Think. What'd he say?"

"What's your deal? Don't think I remember, huh? Me, comin' from there now. I just said—they hung never."

"You want your dough or what? Did he know who the Latino was or not?"

"He knew. Said tightest break he'd ever heard."

"You mean the escape? Did he see the escape?"

"Shit, you nag. My man not there. Not on motivation."

"Girl, if you want the dough, you have to fuckin' talk so I understand you." Mrado was about to snap. Pushed back his chair. Signal: Wise up or I'll leave.

"He, like, in not same block. Not motivation. He somewhere else. You know?"

Mrado knew. Bummed. Mahmud's sis was a dud. There were two units at Österåker. One for inmates who wanted to get their lives back on track, where they got motivation to get off drugs. Learn society's rules. Pedagogical programs, workshops, bullshit psychology and chat therapy. Of course that's where Jorge'd been, the so-called motivation unit. Then it was true what she'd said: Her tired-ass man didn't know zilch.

19

He moved on to another cottage. Stayed there two days. And now he was gonna switch it up again. Had to keep moving.

He walked for over three hours. Wanted to get away from the area where he'd just stayed—watchful neighbors equaled foes. His nigger look a threat. One family has a break-in and suddenly every unknown individual with dark hair in the area's a suspect. A miracle that no one'd stopped by the side of the road yet to ask him who he was and what he was doing there.

A cold wind. The middle of October wasn't his favorite time of year. But Jorge-boy'd planned ahead. The knit sweater and the winter jacket warmed. Thanked the thrift store for that.

He turned off the main road. Read a sign that said DYVIK, 2 MILES. Smaller road. No houses yet. Pine trees all around. He kept trotting along. Hungry. Tired. Refused to lose heart. J-boy: still on the way up. Out. Onward. Toward success. Radovan would yield to him. Give him a passport. Kale. Opportunities. He'd head to Denmark. Maybe invest a few grand in blow. Deal. Make cash. Move on. Maybe to Spain. Maybe Italy. He'd buy a real identity. Start all over. Play drug kingpin with hard-core connections in Viking territory. Hook his old homeys up. Everyone except Radovan would bathe in his glory. The Yugo faggot would have to beg to get in on deals belonging to Jorge, King of Blow.

The road sloped downward. The forest opened up. He saw houses. To his left, a barn with two run-down green tractors out front. Farther down, horses. Not good. Someone lived on the place. He kept going. Found another house. Broke in.

A small kitchen, a living room, and two bedrooms—one with a queen-size bed, the other with a twin. It was cold. He turned on the radiator. Kept his jacket on.

He unpacked his food. The fridge and the freezer were turned off—a good sign that the house was closed for the winter. Fried two eggs. Cut thick slices off the loaf of bread. Put the eggs on top. Checked the pantry. Almost empty: an old box of chocolates, two cans of crushed tomatoes, and beans. Worthless.

Sat down in the living room. Opened the door of a corner cupboard that was painted with florid designs in red and blue: crammed with bottles of booze. Jackpot. City's sickest juice-juju.

Screw safety. Jorge-boy was gonna have a niiiiice night.

No mixers. No ice. No fruit or drinks to blend it with. Fuck that. Real men take it straight. Jorge did a whiskey tasting all by his lonesome. Lined up five glasses on the living room table. Poured out five different brands. Picked the ones with the weirdest names: Laphroaig, Aberlour, Isle of Jura, Mortlach, Strathisla.

Munched on stale chocolate. Turned on the radio on a huge Sharp stereo. A display with blinking yellow stripes and patterns began to glow to the beat of the music. Felt very 1991.

Mortlach was the best. He poured himself another glass. Sang along to the songs from the radio. Tried to wail like Mariah Carey.

Poured water into a glass and more whiskey into another. Not his thing to drink straight, but what the hell. He drained the glass.

The house was spinning. Poorly built. Crooked corners. Tilting windows. He laughed at himself—the countryside's new urban architect. The buzz washed over him.

Joy. At the same time: little Jorgelito, so alone.

Drunken rush. At the same time: He had to be vigilant.

He sat down on the floor to steady himself.

Suddenly, he remembered something he hadn't thought about in a very long time. How he and Mama'd been walking together from the grocery store. He might've been six or seven. Paola was already at home, waiting for them. Preparing dinner. Everything but the rice—they'd run out and so Jorge and Mama'd had to go buy some. Rodriguez'd refused to help out, and Jorge'd been scared to go alone. He saw his mother's face now, clearly: the dark furrows under her eyes and the lines in her forehead that made her look like she was always wondering about something but never could find the answer. He'd asked, "Mama, are you tired?" She'd set the bag of rice down on the sidewalk. Lifted him up into her arms. Smoothed back his hair and said, "No, Jorgelito. If we sleep well tonight, I'm going to be wide-awake tomorrow. That'll be nice."

Jorge reached for the bottle. Poured out more Mortlach.

The living room was spinning like crazy.

He stood up.

Lost control.

Passed out on the floor.

Three days later. Jorge had some serious problems. He'd been out of food for twenty-four hours already and he had only four hundred kronor left. Couldn't even muster sit-ups. Too tired to go to a new cottage. Unfortunately, you couldn't live on whiskey and water.

He needed to get to a store and buy food.

He needed to get cash. The question: Would Radovan agree to his proposition? If not, his need for cheddar would grow even more.

But worst of all: He felt so alone.

He needed to talk to someone—meet some old friend or relative. Human contact.

Was he already fried?

He had to get to the city. Eat. Scrape up some extra dough while he waited to call the Yugos. That's just the way it was.

Jorge checked out map books in the bookcase. The scale was too bad. He checked the back pages of the phone book—he wanted to know how to get back to this cottage when he'd completed his mission in the city. Looked for Dyvik.

Considered boosting a car.

20

It was, without a doubt, the bash to break all bashes—the year's most prestigious, profligate private party.

JW lived off the hype several days beforehand. It was high-gear, high-class, high-line. Most of all, it was so goddamn jet set.

Carl Malmer, alias Jet Set Carl, alias the Prince of Stureplan, was turning twenty-five and was having a courtly revelry in his four-room, sixteen-hundred-square-foot apartment. The apartment was on Skeppargatan and the rooftop terrace'd been booked for months.

The hottest chicks were booked; the kids from the best families were invited; the bottles and models set would naturally be featured at the party.

JW arrived with Fredrik and Nippe. They'd pregamed at Fredrik's. It was eleven-thirty. Overflowing coatracks stood in the foyer, as did an enormous black dude without bouncer tag but sporting a spot-on style: black leather jacket, turtleneck, dark jeans. Fredrik grinned. "A bouncer at a private party?"

The bouncer checked them off a list and waved them through.

They hung up their coats and walked in.

Heat, perfume, party din, and the smell of eau de cash hit them as richly as at the velvet-roped entrances of Stureplan's best clubs. They made their way through a crowd of underage girls who seemed to have just arrived—they were fixing their faces in front of the mirror in the hall. Nippe was drooling, couldn't help himself; started flirt-chatting with one of the girls. Fredrik asked where Carl was. Someone pointed toward the kitchen. They pulled Nippe with them.

The kitchen was nearly six hundred square feet. An island remade as a bar filled the middle of the room. Two guys in bandannas mixed drinks. The place was packed. The music from the speakers: the Sounds. In the middle of it all was Jet Set Carl himself, wearing a white tux and a blinding smile.

"Hey, boys." Carl hugged and welcomed them. Introduced them to the two chicks he was talking to. Top-tier superbimbettes. Fredrik made conversation and Nippe pulled his telltale tail tales. JW looked around with a bored expression. Had to keep the surface ripple-free, couldn't show how impressed he was.

He thought, Carl must make a killing on his parties and club gigs, almost better than you make on C. The kitchen area was redone. Boffi, Italian design for people with black cards. Corian countertops. Slim, discreet cabinet handles. Oven in brushed stainless steel, Gaggenau—four gas burners and a built-in grill. Tap and levers in stylish chrome floated like a swan's neck over the sink. The fridge and freezer were of stainless steel, American extra-wide size, with round, wide handles. To the left of the fridge was a wine cooler with a transparent door, filled with bottles. Having a kitchen like that scored more adult points than having kids.

Right mix of A-, B-, and C-list celebs in the crowd. Bloggers, actors, models. Scenesters and artists. Princess Madeleine plus entourage. He glimpsed former Social Democratic minister Leif Pagrotsky smack in the middle.

Nippe was swallowed up, disappeared on a mingle crusade. Fredrik lit a cigarette.

Jet Set Carl turned to JW. "Good to see you. You haven't been here before, have you?"

"No, but it's a damn nice apartment you've got."

"Thanks. I like it myself."

"How many people did you invite tonight?"

"Many. I've booked the rooftop terrace, too. Probably hundred and fifty people up there already. Gonna be wild. You've got to go up and check it out; that's where the food is. There'll be some stuff happening on the roof later, too."

"What about your neighbors?"

"I booked rooms at the Grand for the families next door and below me. They were happy as hell."

"Who wouldn't be for a free night at the Grand Hôtel? Everything cool with the stuff?"

"Sure thing. Sweet that you could get it on such short notice. It's in the bedroom."

"Sophie here?"

"Yup, check the terrace."

JW thanked him, moved on. Felt good that he and Carl were start-ing to become tight.

He walked out through the foyer, nodded to the bouncer, and took the stairs up.

The terrace looked like a forest of metal mushrooms—gas-powered heaters to soften the October chill. Carl didn't take any risks—a third of the terrace was covered by a party tent. But there were no rain clouds tonight. The gas 'shrooms spurted heat and the girls felt good in their tiny tops and bling. JW was scanning the scene for Sophie. The crowd pushed from all sides. Enormous speakers blared Robyn's latest hit.

A dozen or so girls stood in the middle of the crowd, trying to get the dance party going. Maybe it was too early; in an hour, the terrace would explode. People just needed more booze and a noseful of blow.

The buffet was stylish. Tiny portions on tablespoons: a crouton with fois gras, sour cream with fish roe and red onion, potato salad topped with Russian caviar. You just cleaned the spoon with one bite, tossed it in a bin on the table, and then chose a new gourmet spoon to your liking. Farther down were plates with wineglass holders attached. The buffet consisted of lime-marinated chicken kebobs, tabouleh, and sweet-and-sour chili sauce. The catering crew worked efficiently. The morsel-laden spoons were quickly replaced with new ones; the bucket was emptied in time with the filling of wineglasses.

Real New York vibe in the Stockholm night.

There were ads for Kharma posted everywhere. Jet Set Carl was no dummy—he'd write off this entire party as a company expense.

Sophie was standing at the far end of the terrace, where the party tent began. JW made his way to her. She was talking to a tall guy in a pinstriped blazer and skinny jeans. The guy had some sort of trendy image painted on the back of the blazer. He was unshaven, with hair as short as his stubble. JW recognized him. He was a famous ad guy with a cheesy smile permanently glued to his face. Named Sweden's seventy-third-sexiest man by *Elle* a couple of years ago. Generally infa-mous cunt-catcher. A total tool.

He positioned himself near them, wanted to be introduced. Sophie dissed him majorly, kept talking to the trend tool. JW shoved his hands in his pockets, made a serious effort to nail the disinterested look again. His couldn't-care-less chin hung.

She looked right through him.

He gave up, skipped her. Played the game and went downstairs to the living room.

A single word in his head: *fuck*.

Something was wrong with Sophie. JW worried. Did she see through him? Would she call his bluff? Predetermined tracks were hard to hide. A guy from Robertsfors just couldn't make it with the Stureplan scene's coolest chic.

A thought: What's my yearning for Sophie about anyway? Maybe Sophie was like an incarnation of Camilla. A party girl with brains. Something'd happened to his sister, something he repressed. And still he was doing what she'd done. Moved to the city, partied, spent money. Was falling for girls who looked like her. Was faking Life, like she'd done. Camilla'd lived some kind of double life, definitely in front of his mom and dad, but also in front of JW. That had become apparent after he saw the pictures of her riding in the Ferrari, though she'd never told him about the car. She'd only hinted to JW once. Said, "I make more dough in two months than Mom does in a year." Why? And how was it possible that she'd only had *one* friend at Komvux, Susanne? JW remembered her as Robertsfors's number-one socialite.

The thoughts churned. He thought about what he'd found out three days ago from Jan Brunéus.

It was all so shady.

He had to know more.

The living room was more crowded than a late subway car on a Monday morning. In one corner, a stroboscope was spurting flashes of light. Six different-colored spotlights were moving and painting pictures on the opposite wall. There was a smoke machine on the floor, and gigantic speakers in the corners of the room ensured that everything vibrated. Two flat-screen TVs that were set up on top of the speakers were projecting video installations by the artist Ernst Billgren.

JW got it confirmed once again: People with money party better.

He was dancing wildly with some twenty-year-old silicone celeb from the Paradise Hotel when he saw the closed door from the living room. There was another bouncer positioned in front of the door.

Older, subtler, slicker, with his hair gelled back. The revealing factor once again: his clothes. Black turtleneck, dark jeans, and a thin leather jacket—indoors. JW recognized him. He was the head bouncer from Stureplan's biggest security guard company, Tom Schultzenberg.

He thought, That's gotta be it.

The bouncer checked JW's name off the list. He slid in.

He found himself in Jet Set Carl's bedroom, remade as a Lebanese café—super-*privé*. The bed'd been carried out; in its place were brass hookahs filled with fruit-flavored tobacco on the floor. Purple-and-red fabrics hung on the walls. A thick carpet and tasseled pillows with gold embroidery swallowed the sound in the room. Still, an amped aura: elated, active, sexy. JW clocked right away. In the middle of the room was a glass-topped table. In the middle of the table was a pile of snow.

Magnificent.

Six people were sitting on pillows around the table. Two of them were snorting lines. Two others were preparing theirs. All the people in the room were sniffling, wiping powder with the backs of their hands, sneezing, and babbling about the glory of existence.

JW regarded his work, his delivery. VIP room without borders. What an event, what class.

He sat down on a red pillow. Reached for a razor blade and started to cut a line. A girl across from him was staring him down, sucking him off with her eyes. JW smiled back, snorted the cocaine. The straw was made of glass.

Four hours later. JW was a little too sweaty for comfort. He'd danced, mingled, tried to make out with the girl from the cocaine room in front of Sophie. She kept up her don't-give-a-shit act. They'd talked for a total of only seventeen minutes. He pulled out all the charm cards he had in his deck. Thought, If I can't get her tonight, I'll never fucking get her. He chatted with Jet Set Carl, his friends Fredrik and Nippe, snorted with them, snorted with the silicone bimbo from the Paradise Hotel. Chatted with celebs and silver-spoon babies. He sold himself in.

JW's message was simple: I'm hot as hell and I'm your local cocaine dealer. Buy from me.

He didn't see her coming. Suddenly, Sophie was there, took his hand, looked at him. This time, she wanted something more than to chat. He could feel it.

JW was already on a rush. He couldn't distinguish between the heat in his pants, the heat in his nose, and the heat in his heart. They pushed their way through the party people. It was four o'clock and the party'd peaked. It was still crowded, but not as crowded as before. JW found his jacket on the floor of the foyer. Sophie's was dangling on a hanger. They pushed the button for the elevator. Giggled together. JW squeezed Sophie's hand. Still no other bodily contact. In the midst of the spell he was under, JW felt unease. Was it really all set?

On the way down, Sophie said, "What happens now?"

JW looked at her. Grinned. Pulled a cliché. "Can I come up for a cup of tea?"

She smiled. JW got even more nervous, tried not to let it show.

Out on the street, they could hear the music from the party pounding several stories up.

JW said, "Weird that no one's complaining. Did Carl put the entire neighborhood up at the Grand?"

Sophie, with a Mona Lisa smile: "Maybe they like the music?"

They started walking. JW was unsure of the direction. He thought, Is she playing with me? Is it a joke? She'd done a 180—first ignoring him, as if he were no better than chopped liver, and now taking him home with her.

After a while, she stopped. Looked like she was about to say something. JW's heart skipped a beat. "Of course we should go to my place for a cup of tea."

Was happiness on the horizon?

They kept walking along Linnégatan, past 7-Eleven. At least ten people from Carl's party were stuffing their faces with hot dogs inside the store. JW didn't have the energy to say hi; he didn't want to let anything break the mood.

He and Sophie were quiet, which was unusual for both of them. They just kept walking toward Sophie's place.

They arrived at her apartment on Grev Turegatan—a small studio, 380 square feet. She went into the kitchen. JW, clueless. Was she really going to make tea? He wanted to caress her, kiss her, and hug her, just lie and talk all night with her. At the same time, he wanted to have sex with her more than ever.

The coke kick was wearing off. He got an idea. Went into the bathroom and turned on the tap. Created white noise. He pulled his cock out and began to masturbate. The inspiration came from the movie *There's Something About Mary*. He thought of Sophie naked. He came after two minutes. He was pleased with the security measure—if he was to make it with Sophie, he'd be able to marathon it.

He unlocked the door and walked out.

Sophie was standing by the edge of the bed. Her top'd slid down over one shoulder. Was it a hint?

She looked him in the eyes as though she were saying, What are you waiting for?

He took two steps forward, ended up a few inches from her face. Waited for a reaction from her. Shit, he was such a pussy. Not even now, with all the vibes she was sending out, did he dare make the first move. He was too scared, too nervous. Didn't want to make a fool of himself and burn his bridges with her. Miss future opportunities. Sophie took a tiny step closer. The tips of their noses touched. He hoped she didn't suspect what he was feeling—his heart was pumping 230 bpm.

She kissed him. Finally.

He was flying. Soaring.

JW put his arms around her. Kissed her back. No one had ever tasted so good: smoke, alcohol, and Sophie smell. They ended up on the bed. He took her top off, carefully. Cupped her breasts over her bra. She licked his neck.

JW put his hand on top of her pants, over her butt. Began to kiss her neck, breasts, and belly. He unbuttoned her tight jeans and pulled them off. Kissed the inside of her thighs. She made sounds. JW was dying to put his cock in her, but at the same time he wanted to wait. Sophie started to take her thong off herself. Straight shot, Sophie-style. He continued to kiss around her pussy while he caressed her left breast. Carefully pinched her nipple.

He asked, "May I have a taste?"

Sophie mmmm'ed in response. He licked carefully around her labia. After a while, he let his tongue slip in and slowly swirl around. First around and around, then up and down. He could hardly believe it. He was making her feel good. He was making Sophie whimper.

Sophie pulled him up and pressed him down on his back against the bed. Took off his shirt. Pulled off his pants. Took his cock in her mouth. Sucked him in rapid mouthfuls. He looked down cautiously and saved the image in his mental hard drive—him and Sophie.

JW got up. He was scared he might come. She kept his cock in her hand. Reached over toward the nightstand. Looked for something. He wanted in and didn't get what she was up to. She leaned back. Then she opened a condom wrapper.

JW, filled with angst—he hated condoms.

He asked, "Do we have to use that?"

"Don't kid, JW. Of course we do."

He regretted having said anything. Had to try. She rolled it onto his cock and pulled him down toward her. Right before she guided him in, he went soft. He tried to laugh it off. She looked questioningly at him. JW sighed. Lay down on his back.

Sophie asked, "You and condoms are not a good combo, or what?"

"Damn, Sophie. I'm so happy." Almost told her this was the happiest day in his life but then shut it; he'd already said too much. Unnecessary to open up more, even though she was the most wonderful thing in the world.

"Don't know what the deal is. I just don't work too great with rubber is all."

The condom hung loosely. She pulled it off. Started kissing his cock. He got hard again. She pulled back his foreskin and licked the tip. Kissed his balls. He got rock-hard. She pulled out another condom from the same drawer. JW tried to relax. Took the condom in his own hands. Put it on. Remained lying on his back. Guided her on top of him. She grabbed hold of his cock to put it right.

The smell of latex.

He went flaccid.

She said, "That's okay. It can happen to any guy."

JW thought back to something he'd read in the paper two years ago: a list of the most common lies.

21

Mrado was sitting at a table under the vaulted ceilings on the cellar level of Café Piastowska, on Tegnérgatan. He'd ordered schnitzel Belwederski with sauerkraut and Okocim, Polish beer. He liked the venue. Brick walls and dark wood paneling. A flag with the Polish eagle hung at one of the short ends of the room. Beer ads were glued to the ceiling. Genuine feel to the waitress: middle-aged gray-haired woman with integrity.

He took out pen and paper.

Around him: a racket. It was the weekend. Someone was celebrating their thirtieth birthday—the tables were pushed together to form one long one. The birthday celebrators ordered beer and called down the troubadour from the upstairs level.

A longhaired toothpick with an acoustic guitar attached to a black sash around his neck came down the stairs. Sang a folksy classic with a soft voice. The thirtieth-birthday revelers hooted with joy.

Mrado shut them out. He was tired, had slept worse last night than in the trench in Bosnia.

Was trying to think. Compartmentalize. Analyze. Find leads. In front of him on the table: a ruled notebook. Wrote questions in a column on the left-hand side of the page. What'd Jorge done? Where'd he gone? Who would know where he was? Wrote down probable answers in another column on the right-hand side. The Latino'd asked for a passport; the call'd come from a Swedish pay phone. Conclusion: Jorge hadn't left the country.

Jorge must've planned large parts on his own. In other words, he was on the run, without too many helpers. He wasn't hiding at his sister's, probably not at his mother's. If he was in the Sollentuna area, the Latino was staying indoors at all times. He couldn't have that much money stashed away, either. According to what Mrado remembered, the *blatte*'d been cleaned out worse than Lehman after closing when he'd been locked up at Österåker one and a half years ago. And now he was hitting up Rado for money, too.

In summation: Jorge was hiding somewhere cheap, in Sweden, probably in the Stockholm area. Alone.

Left in the middle of the page: a column for unanswered questions. Who'd last been in touch with Jorge? Where'd he gone directly after the breakout? Mrado underlined two central words: *location now*. He hadn't really gotten anywhere in his search. Figuring out where the *blatte* was hiding was as easy as completing a jigsaw puzzle of a sky with all blue pieces.

He could wait for Jorge's call and scare him then. Threaten to hurt the Latino's sister, his mom. But those weren't Radovan's orders. Instead: Find him, hurt him, and make him understand who's in charge. Also: Jorge'd broken with his family. In that case, threats wouldn't help.

Mrado took a final swig of beer. Asked for the check. Paid. Tipped. On his way up the stairs from the lower level, he felt a vibration in his pocket. Service again. A text. He picked up his cell. Didn't recognize the number. Read the text: *Call me on this number at 8:00 p.m./Rolf.* His cop connect. The pussy used his son's or daughter's cell when he got in touch with Mrado. The text: good news. Maybe Rolf knew something.

It was eight o'clock. Mrado was sitting in his car outside the shoot club, Pancrease, on Odengatan. Called Rolf. Was careful not to be explicit with his own name, Rolf's name, or other details. Kept it brief, as usual.

"What's up? It's me."

"Everything cool?"

"Yep. And you?"

"Sure, sure, but I've had a tough day. Sat hunched in the driver's seat of a car all day. My back's giving out."

"You should work out more. Go running sometimes and do fifty back-ups every night and I'll bet you'll feel better. Whattya got for me?"

"I've checked up on what we talked about. The northern precinct brought a guy in for questioning a month ago. Sergio Salinas Morena, a troublemaker from Sollentuna. He's cousins with your guy. Didn't lead to anything, but apparently he was suspected of aiding."

"Nice. I bow in thanks. Will check it out. That all?"

"That's all. Later."

Mrado started up the car. Drove to the intersection of Sveavägen/
Odengatan. Turned up toward Norrtull. There wouldn't be any working out at the club tonight. He called Ratko—needed his contacts in
Sollentuna. Ratko was with his girl in Solna. Didn't seem too hot on
joining the hunt. Despite that: agreed to be picked up at Råsundavä-
gen. What could Ratko do? The bottom line: When Mrado asks, you
deliver.

They drove on the E4 highway toward Sollentuna. Ratko didn't
know anyone named Sergio Salinas Morena. Called Bobban. He recognized the name. Thought the guy still lived in the Sollentuna area.
Didn't know more than that.

The road was poorly lit. Ratko made calls to old friends from Märsta
and Sollentuna, asked about Sergio. Mrado was strangely unfocused.
Didn't have the energy to listen to Ratko's phone buzz. He was tired.
Thought about Lovisa. His preparatory hearing in family court was
coming up. Annika didn't even want him to see his daughter every
other week. So fuckin' low.

They tore down the highway. Mrado'd busted the speed limit more
times than he could count. He remembered one time in particular:
when Lovisa was born. Immediate cesarean. He'd been at Solvalla with
some buds. Gotten a call from Annika that the contractions'd started
but that the water hadn't broken. She called the hospital. They said,
"Take it easy until the contractions come more frequently." Mrado
stayed at Solvalla. Why go home if it wasn't time? When he was leaving, he called home. No answer. Worry. Had she gone without calling
him? There was a note on the kitchen table. *Went to Huddinge. Had to
hurry.* Mrado ran back out to the car. Gunned it. Drove 110 to Huddinge Hospital. Took the turns on two wheels. Worried more than
he'd ever done in his entire life. Ran the entire way to the hospital's
main entrance. When he arrived, drenched in sweat, Lovisa'd already
been plucked out. Her heart rate'd started to plummet—there'd been
no time to spare. Before Annika went under, she heard the surgeon tell
the rest of the team they had only five minutes of game time. From
emergency to catastrophe. Mrado'd been late to his own daughter's
birth. He would never forgive himself for that. But the following two
hours had been some of the best in his life—in an adjoining room with

Lovisa, 6.9 pounds, lying on his chest. She folded her head in under his chin. Grazed his neck with her tiny mouth. Seemed to become calm. Annika was still not awake after the cut. Just Mrado and Lovisa—the way it should be, always. Maybe the way it could be if he threw in the towel. Stopped with this shit.

Ratko shoved him, "Hey, are you listening?"

Someone'd bitten the bait. Sergio Salinas Morena: worked as a courier driver, lived on Allévägen in Rotebro.

Mrado slammed his foot on the gas. They drove past Sollentuna. Continued on E4 north. Took a left by Staketvägen. His pulse was rising. The tension was soaring. Mrado was in the mood.

Salinas Morena lived on the fourth floor. They looked up at the windows. Six out of nine were lit on the fourth floor. Three apartments on that level. At least one window in each apartment was lit. Hopefully, people home in each of them. The house looked run-down. The sky was darkening, but the crap graffiti was still visible. The paint on the outer walls was peeling.

Ratko positioned himself down in the foyer. Mrado went up. Covered the peephole with his finger as he rang the doorbell.

A girl's voice yelled something in Spanish inside the apartment.

Nothing happened. Mrado rang the bell again.

A guy opened. Mrado assessed him. Around twenty-five years old. Dressed in a black T-shirt with large white Gothic lettering: *Vatos Locos.* Faded jeans. Dark hair. Cocky look. Did he think he was a Los Angeleno, or what?

Sergio looked skeptically at Mrado. Didn't say anything. Raised an eyebrow. Meaning: Who the fuck are you?

Mrado looked beyond Sergio, into the apartment. A hallway with three doors. TV sounds emanating from somewhere. No sign of the woman he'd heard through the door. Generally shabby and ugly. Bare linoleum on the floor. A couple of posters on the walls. Lined up and spread out in the hall: enough sneakers to fill a fucking sporting goods store.

"Are you Sergio? Can I come in?"

"Ey, WHO are you?"

Mrado thought, Kids, no respect these days.

"We can talk about that inside. Can I come in?" No chance in hell he'd repeat the question one more time.

Sergio remained standing. Staring.

Neither one looked away. The guy had to get that Mrado wasn't a cop. But did he pick up that Mrado was one of the most feared men in the Stockholm underworld? Unclear.

Finally, Sergio threw open his arms, gesticulated. "Whaddya want with me?"

"Are you Sergio?"

The guy took a step back. Let Mrado in. The apartment smelled of burned onion.

"Sure. And who're you?"

Mrado thought, What a stubborn motherfucker. Doesn't quit gabbing.

"Let's put it this way: You don't need to know who I am. I don't need to know more about you than that you're Sergio. I only want the answer to one question; then I'll go. Where is Jorge?"

The guy's left hand moved involuntarily. His neck muscles tensed.

The guy knew something.

"What Jorge?"

"Don't play dumber than you are. You know where he is. You'll tell me, whether you want to or not."

"I don't know what the fuck you're talkin' about."

"Exactly which words didn't you understand?"

"*Pendejo*, you think you can come here, to my house, and talk a lotta *basura*?"

Mrado, silent. Just stared. The guy was crazy. Might be king of his anthill, but a nobody in the real world. Clocked *nada*.

Sergio started yelling in Spanish. A girl came out of the TV room, wearing sweatpants and a black tank top. Sergio was freaking out. Mrado was standing calmly. Sergio raised his arms. Got into boxer pose with white-knuckled fists. One arm was out, the other guarding his face. The girl moved toward Sergio. Said something in Spanish. Seemed to be trying to calm him down. Looked at Mrado, her face twisted into a question mark.

Sergio yelled, "Come on, you fat Croat!"

Mrado took another step forward. Sergio struck with his left. His fist'd twitched a heartbeat earlier. Enough for Mrado—he blocked the punch. Put Sergio's arm in a lock. Pressed Sergio's hand up against the arm, his wrist at an unnatural angle. Forced the entire arm back. Sergio howled. Tried to strike with his free hand. Hit Mrado's shoulder. Lost his balance. Fell. The girl screamed. Mrado, on top of him. Continued to force his wrist back.

"Sergio, listen. Tell your bitch to shut up."

The girl kept shrieking. Mrado got up, grabbed hold of her arms. Pushed her down to the floor. She sat down with her back to the wall. Tried to get back up. Sergio, who was still on the floor, tried to kick Mrado's leg. It hurt. Their mistake: to make Mrado lose it. The girl came at him. He slapped her. She fell down again. Hit her head against the wall. Sounded like someone'd bounced a tennis ball on wood. She lay still. The guy started to get up. Fucking mayhem. Mrado punched him in the stomach. The guy doubled over, mouth wide open. Gasped for breath. The girl cried. Mrado pulled a roll of duct tape from his jacket pocket. Had hoped it wouldn't come to this. Gripped Sergio's left hand, pinched between his thumb and index finger. Should hurt like hell. Bent his arm back. Taped his two arms together. Sergio kicked wildly. Mrado tackled him carefully, like it was a training session at Pancrease—but in slow motion. Taped his feet together.

Sergio hollered, "You fuckin' cunt!"

Mrado ignored him. Worked efficiently. Taped up the girl. Dragged her into another room. Fuck. The situation'd derailed. Messier/more dangerous than planned. He called Ratko, asked him to come upstairs.

Leaned over Sergio, "Well, wasn't that really fucking unnecessary?"

"*Pendejo.*"

"You seem to have a limited vocabulary. Don't you know any other bad words?"

Sergio kept his mouth shut.

"It's simple. You just have to tell me where Jorge is. We won't turn him in."

No answer.

"I think you've pretty much figured out what kind of guy I am. I won't leave until you've dished. Don't be an idiot. Why make this such an unpleasant night? Why not just talk?"

Ratko came in through the front door. Locked it behind him. Looked with disapproval at the hall. Clothes and shoes littered everywhere. Both posters torn down. A stool was turned over. A duct-taped *loco* Latino in a pile on the floor.

Mrado slapped Sergio across the face. Immediate effect: the guy's cheek turned red as a blood orange. He still kept his mouth shut. Mrado delivered another slap across the face. Told him to talk. The Latino bit it.

They played good Yugo/bad Yugo. Mrado delivered three, four slaps. Yelled at him to talk. Ratko said it wasn't their intention to hurt Jorge, that they'd take the tape off Sergio, that he'd be compensated if he told them where his cuz was hiding.

No answer.

Mrado took Sergio's hand in his—looked like a baby's hand in a father's palm.

Sergio was rigid. The tape tightened.

Mrado snapped his pinkie finger.

Sergio howled. Lost his cool. The attitude: broken.

He sobbed. Cried.

"I don't even know where he is," he whimpered. "I have no idea. I swear."

Mrado shook his head. Grabbed onto Sergio's ring finger. Bent it back.

Far.

About to snap.

Sergio cracked. It ran out of him. He told them almost everything. "Okay, Okay. You fucking cocks. I helped him a little. When he'd gotten out. He stayed at my aunt's. For five days. Then he started wiggin' out. Thought there were civvies in every car parked on the street. Totally freaked, yo. Made me drive him outta there. I lent him cash. Don't know where he went. Jorge let me down. He owes me for all the help I gave. I haven't seen a fuckin' cent. He's worth less than a bag o' dog shit."

"That's it, there you go. You know where you drove him, don't you?"

"Fuck, man. Yeah, I know. He crashed with this guy, Eddie. Then the cops called me in. That's when he peaced. I swear on my father's grave, I don't know where he went. I swear."

Mrado looked at Sergio. He wasn't lying.

"Great. Now you're gonna go call that Eddie. You're gonna tell him that you need to know where Jorge is. Play it like all's cool. Say you promised to help him with some stuff. And my friend here"—Mrado pointed at Ratko—"understands Spanish. So no tricks."

Mrado pulled out Sergio's cell phone. Told the Latino: "One peep from you about what happened and you can forget all about your left hand."

No one picked up at the first number Sergio called. Mrado checked the contacts list. There were three numbers: "Eddie cell," "Eddie home," "Eddie work." Sergio tried "Eddie home." Someone picked up. Spoke in Spanish. Mrado tried to understand. Hoped his lie wouldn't show. Ratko understood as much Spanish as Sergio understood Serbian. But he picked up a word here and there. The talk was going in the right direction. Sergio wrote something that Eddie said down on the back of an envelope. Ratko was sweating. Was he nervous? The girl stayed calm. The neighbors were chill. Time stood still.

Sergio hung up. His face was expressionless.

"He said Jorge disappeared from his place the same day I was called in for questioning. Said he didn't know where he was going. That he was gonna sleep in parks or shelters and then get dough."

"How can I be sure you're not lying?"

Sergio shrugged. The attitude was back.

"If you want insurance, call a fuckin' corporate boojie, fatso."

Mrado grabbed his ring finger.

Snapped it.

"Don't call me that. Give me something I can trust or I'll break your whole hand."

Sergio screamed. Wailed. Cried.

After a couple of minutes, he calmed down. Seemed apathetic. Spoke quietly, in starts. "Jorge gave Eddie a piece of paper. Coded. Jorge and me came up with the system. A couple of months ago. Eddie read it to me. You can check it with him. If you don't believe me. Just don't hurt me anymore. Please."

Mrado nodded. Sergio showed the letters he'd written down on the back of the envelope: Pq vgpiq fqpfg kt. Bxgtoq gp nc ecnng. Sxg Fkqu og caxfg. Incomprehensible letter combinations. Some kind of code. Shouldn't be impossible to crack, Sergio explained. It was simple. "Every letter is really the one two steps further up in the alphabet. It says: *No tengo donde ir. Duermo en la calle. Que Dios me ayude.*" Mrado asked him to translate. Sergio glanced at Ratko.

Mrado said: "He doesn't understand a word."

The Latino translated, "I have nowhere to go. Sleep on the street. God help me."

———

Mrado and Ratko were silent on the ride home. Mrado'd made a big-enough tear in the tape that Sergio'd be able to free himself in a couple of minutes.

Mrado said, "You thought that was unnecessary?"

Ratko's answer was filled with irritation, "Is there rice in China?"

"Don't worry. He won't say anything. If he does, he'll have to turn himself in."

"Still, risky behavior. The neighbors might've heard."

"They're used to shit goin' down around there."

"Not like that. The *blatte* screamed worse than a Bosnian whore."

"Ratko, can you do me a favor?"

"What?"

"Never second-guess me again."

Mrado kept driving. Dropped Ratko off in Solna. Back with his girl. Mrado thought, Congrats, you've got a life.

New useful information: The Latino fugitive'd left. Planned to sleep outside or at a homeless shelter. But it was colder now. Jorge'd have to be stupid to sleep on the street this time of year. Odds were he stayed at shelters.

Mrado called information. Got the telephone number and address of three homeless shelters in Stockholm. Stadmissionen had two locations: the Night Owl and the Evening Cat. The third: KarismaCare near Fridhemsplan.

He drove to KarismaCare.

Rang the doorbell. Was buzzed in. A small waiting area. A large bulletin board across from the reception desk was covered with hand-outs published for *Situation Stockholm*, a newspaper whose proceeds went to the homeless: opportunities to sell newspapers. Information on community college courses: discounts for the homeless. Information packets about welfare. Pictures from soup kitchens. Ads for yoga classes in the city.

A thin, dark-haired woman was sitting behind the counter. She was dressed in a navy blouse and a cardigan.

"How can I help you?"

"I was wondering if you know if anyone named Jorge Salinas Barrio has slept here in the past four weeks," Mrado said in a matter-of-fact voice.

"Unfortunately, I can't answer that. We have a privacy policy."

Mrado couldn't even get pissed. The woman seemed too nice.

There was only one thing to do. He walked back to the car. Prepared to sleep. Folded down the backseat as far as it would go. He wanted to get the opportunity to talk to all the homeless guys, even the earliest birds, tomorrow morning when they left the shelter.

He slept better than at home. Dreamed he was walking on a beach and was denied entrance to a shelter that was built inside a set of monkey bars at the edge of a forest. Tried to throw sand up at the people in the monkey bars. They laughed. Bizarre.

He woke up. It was 6:00 a.m. He bought coffee and a pastry at a 7-Eleven. Stayed awake from then on. Listened to the radio. The seven o'clock news: anti-U.S. demonstrations in the Middle East. So? Guaranteed they got less beat up by the Americans in Iraq than by their own leaders. Europe didn't get it, as usual. But the Serbs knew. Despite that, all Yankee critique was good. The swine'd bombed the shit out of Yugoslavia.

No movement on the street. Mrado was about to fall asleep again.

Ten minutes past seven: The first homeless guy stepped out. Mrado opened the car door and called out to him. The guy, wearing several layers of jackets and old snow boots, his face covered with gray stubble, seemed uneasy at first. Mrado sugared his tone. Showed the guy pictures of Jorge. Explained that he'd probably changed hair color or something else about his appearance. Explained that the Latino'd stayed at the shelter at some point over the past four weeks. Explained that he'd be served grilled cheese if he said something good. The homeless guy knew nil. Seemed to try hard, especially when he heard about the cheddar.

Mrado waited. After ten minutes, two other homeless guys came out. He pulled the same move on them as on the first one. They didn't recognize J-boy.

He continued. Counted off twelve people. It was now eight thirty. KarismaCare closed in half an hour. No one knew shit, and the worst was that they didn't seem to be lying.

Finally, a middle-aged man stepped out. Shitty teeth. Otherwise, relatively well-kempt appearance. Coat, black pants, gloves. Mrado called out to him. Same routine: explained, exhibited, enticed. Offered one grand. He could see the man was thinking. He knew something.

"I recognize that thug."

Mrado pulled out two five-hundred-kronor bills. Rubbed them together.

The man continued, glanced at the bills. "I've seen that clown at least three times up at KarismaCare. You know, I noticed him; he was always on the floor doing sit-ups. Then he'd shower and smear himself with lotion. Self-tanner. What a damn hustler."

"So he was tanner than in the picture?"

"You know, blacks wanna be white, like that player Mikey Jackson. Whites, like, wanna be brown. That hustler in your picture, he was also kinda coffee-colored, so it was strange. By the way, his hair is curlier in real life. A beard, too. I tried to talk to the guy once. Not much of a conversation. But he knew about other shelters in the city, so maybe you'll find him there."

"How do you know?"

"How do I know? He used to whine so damn much. Claimed the standard was better at other places, like the Night Owl. What an ass. You can't complain when you get a bed, breakfast, and dinner for two hundred. There're a lotta whiners out there, ya know. Don't know what gratitude is."

Mrado thanked the old-timer. Felt genuinely happy. Gave him the two bills. Told him to spread the word: Anyone who knows anything about the nappy, dark thug can report to Mrado and cash in.

22

The first thing Jorge wanted to do was eat.

McDonald's in the Sollentuna Mall: Big Mac, cheeseburgers, extra fries, and ketchup poured into the small white cups. Jorge: in heaven. At the same time: anxiety *masiva*—he was out of money and there were two days left before he had to call Mrado. The word *CASH* pulsed through his body like blood.

He'd left the cottage. Brought a handle of whiskey from the cupboard. Fell asleep on the bus. So fuckin' *nice*—one of the safest spots in town. Golden relaxation. Went straight to Sollentuna. Hadn't dared be in touch with Sergio or Eddie. 5-0 might have eyes there. He'd called some homeboys from way back instead, Vadim and Ashur. Co-dees he used to push powder with in the good old days.

He shouldn't have done it but couldn't resist—thought he'd get the shakes, his withdrawal from actual human contact was so bad.

They welcomed him like a king. J-boy: the legendary fugitive. The blow myth. The lucky Latino. Lent him paper for McDonald's. Reminded him of happier times, asphalt jungle bros, Sollentuna hos.

So ill.

Vadim and Ashur: international friends. Vadim'd come to Sweden from Russia in 1992. Ashur: Syrian from Turkey.

According to Jorge, Vadim could've gone far. The guy was driven, smart, and had a flush family—they ran computer stores outta every single mall in the area. But gangsta dreams got him. Thought dealing a little blow would make him king of the streets. Okay, the clocker'd made out all right, only been in for shorter stints, not like Jorge. But damn, look at the guy today. Worn down like a fuckin' Sven with barrel fever. Tragic. Homeboy should curb his habits.

Ashur: always with a big silver cross around his neck. Stayed straight. Worked as a hairdresser. Kept his eye on the chicks in the area. Highlighting by day, riding by night. Charmed the bitches 110 percent with his talk of bangs and toning.

Jorge should be safe. After all, his appearance was pretty altered. Vadim hadn't even recognized him at first.

After the burgers, they went home to Vadim's. Dude lived in a dump on Malmvägen. Cigarette butts, snort straws, beer cans, and Rizla papers covered the floor. Lighters, pizza boxes, empty booze bottles, and burned spoons on the coffee table. What vice *didn't* Vadim have?

They popped the whiskey. Drank it with lukewarm water like connoisseurs. Plus beer. Later, they built a spliff fat like whoa. Maxed Beenie Man on the stereo. Jorge loved the camaraderie. This was freedom.

They got sloshed. Stoned. Speeded. Vadim spewed fast-cash schemes: We should be pimps. We should build a website and sell mail-order weed. We should sprinkle cocaine in middle schoolers' lunch boxes so they get hooked early. Exchange their Tootsie Rolls for C paste. Jorge joined in. Riled. Get dough. Bake it out. Bake it out.

Vadim looked mischievous, pulled out a matchbox. Unrolled a homemade bag made of plastic wrap. Poured out two grams of blow on a mirror. "Jorge, man, this is to celebrate your homecoming," Vadim said as he cut three lines.

What a party.

Jorge hadn't even dreamed of tasting snow tonight.

Maybe not the most luxurious snort straw—the guys each got a straw that Vadim tore off three juice boxes.

Rapid inhale. First a tickling sensation at the root of the nose. A second later: a tickling sensation in the entire body. Grew into a rush. Felt on top of the world. Everything crystal-clear. Jorge the king. Long live the king. The world was his to conquer.

Ashur buzzed about bitches. He'd arranged to meet up down at the Mingel Room Bar in the Sollentuna Mall with two girls whose hair he usually cut. Good girls. He hollered, "One of 'em, man, you gotta see the back on that female. Beyoncé look-alike. Queen-bee bitch. I gonna promise her free stylin' if one of us get a piece of it tonight."

Course they were gonna get bitches. Course they were gonna go out.

Jorge, stiff, thinking of giving it to the Beyoncé look-alike.

They filled up, more whiskey and another nose each.

The cocaine pounded out the beat of the music.

They went down to Ashur's car.

Mingel Room Bar: Sollentuna's Kharma. But still not. Check Jorgelito out front. Jacked on blow, whiskey, and beer. He didn't feel the chill in the air. Only felt himself. Only felt his party-mood rocket. They eyed the line. Twenty people max, sheepishly cued up. Eyed the chicks approaching the line from the commuter train. Ashur dissed them, "Fuckin' Sweden, man. In this country, chicks don't know howtta walk. Only the guys got it. You should see my home country. Smooth like cats."

Jorge checked them out. Ashur was right: The chicks walked like bros. Straight, with purpose. Without swish, without ass swing, without sex in their steps. He didn't give a fuck. If that Beyoncé broad was inside, he'd butter her into a back bend.

Vadim claimed to know the bouncer. Stepped up. They exchanged Russian pleasantries. Smooth sailing.

Jorge, Vadim, and Ashur were about to glide into the joint, when the bouncer put his hand up. Vadim's questioning look was ignored. The bouncer gazed out toward the road. The line came to a halt. Grew silent. People turned around.

Blue lights.

A cop car parked along the curb.

Mierda.

Two cops got out. Walked toward the line.

Jorge's brain made coke-clear assessments: What were they looking for? Should he book it or have faith in his new look? One thing was certain: If he ran, they'd chase him, 'cause it was shady to dash.

He remained standing. How could he be so stupid that he'd gone out and partied?

Vadim shut his eyes. Looked like his lips were moving, but no sound came out.

Jorge felt stiffer than a substitute on the first day of class in his junior high must've. Didn't move. Didn't think. Did like Vadim—shut his eyes.

Squinted toward the line. Brass with flashlights.

Pointed them in each person's face. The chicks in the way back giggled.

The dudes next to them tried to play cool. One told the cop with the flashlight, "If you don't have a VIP card, you're not getting in."

The cop replied, "Take it easy, buddy."

Cunt attitude.

They continued down the line. People wondered what'd happened. The cops mumbled something unintelligible. They turned the light on Ashur. He cracked a smile. Pointed to the cop with the flashlight. "Hi, I run Scissor Central down in the mall. I think you'd look great with some frosted tips."

The cop actually smiled.

They continued.

Turned the light on Vadim. For a long time. His wasted face attracted the cop's attention.

"Hey there, Vadim," said the guy with the flashlight. "What's up with you?"

"Nothin'. Fancy-free."

"Everything cool?"

"Sure. Like always."

"Yeah, right. Like always." Cop irony.

Jorge stared straight ahead. Felt like it was all a twisted dream. He couldn't concentrate. Time stood still.

What the FUCK was he supposed to do?

Paralyzed.

They came up to him. Shone the torch in his face. He tried to relax. Smile suitably.

23

JW with morning-after angst. He felt like a baked potato with a lead hat on his head. He'd woken up at nine-thirty. Crawled home from Sophie's place. Sat on the floor beside the bed and felt nauseous for twenty minutes. Then drank four cups of water in a desperate attempt to curb the hangover. After the water, he puked in the toilet. Felt considerably better. Fell asleep.

Now he was awake again, after only two hours of sleep. Had gotten what he deserved. Couldn't fall back asleep. He was racked with angst. Things'd gotten weird with Sophie. Felt like the definition of humiliation. On the other hand, he'd done his biggest C delivery ever. So, the night still had to be counted as somewhat of a success.

Promised himself to stick with coke in the future. No booze.

Promised himself to set things right with S.

He stayed in bed even though he couldn't sleep. Couldn't get up.

Promised himself for the six thousandth time: Only coke in the future.

JW woke up again. Remembered why he wasn't allowed to sleep in. There were two projects he had to deal with today. First, he had to make sure the Jan Brunéus story checked out. Then he had to find that Jorge dude. He'd slacked off a little too much on that front. Abdulkarim's expansion plans demanded action.

He skipped a morning lecture at the university. Returned to the Sveaplan high school instead. Went up to the reception desk. The receptionist recognized him and greeted him cheerfully. She was sporting the same pleated skirt as the first time he'd seen her.

JW said, "I have a question for you, ma'am. It may be somewhat unusual."

The woman smiled. JW'd done a good job buttering her up with his manners last time.

"I'd like to see the transcripts for someone who studied here four years ago, Camilla Westlund."

The woman kept smiling but made one of her faces: squeezed her eyes shut, twisted her neck, squinted at JW from the side. Meaning: Aren't you going a little too far now?

"Sorry, we don't release that kind of paperwork."

JW'd spoken with the city agency in charge of academic transcripts. Had expected a reluctant response from Komvux. He was prepared. Had read up, sharpened his arguments. Felt confident. Brought out the heavy artillery right away. No point in mollycoddling the old hag.

"The transcripts are public documents that are to be released unless they are deemed classified for some reason. If you can't prove that they are classified and provide me with the reason for that, they should be considered public and immediately be made available to me. If you refuse to release them, you will be committing a breach of duty, which may be punishable."

The woman made another face but kept that same smile on her lips. Her eyes were staring down to the left. Insecurity.

JW continued as though he were reciting from memory. "Other documents that you draw up here at Komvux are also public and most probably unrestricted. According to the Public Records Act, you have no right to withhold the documents. So, if I may trouble you to please produce Camilla Westlund's grades for all the classes she took here. Thank you."

The woman turned on her heel. Went into an adjoining room. JW heard her speak to someone.

Michael Moore—you can hit the showers.

The receptionist returned.

New expression: The smile on her lips was even phonier than before. Her eyes were glittering in a servile grimace.

"I have to go get them in the archives. Would you mind waiting?" She didn't say a word about being wrong.

It didn't matter. The score was still JW: 1, Grimace lady: 0.

The receptionist disappeared.

She was gone for twenty minutes.

JW got nervous. Sent texts, checked his calendar on his cell. His thoughts flitted from cocaine-selling strategies to Abdulkarim's platitudes, Camilla's Ferrari trips, and the Chilean he still had to track down. Everything hit him at once. No order to the chaos.

The woman returned. She was holding a plastic folder in her hand. She handed it to him.

JW scanned the documents: transcripts. Stockholm's City Continuing Education Program. Sveaplan Gymnasium. Grades for Camilla Westlund. The grades were filled in by hand.

Language Arts: Levels 1 and 2: A
English: Levels 1 and 2: A
Math: Level 1: C
History: Levels 1 and 2: F
Social Studies: Level 1: A
French: Levels 1 and 2: C

JW remained standing by the reception desk. His gaze was glued to the grades. Something was wrong. He tried to get a grip on what. Camilla'd had Jan Brunéus in language arts, English, and social studies. She'd aced them all, just like he'd said she had. She'd only got a C in two other subjects, and failed one. Question was: How come she'd aced Jan's courses?

JW had to know.

He called for the receptionist again. Asked her to get other documents on Camilla.

Less of a wait this time. She knew where to look.

The receptionist came back after five minutes with a similar plastic folder in her hands—other documents.

They addressed Camilla Westlund's attendance record. The same subjects as were listed on the transcript. She had less than a 60 percent rate of attendance. His head was spinning. The Komvux reception area was contorting around him, threatening to swallow him up. He felt hot. Camilla's attendance rate for language arts, English, and social studies—under 30 percent. Something was really fuckin' wrong. No one could ace anything with that kind of attendance. Why had Jan Brunéus lied?

He turned to the receptionist and said, "Do you know where Jan Brunéus usually spends the breaks between classes?" JW made an effort to smile.

"He's probably in the teachers' lounge," she said, and pointed.

JW turned. Booked it down the corridor.

The door to the teachers' lounge was open. He didn't bother to knock. Just walked right in.

Looked around. Seven people were sitting around a large table of pale wood. Eating Danishes and drinking coffee.

None of them was Jan Brunéus.

JW straightened up. "Hi, pardon me for intruding. I was wondering if you know where Jan Brunéus might be?"

One of the people around the table said, "He's left for the day."

JW let it drop. Walked out.

His cell vibrated on the way home from Komvux. At first, JW was going to ignore it—he had enough to think about. Then he realized it might be Abdul. He fished the phone out of his pocket. Too late.

The missed call was from José (cell).

José was one of the guys whose name JW'd gotten from Abdulkarim in the search for Jorge. The guy was a bartender at a place in the Sollentuna area, Mingel Room Bar. JW'd met him two days earlier and taken him to dinner at Primo Ciao Ciao—a moneymaking pizza joint. JW'd offered him two grand in exchange for info on Jorge. José was a perfect hit. Knew who Jorge was, worshiped him like a hero. He'd hung with the same crowd as the Chilean in the early '00s. JW'd told him the truth, more or less: He didn't wish Jorge any harm, wanted to offer the fugitive opportunities, wanted to help Jorge get back on his feet in his new and wonderful life on the outside. Like Jesus, Jr. But José hadn't known anything about Mr. AWOL at the time.

JW waited fifteen minutes to call him back. Walked along Valhallavägen and thought through what he wanted to know and what he had the energy to do right now. Thoughts of Jan Brunéus got in the way. He had to concentrate. The Camilla thing couldn't suck all the energy out of his coke gig right now.

JW said to himself, Focus. Drop the sis angst. It's more exciting to play detective regarding a Chilean on the run than regarding Camilla. The Jorge dude on the run—JW's chance to be part of something big.

He called José.

As soon as the guy picked up, JW knew José had superimportant act-fast-as-fuck kind of info. Someone who looked like Jorge'd been spotted in Sollentuna last night. The *blatte*'d partied hard together with two other Sollentuna gangsters: Vadim and Ashur. Infamous in northwest Stockholm. The Jorge dude'd left the bar at closing, 3:00 a.m. José'd gone out to the entrance, where the stragglers were still hanging. They were juiced up. Blabbered on about the close call they'd had with the 5-0. José asked Vadim if it really was Jorge he'd seen. The hero'd curled his hair, looked darker, more facial hair. Vadim just grinned. He didn't reveal anything directly, but what he did say was enough: "He a new bad boy, yo. Gonna spend the night at my crib 'cause the Five-Oh be chasin' him all the time. Tonight, too." José read him.

JW asked two questions before hanging up: "Where does Vadim live? What time is it?"

José knew the address: Malmvägen 32. Near the Sollentuna Mall. It was 1:00 p.m.

JW stopped short. Tried to hail a cab.

He waited. Not a lot of cabs around at this time.

Thought about the Chilean he had to get hold of. What would he say to him?

Six minutes passed. Where were all the cabs?

Restlessness overtook him once again. Nothing worse than waiting for a taxi.

He waved at a cab that looked empty.

It drove past him.

Hailed another one.

It stopped.

JW got in. The driver said something in unintelligible Swedish.

JW said, "Take me to Malmvägen thirty-two, please."

They drove toward Nortull.

Out on the E4 expressway. Felt like they were crawling.

JW evaluated: There were worse things in the world than waiting for a cab—such as sitting in a cab and waiting for the traffic to move.

Soon he'd have his talk with the Chilean.

24

Mrado'd just completed his weekend training. Murder-machine meeting place par excellence. His guilty conscience—he was there too seldom. Pancrease Gym: Krav Maga, shootfighting, thai boxing, combat tae kwon do. The basement venue consisted of a large room with padded flooring. Four seventeen-pound sandbags suspended by chains along one of the walls. A broad metal locker with sweaty gloves, pads, and safety vests in one corner. A boxing ring in another.

The head instructor was Omar Elalbaoui. Professional shootfighter, fourth dan, Japan. Fastest left hook in town. Middleweight champion in Pride Grand Prix MMA—mixed martial arts, all styles. Swedish-Moroccan prize-podium hunter. Poet of violence. Feared full-contact prophet.

Broken noses, busted knees, dislocated shoulders—legion. And the question: What does fear mean? Omar Elalbaoui's philosophy: "Fear is your worst enemy. Everyone is afraid of something. You're not afraid to get hurt. You're afraid to do poorly, to fight a bad match, to lose. That is the only thing to fear. Never become a loser."

MMA: everything allowed—kicks, punches, knees, elbows, throws, choke slams, grips. No pussy helmets or huge gloves. The only protection: finger gloves, mouth guards, and jockstraps. Sport of sports. Raw strength, agility, and speed were important factors, but above all: strategy and intelligence.

It was the ultimate thing: no props, no complex courses or plans, no complicated rules. Just fighting. The one who gave up first or was knocked out lost. As easy as that.

Mrado's advantages: size, weight, the power behind his punches. Range. But the guys at Pancrease were good. Took punches. Avoided kicks. Blocked tackles. Mrado often got his ass kicked. Once, four years ago, he'd had to be rushed to the hospital. His nose was broken in two places. But the thing was, Mrado liked getting beaten. Made him feel alive. Made him practice not being afraid. To keep feeding jabs even though his head was going numb. To never give up.

Competitions were mostly held in Solnahallen, a large venue in Solna. The organizers easily sidestepped the national ban on boxing. Sometimes they fought in cages, Brazilian *vale tudo*. Mrado knew the guys; a lot of them trained or had trained at Pancrease. He knew their styles, their weaknesses/strengths. At the latest competition in Stockholm, he'd cashed in ten grand. Knew how to place his bets. MMA in its different incarnations was blowing up as a sport.

Mrado knew what was up. Had learned techniques. Trained the right muscle groups. The stronger muscles, tendons, ligaments you have, the more difficult it is to knock you down. The more flexible you are, the lower the risk of pulling something. Maintain your guard. Eye on the punches. Follow your opponent's movements. At the same time, tense the right muscle groups to take the hit. Above all: A strong neck reduces the movement of the head. With Mrado's neck, he was almost immune to knockouts.

Mentally: Pain increases with fear and is reduced with aggression.

Mrado's only problem: Lately, he'd been working out at the gym too much, hadn't been to Pancrease enough. State of contradiction: beefier muscles, less agility. He was starting to lose it. Stiffer joints. Reduced flexibility. Slower punch sequences.

Fighting was a lifestyle.

Mrado pulled on a pair of sweatpants and a sweatshirt after the training. Let the sweat dry. He didn't shower at Pancrease. Showered at home. The guys at the fighting club were too young. Too jazzed. Mrado liked the meatheads at Fitness Club better. He downed a protein drink. When he got home, he'd take his own witch's brew of growth meds.

Went home.

Drove over the Västerbron bridge, the most beautiful spot in the city. Lit up from below. View over a territory: a business empire annexed by the Serbs. No puny AWOL nigger could take that away from them.

Reached Katarina Bangata in four minutes. Home. Now he had to find a parking spot.

The apartment: a two-bedroom. Living room, Mrado's bedroom, and Lovisa's room.

The living room: Eastern European luxury look. A group of black leather corner couches. Glass table. Bookshelf with a stereo, flat-screen TV, and DVD player. Expensive shit. Also on the shelves: CDs, mostly Serbian music and rock, Bruce Springsteen, Fleetwood Mac, and Neil Young. DVDs: action, boxing, all the Rocky films, and Serbian documentaries. Photos of his family in Belgrade, the Swedish king, Slobodan Milosevic, and Lovisa. Three bottles of good whiskey and a bottle of Stoli Cristall. The rest of the booze was in anther cupboard. Four flint-lock rifles on the wall, bought at an arms market in Vojvodina—symbols of the 1813 uprising against the Turks. In a broad glass-front cupboard beside the bookshelf: two Browning pistols, one Smith & Wesson Magnum .41 replica, a bayonet, and a real land mine from the war. The bayonet was well used. Constant question about the mine: Was it disarmed? Mrado kept up the suspense. Never told anyone the truth.

He sat down on the couch. Turned the TV on.

Channel-surfed. Watched a couple minutes of a nature show about crocodiles. Got bored. Kept zapping. Shit across the board.

Fingered his gun. Mrado packed Starfire ammunition. The bullet was hollow at the tip. Effect at impact: explosion. Tore up enough flesh to kill with one shot.

Put the revolver down on the table. Mused.

The Jorge fag was a total fucking fiasco. He was annoyed with himself for not having found the Latino yet, with Radovan for his arrogant style, and with Jorge for lying low.

Flipped through his notebook. Questions and probable answers. In the middle, a column devoted to questions without answers. Two words were underlined and circled: *current location*. The trail'd ended. But people usually slipped up eventually. Ran outta kale. Wanted to bang bitches. Live la dolce vita. Livin' on the lam was hard. But Jorge was keeping a low profile. Nevertheless, Mrado was certain the *blatte* was still in the country/city. It wasn't over yet.

But where to pick up the search?

Mrado leaned back.

His cell vibrated.

A text: *Met Jorge tonight. He at Vadim's now.*

Bingo.

Adrenaline rush.

Mrado called the number. A guy, Ashur, answered. Mrado remembered the name. One of the kids him and Ratko'd shown pics of Jorge to during their runs in Sollentuna. Got the story told to him in crappy Swedish.

Ashur, Jorge, and another hoodlum, Vadim, had been out partying the night before. Cruised to Mingel Room Bar in the Sollentuna Mall and boozed. Jorge'd almost been collared. The Latino'd asked to crash at Vadim's. Ashur's theory: They were still there; it was only noon.

Mrado thanked him. Agreed to stop by later and pay up what he'd promised.

Put on his leather jacket. Stuffed a rubber baton in his inside pocket. Popped the revolver into the holster. Walked down to the car.

Drove the road he now knew by heart. To Sollentuna. To Jorge. It was about fucking time.

What was the smartest thing to do? Head straight into the apartment and do his thing, like he'd done with Sergio? There was a big risk that Vadim, Jorge, and maybe others who were in the apartment would be harder to overpower than Sergio's screaming chick. Risk number two: If neighbors heard and the cops showed up, Jorge'd be put away again. The Latino'd be able to cut down big parts of the Yugo empire with what he knew. Conclusion: Mrado wanted to get at the fugitive alone.

Meanwhile, he called Ratko, Bobban, and other contacts. Asked them if they knew Vadim. Who the guy was. If he was dangerous. Put them to work making calls and finding out more: if the dude worked, where he worked. Who did he hang with? Did he pack heat?

Mrado kept an eye on the entryway to the building. People went in and out. He took note: an unusual number of people around for this time of day. Immigrants, junkies, wife beaters, other criminals—all bunched together in the same kind of concrete towers he'd grown up in.

Mrado was on the phone with Bobban when a guy who looked like Jorge stepped out.

He'd seen the Latino four or five times before. The last time: at the trial, where he'd testified so that Jorge was put away for three years. Radovan and Mrado'd fed him to the wolves—you had to take some losses. Then: The Latino'd been a young, cocky player with modern, gaudy threads. Gold chain with a cross. Gelled hair. Good-looking stubble. Quick movements and machine-gun tongue. Now: The person outside the car looked like a fucking nigger. Nappy hair, dark brown complexion. Walked like a Rastafarian: sluggish with rhythm. Baggy clothes, dirty puffy. Still, there was something about the person's worn appearance that seemed to suggest something else: vigor.

It had to be the Latino.

Mrado hunched down lower behind the wheel. Saw Jorge look around. Then walk toward the commuter rail station. Too many people around to act.

Mrado waited until Jorge rounded the corner toward the path leading to the station before he stepped out of the car. Put on a pair of shades. Wound the scarf a couple more times around his chin. Sent off a prayer to the big Car God: Let my car be left untouched, unscratched, unstolen here on Sollentuna's most dangerous street.

Walked to the corner where Jorge'd turned off.

Jorge didn't turn up the stairs to the station. Kept walking straight. Toward the Sollentuna Mall. Mrado kept his distance, but he didn't want to lose sight of his target.

Into the Sollentuna Mall. Mrado waited a couple of seconds outside the automatic doors before he followed Jorge in. As soon as he stepped inside, he saw Jorge disappear into the grocery store. Mrado sneaked into the photo store across the way. He was such a scout—combat-trained. He called Ratko. In Serbian: "Ratko, where are you? It's important."

In past conversations, Ratko'd been whiny about the over-the-top treatment of Sergio. Now he heard that something real was up.

"I'm home. Watching TV. D'you find him?"

"Yeah. He spent the night at some guy's in Sollentuna. On his way outta here now. Get ready. Go to your car."

"Damn, I was getting so comfortable. Where am I going?"

"Don't know yet. Just get ready for the starting shot."

"Already out the door."

"Nice. I'll call you. Bye."

Jorge walked out of the store. Had two bags in each hand. Looked like they were full of food. The Latino was probably on the way to his hideout.

He trailed him up to the train station. Ground rule: no sudden movements when you're following someone. A guy like Jorge was electrified with tension—would react right away.

Jorge walked out on the platform. Mrado stayed inside the station house. Hoped the outside light turned the glass doors into mirrors. Jorge seemed watchful.

The train headed to the city rolled in. Jorge got on. Mrado got on another car.

He called Ratko again. Told him to drive toward the city.

Mrado looked out the doors at every stop. Jorge didn't get off.

The train slowed down. Rolled slowly into the Stockholm Central Station.

Came to a stop. Mrado looked out. Saw Jorge get off.

Mrado waited outside the train till Jorge walked down the stairs toward T-Centralen, the subway station. He followed. Jorge walked farther up, mixed with the crowd. Mrado concentrated, couldn't lose him now.

They walked the underground passage toward T-Centralen.

A South American band was blowing into pan flutes and banging on drums. A woman in a trench coat standing by a pillar was peddling the *Watchtower*.

Jorge: down toward the subway track. Mrado followed at a measured distance.

Jorge got onto the train toward Mörby Centrum. Mrado boarded another car on the same train.

The car was half-empty. Two punks in baseball hats and windbreakers—potential future recruits—were sitting with their feet propped up on the seats. A misplaced Stureplan brat: blond, knee-length coat, narrow jeans, backslick. Was listening to his MP3 player.

Jorge got off at the Royal Technical Academy, KTH, station. Mrado: same.

Jorge walked out past the turnstiles. Stood and checked out the bus schedules. Went into the bodega. Bought something. His bags looked heavy. He walked up to the bus stop. Mrado followed. The Stureplan brat from the train was there, too, positioned himself at the same bus stop as Jorge. Probably just a coincidence.

Mrado eyed the bus number: 620. Jorge was clearly waiting for a ride to the Norrtälje area.

Mrado called Ratko. Told him, "Drive to KTH."

The 620 bus pulled up. Ratko hadn't shown. Mrado walked over to the hot dog stand by Valhallavägen. Beside it: a taxi stand.

Jorge got on the bus. It pulled out. Drove off.

Mrado told the taxi driver, "Follow the six twenty bus."

They drove for thirty minutes. Mrado was worried. The Jorge-guy was smart. On his guard. Might start wondering why the same taxi kept driving two to five cars behind the bus.

Mrado kept in touch with Ratko.

Switched to his car at Åkersberga.

They kept their distance. Nothing strange about it. There were several cars backed up behind the bus. It didn't make many stops.

The Latino stayed on.

Finally: Dyvik. The bus stopped. Jorge got off.

The Stureplan brat did, too. Weird, but no time to think about that now.

Mrado yelled, "Turn, goddamn it!"

Ratko turned off in the direction Jorge was walking. Mrado ducked in the passenger seat. They passed Jorge at a ten-foot distance. Drove as slowly as they dared. Like people who didn't really know their way around. Looked in the rearview mirror, saw him walking. Worked for a minute or so. Then it got shady. They had to keep driving. Lost sight of Jorge behind them.

They stopped the car. Got out. Mrado walked up into the the woods. Couldn't be seen from the road. Ratko started walking in the opposite direction. Toward Jorge.

Two minutes later, Ratko called. "He's a little over two hundred yards away from me on the road. Still coming at you. What do I do if he recognizes me, gets jittery, and runs?"

"Keep going toward him. Just pass him like it's nothing. Then turn around when you know he can't see you. Start following him. I'll take care of him here."

Mrado waited. No houses nearby. No people. No problems.

His cell was on. Ratko on speed dial. Poised to call him.

Jorge came walking. Bags in hand. Looked tired. He was twenty yards away, down on the road. Mrado called Ratko. Whispered. Told him to run.

Mrado charged out of the woods like an evil Boy Scout, size XL.

Jorge knew right away. Panic in his eyes. Dropped the bags. Turned around. Saw Ratko running from the other direction. In a game of pickle. Tried to run—too late. Mrado grabbed him by the jacket.

Return of the Yugos. Fall of the *blatte*.

Mrado punched Jorge in the gut with full force. Jorge doubled over. Fell. Ratko came up behind, grabbed hold of him, and, with Mrado's help, dragged the Latino up into the trees. Away from the road. Mrado snatched the bags. Jorge puked. Sour stink. Vomit on Mrado's shoes. What a pig. Mrado, with the baton in hand, hit Jorge across the back. Jorge fell to the ground. Stood on all fours. Mrado kept beating him. Jorge screamed. Mrado was careful: didn't break anything. No fractures. No bloodshed. No life-threatening injuries. Nothing that necessarily required medical attention. Just struck with the rubber baton. Across his thighs, arms. Hit across his back, neck, stomach. Whacked. Thrashed. Crushed.

Jorge tried to get on his knees. Folded. Protected his head. Curled into a ball.

Mrado let the baton dance. It bounced up and down over the Latino's body.

Finally, Jorge was a puddle. Destroyed. Almost passed out.

Mrado knelt down.

"Can you hear me? Faggot."

No reaction.

Mrado lifted his head by the hair. "Blink if you can hear me."

The Latino blinked.

"You know what this is about. You tried to fuck with the wrong people. Radovan doesn't dig your style. You only have yourself to blame. Who the fuck do you think you are? Blackmailing Rado. Remember this: We'll find you, always. Wherever you are, on the run, in the joint. With your mom. We never forget. We always punish. If you tell anyone so much as a peep about us, I won't be as nice next time."

Mrado released his grip on Jorge's hair. His head fell back down.

"Oh, and one more thing." Mrado pulled out his cell phone. Scrolled to his photos. Held up the screen in front of Jorge's face.

"You know this chick? I've talked to her about you. Go ahead, ask her. I know her well. Know where she lives. Where she goes to school. What classes she's in. Don't fuck shit up for her. That'd be a shame for such a pretty girl."

25

J-boy, gone/with it. Flashed in and out.

The pain was insane.

Closed his eyes. Waited. Heard the Yugos leave. Crackling in the woods. Their sounds faded out. He waited. Listened.

Alone.

Beaten to bits. Couldn't move. Couldn't feel his legs; they were numb. His arms were totally gone, too. His back, he could feel. Passed out.

Snapped back. Heard a car drive by on the road. Heard the beat of his own heart. Tried to move his arm. Hurt too much.

Vomited.

Just lay still.

Clear flow of thoughts: Jorgelito in the fairy-tale woods. Crushed. Dumped. Disgraced. Thought he'd been the king. Really, the most naïve bitch. They'd been after Paola. God, please don't let them've hurt her. Not humiliated her. He'd call her when he was done here. When he could get up. Paola, the world's best sister.

He descended into darkness.

She'd accepted baby Jorge's attitude. When he was fourteen years old, he'd come home with a letter from school.

I hereby wish to inform you that Jorge Salinas Barrio will be suspended from the Tureberg School for six weeks starting March 1 of this year. The reason for this measure is that he has serious problems cooperating with others and has a negative impact on the other students and the general schoolwork. I have on several occasions spoken with you about Jorge's problems and we have also spoken with the school counselor, Inga-Britt Lindblom, about opportunities for Jorge to reach an understand-

ing regarding his behavior. Unfortunately, his destructive behavior has only increased during this semester, which I also discussed with him and you on February 3 of this year. The school sees no other option but to suspend Jorge during the above-mentioned time. Sollentuna will offer homeschooling. Do not hesitate to be in touch with me if you have any questions.

   —Jan Lind, Principal

Mama'd cried. Rodriguez'd whooped him. Jorge'd thought, If my real dad'd been here, he would've taken me back to Chile. But Paola wasn't angry, not apathetic. Hadn't made excuses. Just been nice. The only one who really talked to Jorgelito. Even though he was a hard-knock, it still felt good to talk. She explained, "You're Mama's and my prince. Never forget that. No matter what you do. You're our prince."

Someone in the forest was calling Jorge's name. He couldn't lay any quieter or stiller than he already was. Were the Yugos back?

No one showed up.

The puke stank.

He was finished. Caput. The Yugos were smarter than he'd thought. He should've been even more cautious. Must've been the hangover. How long'd Mrado and the other guy been following him? They weren't on the bus. They hadn't been on his subway car. Hadn't seen them at the bus stop at KTH. Hadn't seen any one single car following the bus. Had they trailed him all the way from Sollis? How'd they known he was at Vadim's? Suspicions: The Russian fucker must've leaked. Or someone at the bar the night before. Had people recognized him? Cunts.

He tried to move a smaller body part—an index finger. Couldn't feel it at first. Three seconds later, his entire arm was pounding with pain. Too much pain. He screamed aloud. Didn't give a fuck if the Yugos were still around.

Someone yelled his name again.

He vomited.

Prayers on his lips: *La madre que te parió.* Thoughts in his head: Who can I trust now? Sergio? Eddie? Ashur? Can I get in touch with Mama? Do I dare call my sister? His flight from the big cage'd been smooth, slick. Speedy. Best one yet. But life after—Jorgelito'd thought too short-term. Thought it'd be easy. Same mistake as all the others—been weak, partied. Needed social interaction.

He tried to open his eyes.

Fir trees all around. The light peeking through the branches painted the ground a spotty pattern. Brown, bumpy, bare. No birdsong.

What would happen now? It was one thing to risk your own life to get at Radovan's cash. But to risk your sister's?

He thought about his two tattoos. On his left shoulder was a smiling devil. All in black. On his back, a crucifix with the text: *The Man*, in Gothic lettering. He'd thought he was the man with the master plan, when really, he was just a loser. Fucked over.

Down for the count.

26

A deluxe guy on a walk in the enchanted forest. JW was looking for Jorge. Two alternatives: Either the Chilean was lying wounded somewhere in the woods or the Yugos'd taken him with them.

He started on the right-hand side. Walked in a zigzag pattern. First about ten yards forward, then crossed down to the left, then ten yards forward again.

Thought about *Spaceballs*. "Comb the desert!" the Darth Vader caricature orders. In the next scene, his helpers are pulling huge combs over the sand. Mel Brooks—so lame and yet so witty.

JW combed the forest.

Didn't find Jorge among the trees.

An hour and twenty minutes earlier, JW'd reached Malmvägen just in time to see someone who looked like Jorge leave the building. Detective JW took a few steps back, behind the corner of the house—which proved to be the right move. He peered out. Saw an enormous man step out of a car that was way too slick and follow the Chilean. Something wasn't right. The man never walked up to Jorge. Kept a few yards back. It was obvious after a while: The giant was following the Chilean.

The man fulfilled all the criteria of the classic Yugo gangster look: mid-length leather jacket, scarf, black jeans, leather shoes. A neck that put the Hulk to shame. His arms hung out along his sides at an angle, looked like he was constantly carrying a TV. Short, dirty-blond hair, straight-cut bangs. His jaws revealed a hard-core testosterone diet.

Why the hell had Abdulkarim put him in this situation? JW felt like a failed police investigator. Didn't dare approach Jorge, even though he was right on his tail. The biggest question was who the huge Yugo was. Did the Serbian Mafia want to put Jorge's coke know to use, too?

He kept trailing them. Up to the commuter rail station. JW remained standing at the bottom of the escalators and heard the train pull into the station. He ran up and jumped into a car. He could see the Yugo through the glass doors leading to the next car. Thank God.

Total tension. JW completely forgot about the Camilla thing.

The huge Yugo got off at T-Centralen. He couldn't see Jorge, but JW assumed the Yugo was on it. Followed him down.

Got off at KTH. Created a distance between himself and the Yugo. Saw Jorge hanging around a bus stop. JW walked with deliberate steps toward the same bus stop. It had to look like his one and only goal in life was to get to bus 620. He passed the huge Yugo on his way there. Two yards between them. JW couldn't decide if it was suspicious that he was going to the same bus stop as Jorge, but he felt the Yugo's presence as fiercely as though they'd been standing eye-to-eye in a cramped elevator. The man exuded authority.

A couple of people got on after Jorge, but the Yugo wasn't on the bus. Had he given up? Jorge was squeezed in next to a middle-aged lady with a bag on her lap. The woman's two kids sat in the seats in front of them, eating ice-cream cones. One of the seats behind him was free; the other was occupied by an old man in a baseball hat. This wasn't the time to chat up the Chilean; it'd have to wait until he got off. JW took a seat in the way back.

He'd gotten off at the same stop as the Chilean. Followed a couple hundred yards behind him. After a while, a Yugo came running. Understood: They were here. Thirty seconds later, he heard screaming. Panicked. What the fuck was he supposed to do? He ran into the woods. Stood still, listened. Waited. That's where he was now. Was going to look for Jorge. But he couldn't see him. After he'd crisscrossed over a few hundred yards, JW switched sides. It was worth spending another hour searching.

He heard a scream. Not as loud as the previous ones, but still—painful.

He tried to walk in the direction of the sound. Looked around. Saw dark trees, pine needle–covered paths. In some places, the branches of the fir trees dragged on the ground, hiding what might be found underneath. JW stepped up, lifted the branches, looked under them.

Scratched himself on needles. The forest wasn't exactly his scene. And anyway, he was about to shit a brick, he was so scared.

Eight yards farther up, he saw plastic bags filled with groceries strewn on the ground. JW followed the trail. Farther in, he spotted a huddled-up human. Was it the Chilean? Was he alive?

JW looked around. No Yugos in sight. He called out. No answer. Got closer. The guy looked dead. JW knelt down beside him. Said Jorge's name. Really didn't want to find a murdered person.

Finally, he got a reaction.

With his eyes still shut, Jorge mumbled, "Get outta here."

JW didn't know what to say. Thought, Relief the guy's alive. But how much help does he need? Not a good idea to get an ambulance involved.

"Hi. How are you feeling? Is there anything I can do?"

"Beat it."

"Nice to hear you're alive. I know who you are. I recognize you. I've been looking for you for hours."

Jorge opened one eye. He had a slight immigrant lilt to his speech. "And who the hell are you?"

"My name is Johan. I've no idea who did this to you or why. You look like shit. Probably need medical care. You've got to listen to me. I've got good news."

"I said, beat it. You've got fuckin' nothing to do with me. I've never even seen your face."

"Get it together. Your name is Jorge Salinas Barrio and you escaped from Österåker on August thirty-first. You've been on the run ever since. That can't be easy. You know the cocaine business better than anyone else. You're the king of coke in the Stockholm area. Are you listening, or what?"

Jorge lay still. Didn't say anything. But he also didn't say no.

"I work for an Arab—Abdulkarim Haij. Do you know who that is?"

Jorge looked up again. JW read it as: Keep talking.

"He keeps me in the C. I, like, deal to the Stureplan crowd and make a killing. You can get up to eleven hundred a gram from them. That's not bad. But imagine if we could push the purchase price even more. That's what we're going to do when we expand. And we know you; you've got no life without our help. There are clearly others, besides the police, who've got it in for you. You can forget about them now. We'll help you, get you back on your feet. Fix a passport, pesetas, whatever you need. The police don't stand a chance. Not those Yugos, either. If you work for us, we'll make you a rich man."

JW caught his breath. Didn't give a shit that Jorge seemed totally out of it. He felt how excited he was, had thought about this for days. Was hard to take it easy now.

"Listen, man, we've been tracking the development in Stockholm. The coke is on its way to the boroughs, to the projects. It's the big trend, the new everyman drug. It's going to be like weed. And the price is sinking every day. When you were put away it was, what, twelve hundred a gram? Now there are a lot of people out there selling eighty-five percent Charlie for eight hundred. That means the volume's going to be through the roof and we, since we've got good contacts, can buy at lower prices. The aggregate income increases radically. This is where you come in. You're going to help us bring in more. Above all, you're going to deal to the boroughs. You and me, together, are going to own this town. You with me? Own it."

Jorge, with a whimper: "*Maricón.* Beat it."

PART 2

Four months later.

MINUTES
Oral proceedings in the Stockholm District Court
Case number T 3245-06

COURT
Honorable District Court Judge Patrick Renbäck

KEEPER OF THE MINUTES
District Court Clerk Oskar Hävermark

PARTIES

PLAINTIFF
Annika Sjöberg, 690217-1543
Gröndalsvägen 172
117 69 STOCKHOLM
Present in person

REPRESENTATION UNDER THE LEGAL AID ACT
Göran Insulander, Esq.
Box 11244
112 21 STOCKHOLM
Present

DEFENDANT
Mrado Slovovic, 670203-9115
Katarina Bangata 35
116 39 STOCKHOLM
Present in person

REPRESENTATION
Martin Thomasson, Esq.
Box 5467
112 31 STOCKHOLM
Present

THE CASE
Custody, living arrangements, visitation rights, etc.

The judge reviews what has previously been decided in the case.

CLAIMS
Göran Insulander states that Annika Sjöberg, albeit on an interim/interlocutory basis, petitions for sole custody of the daughter, Lovisa.

Martin Thomasson states that Mrado Slovovic's stance is as follows: He contests Annika Sjöberg's claim. He petitions, albeit on an interim/interlocutory basis, to have visitation rights with Lovisa **every** week from **Tuesday** at six p.m. to **Friday** at six p.m.

Göran Insulander states that Annika Sjöberg contests Mrado Slovovic's claim. She agrees that Mrado Slovovic should have visitation rights with Lovisa **every other** week from **Tuesday** at six p.m. to **Wednesday** at six p.m.

GROUNDS, ETC.
Göran Insulander states that the grounds for and the circumstances around Annika Sjöberg's case are as follows: Annika Sjöberg and Mrado Slovovic were married around nine years ago. Together, they had a daughter, Lovisa, two years later. It is in the best interest of Lovisa not to have too much contact with Mrado Slovovic, since he has a very negative influence on his daughter, as well as the fact that it is dangerous for the daughter to spend time with him. Furthermore, he is unable to cooperate with Annika Sjöberg when it comes to picking up and dropping off the girl in connection with his visitation rights. Mrado Slovovic has threatened her on a number of occasions. Despite this, Annika Sjöberg believes that Mrado Slovovic should have limited visitation with Lovisa, since it is important for a child to have a connection with both parents. Lovisa never asks for Mrado Slovovic. In 2002, the parties' relationship began to deteriorate. Mrado Slovovic was never

home at night and slept most of the day. He became angry when Lovisa cried or made noise and didn't take care of her. Annika Sjöberg was the one who fed Lovisa and cared for her hygiene. Mrado Slovovic moved in criminal circles and, in the spring of 2004, Annika Sjöberg decided to file for divorce. Mrado Slovovic was enraged by this and threatened, among other things, to take Lovisa with him to Serbia. On two occasions, he also said that he would break her neck if she didn't let him live with Lovisa. Between 2004 and 2006, his visitation rights with Lovisa have been characterized by problems. Over long periods of time, four months being the longest, he has not seen Lovisa at all. On several occasions, Mrado Slovovic has failed to show up at the agreed time and instead kept Lovisa for up to three days longer without Annika Sjöberg's permission. Lovisa is very stressed-out and sleeps poorly after she has been with him. When she is with Mrado Slovovic, she is allowed to watch movies all night and he does not prepare proper food for her. He still moves in criminal circles and has previously been convicted of several violent crimes. Acquaintances of Annika Sjöberg have reported seeing Mrado Slovovic driving at speeds far above the speed limit with Lovisa in his sports car. It has also happened on one occasion that he took her along to a combat sports club, where she had to stand outside the ring and watch Mrado Slovovic be beaten up. Lovisa was very upset after this. It is harmful for Lovisa to spend time with Mrado Slovovic. Partly because he brings her along to activities that are actually dangerous, and partly because he is involved in criminal activity. Furthermore, Mrado Slovivic is unable to work together with Annika Sjöberg.

Martin Thomasson states the grounds for and the circumstances around Mrado Slovic's case are as follows: Lovisa needs her father. It is untrue that it is dangerous for her to spend time with him. He does not exceed the speed limit when driving with her in his car. He has given her proper food and she does not only watch TV. They do many active things together, such as go to the Skansen outdoor museum and bake. On one occasion, Lovisa accompanied Mrado Slovoic to his combat sports gym, but it is not true that she saw him being beaten. What did, in fact, happen was that he and Lovisa "shadowboxed" for fun in the ring in a completely harmless manner. The reason that Annika Sjöberg makes false claims is that she is jealous of Mrado Slovovic, since he, shortly after the termination of their marriage, had a relationship with another woman. The problems in connection with Lovisa's pickup and drop-off are brought about by Annika Sjöberg, who is at times psychologically fragile. On such occasions, she lies apathetically in bed and is unable to take care of Lovisa. This behavior had already begun during the parties' marriage. When Annika Sjöberg suffers such periods of depression, Mrado Slovovic does not deem it healthy for Lovisa to live with her mother. Lovisa is very happy with the time she spends with Mrado Slovovic and has on several occasions expressed a desire to spend more time with him. On Mrado Slovovic's last occasion of visitation in January, Lovisa said that "she wanted to live with Daddy like she lives with Mommy." She is always very sad when it is time to drop her off with Annika Sjöberg. Annika Sjöberg has refused Mrado Slovovic the right to take Lovisa to Serbia to visit the daughter's grandfather. Mrado Slovovic has never had the intention of taking Lovisa there without Annika Sjöberg's permission. It is in the best interest of Lovisa that the parties maintain joint custody of her and that she spend the same amount of time with her father as with her mother. Presently, Mrado Slovovic is of the mind that visitation from Tuesay to Friday is sufficient.

The judge presided over a discussion during which the parties aimed to come to an agreement. No mutual agreement was reached.

The meeting is adjourned with an announcement that a decision will be made public at the office of the Court on February 23 of this year, at 1:30 p.m.

After careful consideration, the District Court has reached the following decision:

DECISION (TO BE DELIVERED ON FEBRUARY 23 OF THIS YEAR, AT 1:30 P.M.)

Opinion of the Court
The District Court does not find sufficient grounds to terminate joint custody in the present situation. Annika Sjöberg's claim will therefore be dismissed.

As for visitation rights, the District Court concludes that Mrado Slovovic has had irregular contact with Lovisa in recent years. Considering this, the District Court finds that Mrado Slovovic, until further notice, will have visitation rights with Lovisa one day every other week. If the visitation proves positive, the parties can discuss increased forms of visitation independently.

CONCLUSION
Until the issues have been resolved by a final verdict, or by court order, or by a contract created by the parents that has, in turn, been approved by Social Services, or until another decision has been made, the District Court has decided the following:

A. The parties will continue to maintain joint custody of Lovisa.

B. Lovisa's need to see her father will, until further notice, be filled by Mrado Slovovic's right to visitation with her **every other** week from **Wednesday** at 6:00 p.m. to **Thursday** at 6:00 p.m.

27

Psychological borders carved into the Stockholm territory. Kungsgatan was divided into three geographical regions. Farthest down, by Stureplan, were stylish clothing stores, cafés, bars, movie theaters, and electronics retailers. All types of people walked this stretch: Svens, Stureplaners, slumdogs. The next segment led from Hötorget down to Vasagatan. Crap central: shitty dives and rowdy restaurants. Streetfight central: populated by *blattes* and Svens. The last part, the intersection with Vasagatan down to the bridge, was empty of restaurants and regular bars, stores, or cafés. Only places with a specialized profile were found here. An indie theater, a jazz joint, and the gambling pit— Casino Cosmopol. Older clientele. Revitalizing mix of theater fanatics, jazzers, and gamblers.

A slash through Stockholm's nightlife/shopping/entertainment scene. Kungsgatan—the sidewalks were always warm, always clean of snow, always crowded. Always racked by consumer hysteria. Three different strata. Three different worlds along the same street.

Mrado was sitting at the bar at Kicki's Bar & Co., one of the crappy dives in the street's middle section. He was waiting for Ratko. Bar hang with beer & co.: ale, light brew, hard cider.

He was so damn beat.

Staring vacantly. Twenty-year-old bad boys in stolen puffies hung in clusters around the place. Refused to check their coats—the Canada Goose label, with its implied price tag, was a symbol of a world they'd never really gain access to. Stared at a safe distance. They didn't know who he was. Clocked anyway—don't mess with the giant in the bar. If the coat check in this place were his, those downy-lipped niggers' Geese would've been on hangers ages ago.

There was neon lettering on the walls. Formed the words *Kicki's Cocktails*. Written in red, blue, and yellow, interlaced.

Mrado and Ratko'd decided to grab a beer before going to Casino Cosmopol, farther up on Kungsgatan. Mrado had to get some clean cash. The video-rental stores/laundromats weren't working as they should. Weren't able to handle the required volumes. The casino was always a last resort for cleaning cash.

The clock struck 10:05. Ratko wasn't usually late. Had his grouse increased lately? Couldn't be tolerated. Mrado was above Ratko in the Yugo hierarchy. Therefore, he was only gonna wait for ten more minutes.

Ordered another beer. Thought through the past months.

The Jorge situation'd cleared out well. Four months'd passed and the Latino'd taken it easy ever since. Laid low. No more attempts to fuck with them. Mrado'd gotten some indications. Jorge was still in the city, probably still rockin' the dark look in order to survive on the lam. Scraping by the only way he knew how: pushing blow for some dealer. Mrado couldn't care less, as long as the shit didn't affect him.

Mrado'd been trudging along in the same old tracks. Longing for Lovisa. Cursing Annika. On February 23, the district court'd ruled: mixed verdict. A relief that he was allowed to maintain joint custody. Fucking ridiculous that he got a visitation day only once every other week. Sweden betraying the Serbs yet again.

Mrado woke up every night between 4:00 and 5:00 a.m., couldn't sleep. Like an old hag. Usually downed a fat whiskey to fall back asleep. What the hell was going on?

Once, he went into Lovisa's room to find peace of mind. Sat down on her bed. It creaked. The sound reminded him of something. Couldn't think of what. He pulled out a drawer in her desk. Saw the crayons. Realized what the creaking reminded him of. He felt depleted. Racked with anxiety. What would Lovisa think of him if she ever found out about all the shit he'd done? Was it possible to be a good father and still break people's fingers? He should stop.

Other than that, it was the same old. Business was booming. Cash was flowing. Important to-dos right now: fix the video-rental stores and figure out how to deal with the pigs and their new Nova Project. Radovan'd called everyone to a meeting about Nova. All the colleagues were supposed to talk about the cops' efforts to stop them. Mrado, Goran, Nenad, and Stefanovic. Circle-jerk.

The video-rental companies'd been created after thorough research'd been done on the straw man, Christer Lindberg. Mrado didn't want anyone who'd raise suspicions with the Man. He'd checked the public records to make sure the guy was registered as a Swedish resident, that he didn't have any red flag–raising German-imported Beamers, that he was in the clear with tax records, bankruptcy records, and late-payment records. Finally, he'd checked the police's internal lists— everything had to look clean as a Tide commercial. Mrado thanked his police hookup, Rolf, for the latter registry printouts.

Christer Lindberg was, at least on the surface, a responsible citizen. It would work.

Mrado didn't want to meet Lindberg personally, kept his distance. He'd had Goran explain most of it. Mrado'd only spoken with the guy once on the phone. All he was told: Mrado was a friend of Goran and could fix fine flow in exchange for signatures on various documents and possible questions from the tax man.

Lindberg according to Mrado: proletarian caricature. Talked intense Sven Swedish, peppered with clichés and shallow insights. Mrado thought about their one and only conversation. Couldn't help grinning to himself.

"Hi, I'm a friend of Goran. I'm calling about a business idea with video-rental stores. Has he mentioned something about it to you?"

"Yes siree."

"Do you know what it's about?"

"Let's put it this way: I wasn't born yesterday. I get the idea."

"Can I ask you a question? What did you do before you started working for Goran?"

"Yours truly worked as a truck driver for Östman Åkeri, in Haninge."

"And how was that?"

"That was like night and day, so to speak."

"What do you mean?"

"Well, you know, Östman wasn't exactly the type to turn down a drink. Göran showed up one day. Took over the entire operation. Strongly done, so to speak."

"His name is Goran."

"Ha, ha. Right, Goran. I'm not too good with names."

That was enough. Mrado didn't want to get close to Lindberg in any way.

He sent the guy paperwork. Asked him to sign. Explained some more what it was about, that a friend of Mrado and Goran was gonna open video-rental stores. Needed someone registered in Sweden to be on the board of the company. Lindberg would get a one-time fee of twelve thousand kronor if he signed. After that, they'd give him ten thousand every six months, as long as it all flowed smoothly. Mrado instructed him what to do if any nosy authorities got in touch with him.

It was "good as gold," as Lindberg put it.

Mrado got in touch with a company that sold shelf companies. Bought two. Paid a hundred grand per company. Sent in all the paperwork that Lindberg'd signed. Changed the names: the Stockholm Video Specialist, Ltd., and Video Buddy, Ltd. Set up bank accounts. Switched accountants. Landed storefronts.

One of the stores was on Karlavägen. They took over an old video-rental place, Karlaplan's Video. Some poor Turks owned it. Mrado sent Ratko and Bobban to scare them a little. They stopped by ten minutes before closing one night in October. Explained the situation. The two Turks refused. Two days later, when the guys opened the DVD case for *Batman Begins* that'd been returned through the slot in the door—*boom boom*. One of the Turks lost four fingers and the sight in his left eye.

Mrado bought the space a month later for thirty grand. A steal.

The other video-rental store was in the Södertälje Mall. The storefront used to be a dry cleaner's. Business was bad for the previous owner, also a Turk. Chance changed channels—the Yugos against the Turks. Low odds on the Yugos. The dry cleaner's sold for twenty thousand kronor. Didn't need convincing. They just moved right in.

He renovated and rebuilt the storefronts during the month of November. Used a Rado-owned demolition firm. Neat way to give the demolition firm clean, taxable profits.

Mrado threw out the pornos at Karlaplan's Video. Bought a ton of children's films—full-stocked Disney paradise. Lined one wall with shelves of penny candy. Rebuilt the registers, made sure you could buy lottery tickets, magazines, membership. Repainted the place, started selling paperbacks in one corner. The final product: the mildest, most child-friendly video store in all of Östermalm.

Good impression.

The store in Södertälje: Mrado sold the dry-cleaning machines to some old contacts, Syrians. Södertälje was their Jerusalem. Mrado knew—he'd hung out with Syrians growing up. Was even invited to weddings sometimes. The Syrians: one of the tightest networks in Stockholm. Dominated the dry-cleaning and B-list barber biz. Entrepreneurs. Mrado nurtured his connections. Dry cleaners and hairdressers—just as good for money laundering as video rentals. Could come in handy.

Within two months, the video stores were working perfectly. The basic idea was simple. Mrado had 400,000 kronor in cash. Two hundred thousand went to buying the companies. The remaining hundred grand per company, divided into smaller sums, was added to each company's account. The money covered the storefronts, the renovations, and the purchase of DVDs. Guys from the gym manned the stores from 4:00 to 10:00 p.m. every night. Everything under the table. RIP—right in pocket. On paper, Radovan was employed and was a stockholder. Mrado was employed part-time. He added money to each company's account every other day. When it was running smoothly, each store actually made fifty thousand a month. With Mrado's creative bookkeeping: three hundred thousand a month. Left after Radovan was paid a salary of twenty-five grand a month, Mrado twenty, and other general costs and taxes were taken out: around 150,000 kronor per store. Clean. *Summa summarum:* the salaries plus the stores' remaining assets—white as snow.

Money from the coat checks was run through the video business on paper—after tax payments, what came out at the other end were honest bills. Best of all, if the business went to hell, it was Lindberg who went there with it. Mrado and Radovan were not on the board and were not registered on paper anywhere.

Despite the laundromats, he had problems. They weren't enough. In the past months, his insomnia'd only gotten worse. The Radovan situation—more aggravated than ever. Was it because of Mrado's demand for a larger cut of the coat-check business? The Yugo boss seemed patronizing. Gave responsibilities to Goran and the others but not to Mrado. R. was planning something without M. Indications leaked out via Ratko and Bobban. The question: Had R. just put Mrado on building up the video stores in order to keep him busy? Question number two: What could Mrado do without this crap in his life? Would he even exist without it?

He longed for the good old days.

Ratko didn't show. Mrado got up. Paid. Walked toward the casino alone.

Casino Cosmopol: state gambling nest par excellence. The philosophy of hypocrisy perfected. To gamble is a Lutheran sin. To gamble is a waste/stupid/socially deviant. To gamble leads to addiction; at the same time, it sows a clover field for the finance minister. The people need entertainment, bread and circuses. Come on—gambling's just a little thrill, right? The automatic game machines were the worst—cashed in five billion kronor for Big Brother every year. Put people in financial ruin. Sunk families like mini *Titanics*. Crushed dreams. Along with obesity, the new welfare disease was gambling addiction. Up 75 percent since the automatic game machines and casinos'd opened.

The casino bouncers greeted Mrado. He glided past the entry-fee registers. For regular folks, they checked IDs and compared with head shots in their database. The first time you went to the casino, you had your picture taken. Mrado didn't need to do that stuff—he had a membership. Anyway, Mrado was Mrado.

The place was a cross between a well-refurbished turn-of-the-century amusement park and a cheap yacht. Five floors. The street level was the slickest. High ceilings, fifty feet. Nicely painted wood paneling. Original moldings and designs. Four enormous crystal chandeliers. Mirrored walls made the room feel even bigger than it was. Red carpeting. Eight big roulette tables in pairs of two. Between every pair, on an elevated platform, was a tux- or suit-clad casino employee in a black leather swivel chair. Job: to keep their eyes on the game, make sure no one pulled any moves. Minimum bet on the roulette table: five hundred on color, evens, or columns. You could blow a grand in five minutes, easy.

Moving on: five blackjack and punto banco tables. Two sic bo tables for the Asians. Various one-armed bandits everywhere.

Blatant hypocrisy 2.0—someone handed Mrado a pamphlet: *Do you have a gambling problem? Don't be ashamed. Over 300,000 Swedes suffer from the same addiction as you do. But there is help. Call us at THE ADDICTION CENTER.* Dig this shit: They handed out pamphlets against gambling at the same time as it was possible, without a problem, to withdraw 100,000 kronor at Casino Cosmopol's own cash counters.

As usual, the clientele was at least 30 percent Asian. The rest were Sven dudes, older *blatte* dudes, middle-aged women with shirts cut too low, a group of young guys, and the pros—the regulars who came every night.

Mrado greeted a few familiar faces. Headed up toward the fourth floor, where the real game was being played. Poker.

The second floor: brown carpeting, blackjack tables, a couple of midsize roulettes, lots of slot machines. A bar. Mrado went up to the bar. Greeted the bartender. Asked what was up. Things were cool. Frankie boy was crooning in the background. He kept moving.

The third floor: same as the second story, but without a bar. In the stairwell, he ran into the guys from the welcome desk at the gym.

Mrado greeted them. "What's up?"

"Do an old friend a favor. Come to the Klaraberg viaduct and push me in the water."

Mrado laughed. "You blow your whole load again?"

"Yup, goddamn it. This is all *geharget*, totally fucked, man. Dropped thirty big ones tonight. I can forget about that vacation. *It's hard to yell when the barrel's in your mouth.*"

"Get it together. You're always saying that. It's fine. You'll be back."

"I've got to practice more on the guys at the gym. People more in my class. Right? We should organize a little poker night. Sip whiskey, puff cigars."

"Not a bad idea, but a lotta guys are gonna pass on the booze. Too many dangerous calories."

"Yeah, but what the fuck am I supposed to do? I don't have a pissing chance against these guys."

"Just the heavy hitters here tonight?"

"You can say that again."

"You seen Ratko?"

"No, not yet. Didn't see him at the gym today, either. You guys have a date?"

"He better have a good excuse. We were supposed to meet twenty minutes ago."

"If I see him, I'll tell him you're up there and you're steaming. I've gotta head home, or this might get ugly for real."

Mrado resumed his upward climb. The guy in the stairwell was obviously on the verge of becoming a gambling junkie. Mrado wondered what was worse, gambling addiction or steroid addiction.

He pushed through the doors to the upper level. Green carpeting. The same color as the felt on the poker tables. Black ceiling with discreetly angled spotlights. No mirrored walls here—cheaters thrived anyway. Mrado made the rounds. Stockholm's legendary professional players were there: Berra K., the Joker, Piotr B., the Major, and others. Men who'd flipped the day just like Mrado. Worked from 10:00 p.m. until the casino closed at 5:00 a.m. Players who never had less than fifty grand in rubber-banded wads. Maladjusted mathematical masterminds.

Half the room was filled exclusively by one-armed bandits.

The other half housed the poker tables. Thick velvet ropes kept curious bystanders and Peeping Toms at bay. Poker was popular. At the middle of each table's long end stood the state-employed dealer, dressed in a white shirt, red silk vest, and pressed black slacks. The mood was solemn, tense, deeply concentrated.

Two of the tables were reserved for high-stakes play. Someone looked desperate—maybe the family's savings were all blown. Someone beamed—maybe they'd just pulled in twenty, thirty grand in one pot. The rest just looked incredibly immersed in the game.

There were free spots by one of the expensive tables. *No limit:* no restrictions on the stakes, possible to do *all in*. About twenty deals an hour. The state took 5 percent of the pot. Expensive hobby—excluding losses.

Mrado's idea was based on the fact that you were provided with receipts for all wins of over twenty grand at the state poker tables—the money was white as fleece. Mrado wasn't the world's best player, but it happened that he got lucky. In that case, play high stakes. The odds were bad tonight—a lot of good players at the table. On the other hand, that'd make it a higher-stakes game, more money that could be laundered. With luck, he might be able to clean a hundred grand. His plan: play tight. Only bid if he had a good opening hand. Cautious low-risk tactic.

He sat down.

The game: Texas hold 'em. Supertrendy since Channel 5 started airing American competitions. Lured lots of greenhorns to the poker tables, even though it was the toughest type of poker. Fast, most deals per hour meant greatest chances of winning. Bigger pot than in Omaha or seven-card stud, with more players at the table. No open cards except for the five community cards. The game for fast, fat wins.

From the look of it, there were only staples around the table tonight.

Bernhard Kaitkinen, better known as Berra K. Even more famous as the man with Stockholm's longest schlong, which he never passed up an opportunity to point out—Berra with the Boa. Always dressed in a light suit, as though he were in a casino in Monte Carlo. Been paired off with most of the city's society dames: Susanna Roos, editor in chief of *Svensk Damtidning*, the royal gossip rag, was just one in a long line of Botoxed bellas. Berra K.: a loudmouth, a romance scammer, a gentleman. Most of all: a fantastic poker player. Mrado knew his tricks. The dude always buzzed about other stuff, distracted, created a poker face by letting his mouth run nonstop.

Piotr Biekowski: pale Polack. Won the World Championship in backgammon a few years back. Switched over to poker—more money in it. Dressed in a dark blazer and black pants. Wrinkly white shirt with the two top buttons undone. Rocked a nervous, insecure style. Sighed, *oy*'ed, eyes flitted. That might fool the casino rookies. Not Mrado. He knew: Never play too high against Piotr—best way to empty your wallet.

Across from Mrado: a young guy with sunglasses that Mrado didn't recognize. Mrado stared. Did the kid think he was in Las Vegas, or what?

Mrado started with the *big blind:* one thousand that someone—in this particular round, Mrado—had to chip in to incite play. No one could stay in the game without betting at least the same sum.

Piotr sat with the *small blind*—five hundred kronor.

The dealer dealt the cards.

Mrado's hand: five of hearts and six of hearts.

The *flop* hadn't happened yet.

Berra K. was the first to act. Said, "These cards remind me of a game I played on a boat in the archipelago last summer. We had to stop because a huge fuckin' thunderstorm blew in." Mrado tuned out the nitwit nonsense.

Berra K. folded.

The Sunglass Kid posted a grand.

Piotr bet five hundred, up at the same level as the big blind.

Mrado looked at his cards again. It was a pretty shitty hand, but still—*suited connectors* were consecutive cards of the same suit, and it didn't cost him anything to stick out the round. He checked, kept pace.

Flop: the first three cards on the table. Seven of hearts, six of clubs, and ace of spades. Nothing perfect for his hand. Small chance of suit remained. Piotr starting whining—his style.

Mrado had to really think things through. The game was high. Piotr could bluff, try to get the rest of the players to raise the stakes by grumbling and moaning. In that case, Mrado should fold, even though he had a chance at suit or flush. Had promised himself to show tableside restraint.

He folded; the betting went on without him.

The Sunglass Kid called. Put in four grand. Not bad. Maybe he was one of the newbies who'd learned everything from online gaming. But it was different in real life. With hard cards.

Turn: the fourth card on the table. A seven of diamonds.

Piotr first out. Added fifteen big ones.

The Sunglass Kid put in thirty grand. Doubled the bet fast as hell.

All eyes on Piotr. Mrado knew: The Polack could have three of a kind, even a full house. Also possible: The guy could be blowing smoke.

Piotr went for it—put *all in*, 100,000 kronor. A murmur of disbelief swept over the table.

The Sunglass Kid cleared his throat. Fingered his chips.

Mrado eyed Piotr. Was convinced the Polack was bluffing—a brief glitter in his gaze gave him away. Their eyes met. Piotr saw that Mrado knew.

The Sunglass Kid didn't see. The strong offense turned him yellow. He folded.

River: the final card—was never dealt.

Mrado thought, The Polack is shooting high tonight. Playing tough with nothing.

Time for the next round.

The game continued.

Deal after deal.

Mrado stayed afloat.

Piotr played aggressively. Berra K. babbled about broads. Distracted. The Sunglass Kid tried to win back what he'd just blown.

After twenty-four deals: Mrado's hand—the *big slick* of hearts. A classic in the poker world: an ace and a king. You've got a chance to get the best-possible hand, *royal straight*, and you've got the highest cards. And still, you've got nothing. Binary: If it flies, you soar; if it crashes, you're done for.

A single drop of sweat on Mrado's forehead. Could be his chance.

So far, he'd played tight. Piotr, Berra K., and the Sunglass Kid didn't think he'd put all his chips in without having something. But it could be a trick, too. You play steady, trick everyone into thinking that you never take risks. Then you bluff like Abagnale.

His best opening hand of the night. He made up his mind, for the sake of the companies, to save the Rado situation—bid high.

The drop of sweat lodged itself in Mrado's eyebrow. So close to a royal straight and still, hardly one in several thousands of a chance.

He twirled a chip around his fingers.

Thought, Let's do this thing.

Bid five grand.

Berra K. called his bet. Five grand. High-stakes game.

The Sunglass Kid pulled out. Would be crazy to ride out a game this aggressive without really sitting on anything good.

Piotr, with the big blind, raised him. Twenty-five total. Crazy.

Berra K., Mrado, and Piotr all had a sick number of chips in front of them.

Mrado considered: It's make it or brake it now. He knew the odds; his hand was one of the top ten opening hands you could get in this game.

He looked at Piotr. Didn't he glimpse that same glitter in his eyes as in the first deal, when the Polack bluffed? The feeling was the same. Piotr was up to something. Mrado was sure of it—the Polack was trying to pull a fast one—it was Mrado's turn to make it big this time.

He kept going. Twenty into the pot.

Berra K. started prattling again. Jabbered on about other crazy games he'd played and that this one was the craziest one yet. Then he folded. Not surprising.

Mrado faced off against Piotr, waiting for the first cards on the table.

The Sunglass Kid removed his shades; even Berra K. stopped talking. Silence settled around the table.

The flop gave an ace of clubs, a two of diamonds, and a queen of hearts.

Piotr bet another fifteen. Maybe to check Mrado's pulse. Disgustingly high stakes.

Mrado still had a pair of aces, the best pair you could get. He just had to be in the clear, since he had the highest kicker, the king. And still a chance he could land a royal straight. He kept going. Bet fifteen grand. Called.

He was gonna crush that fuckin' Polack.

Turn: jack of hearts. Crazy lucky. Mrado still had a chance at a royal straight. He wasn't going to give up now. And he kept feeling more and more certain: The Polack didn't have jackshit. The guy was crazy bluffing.

Crazier than crazy.

Piotr raised him another thirty.

Mrado thought he saw that gleam again.

He took the chance—played all in, the rest of the money he had in front of him, 120 grand. All his chips on one board. Prayed to God that he was right, that Piotr was trying to pull a fast one.

Piotr shot back the call, didn't miss a beat.

The dealer felt the tension around the table. Both Mrado and Piotr turned up their cards.

Everyone around the table leaned in to get a look.

Mrado: almost royal flush, except for the ten of hearts.

Piotr: three aces.

Mrado's heart sank. The Polack fucker hadn't bluffed this time. That gleam in his eye was something else—maybe triumph. Mrado's only chance was that the river contained a ten of hearts.

The dealer took his time with the river. Piotr shifted uneasily in his seat. Everyone in the poker area stopped what they were doing, sensed that something big was about to happen at one of the tables. If Mrado won, he'd rake in over 300,000.

The dealer dealt the card: three of clubs.

Mrado was dead.

The winner: Piotr. Three of a kind. The entire pot. Mrado'd blown 160,000 on one hand. Congrats.

Mrado could hear his own breathing. Felt dazed, got vertigo. Ready to hurl.

Felt the beating of his own heart. Fast, sad beats.

Piotr stacked the chips. Swept them off the table into a cloth bag.

Got up. Left the table.

Someone called Mrado's name. Ratko was waiting on the other side of the velvet enclosure. More than two hours after the appointed time. Mrado nodded toward him. Turned back to the poker table.

Remained seated, as though in a fog. Felt a flash of heat. He was sweating.

Finally, the dealer turned to him, asked, "Are you in for the next deal?" Mrado knew—for him, a catastrophe had just occurred. For the dealer, it was only a question of when the next round could begin.

Mrado got up. Walked away.

Bobban used to say, "Things happen quick in hockey." Mrado knew—things happen even quicker in Texas hold 'em. Burned more than 160 grand within an hour. Not his night tonight. He should've known. Too many vets at the table.

Ratko stood at a one-armed bandit with his back to the poker table. Fed bills to the machine.

Mrado knocked him on the shoulder. "You were late?"

"Me, late? Sure, but you've been playing for over an hour. Made me wait."

"But you were the one who was late. We were meeting at ten."

"My apologies. How'd it go?"

Mrado, silent.

Ratko asked again. "That bad?"

"It went so fuckin' bad, I'm considering throwing myself off the Klaraberg viaduct."

"My sympathies."

Mrado remained standing and watched as Ratko played. He was done for. Shouldn't have played when he was so beat. Money that belonged to the video-rental stores. This couldn't get out.

Motherfucker.

Ratko fed a final bill to the machine. Pressed the play button. The symbols started spinning.

Mrado's head was spinning even faster.

28

Back in business. The long-lasting feeling: J-boy, baddest bad boy in town. *El choro.* Phoenix out of the ashes. Gotten back up after what they thought was a knockout.

His life vacillated between justified hate and high-level blow business. The hate toward Radovan & Co.: the ones who'd shredded him. The blow business: his job for Abdulkarim.

But Jorge was the man with the plan; he would break Radovan's empire once and for all. Make sure the Yugo Mafia got locked up or wiped out. All he needed was more information and time to plan.

R.'s day would come. Jorgelito was mad certain.

Flashbacks.

Jorge'd recovered surprisingly quickly. First, when JW found him in a thousand pieces in the woods, he didn't clock a thing. Who the hell was this Östermalm creamer? Buzzing about new markets, blow-biz expansion. Did he want in?

Fifteen minutes of explaining to a busted Latino.

Jorge was hardly listening at the time.

JW promised that a car would come. That he'd fix painkillers.

Jorge asked him to leave.

JW walked down to the road.

Jorge left alone on the ground. Half an inch of movement equaled otherworldly pain. The cold crept up on him. Jorge wanted to pass out. Disappear. But the questions were buzzing worse than the pain in his head: Would the Yugos hurt Paola? Would they leave him alone now? Should he skip the country right away? In that case, what were his chances? No money, no passport, no connections. In other words, about as much chance of survival as a twiggy with attitude at Österåker.

Darkness settled over the forest. The weather was getting worse.

The trunks of the trees looked black. The branches hung low to the ground.

Felt like his upper arms and thighbones were broken. Felt as though his back was torn apart. Felt as though he'd gotten a second asshole torn up beside his first. Nature's strange symmetry completed: two eyes, two nostrils, two arms, and two legs. And now, two assholes.

He tried to sleep. Not a chance.

He shivered.

The definition of eternity: Jorge's one and a half hours in the forest before JW showed up again. He had a big guy with him, a gorilla. They lifted him. Jorge thought he was going to die for the second time in four hours. Pest or cholera. First to be beaten to death by a psycho Yugo and then to be carried to death by an enormous Lebanese.

A white Mazda van was waiting on the road. There was a padded gurney in the back. They strapped him down. A Swedish-looking man who Jorge, at the time, thought was a real ambulance EMT poured morphine down his throat. He numbed off. Dreamed of dancing grocery bags.

Fragments of memory.

Woke up in a stark room. Confused. Safe, but scared he'd ended up in a hospital. He'd get treated at the same time as he'd get found out—be sent right back to his cell at Österåker. Then came the pain. He howled.

A big man in the room, the same man who'd carried him to the van. The guy in a turtleneck and dark blue jeans. Jorge realized he wasn't in a hospital. Something about the man signaled the opposite—that face didn't belong in the health-care sector. Dark, coarse features. Scratches/scars along one side of his face. The man smiled; gold gleamed in his upper row. Maybe that's what confirmed it—no one who worked in a hospital would grin with a gold grill like that.

The man, Fahdi, smiled, "*Allahu akbar,* you're alive."

A few days later. He woke up. Someone was dabbing at his arm; it was a sickly green color. On one arm and his left thigh, scabs were healing. Improvement. So, he wasn't beaten black-and-blue anymore—he was beaten green.

The guy dabbing at his arm introduced himself as Petter and said, "You're gonna be fine, man." Jorge let his arm fall down on the bed again. The guy reached for a glass of something red. There was a straw in the glass. He held up the straw to Jorge's mouth. Jorge sucked. It tasted like raspberry Kool-Aid.

The guy left the room. Jorge looked at the wall. Drawn curtains. Was there a window behind them? He tried to turn his head. Hurt too much.

Lay still. Fell back asleep.

Morphine dreams: Jorge was walking on a dark road with Paola. Along the side of the road were tall green stone walls. Spotlights lit up stretches of the road. Soft asphalt. Jorge's feet sank down. Created imprints in the granulated, warm mass. He thought, If I have to run now, how fast can I go? His sister turned to him, "My prince, do you want to play war with me?" Jorge tried to lift his foot. It was hard. The asphalt mass stuck to him. Black, coarse. Felt heavy.

A couple of nights later: Paola was jumping double Dutch. Two ropes. Made out of twisted sheets. Two friends of hers were holding the ropes. Paola: eight years old. Jorge ran toward the ropes. Was about to fall. Stumble. And right then: an enormous blue trampoline. It cushioned the fall. He rolled around. Couldn't get up. The trampoline was too soft. Like quicksand. He sunk down. Tried to support himself with his hands, his elbows, his knees. Paola laughed. The girls laughed. Jorge cried.

Later: The guy who'd dabbed at him, Petter, sat by the bed. Said everything would be fine. That Jorge would look so great. Better than before.

Jorge was too tired.

Didn't ask what they were gonna do.

A bright light blinded him.

He turned his head. Shut his eyes.

Could instinctively feel that something was approaching his face.

A man he hadn't seen before rubbed his nose with something.

Suddenly: extreme pain.

Screams.

Felt like his nose'd been torn off.

He sat up.

The man held him down.

Poured something down his throat.

He fell back asleep.

Someone was shaking him. "Wake up, buddy. You've slept enough today." Jorge looked up. A dark-haired man. Maybe around thirty years old. In a suit. A shirt with broad cuffs. The top buttons undone. A white Craig David hat on his head. "Open your eyes for real."

Jorge stared in silence.

"I'm Abdulkarim. Your chance in life. Your boss."

Jorge, confused.

"You been lying here for over three weeks now. You gonna be a morphine junkie if you're not healed already. You gotta be able to function by now. Raise your arm."

Jorge raised his arm. Yellow at the top, near his shoulder, but otherwise okay.

"You look fine, buddy. Allah is great."

Abdulkarim held up a mirror to his face.

Jorge saw the image of himself: a thin, dark-haired, and bearded man, maybe twenty-five years old, dark eyebrows, bulky nose, almost like a boxer's, olive-colored skin.

A version of Jorge.

He grinned. At the same time, he felt sad. On the one hand, it was his chance. Abdulkarim—whoever he was—had fixed him up. Rubbed him down with a new type of self-tanner, curled his hair, dyed it. Better than he'd done himself. And he was skinnier.

But aside from that, something was different about his nose.

"What've you done to my nose?"

Abdulkarim laughed. "Broken in two places, buddy. Brought in a guy who set it straight. Hope it didn't hurt too much. I think it looks better now. A little flat, maybe, but cooler."

Jorge like Nikita: picked up off the street. Woken up, made up, fixed up to be their new supersoldier. How would the rest of the story go?

Abdulkarim kept talking.

"They pounded you real good. You looked like a fuckin' blueberry when we found you. Then you became like the Hulk. Spotty green. Too bad you don't have his powers."

Jorge turned over in bed.

Abdulkarim tried to be funny. "What jerks. Did they pork you, too, buddy? Who was the bottom?"

Jorge fell asleep.

Everything'd gone so quickly. He was almost completely recovered from Mrado's and Ratko's rough treatment. The only problem: scars on his back and pain in one of his upper arms. He'd been given a chance to stay in Sweden and earn pesetas. That his nose'd been broken and realigned by Abdulkarim's people could be an advantage. It was crooked, broader. Jorge's appearance was even more altered.

Enough time'd passed since his break. The cops no longer had his picture as one of the top one hundred that popped up on their screens as soon as they had a lead. With his new look, the Arab's money and help, Jorge realized he had a chance.

He knew why he was so perfect for Abdulkarim—his blow know mixed with his dependence and debt of gratitude to the Arab would make him the most faithful dog in Abdul's dealer kennel. Abdulkarim's business idea worked the way JW'd explained it. The boroughs were ready for a coke invasion. Blowkrieg. Jorge dug the plans. He'd thought about similar strategies when he was still at Österåker.

Jorge and JW sat in Fahdi's apartment during a couple of days in November and made plans. Abdulkarim stopped by and discussed the big picture. Guidelines, strategy. How much blow did they think they were gonna need for the month of January? In which boroughs were they gonna start? Jorge name-dropped. People they had to get in touch with. Dealers to contract. People to consult. Fahdi brought pizzas and Coca-Cola.

Abdulkarim kept talking about import. They had to get more. Structure smarter smuggling.

Jorge taught JW everything he knew. The Östermalm-boy inhaled the knowledge like a teenager inhales beer at his first kegger. According to Abdulkarim, the dude was a whiz at dealing to the Stureplan crowd. Jorge had a knowledge advantage. Still, JW tried to seem worldly. Snobby. Jorge didn't like his style.

Abdulkarim, shady but good. In every other sentence he praised Allah, in every other sentence he talked blow pricing. One night at Fahdi's, he said, "Jorge, can I ask you a serious question?" Jorge nodded. Abdul continued, "What religion do you have?" Jorge shook his head. "Mom's a Catholic. I believe in Tupac. He lives on." Tried to joke. All ghettoites knew about Tupac, didn't they? The Arab replied, "You know, there's a war going on. You have to pick sides. You think all the Swedes are gonna accept you just 'cause you got cash? Allah can give you guidance."

JW claimed the Arab hadn't always been like that. Before: only talked blow. Allah was definitely a new player on the field.

At the end of November, Jorge hit the streets again. At first, he was paranoid. Kept looking around every third step. The cops or the Yugos reappeared from his nightmares. He slept at Fahdi's. Every time the Lebanese dude came home at night, Jorge woke up, thought it was the 5-o and that he was done for. After a few seconds, the sounds from the pornos calmed him. He realized that he actually looked different. Bonier. Blacker. Broader beak.

He went to a tanning bed regularly. Kept curling his hair. Tried to learn to use a pair of dark brown contacts Abdulkarim'd given him. The rhythm to his step got better with every day; he did his best to walk like a gangsta.

He needed his own place.

Jorge got in touch with Sergio and thanked him for his help. Blessed/praised him. Told him everything was cool but that they couldn't see each other for a while. Sergio understood. He explained: His broken fingers were still crooked; his girlfriend was still shaking like a kitten.

Jorge hated the Yugos even more.

Wrote a text to Paola from a prepaid phone that Abdulkarim'd given him: *I'm alive and doing well. How are you? Don't worry about anything. Say hi to Mama! Hugs /J.*

Two guys, the Sven who'd taken care of him, Petter, and a Tunisian, Mehmed, became Jorge's assistants. Looked up people in the Sollentuna area on his orders. Distributed grams to the right people. Sold on from there. Jorge himself worked the other projects. Places where his face, even if it was new, had never been known.

Everything went beautifully. In January, they grossed 400,000 kronor. After they'd deducted the purchase price and Abdulkarim's cut: 150,000 kronor for Jorge, Petter, and Mehmed to split. Life was sweet. Jorge was royal—Jorgius Maximus.

One thought he hardly ever had time to think: Was this preordained?

Was dealing C as far as an ordinary slumdog from a Stockholm ghetto could get? Was the race already rigged when his mama decided to leave Chile and try to become a normal citizen of a new country? It was like when you get on the subway and realize the train is going in the wrong direction. There's nothing you can do. Can't jump off the train. What happens if you pull the emergency brake? Jorge and his buds'd done that a ton as kids. The fuckin' train didn't stop in the middle of the track like you thought it would; it drove on to the next station before it stopped. What was the point of an emergency brake if you still had to go where you didn't want to go?

Jorge's project for the future slowly morphed. Leaving the country as quickly as possible was no longer a given. To get back at Radovan became more important. And there was still a long way to go on that road. He knew some about Mr. R.'s cocaine dealings from before—but not enough. Radovan must've thought J-boy knew a hell of a lot more than he did. If not, why send Mrado and Ratko after him? Jorge needed more, enough heavy shit to sink Radovan instantly.

Enough to put Paola out of danger.

Enough to sate his hate.

Abdulkarim's plans took time. To establish the blow biz in the western boroughs as well as select areas in the south: Bredäng, Hägerstensåsen, Fruängen. And he was in the middle of planning/preparing a large shipment of snow. Maybe straight from Brazil.

Jorge's new free life was keeping him busy.

29

The inner journey: by train. JW was on his way to Robertsfors.

Was he on his way home? Or away? Where was home, really? The boyz' co-ops, the bathrooms at Kharma where the C deals were brokered, his room at Mrs. Reuterskiöld's, or Robertsfors—at Mom and Dad's?

He was listening to music—Coldplay, the Sadies, and other pop— while he munched on a bag of candy. Tried to see if the gummy colors tasted different from one another. Red, or green, or yellow, or . . . what? Did a blind test.

It was dark outside. He looked at his reflection in the window. JW thought, A wonderful vantage point for a narcissist like me.

The train car was almost empty of people. One of the advantages of being a student was that you could travel any day of the week. Of course, he could've afforded to take any train or flight, almost at any price. But it was unnecessary—stupid to make his parents suspicious.

He should really be studying. He had an assignment to do on macroeconomic theories: the relationship between interest, inflation, currency rates. He even had the laptop open in his lap. But the movement of the train lulled him. He felt tired.

He closed the computer. Shoved his mouth full of gummies and shut his eyes. Chewed and contemplated his circumstances.

It'd been four months since he found Jorge in the woods. Since then, Abdulkarim's coke expansion'd taken most of his time. JW and Jorge were each project managers of an area. The gelt kept growing, an average of a hundred G's a month. Soon he'd be able to buy his BMW—cash—and maybe a co-op apartment. Just had to launder the money first.

He was barely getting by in school. He nearly flunked the exams. Was he on the verge of breaking his promise? The positive effect of his scholarly neglect was that he was becoming a name in the Stureplan jungle. Everyone with a penchant for skating on ice knew of him. JW bided Abdulkarim's orders; he was careful about giving out his cell phone number. Couldn't make it too easy. People called, left messages. JW called back, checked up on people, dictated the terms. Played according to the Arab's strategy—safe.

He hung out with the boyz, more and more with Jet Set Carl and other acquaintances, people raised in rich suburbs like Bromma, Saltsjöbaden, and Lidingö. In Djursholm. Important parentheses: Know-it-all types thought you were supposed to say *on* Djursholm, not *in*, when people who really knew said the opposite. They were people with contacts and cash: party organizers, coke snorters—above all, clients.

JW approached the inner circles around the Swedish royal family. Golden glamour. Progeny of the landowning aristocracy. Wild parties with wild winners and their families. Important C sales. A private arena with exclusive access. Forget pricey tix. This scene was VIP only.

He'd been getting together with Sophie like two or three times a week. Sometimes they went out to eat, got a drink at a bar, or went for a walk.

Their problem, according to JW: The relationship wasn't developing. Felt like they were still playing a game. She wouldn't call for days. JW didn't call back. They waited. Played hard to get.

The sober sex sucked. Embarrassing. JW was all nerves. It took twenty seconds. Tops. He tried to make sure it happened when he was tripping on coke. Worked better that way.

After a couple of months, their relationship'd become more stable. He slept over at Sophie's place several nights a week. At the same time, a certain distance remained. Sometimes she didn't want to get together, without JW knowing why. He missed her whenever the time between their dates got too long.

Nothing wrong with the Jorge dude. Not JW's type, but fine enough. The Chilean possessed sick knowledge about coke. JW tried to absorb all the info, all the know-how, all the tricks.

———

The train slowed down at Hudiksvall. JW glanced out at the station. There was a lake on the other side of the tracks. He was halfway home.

Three days ago, Abdulkarim'd called. Sounded worked up: "JW, I got something big goin'."

"I'm all ears, Abdulkarim. Tell me."

"We goin' to London. Fix a fat import."

"Okay. How? Is your secret boss in on it?" JW felt more and more secure with Abdulkarim—almost dared be cocky.

"Chill, *habibi*, my boss's in on it. Big stuff, you understand. Much bigger than our other imports. We're gonna contact the wholesalers direct. Gonna be ill, *inshallah*. You gotta book tickets for us. Me, Fahdi, and you. We need, like, five days. Have to be there by March seventh, latest. You gotta book hotel rooms, I want it nice. Classy. Fix sweet clubs. Fix a weapon for Fahdi. Fix up London for me. You with me, buddy?"

It drove JW crazy every time Abdulkarim used the word *buddy*. But he didn't feel so safe in his seat that he'd mock the Arab. Sucked it up instead.

"Course. I'll be your travel agent. But I have to check the dates; I've got exams and stuff. And how'll I get a gun there?"

"No, no 'check the dates.' Gotta be there March seventh. Talk to Jorge about guns. And hey, buddy, I want you to fix sightseeing in London, too. Big Ben, Beckham, and all that?"

It sounded exciting. Glam. Abdulkarim and he'd talked about it a lot—they had to get purchase prices down even more in order to increase the import. Find new smart ins. After his visit to Robertsfors, he was going to deal with planning the trip.

The only thing he'd already looked up was how to score a gun for someone in London. Jorge knew a guy who'd done time in England. They contacted him. Contacted his contacts. Promised to pay two thousand pounds. Sent a five-hundred-pound advance via money transfer. Arranged a spot for the handoff. A Yugoslavian pistol, Zastava M57, 7.63mm, would be available for pickup at the Euston Square Tube station at twelve o'clock on March sixth.

Definitely a step up for JW. He felt exhilarated about being invited along to negotiate directly with the big boys. Allowed entrance to the C business's VIP room.

One thing worried him: JW noted that Abdulkarim was changing.

Talked more about Islam and world politics. Started wearing a white Muslim headpiece. Referred to the latest Friday sermon in the mosque. Praised Muhammad in every third sentence, stopped drinking alcohol, and whined about the U.S. running the world. In JW's opinion, the Arab was digging his own grave. There was only one loyalty: sales. Nothing could come before that, not even God.

JW hadn't seen his mom and dad since the summer. Their communication'd been patchy since then. One call from his mom, Margareta, every other week or so and that was it. Her reoccurring questions annoyed him. "How is school going?" "Are you coming up to see us and Grandma soon?" His reoccurring answers were bland, whiny. "School's fine; I'm doing well on all my exams." "I don't have time to come up; I have to do my job as a taxi driver. And no, Mom, it's not dangerous."

Love and guilt baked together. The fear in Margareta's voice was always there; he could hear it. The terror that something would happen to him.

He could see Camilla's face in front of him. What did he know that their parents didn't?

He'd found out some things.

If he hadn't seen the yellow Ferrari over six months ago, things would've stayed the way they were. Silent sorrow. Repressed grief. Conscious forgetting.

Maybe it was the car's speed that'd bothered him. The sound. The roar of the engine. The senselessly cocky move of driving through the city streets at a speed of at least fifty-five miles an hour.

JW'd been forced to choose: either keep searching and maybe discover something unpleasant or just stop right now. Forget it all, try to keep leaving the past behind, like he'd been doing during the past few years. It would probably be best to tell the police what he'd found out. Let them do their job.

He couldn't—not when Jan Brunéus was lying about something.

JW'd called him up. The teacher was obviously unwilling to meet with him again. JW coaxed. Tried. Told him how happy he was that Jan'd known Camilla. Jan armed himself with excuses: He didn't have time. He had to go to a teacher's conference. He was sick. Had to grade papers, was going on vacation.

The weeks passed. JW stopped calling. Instead, he went reluctantly back to the school again.

He pulled the same moves as last time. Positioned himself outside the classroom and waited. The same young black kid who'd come out of the door last time, came out first this time, too.

Jan was still in the classroom. JW got flashbacks to the last time he'd been there—the same girls were still in the classroom, stuffing notebooks into bags.

He remained standing in the doorway and waited for a reaction. Jan was calm. Walked up to JW. Didn't even look surprised.

He greeted him, "Hi, Johan. I've been thinking a lot about you. I understand if you think I've been acting strangely."

JW looked him in the eyes.

Who was Jan Brunéus? JW'd looked him up. The teacher was married, no kids, and lived in a row house in a lower-middle-class suburb. Drove a Saab. Besides teaching at Komvux, he taught high school. Didn't show up in Google searches. He seemed normal on the surface. But, then again, who didn't?

JW replied, "That's an understatement."

"I have a suggestion. Let's take a walk. What about walking out toward Haga Forum. It's pretty there."

JW nodded. Jan had something to say.

It was December. Freezing and snowing out. The ice had set, although thinly, over the Brunnsviken Bay. JW didn't dig the season. It was so difficult to wear nice shoes; they always ended up heavy on rubber and light on finesse.

They were walking behind Wenner-Gren Center when Jan started telling his story.

"I've been a shit. I should've seen you a long time ago and told you. I admit that."

Steam billowed from his mouth as he spoke.

"This whole story has really weighed on me. I have nightmares and can't sleep. Wake up in the middle of the night and wonder. What really happened to Camilla?"

Shared silence.

Jan continued: "She had a rough time. Not a lot of friends. Her talent pushed other girls away, I think. You could tell by looking at her that she wanted to get somewhere. Maybe her ambition scared the others off. Anyway, I took her under my wing. Encouraged her. I used to discuss things with her after class. She really liked studying English, I recall. I mean, she was a grown woman. People who go to Komvux aren't kids anymore. Despite that, I sometimes see them as kids. I mean, most of them haven't made it through the regular school system without problems. There's often something missing."

JW wondered when the guy was going to cut to the chase.

"When you showed up here at Komvux, wanting to know more about Camilla, I got scared. Felt guilty. That I didn't encourage her even more. That I didn't see it coming. Her sorrow and alienation. Her frame of mind. Depression. Suicide."

JW stopped. Thought, What is Jan talking about? No one knows what happened to Camilla.

"Where did you get the idea about suicide?"

"Of course, I can't know for sure, but now in retrospect I can see that the signs were there. She lost weight. Must've had trouble sleeping, came to class with dark circles under her eyes. Pulled more and more away, into herself. She was feeling like shit, to put it simply. I was blind. Blame myself. I should've told someone, sounded the alarm, so to speak. But at the same time, how could I've known?"

The thought wasn't new. JW'd wondered many times how his sister'd really been feeling.

Jan continued: "That's why I've stayed away from you. I guess I haven't been able to deal with this situation. Been afraid. I understand if you've been wondering what I've been up to. I really have to apologize again."

They walked another hundred yards or so. JW didn't have much to say. Jan said he had to get back to Sveaplan Gymnasium. He had more classes to teach.

They shook hands.

JW watched him walk away. Jan was wearing a padded brown Melka jacket. Had bad posture, walked with quick steps toward the school building. Seemed stressed.

JW was standing outside Haga Forum by himself. He was cold, wrapped in thoughts. Had Jan given Camilla good grades to be nice? To encourage her? Because he saw how she was feeling?

He felt low. For his sister's sake. For not finding out anything new. If Camilla had, in fact, killed herself, where was her body? Why hadn't she left a note? Wasn't suicide, as the shrinks say, a call for help? No, even though he hadn't known his sister that well, he'd known her well enough to know that she hadn't killed herself. She wasn't like that.

JW'd ridden straight out to Kista. He knew Abdulkarim would be angry. They'd agreed to meet up and exchange cash for coke, but it'd have to wait.

The Kista Mall'd been newly renovated since the last time he was there: the movie theaters, the restaurants, the clothing stores, you name it. He went straight to H&M. Hoped Susanne Pettersson was working that day. It'd been several months since he'd been there the first time and she'd hinted that he should look up Jan Brunéus.

It was like he was paralyzed for long stretches at a time. Couldn't bear to do anything about the Camilla thing. He blamed the C biz, school, Sophie. When he finally did look into what'd happened, it was always in spurts, with sudden stops and starts.

Susanne was manning the register. There were people in the store. JW asked to speak with her. No problem. Another girl took over. Susanne and JW positioned themselves by the denim section.

She was visibly stressed-out by the situation. Was glancing around, eyeing the customers, her colleagues, anyone who might be listening.

"Pardon me for busting in like this. And I'm sorry for bothering you. How're you doing?"

"You know, fine."

"How're the kids?"

"They're good, too."

"I wanted to tell you that I met Jan Brunéus, your old teacher."

"Yeah."

"I'll make it brief. He says Camilla was feeling like shit. That she must've killed herself. That he tried to encourage her, help her. He blames himself for the way things turned out."

"He does?"

JW waited. Susanne had to say something more.

Nothing.

"What do you have to say about that?"

"I don't know anything more than that. I guess it's the way Jan said."

JW followed her with his gaze.

"Susanne, you know something. Why did Jan give Camilla all A's even though you guys never went to class?"

Susanne folded a pair of jeans. Refused to answer. JW could see plainly: She was blushing.

"What the fuck, Susanne, answer me."

She held up another pair of jeans, tenderly. Fake wear on the knees and thighs. She put one leg on top of the other. Folded the pants in three steps. The back pocket and the label symmetrically aligned. The *Divided* logo in the customer's eye.

Loud background music playing in the store: Robbie Williams.

"You haven't figured it out by now? Didn't you know your sister, or what? Don't you know in what way she was talented? Ask Jan 'Horndog' Brunéus the next time you see him. You think Camilla got top grades in other subjects, or what? No. Just from him. Do you know how she used to come dressed for his classes?"

JW didn't get it. What was she talking about?

"Don't you get it? For an entire semester, Camilla was Jan's plaything. Good grades for sex. That pig fucked her."

The train passed Sundsvall. The conductor called out, "Tickets, please." JW opened his eyes. Conscious again. It had been two months since Susanne Petterson'd almost shrieked out her explanation for Camilla's good grades.

Who was his sister, really? Or, who'd she been? Was she, like he was, a treasure hunter, but one who'd ended up with the wrong crowd? Who hadn't been able to take the pressure and skipped town. Or had someone else made sure she was erased from the picture? And if so, why?

JW was hungry but didn't want to eat. In an hour and a half, he would be sitting at his parents' dinner table, and it was important that he not lose his appetite by then. That he not be too full.

He got up. Walked toward the dining car. Not because he planned on buying anything, but because he was so antsy. The restlessness'd been creeping up on him more and more over the past few months. When he'd sit down to study, during lectures, while waiting for Fahdi or someone else to meet him and load him up with coke. He'd had to move. Direct his concentration on something. He'd learned to deal.

Be prepared. Always kept his Sony player in his breast pocket, often took a paperback with him, downloaded sweet games on his phone. The margins of his college notebooks were filled with doodles.

Now he felt he had to move. Cell phone games wouldn't help. Had to do a few laps. The question that worried him: Was it his new snort habits or the Camilla thing that was making him jittery?

He eyed the people in the train car. Tedious, tired people. Sven squared. JW wore common camouflage: Acne jeans, Superlative Conspiracy sweatshirt, and semi-ratty Adidas running shoes. He blended in. Suitable for his parental reunion.

He'd made up his mind after the conversation with Susanne. Playing private eye wasn't his thing anymore. Even so, it'd felt strange to call the police, to talk to the investigator who'd been in charge of the case. He'd explained what he'd found out: that Jan Brunéus'd had some kind of relationship with Camilla Westlund in the time before her disappearance. That Susanne Petterson was aware of this and had told JW. That Jan'd given Camilla top grades despite her lack of attendance.

The investigator'd promised to look into the info more closely. JW assumed that he meant that Jan Brunéus would be called in for questioning.

That JW'd been in touch with the police was a contradiction. Abdulkarim couldn't know.

But it'd felt like a relief—he'd let go of the burden. Was letting the police do their job.

He'd drifted back into denial. Focused on C, school, and Sophie. Prepared the London trip. Discussed strategies with Jorge. Sold. Dealt. Counted cash.

He'd made up his mind: He wouldn't tell his parents what he'd told the police.

He was arriving in Robertfors within five minutes. His stomach was growling violently. Was it worry or hunger?

In truth, he knew he was worried about seeing Mom and Dad.

It was almost six months since he'd last bid them good-bye and studied his mother's worn face and his father's tight jawline. Would they be feeling better now? JW couldn't stand being reminded of the tragic plodding of their lives. His goal had been to get away, start over. Be accepted as something different. Something better. Bigger than his parents' whole-milk lifestyle with its accompanying angst over a lost child. He'd wanted to forget.

The train pulled into the station. People were waiting for arrivals and to depart themselves. The brakes screeched loudly. His car stopped right in front of his waiting parents. JW saw that they weren't talking to each other. As usual.

Tried to calm down. Look happy and relaxed. As he ought.

He stepped down onto the platform. They didn't see him at first. He walked toward them.

JW knew that Margareta was trying to call out. But for some reason, she'd been unable to raise her voice ever since the Camilla thing. Instead, she greeted him with a tense smile.

Hugs.

"Hi, Johan, let us take your bags."

"Hi, Mom. Hi, Dad." JW handed one of his bags to Bengt.

They walked toward the parking lot together in silence. Bengt still hadn't said a word to his son.

They were sitting at home, in the kitchen. Wood paneling along the walls and stainless-steel counters. A white Electrolux stove, linoleum on the floor, and a shiny wooden table from IKEA. The chairs were Carl Malmsten copies. There was a copy of a PH-lamp in the ceiling that cast a warm purplish glow. Above the sink hung green pots with words painted on them: *Sugar, Salt, Pepper, Garlic, Basil.*

The food was on the table. Thin strips of beef with a blue-cheese sauce. A bottle of red wine, Rioja. A carafe with water. A glass bowl with salad.

JW didn't have much of an appetite. The food was good; that wasn't the problem. It was really good. Mom'd always been a good cook. It was something else—the look of the place, the topics of conversation, and that Bengt talked with his mouth full. Margareta's clothes were all wrong. JW felt like a stranger. The combination bothered him—contempt mingled with a sense of security.

Margareta reached for the salad. "Tell us more, Johan. How are things?"

A few seconds of silence. Her real question was: How are things in

Stockholm? The city where our daughter disappeared. Who are you spending time with? You don't run with a bad crowd, do you? Questions she would never pose directly. The fear of being reminded. The fear of coming too close to the dark scream of reality.

"I'm doing really well, Mom. Passing my exams. The latest one was on macroeconomics. There are over three hundred students in the class. There's only one lecture hall that's big enough."

"Wow. There are so many of you. Does the lecturer use a microphone?"

Bengt, with a chewed gray beef mass in his mouth: "Of course they do, Mother."

"Yes, they do. It's kind of funny, 'cause they draw all these graphs and curves. You know, in a perfect market, the price is where the demand curve meets the supply curve. All the students copy every single graph into their notebooks, and since there are so many different curves, everyone's got those four-colored Bics—you know, the pens with four different colors of ink in them—so they can tell the curves apart. When the lecturer draws a new curve, three hundred students switch colors at the same time. A little clicking sound for each one. It's like a symphony of clicks in the lecture hall."

Bengt grinned.

Margareta laughed.

Contact.

They kept talking. JW asked about his old school friends from Robertsfors. Six of the girls were moms. One of the guys was a dad. JW knew that Margareta was wondering if he had a girlfriend. He didn't bother to share. The truth was, he didn't even know the answer.

A sort of calm washed over him. Warm, safe grief.

After dinner, Bengt asked JW if he wanted to watch sports with him. JW knew that was his attempt at intimacy. Even so, he declined. Preferred to talk to Mom. Bengt went into the living room by himself. Settled into the La-Z-Boy. JW could see him from the kitchen. He stayed where he was and talked to Margareta.

Camilla'd still not been mentioned. JW didn't care if the topic was taboo. For him, his parents were the only people with whom he'd ever consider really talking about her.

"Have you heard anything?"

Margareta understood what he was talking about.

"No, nothing new. Do you think the case is still open?"

JW knew that it should be now at least. But he hadn't heard anything, either.

"I don't know, Mom. Have you changed anything in Camilla's room?"

"No, everything is just like it was. We don't go in there. Dad says he thinks it gives Camilla peace that we don't intrude." Margareta smiled.

Bengt and Camilla'd fought furiously the year before Camilla moved to Stockholm. Now JW looked back on it with nostalgia: doors slamming, crying from the bathroom, screaming from Camilla's room, Bengt on the porch with a cigarette between his fingers—those were the only times he smoked. Maybe Margareta felt the same way. The ominous fights were their last memories of Camilla.

JW helped himself to another slice of blueberry pie. Gazed out at his father in the living room.

"Should we join Dad?"

They watched a movie on TV together: *Much Ado About Nothing*. Modern interpretation of Shakespeare, using the original language. Difficult to understand. JW almost fell asleep during the first half. During the second half, he calculated the kind of money he was missing out on making this weekend. Shit, the alternative costs for spending time with his parents were high.

Bengt fell asleep.

Margareta woke him up.

They bid JW good night. Went to their room.

JW remained seated, alone. Prepared himself mentally. Soon he'd go up to the room. Her room.

He flipped through the channels. Lingered on MTV for five minutes. A Snoop Doggy Dogg video was playing. Asses shook in time to the song.

He turned it off.

Climbed into the La-Z-Boy.

Settled in.

He felt empty. Scared. But, strangely, not restless.

He turned out the lights.

Sat back down.

The silence was so much deeper than by Tessin Park.

He got up.

Tried to walk silently up the stairs. Remembered almost step by step which stairs creaked and what strategies to employ to avoid them. Foot on the thick inner edge, foot in the middle, step over an entire stair, step on the edge, on the narrow section, and so on—all the way up.

Another two steps'd become creaky since he'd moved away from home.

Maybe he wasn't waking Bengt. He was definitely waking Margareta.

The door to Camilla's room was closed.

He waited. Thought Mom might fall back asleep. Pulled the door while simultaneously pushing slowly down on the handle. It didn't make a sound.

When he flipped the light on, the first thing he saw were the three baseball hats Camilla'd hung on the opposite wall: a dark blue Yankees hat, a Red Sox hat, and a hat from her junior high graduation. The text on it: *We rocked and rolled* in black lettering on a white background. Camilla liked baseball hats like a fat kid likes cake. Uncomplicated. If there was one, she wanted it.

The untouched room of a seventeen-year-old. To JW, it was almost more childish than that.

There was a window in the middle of one of the room's short ends. The bed was opposite the window. Camilla'd begged for a whole year to get a double bed to replace her twin. Pink coverlet with flouncy edges. Different-colored throw pillows, some with hearts on them, were spread at the foot of the bed. Margareta'd sewn them. Camilla used to kick the pillows to the floor before going to bed.

A young girl's room.

Every object was a memory.

Every item a chip in JW's armor.

More baseball hats were arranged in a bookcase. On top of the bookcase were framed photographs: the family on a ski vacation, JW as a baby, three friends from school—wearking makeup, smiling, full of expectation.

The rest of the shelves were filled with baseball hats.

Above the bed was pinned a poster of Madonna. A strong, successful woman with a mind of her own. Camilla'd been given it by a guy she'd dated in eighth grade. He was four years older, a secret she kept from Mom and Dad.

JW'd thought about how after the disappearance, when he was still living at home, he'd never gone into the room. It'd been empty for so many years, and the effect of the stored and reinforced memories hit him like a punch in the face.

Camilla at her junior high graduation. Hair in an up do. White dress. Later that night: wearing a camo-colored baseball hat. The stories JW'd heard about her behavior at the graduation party. Next memory: Camilla and JW in a fight over the last glob of Nutella. JW: pulled into the room and beaten up, smeared with his own sandwich—with an extra-thick layer of Nutella. Later: Camilla next to JW on the bed, when they were friends again. She showed him her CDs: Madonna, Alanis Morissette, Robyn.

Read the text on the inserts. Said she was definitely going to leave, go to Stockholm.

Enjoyed hanging out together.

There was a built-in bookshelf and two mirrored closet doors on the left wall.

Unread YA books and CDs were lined up on the shelves, but only the ones she hadn't taken with her to Stockholm. A Sony stereo—a gift on the day of her confirmation. Camilla liked music better than reading.

JW opened the closet doors.

Clothes: skinny jeans, miniskirts, pastel-colored midriff baring tops, a jean jacket. A black corduroy coat. JW remembered when Camilla'd brought it home. She'd bought it herself at H&M in Robertsfors for 490 kronor. Too expensive, Mom thought.

Next to the folded tops was a storage box with reinforced metal corners. JW'd never seen it before. Stiff gray cardboard. JW recognized the type; he'd seen similar ones at container stores in Stockholm.

He pulled the box out and set it down on the bed. It was filled with postcards.

A half hour later, the postcards were all read. Seventeen in total. Camilla'd been living in Stockholm for a little over three years before she disappeared. During that time, she'd been home three times. It made Margareta sad; Bengt angry.

But apparently she'd at least been writing postcards. Cards that JW'd never seen, and that Margareta'd saved and put in Camilla's room. Maybe she thought they belonged there, as though no other place was sufficiently holy to store the fragments of her daughter's abridged life.

Most of it was stuff he already knew. Camilla wrote thin descriptions of life in Stockholm. She worked at a café. She hung out with the other waitresses. She lived in a studio in Södermalm—the south side—that she rented through the owner of the café. She studied at Komvux. She quit the café job and started working at a restaurant. Once, it said that she'd ridden in a Ferrari.

Not a word about Jan Brunéus.

She mentioned her boyfriend in some of the letters. He wasn't referred to by name, but it was clear the boyfriend owned the car.

One postcard, the last one, contained information JW didn't already know.

> Hi Mom,
> I'm good. Things are going well for me and I quit the restaurant. I work as a bartender instead. Make good money. Have pretty much decided to forget about Komvux. Next week I'm going to Belgrade with my boyfriend.
> Say hi to Dad and Johan!
> Love, Camilla

That was news to JW. That Camilla'd been planning to go to Belgrade. With the boyfriend.

He made the rapid calculation: Why go to Belgrade? Because you were from there.

Who was from there? The man with the Ferrari.

He was a Yugo.

30

Stefanovic as lecturer. He probably wasn't familiar with the term *strategic consultant*, but if he'd worked for Ernst & Young, they would've been proud.

It was serious. Organized. The elite were gathered around a conference table in the VIP room on the top floor of Radovan's bar. Radovan, Mrado, Stefanovic, Goran, and Nenad. The conversation was held in Serbian.

Mrado: responsible for the coat checks and other racketeering/blackmail/hit-man jobs.

Stefanovic: Radovan's bodyguard and CFO.

Goran: bossed over booze and cigarette smuggling.

Nenad: biggest supplier of coke to Stockholm's dealers, and also ran the trade in whores, apartment bordellos, and call-service chicks. Was responsible for the entire gamut of services. Nenad was Mrado's closest among the colleagues—he saw in him the same desire he felt to be his own man. None of Goran or Stefanovic's rimming.

The room and the bar'd been searched for hours. The cops were on the hunt. Stefanovic'd looked for any recording devices: under tables, chairs, behind lamps, under ledges. Checked civvies in the bar downstairs, suspicious cars, cameras in the windows across the street. It was the first time Radovan's entire cadre had been together, in person, in over a year and a half.

Dangerous.

Stefanovic began ceremoniously. "Gentlemen, three months ago I was given the task of figuring out what we should do about Nova. You're familiar with it. The Stockholm police began the project four months ago. They've got their sights set on us and other groups. They've already collared more than forty people, mostly those in the western region. Thirty are already convicted. The rest are rotting in jail while they wait to stand trial. All of us in this room appear on their list of the hundred and fifty persons who make up the core of organized crime in this city."

Goran grinned. "Where did they get that idea?"

Stefanovic cut him off. "Funny, Goran. Are you stupid because you're a loser, or a loser because you're stupid?"

Goran opened his mouth, then closed it again without a word. Like a fish.

Radovan looked at him. Most of the time, Goran was his fluffer, but now he wanted seriousness. Mrado thought: One point docked for Goran.

Stefanovic took a sip of mineral water. "During the last five years, we've concentrated our focus on five different areas of business. Then we run some other treats on the side, as you know—freight skimming, tax stuff, et cetera. We have a total turnaround of about sixty million kronor a year. Deduct general costs from that—the price of laundering the cash and paying off the guys. Your net result is something like fifteen. Add your earnings from your own and our shared legal businesses. Clara's, Diamond, and Q-court. The demolition firm and the video-rental stores, et cetera. You're all co-owners in one way or another. You live well on this stuff. But the businesses work differently. The margins vary. The whore biz is rolling. The cigarettes are okay. The blow is flying. Right, Nenad? What's the price today?"

Nenad spoke slowly. "We buy for four fifty. Sell for between nine and eleven hundred. After turnaround costs, we earn an average of four hundred per gram, given that we don't bulk."

"That's good. But everything can get better. If we can zero in on the source, we can press down the prices more. And, anyway, coke is the riskiest of the businesses. You don't want to put all your eggs in one basket. It's important that we have several functioning businesses simultaneously. The risk is really high when it comes to ice. We have to be mobile, be able to switch between different areas depending on the relationship between risk and revenue."

Radovan nodded.

Mrado wasn't surprised about the level of the lecture. He'd talked to Stefanovic two days ago, when he'd told him the instructions Radovan'd given him: "The presentation is for professional businessmen who deal in crime. I want numbers, statistics. Background analysis, prognoses,

constructive solutions. No brainless gangster chitchat." Still, Mrado
was amazed. Unusually open description of Radovan's empire. Mrado
pretty much knew what made up Radovan's domain, sure, but this
was the first time R. himself, through Stefanovic, was giving numbers
in detail.

Mrado regarded the men around the table. All in first-class suits.
Broad shoulders. Broad tie knots like sportscasters'. Broad smiles when
they heard the numbers.

Radovan was at the head of the table. His head was tilted back, chin
in the air. Gave the impression that he wanted to have an overview of
the others. Concentrated, steely look on his face.

Stefanovic: unassuming appearance. Mrado knew better—he was
the other half of Radovan's brain.

Goran was sitting with his arms crossed. Almost as beefy as Mrado.
Almost as bitchy as a teen with a curfew. Followed Stefanovic with his
eyes. Listened and analyzed the strategy. Had a lined notebook in front
of him on the table.

Nenad rocked the Stureplan look. Backslick, pinstriped suit, pink
tailored shirt. Matching silk handkerchief in his breast pocket. What
gave him away was the Serbian cross tattooed on his hands. The
Cocaine King/Whore Boss looked like a cocaine king/whore boss.
Tried to pull a laid-back attitude—drawling voice, slow movements—
but he was always jittery.

Stefanovic rose. Paced back and forth. "Let me give you a quick history lesson."

Goran took notes.

"We've gotten competition over the last couple of years. When they
took down Jokso in 1998, many of us thought the market shares were
up for grabs, that there weren't too many contenders in the cockfight.
Then came the cease-fire between the Hells Angels and the Bandidos
in 2001. You remember the terms. Neither of the gangs was allowed
to expand. They had territories in Malmö, Helsingborg, and in two
places on the west coast. But they were smart. Instead of the main
clubs growing, the hang-around clubs grew, Red & White Crew and
Red Devils, X-Team and Amigos MC. *We are the people your parents
warned you about*, as they like to say. Mischievous boys. Today, they're
like ants and Sweden is their hill; even Stockholm's crawling with
them. As if that wasn't enough, the prisons've really revved up: Original Gangsters, the Wolfpack Brotherhood, Fucked for Life, et cetera,

et cetera. At first, they were loosely knit groups of young criminals and overgrown teen fists. Today, they're almost as well organized as the motorcycle gangs, even outside the walls. What's more, the Russian Mafia, the Estonian crime rings, not to mention the Naser Gang—we all know them—and the fuckin' Polacks with their illegal Benz import have cut into large parts of the market. What's happened?"

Stefanovic stared them down, one by one. The old boys were chastened. What he'd told them wasn't news. Even so, you could see it in their eyes, the flicker of understanding that maybe the Yugos weren't the biggest, baddest, and most beautiful anymore. The golden age was over. They were no longer kings of the hill.

Nenad arranged a well-waxed piece of hair, smoothed it down. "I can tell you what's happened. They're letting too many *blattes* into this country. Fuck, first it was the Kosovo Albanians, Naser's ugly mugs and the rest. Then all the nasty-ass Gambians—they fuckin' own half of the heroin in this city. And this is goddamn unbelievable: The Russians are smuggling cigarettes with the Bandidos. Unholy bedfellows. Worse than Croats, Slovenians, and Americans sucking each other off. It's sicker than what the Svens do to our import pussy. Close the borders. Deport every Eastern fuck who sits his dark-haired, drug-filled ass down on the blond side of the border."

Stefanovic said, "There's a lot to what you just said. But it's not just the new immigrants who've created the competition. We're seeing new alliances. New gangs. They've learned from us and the motorcycle gangs in the States. We've got certain advantages, we all come from Holy Serbia. We speak the same language, have the same habits and contacts, are unified. But today, that's not helping. Especially not now when the peace's been broken. There's a new war on—and it involves us. So far, two from the Bandidos, one HA, and one OG—popped. But we've taken a beating too. You all know what's happened. Two months ago, one of ours was shot, severely injured. Both the war and the Nova Project will continue if we don't do something. I've been thinking about it. Radovan's been thinking about it. Mrado and I've talked to some others, which you'll hear more about in a moment. To conclude, there are a lot more players on the field than five years ago, the cease-fire's been broken, and the police've strengthened their positions through this damn Nova shit. They're pinpointing us, infiltrating us, disturbing the balance. When people within certain groups fall, other groups think it's a free-for-all. We're fighting, when we should be collaborating. But we have a suggestion for a solution to the problem. Mrado will tell you about that."

Stefanovic handed out copies of a paper with a list of names on it. Pointed.

"These are the gangs that control organized crime in Stockholm. Under the name of each gang, I've written down what they do and where. For example, you can see here that the Hells Angels run coat checks all over the city, do some drug dealing, primarily in the southern boroughs, import precursors, run automatic gambling machines all over the city, and do protection racketeering. All you gotta do is compare. Who's in the same business we're in and where're they doing it. I'm about to hand the show over to Mrado. He's already been in touch with some of the gangs on the list. Discussed the solution."

Goran leaned across the table, as if he didn't think the others would hear otherwise. "I honestly don't see why we gotta find a solution. I don't see a problem, since I've got total control over my business. If someone else's got a problem, they should have to solve it on their own."

Clear message directed at Mrado and Nenad: You're not handling your job.

Stefanovic supported himself with both his hands on the table. The sleeves of his suit jacket slipped down over his cuffs and cuff links, which were in the shape of mini revolvers. He leaned over the table, mimicked Goran.

"You're missing the point, Goran. We're in this together. We consider and analyze what's best for Radovan and for us. Not just for you. If you haven't understood that by now, you're welcome to discuss the matter with Rado in private. End of story."

The second time today that Goran'd stepped out of line. The second time he'd gotten his fingers smacked. How much crap would Rado take?

Radovan remained calm. Gaze glued on Goran. Power play.

Goran stared back for a microsecond, then nodded.

Mrado cleared his throat. He'd prepared tonight's talk ahead of time. Some parts were hot; Goran might freak out again.

"As Stefanovic was saying, I've been in touch with some of the groups. Among them, the Hells Angels and the Original Gangsters. And we've come up with the solution; it's all about dividing up the market. Dividing up the different areas we work between us. The groups work differently. The HA are a lot more organized than the OG. On the other hand, the OG are ready to take bigger risks and have better connections in the outer boroughs. You can take a look at Stefanovic's handout to see what they're doing. The HA compete with us over coat checks, cocaine, and booze smuggling. They're bigger than us at racketeering and gambling machines. The OG do cocaine and some racketeering and different loosely planned CIT hits. My assessment is that the OG aren't a direct threat to our business. We could basically give a fuck about them. But they might, for example, be in competition with other groups that, in turn, compete for the same markets we do. We get a domino effect. The Hells Angels, for instance, are ready to discuss a division regarding either the booze import or the coat checks. Stefanovic and I are gonna look into it further. I'm gonna meet up with more people and hear what can be done. The Gambians, the Bandidos, the Wolfpack Brotherhood, and others. The point is that we have to fortify the front against this Nova shit and end the war. You know as well as I do that no one wants to be called a canary, but in a war, the whole sky fills with birdsong. Rat people out rather than rub 'em out, man to man. The Nova Project gains from everyone being at war with everyone else."

Mrado continued to explain. Described the gangs. The rings that divided and ruled the city. Unholy alliances and kinship. Ethnic, racial, and geographic groupings.

The men sat in silence. No one wanted to give up their market. At the same time, everyone understood the problem. Most of all, no one wanted to fight with Radovan.

Mrado thought about the mood he'd sensed earlier. Rado wasn't totally pleased. After this run-through, Radovan's attitude toward him ought to improve. Mrado'd begun a huge job with the market division.

He wrapped up his lecture.

Radovan thanked Stefanovic and Mrado.

Everyone turned their cells back on.

A few minutes of small talk.

Goran excused himself. Said he had to go.

Rado looked satisfied. "Thanks for coming. I think this could be the beginning of something new, something big. You can go now if you want. Personally, I'd planned on enjoying myself tonight."

The doors to the room swung open. Two girls in short skirts rolled in a booze cart. Poured out drinks.

They sang Serbian drinking songs.
Nenad pinched one of the girls on the butt.
Rado laughed.
Food was brought in.
Mrado almost forgot his feelings toward Radovan.
It was gonna be a long night.

***

MEMORANDUM

(Confidential, pursuant to chapter 9, paragraph 12 of the Secrecy Act.)

PROJECT NOVA
COUNTY CRIMINAL POLICE INITIATIVE AGAINST ORGANIZED CRIME

Balkan-related crime in Stockholm

Report Number 7

Background Information

The following memorandum is based on reports and suspicions from the Special Gang Commission and the Norrmalm police's Financial Crime Investigation Unit in collaboration with the Unified County Effort Against Organized Crime in the Stockholm Area (collectively referred to below as the Surveillance Group). The methods employed include mapping, with the help of the combined experience of the Stockholm police; the collection of information from people within the criminal networks, so-called rats; secret wiretapping and bugging; as well as the coordination of requisite registries. The memorandum is being presented due to the fact that new information has been gathered from a person (X) who is currently convicted and incarcerated and who was previously active within the networks described below and also noted internal conflicts within the Yugoslavian network's leadership.

Since the summer of last year, the Surveillance Group has, with increased efforts, tracked a number of persons who belong to the so-called Yugoslavian Mafia (referred to below as the Organization). The members of the Organization are suspicious of new people, which is why the Organization is difficult to infiltrate. This is largely due to the Organization's ethnic homogeneity. The upper levels of the hierarchy solely consist of men between the ages of twenty-five and fifty-five, all born, or with both parents born, in the former Yugoslavia, today Serbia-Montenegro. There are few so-called rats who are ready to provide information about the Organization because of its members' well-documented history of violence. The Organization has become famous for following through on threats, and several incidents of serious violent crimes over recent years can be tied to it and its related groups. See reports 2–4. Wiretapping or other bugging is often unsuccessful, since the people within the Organization search the places where they spend time as well as use prepaid phone cards that are frequently switched out.

Since three months back, the Surveillance Group has suspected that the Organization is preparing itself and its business to face the threat posed by Project Nova.

The Business of the Organization
There are suspicions in regard to the following criminal activities: alcohol and cigarette smuggling, sex trafficking, procuring, and pandering, blackmail, and racketeering, as well as freight frauds and freight theft.

Actors
Radovan Kranjic: The Organization's leader is the Swedish citizen Radovan Kranjic (also known as Rado, Mr. R., and the Yugo boss), born in 1960 at an unknown location in the former Yugoslavia, now Serbia-Montenegro. He came to Sweden in 1978, seeking employment.

Among other things, Kranjic has previously worked as a bouncer and a bodyguard. Today, he owns and runs a restaurant, Clara's Kitchen & Bar, Ltd. (Organization number 556542-2353), in central Stockholm. He reported an income

from the company as well as from certain shares in Diamond
Catering, Ltd. (Organization number 556554-2234), a total
of 321,000 kronor for the past fiscal year.

Kranjic has previously been convicted of the following.
1982: assault, minor. 1985: illegal threats, assault,
illegal weapons possession, speeding (served eight months
in prison). 1989: illegal threats, tax fraud, illegal
weapons possession (served four months in prison). Since
1990, Kranjic has not been reported for any crimes or misdemeanors.

Kranjic is married to Nadja Kranjic, with whom he has one
child. Kranjic is believed to have participated in the war
in the former Yugoslavia, 1993–1995, during which time he
was not in Sweden for long stretches of time. He is said
to have good connections within segments of the Serbian
Nationalist Movement, among them Zeljko Raznatovic, better known as "Arkan," whose private paramilitary army, the
Tigers, led ethnic cleansing actions in Kosovo 1992–1995.
During the later part of the 1990s, he was the number two
in the Organization in Stockholm and was primarily responsible for the racketeering and cocaine businesses. Kranjic
is also believed to have started the sex trafficking, procuring, and pandering business during this time.

Mrado Slovovic: He is Radovan Kranjic's direct subordinate. Slovovic, who is a Swedish citizen born in 1967,
came to Sweden in 1970 from the former Yugoslavia. He has
previously worked as a bouncer and with the import of Thai
wood products. He trains in so-called bodybuilding and
combat sports.

Slovovic reported an income of 136,000 kronor for the past
fiscal year, profits derived from his wood-importing business as well as from gambling.

He has previously been convicted for the following. 1987:
driving under the influence. 1988: aggravated assault,
illegal weapons possession, and illegal drug possession,
minor (served one year in prison). 1995: breaking and

entering, robbery, and resisting arrest (served twenty-four months in prison). 2001: illegal threats. Since 2001, he has not been reported for any crimes or misdemeanors. Slovovic was most recently prosecuted for aggravated assault of a bouncer at restaurant Kvarnen in Stockholm. Charges against Slovovic were dropped on appeal. The other defendant, X, was sentenced to three years in prison for aggravated assault. X is believed to be one of Slovovic's so-called lackeys and has worked with him within the Organization's coat-check racketeering business. Furthermore, Slovovic is currently involved in a custody battle with his former wife, Annika Sjöberg, regarding the care of their daughter, Lovisa.

Slovovic is believed to have been a member of the so-called Tigers, during their attack on Srebrenica in 1995. Slovovic is very violent and has, other than the incident at Kvarnen, without a doubt committed a great number of acts that would be classified as aggravated assault if he were forced to stand trial for them. Among other things, the Norrmalm police's Drug Unit has tried to infiltrate a group of so-called bodybuilders at the Fitness Club gym on Sveavägen in Stockholm, which serves as a recruiting base for crime. The police infiltrator (Y) was, on August 18 of last year, gravely assaulted by Slovovic, who used free weights from the gym as well as threatened him with a gun. Y does not believe that Slovovic suspected his connection with the police, but that the assault was done as an "exhibit of power" by Slovovic.

Slovovic is responsible for the Organization's protection racketeering business as well as other acts of blackmail and threats. The protection-racketeering business is directed primarily against restaurants and bars in the Stockholm area, but also against other business owners who appear to exist in a legal "gray zone."

Stefanovic Rudjman: He is Kranjic's nephew and his and his family's private bodyguard. Born in Sweden in 1977.

He has previously been enrolled at Stockholm University, where his studies have included law and economics. He did not complete a degree in either subject. He has previously been active as an accountant at the accounting firm Rusta Ekonomi, Ltd. (Organization number: 556743-3389).

He reported an income of 859,000 kronor for the past fiscal year, income that mainly originates from interest on stocks and other assets.

The Surveillance Group suspects that Rudjman runs a money-laundering business for, among others, Kranjic. Rudjman has not been convicted of any crime except for a number of traffic offenses since 2000. He is unmarried. Rudjman is also believed to handle Kranjic's investments. Rudjman has, among other things, invested large sums in real estate development projects in the Belgrade area.

Internal Conflicts
The Surveillance Group has gathered information regarding internal conflicts within the Organization. The Organization is well aware of Project Nova and is preparing itself to face the police's efforts. Its leadership is planning to divide the market for certain types of criminal activity in order to avoid insider competition. The method proved effective during the so-called cease-fire between the motorcycle gangs Bandidos and Hells Angels. The Surveillance Group believes that Mrado Slovovic and Stefanovic Rudjman have been entrusted with the job of researching and planning as well as implementing such a division of the market. Slovovic has been in touch with a number of other criminal networks and organizations. He is very difficult to keep under surveillance since he often changes phone carriers. What's more, there is no permit for further surveillance efforts. It is probable that he is planning to meet with more of Stockholm's criminal gangs in the near future. Certain internal conflicts exist within the Organization in regards to the attempts to divide the market.

Based on a tapped conversation between Kranjic and Rudjman on February 15 of this year (tape SPL 3459-045 A), it is apparent that Kranjic no longer trusts Slovovic. The following quotes are translated from Serbian and taken from the transcript of the conversation:

Kranjic: We probably have to get rid of the coat checks or knock him off [Mrado]. I don't trust M.

Rudjman: But he means a lot to us. Does a good job. Got a hold of that Chilean snitch whore. Puts people in their place. Hookers, bouncers, live wires.

Kranjic: Sure, but he doesn't know his place anymore. This fall, he demanded a bigger cut of the profits. He can forget about that. After the Kvarnen shit show. Bad and poorly planned. But, most of all, and now I know I'm getting personal, it's about history. He can't accept that I'm in charge. We worked on the same level a long time ago. That's another reason he's gotta go. His loyalty falters.

The Surveillance Group believes that this is another sign that Project Nova has succeeded in its initial stage: to disrupt the organized crime scene and weaken it.

Measures
The Surveillance Group suggests the following measures to be taken, based on what has been described above:
1. Increased surveillance operations against Mrado Slovovic and Radovan Kranjic, to the extent that permission is granted.
2. Continued attempts to gather information from X.
3. Continued attempts to infiltrate the Organization.

Regarding the budget for the above-listed measures, see attachment 1.

Criminal Investigation Department Superintendent Björn Stavgård
Special Investigator Stefan Krans

31

Jorge had to pee so bad, he could've pissed a whole ginger ale bottle full. Funny thought, maybe treat someone. "Here, have some ginger ale." The color deceptively similar.

It would be weeks before he finally understood a basic ground rule for people in the surveillance business: Always bring a bottle to pee into when you're staking out in a car. If it's an empty ginger ale bottle or not doesn't matter.

The car's back windows were tinted—it was necessary so no one could see him. Regular windows would be too much of a hassle; he'd have to lie with his seat lowered all the way back. And then there'd be the risk of falling asleep.

Radovan's house was peaceful. It was the first day he'd spent sitting out here. The first of many days to come.

He'd stolen the car, a Jeep Cherokee, in posh Östermalm at 3:00 a.m. Switched out the license plates. Reduced the risk of being outed by the cops.

Jorge, the Angel of Revenge, was gonna bring Radovan's empire to its knees. He just had to figure out how.

All he knew right now was that hate went a long way. A vendetta that demanded even more patience than the escape from Österåker. He had to investigate, stake out, add things up. Dig up dirt on Radovan. To start, figure out Mr. R.'s routines. A good start: sitting in the car, thinking, and waiting to see if something shady would happen.

Nothing was happening on the street.

He looked at the house.

There was snow on the roof.

Unclear if anyone was home or not.

He kept staring, as if he'd enrolled at Komvux again—a course in suburban architecture.

Nodded off between five and six o'clock in the afternoon. Not good.

Had to stay awake. Tomorrow, he was gonna bring cigarettes, Coca-Cola, maybe a Gameboy.

The day slipped by.

The hate remained.

A few days later, he was staking out the house again.

Forced himself to think about an outlet for his feelings toward Radovan. The ideas'd found their way into his mind a week ago for the first time. Earlier, he'd pushed the thoughts away, into the future. Had only wanted to survive on the run. Get in with Abdulkarim. Do a good job. Make some money. Fix a passport. Skip the country. Now, he enjoyed walking the city streets, being unrecognizable. The thought of leaving Sweden was starting to seem like too much of a hassle. Instead: When he'd made enough money, he'd start some kind of assault on Radovan.

A thought: There was the possibility that he was actually working indirectly for Radovan right now. Jorge knew coke Stockholm inside out. There weren't many players out there with muscles big enough to deal on Abdulkarim's massive scale. The Arab seemed ridiculous sometimes, but Jorge knew the dude had an iron grip on cocaine. Knew his shit. Jorge could have cared less either way. It wasn't probable that Rado actually controlled Abdul—Serbs and Muslims didn't usually mesh. And, if Radovan really was the boss, the irony was just too perfect.

He needed to plan other projects, his first real job for the Arab. Make sure a coke shipment had a smooth arrival, directly from Brazil.

That was his area of expertise.

Founding principle: An old trick can fly if you play it right. Jorge was prepared. A much bigger load than usual was being delivered. Cocaine acquired through contacts of contacts in Brazil. Priceworthy. Forty American dollars a gram. Heavy phone traffic the last couple of months. The deal was done: The tickets had been bought, a new prepaid cell had been acquired, the necessary people had been informed, customs officers in São Paolo had been bribed, and a hotel room had been booked. Most important of all, the courier had been secured. It was a woman.

Troubleshooting: done. Abdulkarim: double-checked everything.

Again: An old trick can fly if you play it right. The Arlanda airport police/customs were after suspicious couriers worse than baby ballers in the projects were after the gangs they wanted to belong to, like leeches.

Jorge repeated: He would play it right.

He went over his revenge project once again, which led to questions. What did he really know about R.? Some from the time before he was locked up, when he'd pushed powder for the Yugos. Their routines were tight. He'd pick up a key in a storage locker at the Central Station about once a week. Then he'd ride out to a Shurgard storage unit in Kungens Kurva, where he'd measure out ten to twenty grams per visit. Dealt the shit in the northern boroughs, sometimes at bars in the city. Sometimes to other dealers, sometimes directly to the customers. Simple jobs. Still, he'd banked. Been glossy.

He knew so much more about snow now. Österåker'd had its good sides—J-boy was a walking Stockholm coke encyclopedia.

Then: He'd always known Rado, the Yugo king, was behind it all. But he'd also known that nothing led back to Mr. R. The guys that delivered the coke to Jorge had never mentioned his name. He'd never run into them at the Shurgard storage unit. Strange that Mrado hadn't killed him out there in the woods. The Yugos must've been scared that he had so much dirt on Radovan, he'd be able to hurt them for real.

He wished he had as much on the Yugo boss as they thought he did.

Something Jorge had to consider: If he tried to gather info about R. within the field he knew best, coke dealing, didn't he risk his own skin? Didn't he risk his buddies: Sergio, Vadim, Ashur? Dudes who'd all been involved in Radovan's coke pyramid in one way or another. He ought to find out other stuff about the Yugo Mafia.

What else did he know about Radovan from his time at Österåker? First and foremost, what everybody knew: The Yugo boss was involved in a ton of other businesses besides ice. Racketeering, doping, cigarette smuggling. But what did he know of substance? Only a couple things: Radovan's blow came in via the Balkan route, over the former Yugoslavia, where the shit was refined and packaged. Not like most other blow in Sweden, which came in through the Iberian Peninsula, England, or directly from Colombia and the rest of Latin America. The Balkan route was usually the heroin channel.

Moreover, he knew which restaurants Radovan was said to control and use for laundering. He knew a number of people who'd been threatened or gotten the shit kicked out of them because they'd challenged parts of Radovan's empire: the blow biz in the inner city, Jack Vegas gambling machines at bars in the western boroughs, moonshine instead of smuggled stuff at restaurants in Sollentuna.

But again, nothing could be linked directly to R. Nothing could be proven.

Jorge figured he should give up. Eat the humiliation. Lots of people got the living daylights beaten out of them by men like Mrado. Who did he think he was? What could he achieve? On the other hand, J-boy, the big-balled Latino, escape artist extraordinaire, was bigger than the regular ghetto gophers with dreams of bling and expensive rides. He was gonna be somebody. Cash in, for real. If Österåker hadn't been able to stop him, no flabby Serbo-Croatian would, either.

The sky was darkening.

A crappy day.

The house was the wrong place to start. Jorge had to think. Be systematic.

He drove off. Parked the car in Södermalm. Dangerous to ride around in it for too long.

Couldn't let go of the thoughts of R. and his connection to the Balkan route. Jorge knew a guy, Steven, at Österåker. The dude was doing time for smuggling horse from Croatia. Might be a starting point. Find out if Steven was out yet. Otherwise, find Steven's partners. Guys who knew more about the Balkan route.

The next day, he called Österåker from a pay phone. Disguised his voice. Asked if Steven'd been released yet. He was met with a mocking tone on the other end of the line. Jorge didn't recognize who it was. "Steven Jonsson? He's got at least three years left. Call back then."

Pigs.

Jorge called Abdulkarim, Fahdi, Sergio. Everyone he trusted. No one knew much about Steven and H smuggling. Some of them knew his name but had no idea who he'd worked with.

Three days of making calls. No success.

He couldn't even get in touch with Steven himself in a safe way.

Phone calls could be tapped, if they were even allowed. Letters could be opened and read. E-mail wasn't allowed at the facility.

He staked out the house. Waited for something without knowing what.

Stared at the flat roof, his gaze glued to the snow.

Thought: How do I get in touch with Steven? Learn about heroin via the Balkan route. It was a perfect area. Jorge himself'd never been involved in it. No risk for him or his friends.

It became an obsession. A manic goal with Rado's and Mrado's heads as bounty.

Sometimes he saw people at the house. R. himself came home. A woman with a thirteen- or fourteen-year-old girl arrived at the house at around six o'clock every night. It had to be R.'s wife and daughter. Home from school and work. Never alone. Always accompanied by a big dude with a Slavic look—obvious capo in the Yugo hierarchy. Later, Jorge learned who the guy was. His name was Stefanovic, private bodyguard and murder machine for the Radovan Kranjic family.

The woman drove a Saab convertible.

Radovan drove a Lexus SUV.

A happy little family.

When Jorge saw the girl, he thought about the picture of Paola that Mrado'd showed him in the woods. They played dirty. Jorge could play dirty, too. Do something to the girl. Still, it didn't feel right. The girl was innocent. Besides, it seemed too dangerous.

The house was heavily guarded. Every time someone approached it, floodlights automatically lit up the path leading to the door. Sometimes, if Stefanovic was home, he came and opened the door for Radovan. That indicated that some sort of indoor alarm system forewarned him as soon as someone approached the house.

Jorge abandoned the idea that waiting outside the house would yield anything. It seemed half-baked.

Four days later: another idea. He called Österåker again. Asked about Steven. Asked what he'd been convicted of. Asked when he'd been convicted. At which district court.

Thanked Sweden for the law about open access to public records, whatever it was called. Jorge called the district court. Asked them to send him information about Steven Jonsson's conviction. No problem—they didn't even ask his name.

A day later, in Fahdi's mailbox: trial documents. Stockholm's district court. Aggravated drug possession. Thirteen pounds of heroin. Straight from Croatia, fresh. The defendants were Steven Jonsson, Ilja Randic, Darko Kusovic. Steven'd been sentenced to six years, Ilja to six years, Darko to two years. The last guy should be out by now.

Darko wasn't difficult to get hold of. His cell was listed in the regular directory.

Jorge called.

"Hey, my name is Jorge. Old buddy of Steven's from Österåker. I was wondering if it'd be okay if I asked some questions."

"Who the hell are you?" Darko sounded on edge.

"Chill out, man. I did time with Steven. We were on the same hall. Would like to get together if you've got the time."

Jorge cajoled. Sounded pleasant. Pulled some slammer stories about Steven. Made Darko understand that he'd really been in the cell next to Steven. Jorge giggled. Played like a cob. Harmless tool.

That always worked.

Finally, Darko said, "It's cool. I've kicked that habit. Refurbishing Saabs full-time now. I'll meet you, but only on one condition. I don't wanna get pulled into anything. You get me? I quit that shit. I can tell you what Steven and I were up to, but it's gonna be my way. Nothing more. I'm straight these days."

Jorge thought: Yeah right, superstraight.

They arranged to meet up.

He was gonna meet Darko in four days. Five hot G's burned in his pocket. A large part of his income from the job with Abdulkarim went to his hate project: It was both completing and depleting.

They met up at a coffee shop on Kungsgatan. Blueberry muffins and a hundred different types of coffee behind the counter. Place packed with teens and maternity-leave moms. The clientele's conversation topics recapitulated: guys, girlfriends, stroller models.

After some polite small talk and the three thousand kronor as promised, Darko started talking. His dark voice carried over the shrill cackle as he recounted the preparations the heavy hitters'd made four years ago. Despite all his objections over the phone, he didn't seem to give a shit if people heard him.

Darko was a Balkan route pro. Was familiar with every single smuggling route between Afghanistan, Turkey, Tajikistan, and the Balkans. He knew the 20 of every customs station along the entire stretch of the former Yugoslavia's border. Which customs agents would turn a blind eye for dead presidents. Who was expensive, who was cheap.

Jorge was impressed. He asked about Radovan specifically.

Darko shook his head. "I can't tell you. Can lead to trouble. I've got a son, eight years old."

Again, Jorge thought about the cell phone picture of his sister that Mrado'd held up to his face in the woods that afternoon.

Kept applying pressure.

"Come on. Help me, just a little. Two more G's for the info?"

"Why should I trust you?"

"Fuck it, man, call and ask Steven if you think I'll sing. We used to sneak a blaze in the bathroom my whole time on the inside. I'd never jux a friend of Steven's."

Darko seemed to relax when he heard Steven's name.

"You're stubborn. I'll tell you the whole story for five."

No point in haggling. Jorge said, "Agreed. Five."

Darko kept talking. Told how he and Steven hadn't really worked for R. except on two occasions. The first time, they smuggled in nine pounds of heroin hidden in a tractor-trailer crammed with timber. Value on the street: over one and a half million. They'd cooked the whole dish from scratch: fixed the dudes who drove, kept their eyes on the dudes who drove, bribed customs agents, landed protection from other organized naughty boys in Belgrade.

The second time, he hadn't smuggled H, something else. Worse.

Jorge got interested. Poured on the questions.

Darko looked strained. His eyes danced around the room. Downed his coffee. Suggested a walk instead.

They went out.

It was a cold February day. Crispy air and blue sky.

Jorge spewed chatter. Created trust. Babbled on.

"You should've been there. In the summer. Steven smuggled in fifteen cannabis seeds hidden in raisins that he planted in the rec yard. You know, cannabis is thirstier than an Arab in the desert."

Darko listened. Let himself be entertained. Looked like he was unwinding somewhat.

"Major problem, watering the plants. Steven got the sickest idea, stood and pretended to piss on 'em at the same time the dude poured a glass of water on the shits. A screw found him out, of course. Walked up. Flipped the fuck out and was all 'Are you urinating on the lawn?' Steven denied it, straight up. The screw was all gonna prove he'd pissed, got down on all fours. Started smelling the grass. You follow? Like a fucking dog. Steven told the CO fag, 'Now you proved it. I suspected it a long time—screws and bitches, you got the same genes.' Man, everyone in the yard just howled."

Darko smiled. "I've heard that story before. Steven's a cool bro."

They walked up Kungsgatan.

After another five minutes, he started telling the story. "Me and Steven worked with a Serb, Nenad. Cruel bastard. The dude had good connections in Belgrade. There were rumors he'd belonged to the Tigers, that he'd slaughtered thirty Bosnians in Srebrenica with his bare hands. First brought the men out into the square, their hands tied behind their backs, and beat them until they crawled in their own puke. Then they raped their wives, in front of them. We didn't know then that he was Radovan's man. When we did the H job, it was on direct orders from R. We got a twenty percent cut. Partied for six months, then time for business again. So, the second time we worked for Radovan, it was on Nenad's orders. Think that was a year before I was put away. We met up at Café Ogo—you know, Jokso's old place. Nenad introduced himself, said we could call him the Patriot 'cause he always supported Serbia. That was serious for those guys. He was rock-hard, Nenad, with war tattoos all over his knuckles. Two other dudes were there at the table. Kept their mouths shut the whole time, I think. But I recognized one of them from the club scene, Stefanovic. Younger guy who worked for Radovan at the time. Nenad buttered us up. Kept talking about the good job we'd done with the last transport. What a success it'd been. He knew a lot about me, but that wasn't strange, since we often worked for Yugos. I mean, I'm a Serb myself."

Darko paused. His eyes glowed like embers. Fired up by old memories. By the kicks. The suspense. Or?

They walked across the square at Hötorget.

"Nenad went over the plan. It was a big load of H. We were gonna bring it on trucks, like before, from the Belgrade area. And it'd be real bulked, take a lotta space. We didn't clock shit, then. Planned the whole thing. Landed two German-registered semis, took two containers each. Fixed the drivers, the customs crap, the permits. The whole enchilada. Officially, machine parts were being driven from Turkey over the Balkans. Nenad had rules. Needed at least seventy cubic feet for the load in each container. When we met up with our contact people outside Belgrade, they drove up in two old army buses, dressed in military uniforms and carrying machine guns. Had four women with them. I thought they were gonna give us vodka and a nice time with the girls. It took me a minute to get it. We were never bringing any H. It was people we were smuggling. At first, I thought they were refugees."

Jorge and Darko kept walking along Vasagatan at a leisurely pace. Past the Central Station. The taxis in line. Jorge asked, "Who were the contact people?"

"No idea. But we drove the girls all the way here. Wouldn't let 'em out even once. It was hot as hell that summer. When we drove through Germany, the thermometer showed over ninety-seven degrees. Fuck knows how they survived the trip. Thirty hours in seventy cubic feet— suck on that. At least they had water. We unloaded them in the harbor at Södra Hammarbyhamnen, which was an undeveloped industrial area at that time. I can still see their faces when they came outta those containers—puffy from crying, a dark gray color. Bags under their eyes that added twenty years. If I'd only known ahead of time what I'd be carrying, fuck. I could've said no. But they had water."

Jorge ignored Darko's remorse. Right now, it didn't matter if the whores'd had water or not. He asked, "Who met you?"

"Radovan, Nenad, Stefanovic, and a couple others."

"Radovan?"

"Yeah. I recognized him from pictures I'd seen at Café Ogo."

"You sure?"

"As sure as I am that it wasn't H I was driving that time."

"Who were the others?"

"No clue who the others were, other than Nenad and Stefanovic. Sorry."

"How much did you get?"

"Hundred and fifty each. To cover everything. Including bribes and salaries for the drivers."

Jorge with a fire inside.

So hot.
Hate.
A lead.
Radovan—wading in the whore trench.
Jorge picked up the chase.

32

JW's luxury problem: He'd put away 300,000 kronor in three months and still been able to consume like an oil sheik—what to do with all the money?

It would soon be time for the Beamer. Maybe in a month. Maybe in two. Probably a used one after all. He was choosing between a slick BMW 330Ci with M sport pack from '03, an even slicker BMW 330 cab with navi from '04, and, slickest of them all, a BMW Z4 2.5i. He was eyeing the last-named car online. It was ill, silver with leather interior, and made zero to sixty in five seconds. Cash car. Class car. Cavalier car for the incomparable. It was soooo him.

Faced the classic caveat for off-the-bookers. On paper, JW didn't make any money and lived, according to Big Brother's records, on student loans—a total of 7,500 kronor a month. The car had to be registered and insured. As a result, Big Brother would see that he'd bought a car for three hundred G's, even though he didn't report any income or assets. Big Brother would wonder. Worst-case scenario: Big Brother would get suspicious, start eyeing JW more closely.

The standard solution for naughty off-the-bookers was to launder the dirty money.

JW did some research. These economic models weren't the most openly written about. Hard to find info. He asked Abdulkarim about smart ways to do it.

The Arab responded, "JW, man, you know, me, I'm no economist. Me, I'm a regular *blatte*. Sweden don't trust me anyway. I don't need clean cash. I'm outside all that."

JW tried to explain the advantages of being good with the system.

Abdulkarim offered a crooked smile. "You comin' to London 'cause you're my economist. You do the thinking. You come up with a smart way—you tell me. In that case, I'll wash ten percent."

The Arab had a point: One alternative was to stay completely outside the system. Not register any cars, not insure any cars, not buy any co-ops, always pay cash.

But that wasn't JW's way. He wanted in—for real.

Three days after he came home from Robertsfors, JW asked himself, What do I have with me from that place? The easy answer: nothing. But still, deep inside, he knew that it'd felt good to be there. Felt good to be safe. Not have to pretend. Be able to speak with his regular dialect again. Be able to walk around in any crappy old threads. Be able to lie on his bed all day without having to call people and ask them what was happening that night.

At the same time, he felt contempt. His parents were clueless. Where he came from—it just didn't cut it.

And he'd brought a new lead home with him: Camilla's guy'd been a Yugo. What did that mean? That was probably information he should give to the police.

But were the police finding anything? JW'd provided them with the Jan Brunéus story, the teacher who'd obviously used his sister. Why didn't they call? Didn't they give a fuck about the Westlund family's anxiety and grief?

At the same time, it was such a relief to have handed it all over to the police. He could do other things. He couldn't let Camilla take too much of his concentration; he had to focus on his career.

JW learned about money laundering. The key to success was moving money from one economic system to another. Moving from dirty to clean areas of business. Moving in a cycle. Moving in three vital steps: placement, concealment, laundry. Without them, the circle wasn't complete.

Placement was necessary since you were dealing in cash. No C sales, no matter how posh the people, happened through any other payment method. Catchy phrase: *Cash is king for cocaine consumers.* The advantage of cash: left no trace. The disadvantage: It was suspicious. People raised their eyebrows at fat rolls of big bills. The cash had to be moved. Placed. Converted. Into another currency, into electronic ones and zeros in a bank account, into stocks, options, or other financial instruments. Into something that didn't attract attention, that wasn't easy to maneuver, that was one step away from your illegal source of income.

The second move was all about concealment. Use businesses as a front or use other methods that would conceal the source of income: bank accounts in countries with good confidentiality policies. You had to break the chain. Create layers of transactions. Couldn't show where the money'd come from. Use decoys. Use numbered accounts. Use systems that cut your connection to the sweet sums.

The final move was the most important; it regarded the actual laundering, the reintegration of the money into your finances. When the cash'd been placed, been put into accounts, the money concealed and impossible to trace back to you, it was time for the final step—the focus on where it'd come from, the creation of a chimera of legitimate sources. Often taxed sources. Normal sources.

Money laundering forced you to play by the rules of the state. You lost the sweet flexibility of cold, hard cash. Entered it into the financial system, where everything was meticulously regulated. All information was saved. All assets were checked off on lists. Every move was registered. No assets arise out of thin air. But it's possible to fake it.

You want to do some laundry. You want to break the chain. At the same time, you want to create a good-looking chain to show the authorities. There are two alternatives. One, you put the money somewhere where the confidentiality laws stop Big Brother's investigations in their tracks. The answer to probing questions: There is a registered transaction, but, unfortunately, there is no authority to release it. Or you use the system itself to create a trail. The answer you offer Big Brother: Of course there's a registered transaction. Look here.

The whole thing demanded preparation. JW was going to get that BMW, no question about it. Registered and insured. Time was of the essence. He wanted to get going right away.

A week later, he'd bought three shelf companies online for six thousand kronor each. Registered himself as a director. One was an events-marketing company; the other two dealt in antiques. Perfect. He placed share capital of one hundred thousand in each company by creating promissory notes. He made himself the debtor—a way to avoid actually investing any real money. He wrote up a hiring contract with himself in the events-marketing firm. Finally, he named the companies: JW Empire Antiques I, Ltd., JW Empire Antiques II, Ltd., and JW Consulting, Ltd. Sounded professional enough.

He got in touch with people in London, friends of Fredrik and Putte who studied at the London School of Economics. Creamy kids whose parents dropped 100,000 kronor per semester for a fine education. They knew others there who were already working, investment bankers. JW made calls. Nasal upper-class voices on the other end of the line. Guys who worked day and night and tried to legitimize their own self-image. He always referred to the guys he'd gotten their names from. That opened doors. Led to new names. Brits, Indians, Italians. Half the world worked in London.

Finally, after four days of calling London—his phone bill would probably land upward of three grand—he was able to speak to a man at the Central Union Bank, Isle of Man. A tax paradise with one huge advantage: bank secrecy. Perfect.

They agreed to meet during the same week that JW was in London with Abdulkarim.

That night, JW was going to have dinner with Sophie at Aubergine on Linnégatan.

He was at home in his room, surfing the Web. Drooling over buyable gadgets. Überhot cars. Used Excel to calculate his own purchases as of late. New sales methods. Cash-flow analysis. Laundering advantages.

Shut down the computer.

Got up. It was time to see Sophie. JW rocked his usual look: Gucci jeans, loafers, blue striped Pal Zileri shirt with double cuffs. He put on the cashmere coat.

Walked toward Aubergine. Dirty snow lined the streets. His shoes were more slippery than a banana dipped in K-Y. He saw Sophie through the window. She always looked good, always. But you couldn't appreciate it 100 percent while she was sitting down. When he walked in, she stood up. Her hotness hit him in the face like a rock-hard right jab. Shit, she was fine.

She was wearing tight blue jeans, Sass & Bide, pointy black shoes,

and a low-cut black top, probably from the Nathalie Schuterman boutique on Birger Jarlsgatan. Sophie was a regular.

He winked, fake-flirted with her.

She smiled. They hugged. A quick kiss.

JW sat down. Ordered a beer. Sophie was already nursing a glass
of red.

The restaurant was shaped like an L. The windows were big. The
black lacquered tables discreet. The bar was located in the corner of
the L. Intricate iron structures suspended from the ceiling served as
lamps, casting a soft light over the room.

The clientele consisted of lawyers and finance guys grabbing an
after-work beer, club-scene gals pouting over preparty cocktails, and
Östermalm couples out for dinner, tête-à-tête.

They ordered food.

JW put his arm around Sophie.

She sipped her wine. "You look tired."

Sometimes she had a way about her that made him nervous. When
she fixed her gaze, she never looked away.

"I don't think I've been sleeping enough."

"But last week you told me you were tired 'cause you'd been sleeping too much. You'd slept till three in the afternoon. Is that a record
for you?"

JW ran his finger along the frosted beer glass. "I don't think so. That
was the weekend I got back from Mom and Dad's. You get drowsy
from sleeping too much. I relaxed too much at their house."

"That stuff's so weird. There's, like, always a reason to be tired. Can
be totally opposing things. Kind of messed up, when you think about
it. You're tired 'cause you've slept too little, or too much, from the
winter darkness, or from the spring light. People say you get tired
from vegging out one day or from being too active another."

"It's true. Everyone wants an excuse to be tired. Tired 'cause you
had a hard workout at the gym or 'cause you bent your mind all out
of shape for an exam. Tired 'cause it's too hot or 'cause the cold takes
it out of you. People always have a reason to be tired. But I know why
I'm, like, falling asleep right now. I went out last night."

JW kept talking. About his night out. About his buddies' crazy antics.
About the snort rush. Babbled on. Sophie was a good listener, asked
follow-up question at the right pauses, nodded in the right places,

laughed at the right jokes. Sophie knew part of the true story—she knew that JW dealt to the boyz—but she didn't know the scale of it. Not by a long stretch.

Sophie leaned back. They were quiet for a moment. Eavesdropped on the conversation at the table next to them.

Finally she asked, "What other friends do you have besides the boys?"

In JW's head: process of analysis in turbogear. Fumbled for false phrases. What the fuck was he gonna say? That the boyz were his only friends—appear like someone with few friends. Make up other friends? Like Casper. No, he couldn't keep more lies straight in his head. The answer: compromise, tell her half the story.

"I hang out with another group sometimes. You're gonna laugh."

"Why would I laugh?"

"'Cause they're, like, *blatte* guys, sort of."

"*Blatte* guys?" Honest surprise.

"Kind of, yeah. We party, work out. Chill." JW felt a need to explain himself. "They're cool, actually."

"I would never have expected that of you. Sometimes I wonder how well we really know each other. When do I get to meet them?"

A miscalculation. JW hadn't thought she'd want to get involved. Usually she didn't take much of an interest in people outside her immediate circle. Now she suddenly wanted to meet Abdulkarim, Fahdi, and Jorge.

A joke, or what?

JW made an effort. Had to maintain the mask. He said, "Maybe. Sometime." His need to change the subject got desperate. He started talking about Sophie instead. That usually worked.

Brought up her relationship with Anna and other Lundsberg chicks. Relationship talk. Sophie's favorite. JW wondered if she knew what'd happened between him and her friend Anna at the rager at Lövhälla Manor. But why should she care? It was almost six months ago.

Sophie reminded him of Camilla. It was frightening.

Camilla was like Sophie except for one difference—Camilla hadn't been as savvy somehow.

And then it hit him. It still felt like Sophie was playing a game with him, playing hard to get, maintaining a distance, and maybe it was just her way of saying that she wanted him to give her intimacy. Let down his guard. Let her in. Tell her who he really was. Tell her all he didn't dare say. Just like Camilla'd been. Maintained a hard shell and a distance toward Mom and Dad, especially toward Bengt, when it was probably just a way to shut down because there wasn't really any intimacy available at home. Playing hard because she didn't dare be vulnerable. And was it that lack of intimacy that'd lured her to that fucking Jan Brunéus? JW wasn't even sure he wanted to know.

A couple of days later, planning for the London trip was in full swing. JW bought tickets. Booked luxury hotel rooms. Made sure they were written up on club guest lists: Chinawhite, Mayfair Club, Moore's. Arranged for a private London guide, booked a limo for their personal use, made reservations at the sweetest restaurants, looked up the best strip joints, got in touch with scalpers for tix to Chelsea games, researched the directions to the luxury department stores and checked when they were open: Harvey Nichols, Harrods, Selfridges.

Abdulkarim would be pleased. The only thing that irritated JW was that he didn't know whom they were meeting and why. The only info Abdulkarim'd given him: "This is big business."

They often hung out at Fahdi's. JW, Fahdi, Jorge, and Abdulkarim sometimes. Fahdi watched old Van Damme flicks and pornos. Talked about dudes he'd crushed and Evil with a capital *E: USA*. JW and Jorge mind-mapped their contacts and dealers. Planned new storage spots, safe turf for deals, sales strategies, and, above all, import. A massive import from Brazil was up first.

The Chilean exuded hate and resolve. The guy had his side project, revenge against the guys who'd torn him to pieces.

JW generally felt relaxed when he was with them. They were unaffected compared to his Stureplan buds. Somewhat B-list in their habits, but at the core they basically shared the same values as the boyz—chicks, money, living it up.

One night at Fahdi's he realized there were aspects to the C biz he'd been spared from dealing with.

JW, Jorge, and Fahdi were on the couches. Had made calls to dealers and arranged drop-off spots.

The TV was on in the background. Slow-motion action scenes from *Mission Impossible II* streamed out.

Enjoyable, bloody kicks and punches. For Fahdi—inspiration.

He started telling them about a guy he'd shot two years earlier.

JW laughed at first.

Jorge wanted to hear more.

He asked Fahdi, "Aren't you scared you'll be put away?"

Fahdi laughed and said proudly, "Me, never scared. Scared is for fags."

"So whattya do if the Five-Oh show up?"

"You seen Léon?"

"*¿Qué?*"

"Don't get it?"

"What, you got heat at home?"

"*Habibi*, obviously. You wanna see my arsenal?"

JW was honestly curious. They followed Fahdi to his bedroom. The closet door creaked. Fahdi fumbled in the dark. Threw something on the bed. At first, JW didn't see what it was. Then he understood. In front of him on the bed was a sawed-off shotgun, a Winchester. Double barrel. Five yellow boxes of shells of the same make as the shotgun. Two Glock pistols. One machete with duct tape around the grip. Fahdi's face glowed with joy, like that of a happy child. "And I show you my best thing." He leaned into the closet again. Brought out an AK-5. "Swedish military issue. Hot, yeah?"

JW played cool. Really, he was shocked—Fahdi's home was a veritable Eagle's Nest. A loaded war bunker in the gray projects . . . with the safety off.

Jorge grinned.

When JW got home later that night, he didn't call Sophie. He had trouble falling asleep.

33

Mrado debuted as peace mediator. Worked well. Thought, Maybe I could've had a career in the UN. Then he cut himself off. Sodomize the shit out of the UN. They betrayed Serbia.

He'd been having meetings with head honchos for three weeks now. Magnus Lindén, a hard-boiled, half-cobbed right-wing extremist. Leader of the Wolfpack Brotherhood. Ahmad Gafani, leader of the Fittja Boys, with the classic ACAB (all cops are bastards) tattoo on his neck. Naser, leader of the Albanians. Hardly spoke Swedish but gypped the Swedes out of millions every year. Men with too much power. And yet, men without potent plans. The Yugos were still better, he realized. The rest of 'em needed to shape up. Get organized.

The Hells Angels and the Bandidos'd resumed the war. Two people were already dead, one from each club. The Fittja Boys were fighting over cuts of three CIT heists they'd done with guys from the Original Gangsters. At the Kumla penitentiary, members of the OG and the Bandidos were at war with each other. A Hells Angel at the Hall penitentiary'd recently cut one of Naser's men dead with a ballpoint pen. Four quick ones to the throat. Chop chop. In other words, a third world war'd just broken out in the Stockholm jungle and the adjoining satellite boroughs. The cocksucking cops' Project Nova was icing on the cake. Mrado was convinced they were manipulating the war. Taking advantage of the growing hate and violence. People were ready to snitch to fell the enemy. People were ready to takes risks in a war; they lowered their guard, compromised with security measures. The cops could nestle their way into the gangster teat. Suck out info. The result so far: over thirty convictions.

Mrado was on his way to an industrial area in Tullinge, near the Bandidos' headquarters. It was important to Mrado that a meeting like this not take place *in* the Bandidos' bunker. Had to be on neutral ground.

He'd slept like a dog the night before. Woke at three-thirty. Sweaty. Nasty. Sheets all tangled. Images of Lovisa flashing through his head: playing in the building's courtyard, in her room, watching a movie on the couch, building a snowman and using her crayons for a nose. Insomnia wore him down. Whiskey didn't help. Turning on the stereo and listening to Serbian ballads didn't help, either. He could function okay with three or four hours of sleep a night for a few days in a row. But not for weeks in a row. He had to do something about his life.

Three days earlier, he'd talked to a Bandidos member. Asked him to give a message to Jonas Haakonsen, the head of the Bandidos' Stockholm chapter, saying that Mrado wanted to have a conversation about certain areas of their operation. Gave him one of his cell phone numbers. Two hours later: a text. A location. A time. And: *Come solo*. Nothing more. It fit with what Mrado'd heard about Haakonsen's style. Dramatic. Didn't take risks. Mrado thought, Come on, this isn't some fucking Cold War spy thriller.

Mrado'd met Haakonsen at the Gangsta Golf meet the previous year. Gangsta Golf, a fantastic initiative by an old OG member. Anyone who'd spent more than two years in an iron pen and had a decent swing was welcome. Last year, they'd played at the beautiful Ulriksdal golf course. Forty-two players. Bull necks and tattoos ad absurdum. Mrado felt tiny in comparison. If Mrado'd had the assignment at the time, it would've been the perfect opportunity to talk about the market division. Except for the fact that every single tree, bunker, and green was probably bugged.

What was there to know about the Bandidos? The brightest star in mid-Sweden's gang sky. Recruited from the immigrant boys' hardest cores, via the prospect club, X-Team. Two bases in the Stockholm area: Tullinge and Bålsta. Their latest feat was kidnapping an HA member. The guy was found three days later. Skin like a leopard, round burn marks from stubbed-out cigarettes on every inch. Kneecaps in shards. Nails yanked out. Ultimate cause of death: forced consumption of gasoline. No wonder the MC gangs were at war.

The Bandidos did the same kind of business as the Hells Angels, except heavier on the drugs. That is, they engaged in booze smuggling, protection racketeering, some financial crime, like invoice fraud and tax fraud. Heroin and weed sales were sprinkles on top.

Mrado kept his eyes peeled for traffic signs to Tullinge. Being behind the wheel of the Benz was always a true pleasure. V-8 engine. Curved leather seats. Seriously broad tires.

He downshifted; the car growled from pure power. Driving delight at max.

Radio drone in the background, broke off for the news. Something about the Americans' war in the Middle East. Mrado's mixed feelings. He hated the U.S., while he loved that they were rubbing out towelheads. The fight. Light facing off against the darkness. Europe facing off against the Orient. The Serbs' everlasting duty. And who thanked them for it? That they'd resisted for centuries. Kept the gate to the rest of Europe shut. Sacrificed themselves. Mrado'd fought, too. Now people whined about fanatic fundamentalists and girls being forced to wear veils. Europe, you only have yourself to blame. The Serbs'd done what they could. Been reamed royally by the rest of the world, and the U.S.'d been the first to climb on top. The Serbian people didn't owe anyone anything.

He lowered the volume. Highways were so damn dull. He was planning on taking Lovisa to Kolmården, the big animal park outside the city, next week. Visit the dolphins. Maybe take the back roads. Enjoy.

The sky was gray. Was February the crappiest month? Mrado hadn't seen the sun in four weeks. The other cars on the road were snow-stained, sans style, soiled. Boring.

The problems spun. Worry/angst as mood music instead of the radio.

Radovan was losing faith in him. Maybe it'd been eating at Rado for a long time. What the hell did Mrado know? The more he thought about it, the more obvious it seemed that Rado'd never trusted him.

He kept certain things secret, like how crappy the laundromats/video-rental stores were working. Above all, he hadn't said anything about how he planned to rig the market division in his favor. Rado was probably ticked off about his demand for a bigger cut of the profits. Irked about the Kvarnen fiasco. Pure luck that he'd actually gotten away without a prison sentence. Meant an extra bonus for the Yugos' own lawyer, Martin Thomasson.

Mrado needed to insure himself against Rado's capriciousness. He ought to talk more with Nenad.

On the bright side: Mrado'd dealt with Jorge. Best of all: Mrado was needed to divide up the market in the gangster war.

Wet snowflakes were falling. The windshield wipers were moving back and forth on the lowest setting. He turned up the warm air blowing toward the window. His hands were resting on the wheel. His movements felt stiff—the bulletproof vest was heavy.

He took the exit toward Tullinge. Followed the signs.

Seven minutes later, he'd found the place. A row of low gray storage buildings. Snow on the roofs. Green containers lined up. Ads for a recycling company on the façade of one of the buildings. The area was fenced in. Mrado knew where the Bandidos' bunker was, and it wasn't here. Still, this felt like their home turf. On the other hand, if they messed with him, they'd have to count their losses—in lives.

He parked the car. Remained sitting for a minute. Made sure the switchblade was in its place in his boot. Pulled out his revolver. The chamber was loaded. No bullet in the circuit—honest old safety measure. Finally, he sent Ratko a text. *I'm on my way in. Will be in touch in max two hours. /M*

Took a deep breath.

The first time he'd gone alone to a meeting. Ratko was usually at his side.

Squeezed his eyes shut for ten seconds.

No wrong moves today.

He stepped out of the car. Big snowflakes settled on his eyebrows. Poor visibility.

Farther away, on the other side of the fence, two people were walking toward him. Mrado remained standing where he was. Hands at his sides. The people came into better view. Big guys. Leather jackets, patches on their breast pockets: the Bandidos logo. One had a dark, full beard, probably a *blatte*. Bandanna on his head. The other was a blondie with a pockmarked face.

The bearded one pulled off a leather glove and extended his hand. "Mrado?"

Mrado shook his hand. "That's right. And you are?"

"Vice president of the Stockholm chapter. James Khalil. Are you alone?"

"That's what we agreed on. I keep my end of agreements. Does that surprise you?"

"Not at all. Welcome. You'll soon meet Haakonsen. Follow me."

Mrado knew the lingo. The key word was *respect*. Short, hard one-liners. No signs of insecurity. Second-guess when you can second-guess. Respectfully.

They walked toward one of the containers. The Bandidos boys' boots made deep impressions in the snow. Thirty or so yards farther off, a truck engine rumbled to a start. Drove out of the area. Mrado took note of several other noises coming from the same direction. Understood that normal work was actually being done on the premises.

James turned a key in a gigantic padlock hanging on a freight container. Opened it. Turned on a lamp. Mrado saw a table. Three chairs. A couple of bottles on the table. A construction site lamp suspended from a steel setting in the ceiling. Simple. Practical. Smart.

Before Mrado took a step in, he said, "I assume the place has been secured."

James looked at him. Seemed to consider piling on the sarcasm but then thought better of it. "Of course," he said. "We work according the same principles as you do. To act but not be seen."

James pulled out one of the chairs. Kept his leather jacket on. Offered Mrado a seat. The guy with the pockmarked face stayed outside the container. James sat down. Offered him a drink. Poured out whiskey for Mrado. They exchanged pleasantries. Sipped the whiskey. Waited in silence.

Three minutes passed.

Mrado thought, If he's not here in five, I'm out.

He lifted his gaze from the glass and looked at James. Raised one eyebrow. James understood.

"He'll be here any minute. It's not our intention to keep you waiting."

The answer was enough for Mrado. Important that they really knew whom they were dealing with.

Two minutes later, the hatch to the container was opened. Jonas Haakonsen walked in, hunched over.

Mrado got up. They shook hands.

Haakonsen sat down on the third chair. James poured out whiskey.

Jonas Haakonsen: at least six two, hair in a ponytail, and a thin blond beard. Bloodshot eyes. Leather jacket with the customary patches. On the back: *Bandidos MC, Stockholm, Sweden*. The logo in big block letters, surrounded by embroidered machetes. He had a crazed look in his eye. Reminded Mrado of what he'd seen in the faces of some of Arkan's men. Glazed eyes, shark eyes. Psychotic warrior eyes. Could go to attack mode at any moment.

Haakonsen was the kind of man you'd take a mile detour to avoid bumping into. The dude could silence an entire chow hall just by opening his mouth.

He took off his leather jacket. Apparently, the chill in the container didn't faze him. He wore a leather vest under the jacket. Under the vest: a long-sleeved black T-shirt with the text *We are the people your parents warned you about.* His neck: covered in tattoos. On one of his earlobes: the *SS* lightning bolts. On the other earlobe: the letters *BMC*—Bandidos MC.

Mrado didn't give much for the attitude. But the eyes. He knew what those eyes'd seen. Everyone knew. Jonas Haakonsen as a nineteen-year-old in Denmark. Leader of a gang of guys from south Copenhagen who robbed post offices and pushed lighter drugs. They made a big hit, the post office in Skanderborg's mall. Three guys. Rushed in right when the armored van was about to pick up the banknotes. Their weapons: a sawed-off shotgun and two axes. One of the guards thought fast. Locked the bills into a security bag. But Haakonsen thought faster, grabbed the security bag—and the guard. The robbers switched cars somewhere on the freeway. Drove out into the Danish countryside. The guard was in the trunk, like in an American gangster flick. He was found three days later, staggering along a road near Skanderborg. Delirious, with a T-shirt wrapped around his head. Coagulated blood everywhere. The EMTs removed the T-shirt. The guard's eyes were poked out. Haakonsen'd asked him for the combination to open the security bag. The guard hadn't known it, but Haakonsen'd been persistent. The guard hadn't had anything to say. Haaksonsen'd popped the man's eyes out with his thumbs. One at a time. He managed to stay on the lam for three weeks. Then they got him. Haakonsen was slammed with only five years, because he was so young. He caged out after three. Angrier than ever.

Haakonsen downed a gulp of whiskey. Then, with a light Danish accent: "So, the infamous Mrado. Floored any bouncers recently?"

"It happens, it happens," Mrado said, and laughed. "Even I've gotta stay in shape, right?" Mrado, surprised. Didn't know a guy like Haakonsen knew about the Kvarnen incident.

"And how is the Godfather himself?" Haakonsen went on.

"Just dandy. Radovan is alive and well. Business is booming. And you?"

"Better than ever. The Bandidos are in Stockholm to stay. You'll have to watch out."

A joke or a warning?

"Watch out for what? Greasy-fingered kids with biker dreams?"

"No, I'm not talking about the HA."

Mrado and Haakonsen laughed loudly. James grinned.

The tension lifted. They talked about Mrado's Benz, about the weather, about the latest news in their world, that a man from the Naser gang'd been offed with a ballpoint pen. According to Haakonsen, the job'd been professionally done: "Hitting the right spot with a pen isn't so hard, but the trick is, you gotta twist it around so you kill with the first jab."

Ten minutes in, Mrado interrupted the conversation to cut to the chase. "I think you know why I wanted to see you." He looked Haakonsen in the eye.

"I can only suspect. A little bird whispered in my ear that you've already talked to Magnus Lindén and Naser."

"So you know what I'm after?"

"My qualified guess is that you want us to end the war with the HA. You want the other gangs to cool it?"

"That's about right. But let me explain."

"In a bit. First, I have to make a couple of things clear. We are men of honor. I am sure that you Serbs have your rules. We have ours, in any case. The Bandidos are a family. If you hurt one of us, you hurt us all. Like an animal—if you cut one paw, the whole body feels the pain. Two months ago, Jonny 'Bonanza' Carlgren was shot dead in Södertälje, in the middle of the square. Bonanza'd been at the liquor store with his wife and two of his brothers. Four shots to the stomach, but the first one, it was in his back. In front of his woman. He bled to death in thirty minutes. You get me. They put the first shot in his back. He didn't even have time to turn around."

"With all due respect, I know all that."

"Just let me finish."

Mrado backed up. Wanted to keep the mood good. Nodded.

"Bonanza was my brother. Do you understand. My Bandidos

brother. We don't forget. Nothing can get us to stop what has to be done. The Hells Angels are gonna pay. It's gonna cost 'em. A fucking fortune. We popped the guy who planned Bonanza a month ago. Now we're gonna get the guy who pulled the trigger."

They were quiet for ten seconds, their eyes glued on each other.

"You've got every right to avenge a fallen brother. But, as you said, you've already done that. If I'm not mistaken, you guys shot Micke Lindgren. One all. What matters is that you're only tripping yourselves up if you keep going. The situation's just that simple, even if I sympathize. It's not just about the Bandidos and the HA. Jonas, we've been in this town much longer than you guys. You're big now, and I like your style, definitely, but you were pedaling a BMX and chewing gum when I first started breaking human bones. You'd robbed a couple of bodegas when I'd made my first million on blow. I know the opportunities this city has to offer. There's room for all of us. But we have to act right. Why are we in a fucking container right now? In the middle of winter? You know the answer. You and me, we're both targeted by that damn Nova Project. The cop offensive. They're on it. If you just plan your next kick to the HA's balls instead of planning your defense against the next Nova hit, you'll be tripping BMC. We're splitting ourselves into pieces in these wars while they pick us up, one by one. With my plan, we break these cop faggots."

Mrado kept convincing. Haakonsen was opposed to everything that had to do with peace with the HA, but he listened to the rest. Nodded at times. Delivered his own monologues. Got fired up. James Khalil was invisible, sat completely silent. Mrado and Haakonsen discussed market shares for an hour.

The Bandidos president bought the basic concept.

Finally, they reached a preliminary agreement.

Mrado downed his glass. Haakonsen stood up. James got up. Opened the hatch. Mrado stepped out first. Outside, the snow kept coming down.

Homeward bound in the Benz. Mrado thought the agreement was pitch-perfect. The Bandidos would reduce their coat-check racketeering in the inner city. Would reduce their blow biz in the inner city. Would do whatever financial crime they wanted. Would increase the other protection-racket stuff. Would increase the marijuana trade.

Perfect. That served Rado. That served Nenad. But most of all, that served Mrado. The coat-check business was saved, which meant that Mrado's seat was secured.

He called Ratko. They chatted for a minute or so.

He decided to call Nenad, too, his closest man among the colleagues. Told him what'd just happened. Nenad: clearly pleased.

"Nenad, maybe you and me should start talking about some business of our own one of these days. What do you think?"

The first time Mrado'd suggested anything that bridged on betrayal of Radovan. If Nenad was the wrong man, Mrado could count his days in computer code—one or zero.

34

The strategy: to import directly. Buy at the source, South America. In this case, no direct deal with a syndicate. They weren't that big yet. But Abdulkarim's connections plus Jorge's brains might equal jackpot.

Import was the vital point. As large and low-risk as possible.

So far, they'd brought home smaller portions. Through mules, through the mail, in shampoo bottles, in toothpaste tubes, bags of candy. Expansion demanded larger quantities.

Jorge's main job: to work home the product. To push the stuff wasn't a problem; the bottleneck was working it home.

Jorge'd spent the past couple of weeks as follows: in the car outside Radovan's; at Fahdi's place, planning import; south of the city, networking.

He needed kale to hate Rado.

Needed Rado hate to keep making kale.

Life on the lam. Hate, plan, sleep—life was simple.

Everything at the mercy of Abdulkarim. A miracle that the Arab accepted Jorge's hate project. He probably didn't grasp the scope, didn't know the Latino planned on completely breaking the Yugo boss. Jorge indirectly owed the Arab loyalty for taking him under his wing, giving him a roof over his head and medical attention after Mrado's assault. Abdulkarim'd invested heavy in Jorge-boy. Really, it couldn't be measured in money. Abdul never said anything. But Jorge knew: He expected returns on his investment.

Today the first serious import of his own would go down, been planned for months. The Brazilian courier. *De miedo*.

The rule was to use someone who wouldn't attract attention. Jorge knew more than he ought to know about her—Silvia Pasqual de Pizzaro. The contact person from São Paulo'd told him. She was twenty-nine years old. From Campo Grande, near Paraguay, where unemployment was sky-high. Only finished elementary school. Had her first baby, a daughter, at eighteen. Since then, she'd been living with her kid and her mother. The second kid came at twenty, the third at twenty two. All the babydaddies were long gone. Silvia's mother worked as a seamstress but had respiratory problems.

He could figure it out easy: The little family was on the brink of total destitution. Silvia Pasqual would do anything for a couple of reais. Tragic? No. That's life. You have to take risks if you want to get somewhere. Jorge knew.

Jorge gave the how-to orders. Two cabin bags were bought. Make: Samsonite—large, magnesium-light. The genius devil in the details: The retractable handle was made of aluminum—hollow. Drilled into with a 0.1-inch drill under the rubber handle at the top. Six hundred grams of blow fit in each bag's handle. Total value on the street: at least three million. Easy money.

The final pour-in was pulverized mothballs. In the unlucky case of dogs, the sharp smell might distract their sniffing. The drill hole was welded shut. The rubber handles were put back. They could check the bags' contents as thoroughly as they wanted. They could check Silvia all night, feel her up everywhere, X-ray her, make her sit on a toilet in a customs holding pen for three days. They'd find *nada*.

But that wasn't enough. He nagged at himself: Do it right. Jorge'd heard about tons of smart freight methods that'd been blown 'cause customs got suspicious. If they thought something was shady, they wouldn't let it go. Jorge's solution lay in careful instructions to Silvia, conveyed through his contact in Brazil. She learned the spiel by heart: She was going to Sweden to visit relatives who lived outside Stockholm. Stay for a week. He gave her a number to give in case they asked: one of Jorge's prepaid cell numbers. He gave her an address: a house that belonged to Fahdi's godfather. She got over fifty bucks' worth of clothes—couldn't be obvious that she was an impoverished illiterate from the Brazilian *campo*. He had her learn simple English phrases. Maybe most important of all: She flew via London; the ticket wouldn't show she'd flown from Rio.

Should be just right.

Saturday afternoon. A clear day. Finally.

Jorge leaned against the fence that surrounded the yellowish church at Odenplan. In front of him was the Hotel Oden. Jorge'd been standing there for two hours already. Waiting for Silvia Pasqual de Pizzaro.

She should've been there over an hour ago. Jorge: a little anxious, but everything was probably under control.

He called the airport. The plane was delayed by thirty minutes. Maybe the woman'd had trouble with the buses. With the passport controllers, the dogs, the airport police. Jorge hoped for *suerte*'s smile.

Their two cars were parked farther down on Karlbergsvägen, within sight. One boosted by Petter. The other rented by Mehmed, using a fake driver's license. *Elegantish.*

His co-dees, Petter and Mehmed—hustlers with skill. Made the blow go like never before. Jorge organized from the top. Petter and Mehmed kept the buzz alive with underlings and dealers, kept their contacts fresh, sold, spread rumors. Produced profit. Both were housing-project kids from the outer boroughs. Both pulled a line themselves now and then.

Petter: south of south side supporter. Thought he was abroad as soon as he entered the inner-city limits. Soccer fanatic. Party boy. Perfect sales channel to the Swedish working class.

Mehmed: Tunisian. *Blatte* bad boys' distributor. Loved to coast in his Audi A4 along the cracked streets of Botkyrka. A hero on his turf: the asphalt jungle.

Now Mehmed was waiting in one of the cars. Was gonna meet Silvia at her hotel room as soon as she got there. Empty the Samsonites of blow. Go down to the car. Drive to Petter's apartment. Give him the gear. Petter would weigh it, check the grade, repackage. Then bring the bags out to Jorge. The plan ought to be waterproof.

Jorge's job was mostly to survey the transaction. Petter and Mehmed were good guys—but also typical guys who'd do anything for cash. Like shovel the snow on their own. Blow Abdukarim and Jorge off. No one trusted anyone. But J-boy was smarter than that, had gotten an extra involved, an IT guy who used to be a customer of Jorge's in earlier days. The IT dude was just payrolled for the day. Was gonna put on a little show for the sake of security. The dude was sitting in his car farther up the street. Jorge commended himself: What a fuckin' ill plan.

He waited. Reminded him of the wait outside Radovan's house. But the difference was that here he knew something would happen.

Was thinking. What'd surfaced about Radovan? Above all, Jorge's hate'd surfaced at full force. Stronger with every day. He breathed hate. Ate hate. Dreamed hate. To whip Rado with a baseball bat, across his kneecaps, mouth, forehead. Shoot Radovan in the gut with a shotgun. He tried to cool down. Think pragmatically instead. How could he nail Rado without risking his own livelihood?

Darko's info was helpful. Jorge'd looked up that Nenad guy. The dude bossed over huge stores of whores. Jorge recognized the name from way back; Nenad was a well-known personality on the blow circuit, too. No one knew how. Everyone just knew that. No one could connect Rado and Nenad. But it would come. Jorge felt certain. It was a lead anyway.

Jorge asked around among contacts who visited hookers. Not hard to find—Fahdi was one.

Got bored waiting for Silvia Pasqual de Pizzaro.

Jorge scrolled through his memories. A couple of days ago Fahdi'd taken him to the brothel, an apartment in Hallonbergen. External balconies, echoing stairwells, dried-up potted plants. Fahdi made three calls before they went. Explained how it worked: mouth-to-mouth method. All the clients gave their real names at their first visit, told the brothel madam, Jelena. After that, they used aliases and passwords. Agreement: The real name was not recorded anywhere. All the whores worked under aliases. Visitors had to be recommended by someone else before they were let in. The madam probably checked up on people somehow.

There was an anonymous website—the server was somewhere in England—with pictures of the girls. You could sit at home, pick and choose. Either they came to you or you went to the apartment in Hallonbergen. Fahdi preferred Hallonbergen.

Jorge'd imagined something lavish/luxurious.

Instead, the dankest shit J-boy'd ever seen. Bad energy washed over him as soon as the door opened. A red wallpapered hall. Two stained velvet couches and a fake Persian carpet. Stank of sweat and smoke. In the background: Tom Jones. What bullshit.

Jorge and Fahdi kept their jackets on. A woman approached them. Heavily made-up face. Short hair, dyed red. Enormous bust. Long, curled fingernails that had to be plastic. Fake pearls hung around her neck. Fingers studded with stones. Strangest outfit Jorge'd ever seen. A black tailored blazer, looked proper enough, but when she turned around he saw the blazer had a deep V cut into the back, almost all the way down to her *culo*. She spoke bad, broken Swedish. Recognized Fahdi. They exchanged pleasantries. Jorge understood—it was the madam herself, Jelena.

Jorge and Fahdi sat down. Waited.

After fifteen minutes, a man walked into the hall. Turned his face away as he left the apartment. Silent agreement: They'd never seen each other. The woman came and got Fahdi. Through the kitchen door, Jorge glimpsed a coffeepot on the counter. Bizarre feeling. The brothel madam was having her coffee break, like at any regular workplace.

Five minutes later, the woman showed Jorge into a room. A wide bed stood in the middle. Poorly made. An armchair. Shades pulled down. On the bed: the whore.

Jorge remained standing in the doorway. Looked at her. She was thin. Small nose. Maybe been pretty once. Today, expressionless. The clothes: a gray tank top, black tights, miniskirt, high-heeled shoes. Classic hooker look.

No, he was wrong. She was still pretty and was checking him out as much as he eyed her.

"Hi," Jorge said.

"Hi, hot stuff. What up? You first time here?" Thick Eastern European accent, but still comprehensible. Good. Jorge'd expressly asked for one who spoke Swedish.

"How much for a suck?"

"Four hundred. For you. You hot."

"Skip the talk. I'll pay five hundred if you'll tell me some stuff."

"What? Talk dirty?"

"No, I wanna know how you got to Sweden."

The girl froze. Not unexpected. Probably had strict instructions not to talk about anything but fuck/cunt/cock with anyone.

Jorge tried to make her relax. "Forget it. I'll pay three hundred for the BJ."

The girl agreed. Unbuttoned his pants.

Tugged down his boxers.

Jorge, no erection.

She started sucking him.

Felt strange. Filthy.

Jorge was surprised—hadn't thought he'd feel anything at all. He asked her to stop. Felt nauseous.

She didn't seem to notice anything. Or, more likely, she could have cared less that he'd gone pale and sat down on the bed.

Two minutes of silence. He fingered the money.

Made another go of it. "I'll give you a G on top of the three hundred if you tell me something about Nenad." He held up two five-hundred-kronor bills.

Strangely enough, she started talking. Jorge's theory: Now that he'd dished for sex, he couldn't be a cop. Instead, he'd become a creature she knew well—a john was always a john.

"Me, I not know much. But all know Nenad."

Jorge thought her voice sounded frail. "So, what've you heard about him?"

"Nenad in charge. Nenad danger for life. They scared of him."

"Who? You girls or your pimps?"

"All. Girls, pimps. Johns. He done stuff to people. He work for Mr. R."

Jorge thought, She's saying a lot but really nothing. "What's he done?" he asked.

"Rape, beat, sick stuff, use girls for sick stuff. All scared. But me, no. Not give shit about him."

"And Mr. R., what do they say about him?"

She looked up. Jorge thought it looked like she was smiling.

"Mr. R. They talk, say him always with guns, him kill if offend, him control this city. Boss Nenad, who boss little pimps, who boss us. They say R. ice-cold. All power. Spread bad air. But me, I think exaggerate. Mr. R. not ice-cold. Mr. R. not spread bad air. Mr. R. spread Hugo Boss smell."

Jorge sat beside her on the bed. She was special. He couldn't say what it was, but she had something. For sure.

A knock at the door. Jorge got up.

The madam poked her head in the door. Asked how long they were gonna go at it. Saw they were both dressed. Jorge on his way out. She nodded.

The madam led him out.

In the hall, Fahdi was talking to a guy wearing a hoodie under a blazer.

Jorge and Fahdi left the apartment.

"Who you talkin' to when I came out?"

"The girls' pimp. The guy in charge. What a fucking cushy job."

Jorge woke from his reverie. Checked his cell. Back to the present— Odenplan, waiting for the courier: Silvia Pasqual de Pizzaro.

Jorge saw the number on the screen. Recognized the digits before he heard the signal. It was Mehmed.

He was wondering why nothing'd happened yet.

Silvia should've been at the hotel ages ago. Something was crooked.

They hung up.

He kept waiting.

Stared at the Hotel Oden.

A taxi pulled up on the other side of the street: Top Cab. Fixed price from Arlanda Aiport: 350 kronor. The driver stepped out first. Opened the trunk, lifted out two Samsonite bags. A woman got out of the passenger seat.

Obviously her. Dressed in black jeans, black wool jacket. Hat with earflaps.

Silvia Pasqual de Pizzaro. Finally.

Rolled the bags behind her to the hotel. The sand that'd been poured on the icy sidewalk crunched under the wheels.

Jorge remained where he was. Mehmed stayed in the car, waiting for a green light from Jorge.

Jorge eyed the entrance to the hotel for ten minutes. No one else went in or out. Good sign. If the 5-o were on their backs, they'd probably want to bust the hotel, pluck the courier at the handoff.

Jorge called the reception desk at the hotel. Asked if the woman'd checked in. He got the direct number to her room. Called Silvia. She answered. Shit English. She'd made it fine through customs. No one'd followed her. Everything seemed clear.

Jorge texted Mehmed. Saw him go into the hotel. His instructions were to order lunch and send it up to Silvia. When the waiter came back down, Mehmed would ask if Silvia'd been alone in the room. If the answer was yes, time to go up and collect the blow.

Jorge'd walked around to the other corner of the hotel. Saw the entrance from a side angle.

Waited.

Phone in hand. If someone suspicious-looking entered the Hotel Oden, he'd call Mehmed, stat. Plan B, in case of a chase: Mehmed would drop the gear out the window toward Hagagatan. Jorge could pick the shit up there. Book it to the car. Step on it.

Nothing shady happened.

Darkness was falling. The hotel's vertical neon yellow sign glowed softly.

Ten minutes passed. Jorge'd calculated that it'd take fifteen minutes to get the blow out of the bags.

Five more minutes passed.

Mehmed came out. Scratched his head—the sign that everything was under control. He had a plastic shopping bag from the NK department store in one hand. Started walking toward his car. Jorge watched from a distance. No one was following, as far as he could tell.

Jorge saw his very own controller, the IT dude, get out of his car. Timing smooth as hell.

Walked quickly after Mehmed. Caught up with him right at the car. Exchanged greetings. Jorge knew what they were saying to each other. Traded memorized phrases. A lot of people on the street at this time on a weekend. Made it worthwhile to put on a show. The IT dude asked loudly what Mehmed'd bought at NK. Mehmed told him about a jacket. Jorge saw the IT guy look into the bag.

It all went fast. The IT dude put his hand in the bag.

Pulled his hand out.

Licked his finger.

Tasted.

They talked for another forty seconds. Split up. Mehmed got into his car. Started it.

The IT guy kept walking down the street, his cell in hand.

Jorge got a text: *Clean*.

Neither Silvia nor Mehmed'd ripped him off. The gear in the NK bag was real. The IT dude was a genius call.

Jorge started his car. Pulled in behind Mehmed's car, up by the red light at Dalagatan.

Then they drove off.

They were heading to Sätra. Petter's apartment. Jorge looked around. Compared cars. Took note if anyone'd been driving behind them unusually long. He and Mehmed'd decided on a more roundabout route than necessary. If anyone trailed them, they'd know right away. Jorge wouldn't make the same mistake as when Mrado and Ratko'd followed him so easily into the countryside.

They took St. Eriksgatan. Over to Kungsholmen. Between Mehmed and Jorge the whole way: a red Saab 900. Behind Jorge the entire time: a Jaguar. But Jorge and Mehmed'd driven the straight shot so far. At this point, there was nothing strange about the same cars caravanning the whole way to Fridhemsplan.

Vigilance.

They took a left after Fridhemsplan. Through the Rålambshov Park. The red Saab was still sandwiched between them.

Up on Västerbron bridge. It was dark out by now. The skeleton of the bridge was illuminated from below by floodlights. Jorge thought it was the city's prettiest spot.

Nerves electrified. Thought he could feel the fabric of his shirt move over the left side of his chest with every heartbeat. To himself: Do this right. Become seven pounds richer.

Something in the red Saab caught his eye—a movement in the backseat.

Jorge looked again.

Something was off.

They came to the crest of the bridge.

The city's silhouette draped in a dark blue shroud. The narrow bodies of the church spires like needles in his field of vision.

Jorge picked up his cell phone. Called Mehmed. Told him to change route at the end of the bridge.

Jorge kept his eye on the Saab. Saw more movements in the backseat. The people were putting something on. He hit his high beams. Shone straight into the back of the Saab.

The men in the backseat were as visible as on a sunny summer's day.

They were putting something on that looked like heavy vests. Could only be one thing—bulletproof vests.

Cunt.

Jorge slammed on the breaks. His forehead smacked into the windshield.

He looked toward the Saab. It stopped, as well.

Looked toward Mehmed's car. He'd stopped, too, about thirty yards farther up. Probably hadn't clocked more than that something was whack.

Jorge looked farther out, over Hornstull.

Blue lights every fucking where.

Mierda.

Quick calculation. The Saab between Jorge and Mehmed's car was crooked. The enemy, the cops? He had to act now.

The dudes in the Saab stepped out of the car. Three. Two of them ran toward Mehmed's car.

Someone behind Jorge honked. The natural question in rush-hour traffic: Why'd someone panic-braked in the middle of the bridge?

Jorge leapt out of his car. Ran toward Mehmed's car.

The guys from the Saab turned around. Ran faster.

Jorge's luck—the training from his escape still did the trick. He had speed. Reached Mehmed's car at the same time as the men from the Saab.

Everything went so fast.

One of the men opened the door to Mehmed's car. One turned to Jorge. Grabbed hold of his hand, tried to get him in some kind of grip. Mehmed yelled to Jorge, "Fuckin' run. It's the Five-Oh."

The third man, who came running from the Saab, threw himself at Mehmed and tried to push him down into the seat. The guy holding Jorge's arm pulled out a pair of handcuffs. Roared, "Police. You are being arrested on suspicion of possessing illegal drugs. Don't fuckin' give us a hard time. The entire force is waiting for you down there at Hornstull." Jorge panicked. Kicked with all his might at the cop's cock. The man howled. Only one thought in Jorge's head: the blow in the trunk. Got a hold of the handle. Opened the trunk. Grabbed the NK bag. The cop standing by the door to Mehmed's car threw himself at Jorge. Jorge took a step to the side. Remained free. The cop who'd taken the kick to the balls pulled a gun, yelled something.

Jorge ran. The cop who'd tried to throw himself at him picked up the chase. Jorge accelerated. The man at his heels was fast. Jorge was faster. Thank God for the time at Österåker and the little training he'd done lately. The cop behind him hollered.

Jorge: focused. Come on now, pick up the pulse, *hombre*. Light steps. Long steps.

He ran along the bridge's railing. People got out of their cars and stared at the mass of flashing lights moving its way up the bridge in the opposite lane.

In Jorge's head: Run now, J-boy. No Asics DuoMax with super soles. No laps around the blocks at Österåker in his legs. Hardly any training except for some jump rope in recent months.

Still, he was fast.

His feet rolled with each step.

The pavement pounded.

The Stockholm night screamed blue.

He turned his head. His lead'd increased. The cop faggot was too winded.

Jorge saw Långholmen under the bridge. How far could the jump be? Worse than the twenty-three feet from the Österåker wall?

He didn't give a fuck. Did it once. Could do it again.

Jorge, master escape artist. Chain-busting legend. Nothing would stop him.

He gained momentum. Leapt up on the railing. Looked down. Hard to see in the dark. The handle of the NK bag hung in the crook of his arm. He swung himself down, hands gripping the railing. Should reduce the fall by about six feet. Let go.

Fell.

35

JW sat on the bus to the Skavsta Airport, thinking, Two hours of restlessness ahead. God, I regret not flying from Arlanda Airport. So much closer.

He tried to play games on his phone: mini-golf, Chesswizz, Arkanoid. He'd become a master at downloading games. Was even starting to beat the phone at chess. Pride mingled with thrill: How good could he get?

Abdulkarim was flying two days later with British Airways, business class. From Arlanda.

Fahdi was flying SAS. Also from Arlanda. Typical.

He just had to stick it out. Deal. They were spreading their flights out over different carriers, different times, different locations. According to Abdulkarim's philosophy, caution was a shortcut. JW thought, Shortcut for who? Not for me, that much is for fucking sure—two hours on a bus, at least an hour and a half wait estimated at Skavsta, then from Stansted Airport into central London, at least two hours. Congrats.

He started a new game of chess. Had trouble concentrating, was always sensitive to stress. Started searching for the slip of paper where he'd written down his confirmation number—Ryanair didn't even do paper tickets.

Skavsta Airport, in JW's opinion, was an embodiment of the word *beige*. Broad fluorescent tubing lit up the departure hall. A white propeller plane was suspended from the ceiling, which looked like it was made of thick metal pipes. The floor was made of laminated plastic. The walls were of laminated plastic. The check-in counters were made of green—guess what?—laminated plastic.

A line unfurled itself from two counters. JW set his bags down. One of them was a large Louis Vuitton. Price: twelve thousand kronor. The only problem at a place like Skavsta was that everyone would assume it was a fake. But there was still a risk it'd be stolen by the baggage loaders if they realized it was real.

He kept playing chess. Pushed the bags in front of him with his foot. Focused on his phone. The line took over forty minutes. He thought, Ryanair—go shit yourselves.

After he'd checked in, the only carry-on he had was a black shoulder bag from Prada.

Security was overambitious. He guessed the Brits were scared of Muslim bombers. JW hoped that Abdulkarim traveled without his prayer hat. JW's Hermès belt set off the metal detector. He had to take it off and run it through the X-ray machine in a blue plastic tray.

After security, JW called Sophie. They chatted. She already knew about his trip and with which friends he was traveling. After a couple of minutes, she repeated her question from earlier: "When do I get to meet them anyway?"

JW changed the subject. "Can you recommend some sweet bars in Mayfair?" Sophie'd been to London more times than JW'd been to Stockholm before he moved there. She listed some places. They talked on: about Jet Set Carl's latest party, Nippe's latest chick, Lollo's latest C trip. Nothing about JW's buds.

He was hungry. According to the signage, there was a restaurant around here somewhere.

He found it—a supergrimy place. Three dishes on the menu: fish and chips, spaghetti Bolognese, and pork chops with french fries and béarnaise sauce. In front of him in line: two seventeen-year-old girls wearing Palestine scarves and wool hats pulled down low. They complained about the lack of vegetarian options.

The cashier muttered, "You could have french fries with béa."

The activist broads declined. Whined for a bit and then went to the airport kiosk and bought Snickers and soda.

JW ordered fish and chips and grabbed a seat. Waited for his number to be called.

He pulled out the latest issue of *GQ*, which he'd bought at the bus station. Absentmindedly skimmed an article about the latest florid fashion for men. Really, he was uninterested. Just needed something to busy his fingers.

The food arrived. At least half a pound of thick white sauce covered the fish—heart-attack grub, yes siree. He ate, thought about calling his mom when he was finished. Tell her what he'd found out about Camilla's relationship with one of her Komvux teachers. Or about the Ferrari.

There was so much that was shady. Still, it wasn't a good idea. Would make her head spin with unnecessary thoughts. Better that the police finish their investigation. Better that it be done professionally instead of through JW's own inquiries. Find solutions. Inspect, interrogate, investigate. Sort out Camilla's life.

Boarding at the gate. People lined up. JW felt tired; it would feel good to sleep on the plane.

A second security check. They checked passports again. The passengers were ushered outside, where it was piss-cold and windy. Then into the plane. Even the flight attendants were uglier than on flights from Arlanda. He found a seat, set the Prada bag down on the floor. A stewardess asked him to stow it in the overhead bin. JW felt pissy. Gave her attitude. The stewardess didn't even try to be polite. The bag went up.

Fuckingmotherfuckingcuntfucker. JW promised himself: business class next time.

They ran through the safety procedures. JW read his magazine.

The plane started up.

He leaned back. Closed his eyes.

Relaxed.

"Beep! Beep!" someone yelled behind him. He turned around. Thought, No end to the misery. JW hadn't seen them when he boarded. Behind him was a group of soccer fans, already smashed. One of them was shrieking himself red in the face. The other guys roared hysterically.

A flight attendant walked down the isle with determined steps. "Excuse me, can I help you with something?"

The guy pointed to a button in the ceiling. "I pressed the button here, but no one came, so I beeped myself."

The guys doubled over.

The flight attendant fired off a snide remark. More laughter.

What a day. JW thanked God for his MP3 player, but the soccer asses' laughter even penetrated the music.

Two hours later: landing at Stansted. JW followed the sleepy flock of passengers out through the passport control to the baggage claim. Played Chesswizz on his phone. His two bags came riding on the baggage belt. They looked unharmed. Relief.

Out through customs. Took the escalators down to Stansted Express.

JW calculated his total travel time. The flight: around two hours. With the accompanying trips—buses, subways, taxi—plus waiting, it would total six hours. Ryanair blew horse cock.

The train rolled into the station. An automated woman's voice blazoned out: "This train leaves for London's Liverpool Street Station in three minutes."

He got on. Sat so he could see his Louis Vuitton bag in the luggage rack. Fished out his *GQ*. England was significantly warmer than Sweden. He sweated. Took off his Dior coat. Draped it over his lap.

The train conductor rocked an ultra-Cockney dialect. JW barely understood what he was saying when he suggested JW buy a return ticket now.

JW got out his cell phone and texed Abdulkarim, telling him he'd landed. Sent another text to Sophie: *Hi, hot stuff. Just landed. It's warm here. Slept on the plane. What are you up to? Talk in a couple of days. Luv /J.*

A couple of hours later he was splayed out on the hotel bed, tired and still wet from the shower. He'd made a few calls to Fredrik's and Jet Set Carl's friends in London. Wanted to get plans lined up for the evening. Test the nightlife. Party and, above all, network.

The hotel was in Bayswater. A tourist trap—wall-to-wall carpeting in every nook. Even in the bathroom.

He'd booked rooms for Abdulkarim and Fahdi, too; he was going to cancel them tomorrow and get safe rooms at a luxury hotel instead if anything seemed fishy. In JW's opinion: a fucking hassle. According to Abdulkarim, their phones could be tapped. The police could find out where they were staying, whom they were seeing, what they were doing in London. Therefore the quick changeability.

JW thought about Sophie. She'd really pressured him to tell her who his other friends were. What was she after? Why was she interested? He still didn't know if it was intimacy she really wanted. After all, superficiality was a virtue in their crowd. In his darkest moments, JW suspected that she saw through him. That the show he'd been putting on was coming close to curtain. And why was it so important? Why didn't he ever feel like he was good enough? What did he want to achieve? The last question mirrored another question: What'd Camilla wanted to achieve? Something'd been driving her. JW couldn't decide if it was his job or the police's to find out what.

36

Things had to turn soon. Things would turn.

He would get everything squared away. Radovan's frostiness—a bad omen. R. sensed that Mrado didn't see him as he had Jokso. And there was a difference. Jokso'd been a true guru, the man who'd brought the Serbs to the absolute top of Stockholm's underworld. United, strong, loyal. Radovan didn't have what it took. A weakling, a divider. Two-faced. Mrado was beginning to envision a path of his own: Maybe one day it'd be him and Nenad, alone.

But it would work out. He wasn't gonna think about all that crap today. Today was his day of visitation with Lovisa. Planned. Pictured. Pined for. Wednesday night to Thursday night. Too short—but still.

The night before, they'd rented the latest Disney movie. Popped popcorn. Drunk orange soda. Mrado'd fried meatballs and boiled potatoes. Even made sauerkraut. Helped Lovisa peel, cut, and squirt the ketchup. Unfortunately, she didn't like the sauerkraut, the only Serbian thing on her plate.

What an idyllic fucking scene.

The whole day was theirs. Last time, it'd all gone to hell. Mrado hadn't been able to pick Lovisa up from school, had to flex his muscles for a junkie in Tumba who'd threatened Nenad. The guy'd gotten hold of Nenad's number somehow and called home to his wife and kids. Go ahead, shoot up and buy as much smack as you want, but don't disturb Nenad's family. Mrado and Ratko'd looked the bum up. Punished him: broken nose and severe cuts to the forehead. The effect of getting your head pounded into a concrete wall in a stairwell at Gödingevägen 13.

The duality: Mrado wanted to see his daughter, but he still often managed to fuck it up. He always regretted it after. Rationalized:

Someone's gotta make cash to give Lovisa a good life. Better that than just whining, like her mom, Annika "Cunt" Sjöberg, did.

It was eight-thirty. Lovisa was watching morning cartoons. Her hair, one big bird's nest. Mrado lingered in bed for three minutes. Got up. Kissed Lovisa on the forehead. Went down to the 7-Eleven and bought Tropicana with extra pulp, milk, and granola. Prepared breakfast: brewed coffee, poured out the juice, buttered a piece of bread for Lovisa.

They sat in front of the TV. Lovisa made a mess on the floor. Mrado drank coffee.

Two hours later, they were on their way to the Gärdet area of the city by bus. Mrado'd chosen not to drive because of all the complaints hurled at him about speeding with Lovisa in the car. Hated that he gave way to Annika's criticism, but it was better to be careful, at least in the inner city.

The snow lay like a thick white blanket over the big field by Gärdet. Lovisa talked about a snowman she'd built at school.

"Me and Olivia built the biggest one. We borrowed a carrot from the lunch ladies as a nose."

"That sounds really nice. How many snowballs did you use to make him?"

"Three. Then we put a hat on him. But the boys ruined it."

"That was mean of them. What did you do when they did that?"

"Told the teacher, of course."

Mrado could hardly believe it himself; he glanced around the bus. No one seemed to notice—here was the guy who'd crushed a junkie's head two weeks ago and now was being the perfect father figure.

They got off the bus at Tekniska Museet, the museum of technology.

Lovisa ran toward the machines and installations right outside the entrance. She was wearing a red puffy jacket with fluffy stuff around the collar. On her legs: green snow pants. On her feet: leather boots for kids. Mrado's contribution: the boots. His daughter wasn't gonna go around in crappy foam-rubber shoes.

His daughter was so full of life and careless energy. Just like he'd been as a kid in Södertälje. He remembered: As a three-year-old, Lovisa used to run headfirst downstairs—not a thought about falling. Just rush on down. Full attack. One thing was certain: Her energy wouldn't be wasted on the same stuff as his.

Mrado reached the installations. He was cold. Lovisa jumped up on a platform in front of something that looked like a giant satellite dish. Mrado walked up to her. Lovisa asked him to read the sign. Something about whispers being audible despite the distance. Lovisa didn't get it. Mrado understood.

Showed her. He walked over to an identical satellite dish twenty yards away.

"Stay there, Lovisa. Daddy's gonna show you something really cool."

The whispers were audible despite the distance, as if they'd been standing with their mouths up to each other's ears. Lovisa loved it. She whispered to him about her snowman. About Shrek. About Daddy's meatballs and sauerkraut the night before.

They laughed.

Inside the museum, they checked their coats and her snow pants. Mrado'd prepared himself—he was wearing a blazer under his jacket. Didn't want the holster to show. It smelled like a cafeteria. Mrado'd done his homework—after they made the rounds, they would have a snack in the café.

They walked from room to room. Teknorama: the museum's experimental wing for kids.

In one room: power measurements. Showed how you could become stronger than you really were. Pulleys/blocks/levers/screws/wedges. Mrado on the short end of a seesaw, Lovisa on the long end. Mrado: 265 pounds of pure muscle. Lovisa: fifty-seven pounds of girl. Still, her side weighed down. Mrado shot up. Seemed as though Lovisa was heavier than Daddy. Lovisa clucked. Mrado's spirit: laughed.

They went on. Tested machines/inventions/installations/mechanisms in every room. Lovisa chattered. Mrado asked questions. Swedish/Serbian mixed.

After they'd had a snack, they went home. Lovisa watched the Disney movie again. Mrado prepared a real lunch: sausage with whole-wheat macaroni, ketchup, and salad. They rested an hour on the couch. Napped. Lovisa in Mrado's arms. Mrado thought, I don't need anything more in life.

On their way out. Lovisa put on her snow pants and jacket. Mrado didn't give a shit if Annika complained—there was no way he was taking public transportation to the gym.

Four o'clock in the afternoon. Not a lot of people at the gym. Mrado worked his legs. Grimaced. Growled. Groaned.

Lovisa played on the mats on the floor. Mrado tried to smile between grimaces. Lovisa had been here before, knew the drill.

A guy from the reception desk crouched down by the mat. Talked baby talk. "What did you do with Daddy today?"

Mrado loved Lovisa's reply: "Why are you talking like Grandma?"

It was five-thirty. Mrado: watching the clock. The mood was already bad after the blunder two weeks ago when Lovisa'd waited for him for forty-five minutes outside school. Mrado'd been off cracking the junkie's skull. Finally, the teachers'd called Annika, who came and picked her up. Not good.

After the gym, they drove to Gröndal. The freeway was clogged with rush-hour traffic. Listened to Serbian music in the car. Lovisa tried to sing along.

Turned off above Stora Essingen. Drove down to Gröndal. Drove seventy in the forty-five zone. Mrado couldn't help himself. Hit the breaks. Did twenty on Gröndalsvägen. Mrado reined himself in. Kept to the speed limit.

Drove carefully all the way up to her apartment building.

Dropped her off at the curb. Waited in the car.

Saw her enter the key code to unlock the door to the apartment building, open the door with both hands—it was heavy—disappear inside.

Away.

He was elated, high on human warmth.

A day of fatherhood.

The day after his visitation day: back to reality. Over the past couple of months, Mrado'd met with the most important people/leaders of Stockholm and middle Sweden's underworld. Robbers/rapists/murderers/drug lords—it didn't matter what they'd done as long as they had influence.

Unanticipated success. Mrado, surprised. They listened, meditated, deliberated. Most of them came back with answers. They were in line with his thinking: Dealing with the pigs demanded a market division and an end to the war.

The result: The deal creating Stockholm's criminal cartels was taking shape. Could be a triumph for Mrado.

The downside: Nova Project reaped its victims, including some of the Yugos. Two of Goran's men'd been collared. On suspicion of aggravated tax fraud.

A summary of the market division: The Bandidos'd agreed to drop their coat-check racketeering and cocaine dealings in the inner city. Instead, they'd increase the protection racket, especially in the southern boroughs. The HA would increase their booze smuggling in all of middle Sweden. Reduce their protection racket. Expand whatever financial crime schemes they wanted. The Naser gang: difficult to sway. They were gonna keep running H as usual. The Original Gangsters: did CIT heists all over Sweden. Not really a competitive field. On the other hand, they'd promised to reduce their blow biz in the boroughs. They had the run of the northern boroughs. Fucked For Life kept the weed business in southern Stockholm, would reduce their scope in the north.

Mrado'd organized it all. Valued the different markets. Shares. Areas. Weighed. Analyzed. Talked to over forty different people. Lobbied. Buttered up when necessary. Been hard as bone when the situation demanded it.

Most people trusted him, treated him like a Yugo with honor. Saw the advantages to his proposal. Saw the risks with Nova.

Summa summarum: He was close to a market division. Best of all, the coat checks in the inner city, his own pet project, were becoming protected ground.

According to Mrado: He was a genius.

Left to convince: Magnus Lindén, the Wolfpack Brotherhood.

They were meeting up at the Golden Cave pub in Fittja. Neutral ground.

Mrado loved his Benz more than usual. It was the effect of the crayons Lovisa'd left behind. Mrado'd pinned the box on the dashboard like an icon. Crayola. Thought, Soon it'll be Wednesday again.

No traffic. Smooth driving. He thought about the Wolfpack Brotherhood.

Created by a couple of inmates at Kumla seven years ago. The founder was the self-appointed president, Danny "the Hood" Fitzpatrick. According to him, he got the idea of creating the Brotherhood after a couple of years on the inside, when he "realized that there were a lot of us who had to live with a reality where the cops threw tear gas in our apartments now and then and came after us with machine guns." The goal'd been to copy the Hells Angels' hierarchy: hang-around, prospect, member, sergeant at arms, and president. But after a couple of years, the shit really hit the fan. The Brotherhood's president found himself in a power struggle with Radovan's brother. War broke out between the Brotherhood and the Yugos. Went on for two years; three people lost their lives. But that was many years ago now. The Brotherhood had gotten a new president: Magnus Lindén. The Yugos calmed down. But the scars remained.

Mrado parked the car. Before he locked it, he said his customary prayer to the Car God.

Didn't feel anything before his meeting with Lindén besides a weak hope for a successful market division. No nerves. No fear.

He entered the pub.

Spotted Magnus Lindén right away. The dude exuded cruelty.

The pub was almost empty. A middle-aged woman behind the bar was stacking glasses. Lunch had been over for two hours. The place was dimly lit. In the background: Led Zeppelin, "Stairway to Heaven." A classic.

Lindén rose, arms hanging by his sides. Not so much as a hint of a greeting. Was rocking some serious attitude.

Mrado in his new role as mediator: ignored that Lindén ignored. Extended his hand. Met Lindén's gaze.

He remained standing like that for three seconds too long.

Lindén backed down. Extended his hand. Shook Mrado's.

"Welcome. Want something to eat?"

The ice was broken.

They ordered beer. Made small talk.

Mrado knew the game by now. Discussed engines, cars, bikes.

Lindén imparted his words of wisdom, sounded a lot like HA philosophy to Mrado's ears: "If you drive Japanese, you're a faggot."

Mrado agreed. Honestly. He'd owned a lot of cars in his life, but never an Asian, and he planned to keep it that way.

The conversation was easy.

Lindén's approach was different from that of a lot of others. The dude was a roaring racist. Kept sliding into talk about nigger decay/commie Jews and the Swedish Resistance Movement, some sort of organization made up of old skinheads. Mrado was uninterested. Where was the money in this bullshit?

Lindén shook his head. "Why'd I think a person of the Slavic race would understand?"

Mrado got fed up. "Listen, li'l Hitler. I don't give a fuck about your race theories. You know what I want. It's about all of us. Cut the bullshit and answer the questions already. Will you agree to the market division or not?"

Risky to push Lindén. He'd made a bloody mush of people for less. But Mrado wasn't "people."

Lindén nodded. Had made up his mind.

It was decided.

Mrado on a happiness high on his way home.

Called Ratko with the news.

Called Nenad.

"Sealed the deal with the Brotherhood, too. Like I told you, we're sitting pretty. Our markets are protected."

"Damn, you've done a fucking fantastic job, Mrado. Pray to God they keep their promises. The blow biz in the boroughs is soaring at record speed. The sky's the limit. We're gonna do some serious revving up now."

"Real good odds."

Mrado'd been thinking about where Nenad stood for a long time. Was he with or against the boss? Mrado'd heard the talk, knew that Nenad'd had conflicts with Radovan, too. There was a possibility that Nenad was as ticked off as he was. A possibility he had to test.

Mrado went for it. "No matter what Radovan does, we're safe."

"Yes, no matter what Radovan does."

Nenad paused. They were silent.

Then he went on. "Mrado, we're on the same team, right?"

Nenad tested Mrado the way Mrado'd planned on testing him.

Nenad in the game. Mrado and Nenad on the same side against Radovan.

EASY MONEY

***

Stockholm City, daily
March

PROJECT NOVA—THE POLICE'S NEW WEAPON AGAINST ORGANIZED CRIME IN THE REGION. **The gangs have long criminal records, are becoming increasingly organized and violent, and are training their successors to rob and sell drugs.**

Aggravated robberies, severe drug crimes, aggravated assault, procuring and pandering sex, and severe illegal weapons possession constitute their everyday lives.

Despite special police efforts, gang crime in Stockholm has become increasingly sophisticated, violent, and organized. Hardly a day passes without newspaper reports about new CIT robberies, procuring and pandering sex, or cases of assault taking place in the Stockholm area.

Organization

Many of the persons in question are experienced criminals with substantial criminal records who previously worked largely alone or in smaller groups. The new development points to improved organization and unity.

Cracking down on gang crime is a central issue for the regional head of police, Kerstin Götberg, and the Stockholm police's Project Nova began last year after a period of critical escalation of violent crime in the region.

150 persons have been given a so-called Nova mark. This means that all police officers know that an arrest of such a person has top priority, no matter the crime in question.

"We can't wait around for trophies. Sure, locking them up for seven, eight years would be good if it was possible, but it might not always work. We are going to maintain constant pressure on them. If you combine all the units in the region, you can, as a rule, find a way to convict them of something," said Leif Brunell, head of the region's Drug and Surveillance Unit and operative head of Project Nova.

Status Among the Criminals

When the Nova marks were instituted, having one in the police's registry was almost considered a status symbol among criminals.

"It becomes some sort of status, but in the long term it gets pretty annoying for them, since they become more visible, and that isn't something they want," said Lena Olofsson, criminal investigator working with Project Nova.

The heavy criminals are organized in unified networks and they specialize in different types of crimes. Conflicts can arise when different gangs compete for the same market. "There is a code of honor that has led to confrontations between different gangs, for example the Hells Angels and the Bandidos MC. Even the so-called Yugoslavian networks have had internal conflicts. Right now, the problems are especially big in southern Stockholm."

Young People Seek Out the Gangs

Recruitment to the criminal gangs is large. It is common that the more experienced criminals plan, while the younger ones, the so-called chips, actually carry out the crimes. Sometimes the older and more experienced members participate as "mentors."

37

They met up in the Sollentuna Mall. Jorge felt at home there. Indoor streets, the usual stores: H&M, the Systembolaget liquor store, B&R Toys, Intersport, Duka, Lindex, Teknikmagasinet. And the ICA supermarket. Jorge remembered how the food he'd bought there'd fallen to the ground when he was jumped by the Yugos. Then he remembered all the times he'd shoplifted there as a kid.

Jorge's fear of being recognized returned. It'd happened once three weeks ago, right here in Sollentuna. The danger zone for Jorge, highest density of people who recognized him. That time, he'd been there to meet a guy who dealt for him. In the stairwell of the apartment building on Malmvägen, a woman'd walked past who knew Jorge's mom. She'd tried to joke, yelled at him in Chilean slang: "Jorgelito. You been tanning in Africa?" He'd ignored her. Kept walking out of the building, with his panicked heart beating faster than a drum 'n' bass rhythm.

Told himself, It's cool. I'm way down on the 5-o's lists by now. I've changed my appearance. I'm a different guy. She was the first one in months who'd actually recognized him.

They each bought a Coca-Cola at a bodega: Jorge, the prostitute from the brothel in Hallonbergen, and her sidekick, a dude Jorge hadn't seen before.

The dude: an enormous Sven—six eight, at least. His chest was three feet across and there was no difference between the width of his neck and his head. Doubtful if the guy could walk without his thighs rubbing, friction between Black Angus beef shanks.

"This is Micke," the girl said.

Jorge wondered if the giant was her boyfriend or her pimp. Didn't dare ask. He was ashamed that he'd paid her for sex a week ago. The real question: Was he ashamed 'cause it was embarrassing or 'cause it was wrong?

Jorge raised an eyebrow. Signal to the chick: What's with the guy?

The girl understood. Said, "Chill. He just wanna come along. See nothing happen to me."

"Is he gonna listen to everything we're saying, or what? Can't have that."

The dude answered with a shriller voice than expected. "Relax, twiggy. I'll just walk a few feet behind you."

Shady as hell. Why'd she brought this guy? J-boy didn't take any risks. J-boy knew what could happen when you let meatheads out of your sight. He said, "You can keep close, but you gotta walk in front. So I can see you."

The giant stared him down. Cracked his knuckles. Jorge ignored him. Said, "If she wants the cash, you'll do what I say."

The chick okayed it.

They walked out of the mall. Through the sliding doors. Toward the park. In silence. The giant always twenty or so feet ahead.

Jorge: happiest dealer in town. Tricked the popo *grande*. Clearly, cockiest cocaine coup ever. Plucked that NK bag with blow right from under their snouts. Booked it—pigs were wheezy geezers—swung himself down from the bridge, and jumped. Landed in the snow on Långholmen. Foot fixed the fall: flourishing feat. Almost lost it when he realized Långholmen was an island. Then he thought, Sweden is a wonderful country. There's winter; there's ice. He made his way to the south side of the island, toward Hornstull. Ran over the ice. It was thin, but it bore him. He ran between the houses lining the water on Bergsunds Strand. Came out on the other side, by Tantolunden. All clear. He hailed a cab at Ringvägen.

The second-best thing about the whole deal: They might have a hard time pinning anything on Mehmed. Hopefully, they couldn't prove that he'd been in possession of cocaine. On the other hand, Big Brother usually managed to prove what Big Brother wanted to prove. They'd been caught with their pants down, *claro*. Usually, they switched out the cocaine for something else, kept the authentic gear as evidence. But this time, they'd let Mehmed drive off with the real stuff. Probable reason: They knew that someone was gonna test the shit and they wanted to get at the true bad boys, the higher-ups. Losers—J-boy wasn't an easy catch.

The only piss on his parade: How'd it gone down?

The most probable answer was that Silvia, the courier, had fucked it up. Maybe she'd answered all wrong in customs. Maybe there'd been dogs. Maybe—terrible thought—someone'd tipped them off.

He didn't give a fuck right now. The blow was his/Abdulkarim's. At least three million kronor gross on the street. Stockholm's boroughs were theirs for the taking.

Jorge and the chick were approaching the wooded area. The giant stayed up front. The snow lay thick, beautifully white. The path was well sanded. Jorge, with slippery sneakers on his feet, was grateful for the park service's diligence.

She turned to him, made it clear she was ready to talk.

"Good that you came," he said.

"It cost."

"Of course. What we agreed on."

"Yes. Where I start?"

"Why don't you start by telling me your name?"

"Call me Nadja. What I say?"

"Start from the beginning. How'd you get here?"

She didn't gush, told her tale in few words. Jorge thought, She's pretty. That special something remains: She was playing hard-boiled, while at the same time there was something she wanted to say. He could tell. She was easily persuaded. Too eager. The first time he'd met her in the apartment brothel, she'd told him that Mr. R. spread a Hugo Boss scent. Jorge'd checked it out with people who knew. It was correct. Radovan loved Hugo Boss. Everything Boss—suits, shirts, coats. Aftershave.

How could she know Rado smelled like Hugo Boss? Only two answers. Either someone'd told her, but that was improbable. Or she'd met him up close.

Possibility number two made her into Jorge's most interesting lead yet.

There was something she wanted to say. He was impressed by her courage.

She told him how she'd come to Sweden from Bosnia-Herzegovina six years ago. Eighteen years old. Raped four times by Serbian militia during her early teens. Applied for asylum here. Lived in a refugee camp outside Gnesta for two years. Thought she'd known what the word *bureaucracy* meant from her home country. Now she *really* knew what it meant. Life sucked. She took Swedish for Immigrants classes two hours every day. She was talented. Learned quickly. Other than that, she spent her days sprawled on a bed. Watched shopping shows and matinee movies in a Swedish she didn't yet understand. Once tried to go shopping on her own in Stockholm: her two thousand kronor a month—one thousand after she'd sent money home to her family in Sarajevo—wasn't enough for zilch. Never did that again. Stayed in her room. Slept, watched TV, listened to the radio. Near the edge of apathy. Thought only money could save her. One night, a neighbor on her hall at the camp asked if she wanted to smoke up. The feeling: the only nice experience she'd had since the time before the Bosnian catastrophe. It continued like that: They gathered in the neighbor's room a couple of times a week. Just sat. Smoked. Relaxed. The downside: The need for cash flow became desperate. She stopped sending money home. Hardly helped. Her debt grew. The solution came through the same neighbor, who did it herself—let some guy come to her room once a week or so, gave him a hand job, sometimes sucked a little. Made a couple hundred kronor. Later that night, they gathered in the neighbor's room again. Built bigger roaches. Took deeper hits. Forgot all the shit.

It worked for a few months. Then other men showed up—ex-Yugoslavs, Serbs. She didn't recognize their faces. But she did recognize their style. Arkan's boys. Told her and the neighbor what to do, when to do it, what to charge.

The number of customers increased. The money rolled in.

She wasn't granted asylum. The choice: stay illegally or go back to her war-ravaged home and the rape memories. She chose to stay. Sank deeper into the pimps' system.

They let her live together with other girls in a heavily guarded apartment. Sometimes the guys came there. Sometimes they were driven to other places. They thought she had a talent for more than the Swedish language, so they let her do the so-called luxury jobs: go along to restaurants and just look pretty. Maybe be picked up by some guy who'd buy her drinks. Maybe go to parties in huge houses in a miniskirt and act like a waitress. Old guys who'd grope/feel her up, pull her into adjoining rooms. Johns who never paid directly to her.

And every night when she came home, she'd roll a joint. Take some Sobril. Sometimes she topped the roach with aimies—in junkie lingo: dusting.

The Serbian pimps provided the drugs. Made sure they stayed calm.

After six months, she went into withdrawal if she didn't get her daily dose of weed or amphetamine.

Jorge asked few follow-up questions. Let her tell the story at her own pace. Felt like a head doctor. Like with Paola, who'd always listened to him. But it wasn't just that; he felt something for Nadja, too.

It hit him what it was: empathy. And something more: a kind of tenderness.

It wasn't till now that they'd gotten to the interesting stuff. The giant looked back at them every now and then. Made sure they were still there. That the distance hadn't gotten too big. Jorge guessed that they never let the whores out of their grip.

Jorge looked at Nadja. "Could you tell me some more details about the luxury jobs?"

"For, like, two year. Many time, they first drive us to makeup place. Get fix up. Choose what we wear. Sometime expensive: silk, satin skirt. High heels in nicest leather. A makeup girl learn me to walk in shoes like that. No wobble. They learn us what we talk about, what we do with old guys."

"Where?"

"Everywhere. In big houses, nice suburb, I think. Restaurant by Stureplan. Other part of town. Four, five time I go with old man for weekend. Swedish girls there, too."

Jorge sharpened his interview technique. Wanted to ask the right questions. Not push her too far. She had to keep talking. He wanted her to tell him, for her sake.

"How do you get the privilege of going to one of those parties?"

"What you mean?"

"I mean, if I wanted to go to one of those house parties. How would I do that?"

"I not do luxury job anymore. I not young and pretty enough. I almost over. Too much fucking amphetamine. You want to go to party, you need much money. Girls there not cheap." A fake smile.

"But if I still want to. Who do I talk to?"

"There are many. You ask about Nenad. Talk to him."

"I can't do that. Are there others? Who would organize those nicer parties?"

"Swedes. Upper-class."

"You got any names?"

"Try Jonas or Karl. They use to boss makeup girls."

"You know what their last names were?"

"No. Swedish last names hard. They never tell us. But nickname."

"They had nicknames?"

"Yes. Jonas, 'Jonte.' 'Karl,' called sort of like 'Giant Karl.'"

"Who else was involved?"

"Talk to Mr. R. if you dare."

"He was there? Does your boyfriend know you've been with him?"

She stopped. "How you know?"

Jorge: Sherlock fuckin' Holmes. "I just know."

They kept walking. Back toward the mall.

"Micke not my boyfriend. He Nenad's eye on me. Mr. R.'s eye. He not know who I be with. Why he got to know?"

"Why does he let you talk to me like this?"

"Micke not like others. He hate Mr. R. Micke promise help me out of the shit."

"Why?"

"I told you: He hate R. Only work for money. Been beat up before."

"What're you talkin' about?"

"Micke good man. Got foot crushed by a Serb swine who work for Mr. R. At gym. Mrado drop weightiest weight on foot. Then Serb just hit him down, no reason. For him, no big deal. That why Micke can work for Nenad instead. You understand. Micke is big. Still. You understand the men you ask about?"

Jorge understood.

The hate.

The drive.

The hunt.

38

Abdulkarim and Fahdi arrived in London two days after JW.

Picking up the gun was the first thing they did after landing. Cabbed it to Euston Square, where a black guy waited by the newspaper stand at the station. They handed over an envelope with the agreed-upon sum. The guy counted quickly and nodded. Then gave them a slip of paper.

Abdulkarim refused to be ripped off, made sure the guy didn't vaporize, held on to him. If there was no weapon, the guy'd have to take the hit.

The storage boxes had combination locks. The guy showed them to the correct box right away. The combination on the slip of paper worked. In the box was a sports bag. Fahdi took hold of the bag and reached his hand in. Copped a feel. Smiled broadly.

JW took them sightseeing with a hired tour guide for the rest of the day. Abdulkarim was in rapture, hadn't been abroad since he'd come to Sweden as a boy in 1985.

They saw the Houses of Parliament, Big Ben, London Dungeon, took a spin in the London Eye. Abdulkarim's favorite: London Dungeon, the horror museum with distorted wax dolls, guillotines, garrote irons, gallows.

The guide was a middle-aged Swedish man who'd lived in London for seventeen years. Was used to teens on language-course trips and traveling groups from middle Svenland. The guide couldn't really get a grip on his customers that day, maybe thought they were nice, normal guys. Instead, Abdulkarim and Fahdi poured on the questions. "Where's the closest strip club?" "Any idea about the price of snow?" "You gonna help us buy cheap ganja?"

Nervous drops gleamed on the guide's brow. He was probably sweating bullets.

JW grinned.

By the end of the day, the guide appeared visibly shaken. Shifty-eyed, probably scared a bobby'd pop around the next corner and collar him. They thanked him and gave a fat tip.

Before they parted ways, Abdulkarim said, "We're planning on going to Hothouse Inn tonight. Wanna come?"

The Hothouse Inn: JW'd scored tix. It was one of Soho's glammest strip joints.

The dopest part: The geezer guide said yes.

Abdulkarim's grimaced. "Oh my. I was just joking. We definitely weren't gonna go there. That's dirty. You do stuff like that?"

The guide: like a Jersey tomato. The red lights on the streets paled in comparison. Turned and hurried off.

They died laughing.

Day two. JW, Abdulkarim, and Fahdi invaded the shopping districts.

London, the Holy Land of luxury department stores: Selfridges, Harrods. But best of all: Harvey Nichols.

They'd booked a limo for the whole day.

JW'd moved to Abdulkarim's hotel the previous day, when Abdulkarim deemed it safe. Fahdi'd moved somewhat later the same day.

They began with a hotel brunch, model XL: sausages, bacon, spareribs, chicken clubs, fried potatoes, pancakes with syrup, seven kinds of bread, granola, Kellogg's cereal, scrambled eggs, three kinds of fresh-squeezed juice, marmalade, Marmite, Vegemite, tons of cheeses—Stilton, cheddar, Brie—jam, Nutella, ice cream, fruit salad. No end to it.

They binged. Fahdi loved the scrambled eggs, loaded up two plates. The middle-aged women one table over stared. Abdulkarim ordered new fresh-squeezed juice four times. JW was ashamed, and still not. He straightened his cuff links and looked toward their neighbors at the next table. Winked.

Enjoyed it somehow.

The limo picked them up at one.

Abdulkarim was coasting, boasting about how much they were going to make on the blow Jorge'd scored through that Brazilian. Blabbered on about all they were going to do in London. All the *bea-ches* were going to get a piece of Abdulkarim. All the knuckleheads were going to get a taste of Fahdi.

Abdulkarim hadn't talked about anything else the night before, couldn't let it drop: Jorge's infamous flight from the Västerbron bridge. JW was impressed. Seven pounds of coke was theirs. Exactly what they needed—quantity.

They stopped outside Selfridges. Abdulkarim opened the door and looked out. Roared in crappy English, "Get us outta here. This place don't look fancy enough."

JW glanced at Fahdi and laughed. Had Abdulkarim sucked a nose before breakfast?

The driver remained impassive. Abdulkarim's behavior was probably nothing compared to the really rich and famous people he'd chauffeured around.

They drove on. The sidewalks were crammed and the streets teeming with cars. Classic double-deckers squeezed past, pulled up to bus stops.

The limo stopped outside Harvey Nichols.

They walked into the department store and quickly found the men's section. It was gigantic. For JW, the shopping freak, the luxury leech, this was one of life's happier moments.

He drooled, dug, danced the consumer dance. Merch Mecca. Brand Bethlehem: Dior, Alexandre of London, Fendi, Giuseppe Zanotti, Canali, Hugo Boss, Cerruti 1881, Ralph Lauren, Comme des Garçons, Costume National, Dolce & Gabbana, Duffer of St. George, Yves Saint Laurent, Dunhill, Calvin Klein, Armani, Givenchy, Energie, Evisu, Gianfranco Ferre, Versace, Gucci, Guerlain, Helmut Lang, Hermès, Iceberg, Issey Miyake, J. Lindeberg, Christian Lacroix, Jean Paul Gaultier, C. P. Company, John Galliano, John Smedley, Kenzo, Lacoste, Marc Jacobs, Dries Van Noten, Martin Margiela, Miu Miu, Nicole Farhi, Oscar de la Renta, Paul Smith, Punk Royal, Ermenegildo Zegna, Roberto Cavalli, Jil Sander, Burberry, Tod's, Tommy Hilfiger, Trussardi, Valentino, Yohji Yamamoto.

It was all there.

Abdulkarim had a sales rep guide him around the store and drove around with his own little shopping cart. He plucked suits, shirts, shoes, and sweaters off the racks.

JW made the rounds by himself. Chose a club blazer by Alexandre of Savile Row, a pair of Helmut Lang jeans, two shirts—one from Paul Smith and one Prada—and a Gucci belt. Total damage: one thousand pounds.

Fahdi looked lost. He was most comfortable in a simple leather jacket and blue jeans and so he bought a pair of Hilfiger jeans and a leather jacket from Gucci. Price of the leather jacket alone: three thousand pounds. Gucci—all luxury lovers' favorite feature.

JW thought about how much easier it all would be when he had clean fleece. The ability to use proper credit cards: a dream on the British horizon. The feeling he longed for: to be able to toss an American Express platinum card on the counter.

They got help lugging all the bags out to the limousine. The salesclerks seemed used to this kind of thing. London was the place for the disgustingly rich.

The limo kept driving along Sloane Street, the flagship stores' mainline: Louis Vuitton, Prada, Gucci, Chanel, Hermès in a row.

JW's eyes were glued to the logos' luring lines. After a minute or so, Abdulkarim started yelling.

They got out.

Abdulkarim ran toward the Louis Vuitton store. JW saw his billowing pants and too-short jacket over his blazer and thought, Dressing like that ought to be a criminal offense.

At first the bouncer at the boutique looked skeptically at Abdulkarim—a swarthy maniac? Then he saw the limo. Waved him in.

They spent another hour and a half pillaging the street.

JW's final count was four thousand pounds, not including what he'd dropped at Harvey Nichols. Trophies to show the boyz back home: a leather briefcase from Gucci, a coat from Miu Miu, a shirt from Burberry. Not bad.

A thought flitted through his head: Is this Life, or is this a sham? JW felt elated, almost ecstatic. Still, he couldn't help but connect it to how Camilla must've felt when she'd been given a ride in the man from Belgrade's yellow Ferrari. How similar were she and JW?

They had lunch at Wagamama, at the end of Sloane Street, a trendy Asian restaurant chain with minimalistic interiors. Abdulkarim complained that too many dishes contained pork.

"Tomorrow night, we gonna celebrate," he said, "by eating at some halal place."

Fahdi looked surprised. "What're we celebrating?"

Abdulkarim grinned. "Buddy, tomorrow we gonna meet the guys we came here to meet. Tomorrow we gonna know if we gonna be millionaires."

39

Mrado was sitting on the couch at home postgym. Tired muscles. Wet hair. And full—he'd gorged on two tins of tuna with pasta, plus a protein powder cocktail. To top it off: Ultra Builder 5000, two tablets—Metandeinon, grade-A anabolic-androgenic steroids.

He vegged, watched *Fight Club*, Europsport. K-1, Elimination Tournament. The former K-1 champion, Jörgen Kruth, was the commentator. Analyzed the punches, kicks, and knees. The message his dragging, nasal voice sent was crystal-clear—the guy'd taken too many hits to the nose.

One of the masters, Remy Bonjasky, was crushing his opponent in the ring. Got the guy up against a corner. Kneed him in the gut. Low-kicked to his shins. His opponent screamed in pain. Bonjasky, two rapid left jabs. The guy didn't get his guard up in time. Mouth guard went flying. Before the ref had time to call it, Bonjasky finished with a round kick, impact on the left ear. Pure knockout: the opponent unconscious before he hit the floor. Mrado couldn't have done it better himself.

The past few days, Mrado'd been in a fantastic mood. He'd kicked his training into high gear. Serotonin surged. He was sleeping better. The gangs were under control—he'd succeeded. Most of them were in agreement enough for the idea to work. They knew the drill: As long as everyone kept to their own playpens, biz would soar. Cops lose. Cash flow.

His cell phone rang.

On the other end of the line: Stefanovic.

"Hey, Mrado, how are you doing?" He sounded formal. Mrado wondered why.

"All's good with me. And you?"

"Good, good. Where are you right now?"

"At home. Why're you asking?"

"Stay there. We'll pick you up."

"What, what's going on?"

"It's your turn, Mrado. To see Radovan. *Bilo mu je sudeno.*" Then he hung up.

Bilo mu je sudeno—it is your fate, Mrado.

His head spun. The couch felt uncomfortable. He stood up. Lowered the volume on the TV. Made a loop around the couch.

Gangster code: If you get picked up, you're never coming back. Like in Mafia movies. The Brooklyn Bridge with a rainy backdrop. They drive you across it. You don't return.

Thoughts like in wind turbine. Should he jump ship? If so, where could he disappear to? His life was here. His apartment, his business, his daughter.

What was Radovan's problem? Was it that he couldn't forget that Mrado'd asked for a bigger cut of the coat-check profits? Did he know Mrado'd rigged the market division in a way that curried his coat-check business? Worse: Did the Yugo boss sense his low loyalty? No, that was impossible.

Mrado'd just served Radovan Stockholm's criminal market on a silver platter. The Yugo boss should be grateful. Maybe everything was okay, after all. Maybe R. wasn't planning on hurting him.

He sat back down on the couch. Tried to think clearly. No point in leaving. Better to take it like a man. Like a Serb. Mrado still had some kind of advantage; his businesses were the ones that were protected with the market division. He should be safe.

Twelve minutes later, his home phone rang. Stefanovic again. Mrado put his holster on, slipped his knife in place under his pants, against the inside of his shin. Walked down the stairs.

Out on the street was a Range Rover with tinted windows. Mrado'd never seen the car before. Not one of Radovan's or Stefanovic's vehicles.

The passenger door was open.

Mrado got into the passenger seat. At the wheel: a young Serb. Mrado'd seen him before, one of Stefanovic's boys. In the backseat: Stefanovic.

The car started up.

Stefanovic: "Welcome. I hope you're doing well."

Mrado didn't answer. Waited to gauge the mood. Read the situation.

"Something on your chest. Why so quiet?"

Mrado turned his head. Stefanovic: impeccably dressed in a suit. As usual.

Mrado looked straight ahead again. It was still light out, but the sky was beginning to darken.

"All's good with me. I already told you that on the phone. You forget quickly. Or do you have something on *your* chest?" Obvious diss in his mimic of Stefanovic.

Stefanovic fired off a forced laugh. "Maybe it's best we don't talk if you're in a bad mood. Might just be a load of bull if we do. Don't you agree?"

Mrado didn't answer.

They drove through the city and out onto Lidingövägen.

The silence spoke loud and clear. The situation smelled like shit.

Mrado examined expedient exits: to pull his Smith & Wesson and shoot the driver's head off. Might work, but Stefanovic could be armed. He'd have time to bust some major holes in the back of his head before the car even came to a stop. Other way out: to turn around, take a well-aimed shot at Stefanovic's mug. Even if he did that—just like popping the driver—Stefanovic could beat him to it. Last idea: to shoot both men when they got out of the car. Best idea yet.

He thought about Lovisa.

The car slowed down. Turned up a narrow gravel path and then up a steep hill in the Lill-Jansskogen forest. The Range Rover was a good call, Mrado thought.

Finally, the car stopped. Stefanovic asked him to get out.

Mrado'd never been to this place before. He looked around. Stefanovic and the driver remained in the car. Typical veteran move. Nothing Mrado could do—he couldn't even see them through the tinted windows. To shoot would be meaningless.

They were on a height. A single building in front of him: a sixty-five-foot tower. Surreal.

Or? His eyes ran up the length of the red-painted cement body of the tower—saw the explanation: It was a ski-jumping hill.

Apparently, he'd ended up somewhere at the edge of the Lill-Jansskogen forest, by a ski-jumping tower that didn't look like it'd been used in ages. A bad omen.

The door at the base of the tower opened. A man he recognized waved at him to come inside.

The inside of the tower's base was spruced up, nice. Renovated. A small reception desk. Signs on the walls: WELCOME TO FISKARTORPET'S CONFERENCE HALL. WE CAN ACCOMMODATE UP TO FIFTY GUESTS. PERFECT FOR YOUR KICK-OFF, COMPANY PARTY, OR CONFERENCE.

Quick glance back—Stefanovic and the driver'd gotten out of the car.

No time to try any tricks. The man who'd met him asked for his gun.

He handed it over. The walnut grip felt slippery.

There was only one room at the top of the tower. Large windows facing in three directions. It wasn't completely dark outside yet. Mrado could see out over the Lill-Jansskogen forest. Off toward Östermalm. He saw City Hall in the distance. Church spires. Farthest off on the horizon: the Globe Arena. Stockholm spread out before him.

Mrado's thought at that moment: Why didn't someone build a luxury restaurant in this place?

In the middle of the room was a square table. White tablecloth. Large candelabras. Set for a meal.

On the other side of the table: Radovan in a dark suit.

He said in Serbian, "Mrado, welcome. What do you think of the place? Elegant, huh? I found it myself. Was out jogging in the woods down here one day. Exploring the paths in either direction and got curious. Kept running uphill. Found this."

Mrado selected strategies. Stony style. Self-confident style.

Straight-to-the-point style was what he chose. "It's nice, Radovan. To what do I owe the honor of being invited to dinner?"

"We'll get to that later. Let me finish my story. This is actually an old ski-jumping hill. They closed it in the late eighties, and it's been empty and rotting ever since. I bought the place this summer and I'm in the process of refurbishing it. It's gonna be a conference hall. Party venue. Could be a damn nice hullabaloo joint. What do you think?"

Radovan walked around the table. Pulled out the chair for Mrado. The simple fact that Mrado'd been left standing for over a minute was yet another bad sign.

Radovan went on and on about the tower.

"Do you realize how many forgotten places like this there are in Stockholm? I flew in seven Polacks last week who're gonna redo the ground floor. It's gonna be a restaurant, with the finest VIP room up here, at the top. People can do what they want here. Radovan invites the girls, brings the food, the booze, the whole nine yards."

A woman came in, pushing a drink cart. Served dry martinis. The olive gleamed, speared by a toothpick. When the door opened, the hair rose on Mrado's neck. He knew instinctively that they were out there: Stefanovic, the driver, the man who'd met him downstairs. Ready for violence if needed.

Radovan didn't take any risks.

Mrado thought, Not smart to do something rash now, but then again, it probably never was.

The woman came back in with the appetizers: toast Skagen, a Swedish seafood specialty. Poured out white wine. They began eating.

After a few mouthfuls, Rado laid down his utensils. Chewed. Swallowed. "Mrado. It's important that you understand our situation. You already know what I'm about to say, but just listen to Radovan. We're moving into a new phase. New times. New people. New ways of working. As you know. Today, there are a lot more players on the Swedish field than there were when we began twenty years ago. Back then, it was just us and a couple of old bank robbers, Svartenbrandt and Clark Olofsson. But Sweden is different now. The MC gangs are here to stay. The youth and prison gangs are well organized; the EU dissolves the borders. Biggest change is that nowadays we're also competing with the Albanians, the Russian Mafia, a ton of nasty types from Estonia, just to name a few. It's not just Western Europe that's gotten smaller. The East is here. Globalization, yada yada."

Mrado sat calmly. Knew that Rado liked the sound of his own voice.

"We're playing in an international market now. And the solution is in that very term. Tito chose a middle ground. So we knew a little about market economics. But here in the West, and in the free countries in the East, we make sure people get what they want—the ultimate consumer-driven market. 'Cause crime really isn't much more than that: the essence of market economics. Crimes are deregulated, free, supply-and-demand controlled. Without state intervention. Without planned economics, Commie rules, or chief guardianship. On the contrary, the strongest survive, just like in the market. That's the future. And to get there, we have to adjust the way we work. Choose areas of work depending on what, at the moment, maximizes profit in relation to risk. Consider the opportunity costs. Constantly invest, inject assets into new fields. Market our capital of violence. Recruit, merge, cut. We can't be slow, gotta be nimble. It's much more efficient to use consultants and work in small cells—like small business owners, if you like that analogy. We can learn from these Muslim terrorist networks. They hardly know each other. Still, they work toward the same goal. If one band gets plucked, it doesn't mess up the big picture. We've got to work that way. 'Cluster thinking,' that's what it's called in fancy talk. Get rid of the old hierarchical organization. Some Swedish business dude put it this way: 'Tear down the pyramids.' Sounds good to me."

Mrado just stared in reply. He'd stopped eating.

The woman came in. Cleared the plates. Refilled the wine.

"We know our fields. But we're organizing all wrong. That's the hitch. A few years ago, there was a lotta talk about the new economy. I don't know if it worked for regular folks. But for us, Mrado, the new market is the new rule. We've got to integrate a new way of thinking. Reach out beyond our narrow ethnic group. Recruit from the boroughs. Make alliances with Russian and Estonian organizations. Decentralize. Invest more in outsourcing. Control the cash flow, but maybe not always the core businesses. You with me?"

Mrado nodded slowly. Best to wait out Radovan's half-hysterical monologue.

"Good. Drugs've got wings. The blow's damn successful. The whores are even better. You can't even imagine what Swedish men've been longing for during all these years of political correctness. They're ready to pay anything. And this faggy law against purchasing sex, it's only strengthened us. The indoor brothels are as big as in Vegas; the luxury hookers are at every potbelly party in the suburbs. It's glorious. You were a part of building up our call-service biz. Remember?"

"Radovan, what you're saying is interesting. But I already know this stuff, and where exactly are you saying I come into it?"

"Thanks for bringing it up yourself. You've served the organization well. Served me well. Served Jokso well, too. But times change. You've got no place in what I'm describing. Unfortunately. Sorry. What you've done, the market-division agreement, it's wonderful. Thanks to your contacts. Your image. But that's all over now. I can't trust you. Why? Deep inside, you know the answer. It's been brewing in you for years. The answer is: because you don't trust me. You don't see me as our leader. As the one whose word should be followed without compromise. You demand too much. In the new market, individuals must act on their own. But never, ever act against their Radovan's interests."

Radovan's tone hardened.

"Mrado, look out the windows. Out over Stockholm. This is my fucking city. No one can take it away from me. That's the point of everything I've been talking about just now. This is my market. That's what you haven't understood. You think it's thanks to you that the money's rolling in, that you and I still work side by side. Forget that. I'm the new Jokso. I'm your new general. You have only me to thank for your livelihood. Your little life. Your pathetic position. And still, you've got the balls to demand a bigger cut of the coat-check profits. Demand. That's when it stops working. But worst of all is that you've tried to two-time me. Your only motivation for the market division has been your own self-interest. It's okay to work for your own self-interest, but never against me."

Mrado tried to interrupt Radovan. "Radovan, I don't know what you're talking about. I haven't two-timed you."

Radovan cut him off, almost screamed. "Don't bullshit me! I know what I know. You're out of the game. Don't you get it? No one challenges Radovan. You're out of the coat-check business. Sent off. Benched. You know me after all these years. I've had my eye on you. Know how you think. Rather, know that you don't think. Don't see me as your boss, your officer, your fucking president, as you should. But that's all done now. Game over. Fatso."

Mrado expected a bullet to the back of the head.

Nothing happened.

Radovan waved in the woman with the food cart.

She served the main course.

That's when Mrado knew he would live.

In a new situation. Demoted.

Shamed.

Radovan said, in a normal tone of voice, "Isn't this steak fantastically tender? I fly it in straight from Belgium."

40

Not counting the Radovan Revenge Project, Jorge was on top. Living large. Making fat stacks. Liked Abdulkarim, Fahdi, Petter, and the others lower on the dealing totem pole. He'd liked Mehmed, too, and now the guy was in trouble—still unclear if the cops were gonna muster a wrapping. He even liked the Östermalm brat, JW. But the dude was weird. Seemed to be double-dipping. Hanging in different worlds. Rocked a snooty style. At the same time, obviously horny for Jorge's know, honestly curious. Most of all, the guy desired dirty dough.

At the same time, Jorge had the hots for JW's other life—Stureplan. Jorge'd partied at the bars around there tons of times. Champagne-*chinga*'d *chicas*. Palmed some bills and the bouncer'd let him glide past the line. Brought some prime rib home from the meat market.

But still, something was missing. He saw the Swedish guys. No matter how much money he spent, he'd never be at their level. Jorge could feel it. Every *blatte* in the city could feel it. No matter how hard they tried, waxed their hair, bought the right clothes, kept their honor intact, and drove slick rides, they didn't belong with Them.

Humiliation was always around the corner. You could see it in the salesclerks' reactions, in old ladies' sidewalk detours and cops' stares. It appeared in the bouncers' gazes, the bitches' grimaces, the bartenders' gestures. The message clearer than the city of Stockholm's segregation politics: In the end, you're always just a *blatte*.

JW, Abdulkarim, and Fahdi were in London. Doing something big. Jorge's job at home was to hold down the fort. Make sure to move the gorgeous gear Silvia'd brought in. No problem. It'd melt faster than Popsicles in the sun.

Jorge'd gotten an apartment in Helenelund. The proximity to his old hood felt good. Sublet from one of Adbulkarim's contacts. Tricked it out with crib capital: forty-two-inch flat-screen, DVD, stereo, Xbox, laptop.

Loved life as Jorge Nuevo. Zambo Jorge rolled with flow.

Loved his new friends. Habits. The beautiful bills.

What ate away at him—the hate.

Three days ago, he'd met the hooker, Nadja. There were still some unanswered questions. Who was the giant, Micke, really, and how could he help Jorge? Who were the guys she'd mentioned? Jonas and Karl, alias Giant Karl. How could he weasel his way into Radovan's whore trench?

He was stressed-out. Hadn't gotten anywhere. Had stopped sitting in cars outside Rado's house, since it was pointless. Maybe he should rethink things. Invest in info about Radovan's dealer biz instead. Still, no. That was too much of a threat to Jorge himself and to the people he cared about.

The whore trail was better. Anyway, the job for Abdulkarim was taking more and more of his time. Mehmed had to be replaced. Fresh meat had to be recruited. Jorge's ideas: maybe his cousin, Sergio. Maybe Eddie. Maybe his bro Rolando, when he caged out of Österåker. Sergio was the hero who'd helped Jorge out of Österåker. So far, he'd been repaid in a few measly moneys. Should be paid better. Jorge wanted to offer him the chance on an in of the C profits. Same with Eddie. And Rolando—player'd been the most competent coke coach J-boy'd had. Should pay off. He'd called the brothel madam at least twenty times over the past few days. Wanted to book a time with Nadja. See her again. Didn't need a walk. Just needed ten minutes to ask more questions. And something else—maybe get sucked off again. He thought, No, that felt fucked even before I knew her. There was another reason he wanted to see her.

Finally, Jorge got hold of the hooker mama. Gave the alias he'd been given the first time he was there. She okayed him, said he could come that same night.

Took the subway to Hallonbergen.

It rained. Warmer in the air. Smelled like a halal cart. Last time, Jorge'd come by car, but now the map master'd quested it. Memorized. Could find the way with a blindfold on.

The red apartment building with the brown external balconies was haloed by a rose-colored sunset glow.

He entered the combination for the front door. Took the elevator up. Out onto the balcony. Rang the doorbell. Dark in the peephole—someone's eye on the other side. He gave his alias aloud.

The door was opened by the man that Fahdi'd been talking to the last time he was there. Same clothes. Blazer over hoodie.

Jorge gave his alias again. Was let in.

Asked for Nadja.

Same music in the wait room. Shitty imagination in this joint.

The man just nodded and led Jorge to the room. Opened the door. Let him in.

Same bed. As poorly made as last time he'd been there. Same armchair. Same drawn blinds.

On the bed: a different whore.

Jorge stopped short in the door, turned around. The dude wasn't standing behind him anymore.

He looked at the girl on the bed. She was pretty, too. Bigger tits than Nadja's. Miniskirt. Tight, low-cut top. Fishnets.

"I was supposed to see someone else. Nadja?"

The girl answered in quasi-intelligible English.

"I not understand."

Jorge said in English, "I want to see Nadja."

Maybe it was instinct. Jorge wasn't just anyone—he was the chain-buster on the run, after all—was always tensed to the max. Usually, his nerves were pricked for cop fuckers. But also for Radovan.

He turned in the door. Ran out through the wait room. Heard the man in the blazer *y* hoodie yell his alias. Didn't turn around. Jorge already through the door. Ran across the exterior balcony. Down the stairs. Out. Away.

Jorge'd never seen a face contort as gruesomely as when the new chick in Nadja's room understood who he was asking about. Obvious: The name Nadja equaled terror.

Something wasn't right.

Something was revoltingly wrong.

The next day. Jorge was on the toilet, doing number two. Incoming call on his cell—restricted. Not unusual on Jorge's cell. Those who called him often hid their numbers. He decided to pick up despite his embarrassing position.

"Hi, my name is Sophie. I'm JW's girlfriend."

Jorge, surprise squared. Had heard about Sophie from JW. But why was she calling him? And how'd Sophie gotten his number after all of Abdulkarim's strict rules about not giving numbers to strangers?

"Yeah, hi. I've heard a lot about you."

She laughed. "So, what've you heard?"

"How much he dreams about making a family."

A short silence on the other end of the line. She hadn't gotten the joke.

"Hey, JW's in London, so this might sound strange, but I was wondering if you'd want to get together. Grab a coffee or something?"

"Without JW?"

"Yes. I want to get to know you, his other friends. But he's such a clam. You know how he is—doesn't talk about certain stuff."

Jorge knew what she was talking about. JW played two games.

"Come on, let's get together sometime before JW gets back? It's nothing weird, promise."

Jorge's instinct said no. But the curiosity, really, why not? He was interested in knowing more about JW, too. Maybe one day get the chance to go with him to his other world.

"He'll be back in four days, I think. Want to meet up tonight?"

They set a time. Sophie sounded pleased.

He remained seated, finished his thing.

Ruminated. Had to be careful. Something off about Nadja's disappearance. Something off about the hoodie man's behavior. They knew he wanted to see Nadja. Why didn't they tell him she was gone? The biggest question: Where was she? And now: suddenly JW's *polola* calls. Was there a connection?

Conclusion: Don't take any risks with the Sophie chick. Could be a bluff.

That night, he took the commuter rail to T-Centralen. Jorge still didn't have a car. Top priority when Project Rado was completed: Buy a fine ride.

Was gonna meet the girl who claimed she was Sophie. He walked from T-Centralen. The streets were clear of snow.

Jorge remembered his guarded parole from Österåker, when he'd walked the exact same street. Warm day in August. Three COs in tow. If they'd only known what he was gonna use the Asics shoes for. Tools.

Took a right on Birger Jarlsgatan. Neon signs blinked above the Sturegallerian shopping center. Endless repeats of the Nokia logo.

Ten yards outside Café Albert, he took hold of a young dude. Sideways baseball hat. *Blatte* kid on the wrong turf. Offered him a hundred kronor for a favor.

The guy went into the café.

Came back out a minute later.

Another minute.

Sophie came out.

Jorge stared. Sophie: matchless *mina*. Sex appeal personified. Black knit scarf nonchalantly wrapped. Tight black leather motorcycle jacket, without reinforced elbows or shoulders. Tight jeans.

He knew JW belonged to Stureplan. But this—*abbou*, what a cat.

Sophie looked questioningly at him.

She was clearly alone. Jorge was satisfied. Felt safer. *Sonrisa*'d up.

They said hi. She suggested Sturehof. No problem getting in. Reason was obvious: Sophie always got in.

Walked past the restaurant and entered the bar area.

Jorge ordered a beer for himself and a glass of red for Sophie.

"So, Sophie, good to meet you. Sorry if I was weird outside Café Albert. I get a little wigged-out sometimes."

She tilted her head at him. Jorge thought, Did she understand why he hadn't wanted to meet at a place she'd decided?

"You don't like it there, or what?"

"Nothing wrong with Café Albert, but it's so loud in there."

"And you don't think it's loud here?"

"Just joking." Jorge careful. Spoke the words as un-*blatte* as he could. The Swedish sounds at the front of his mouth. No ghetto pronunciation.

They dropped the subject. Sophie started questioning him. What did he do? How long had he known JW? In between answers, he asked control questions. Wanted to be sure that Sophie was who she said she was. She seemed green.

Jorge's impression: Sophie, genuinely interested in JW's life. But also something else—she was interviewing him. Digging. Wanted to know things Jorge wasn't sure JW wanted her to know. Not sure Abdulkarim would've liked it, either. No matter how smokin' this someone looked.

He held back. Told her he and JW hung out, chilled. Watched movies. Played video games. Drank beer. Played soccer. Partied sometimes. But nothing about the C biz.

"Party?" Sophie asked. "Where?"

Jorge without a good answer. Mumbled something about a bar in Helenelund.

Sophie asked, "You guys do a line now and then?"

Jorge took a big gulp of beer, thought about what he should say. Chanced it. "It happens. You?"

She winked with one eye. "It happens. Sometimes I wonder if JW does one too many now and then."

"Don't think so. He's got it on lock. Guy with style. With class. You know, he's schooling me about your world." Jorge surprised himself. Opened up to a stranger.

Sophie opened up in return, told him about her thoughts. That JW'd gotten all twitchy lately. Wasn't studying. Kept a weird schedule. Slept badly. That she wanted to get to know JW in order to be able to help him.

Jorge listened. Understood why she'd wanted to meet up.

Time flew. They talked about other stuff: film, the bars around Stureplan, Sophie's studies, JW's way of dressing, Jorge's family.

Strange combination: the fake-Zambo fugitive, the borough blow baron. Together with the city's hottest brat broad.

Even stranger—they had a good time.

The clock struck midnight. They'd been talking for over three hours.

Afterward, Jorge thought, Chance plays strange tricks. You meet someone for the first time in your life. One day later, you see the same person again. You hear a word you've never heard before. A few hours later, that same word is used for the second time in your life. Or, turns out someone you know is related to someone else you know, and you'd never talked about it before. Or, at the very moment you're thinking about a person, that very person walks into the subway car. What're the odds? Still, it happens.

Or maybe it's not chance. Maybe reality is made up of a complex lattice of coincidence. Clumps of information. Connected, linked to one another by what we call "chance."

Jorge made it easy for himself. His only creed: Cash is king.

Still, couldn't help but wonder. What happened at that moment at Sturehof must've been an instance of pure chance.

Or not.

A group of guys walked by. Blazers, shirts unbuttoned at the collar, straight-leg jeans. Cuff links, expensive watches. Broad belt buckles in the shape of the luxury brands' monograms.

Most of all—slicked-back hair.

Stureplan's swift golden gods.

Sophie got up. Hugged and kissed them on the cheek, one by one. Tittered at their jokes.

In Jorge's opinion: obvious that she acted excessively happy to see them.

She didn't introduce Jorge. Maybe that was expecting too much. Still, it stung.

The brats disappeared into the O Bar, Sturehof's inner party spot.

He asked, "Who were they?"

"No one, really. Just some acquaintances." Sophie seemed uncomfortable. Jorge thought, She's ashamed she didn't introduce me.

"JW's friends?"

"Some of them know JW."

"Which ones?"

"The guy in the striped blazer, that's Nippe. The guy in the black coat, his name's Fredrik. He's friends with Jet Set Carl, too. Have you heard of him?"

In Jorge's head: Jet Set Carl? Sounds familiar.

Thought again.

Jet Set Carl.

Jogged his memory.

Giant Karl.

"Jet Set Carl. Who's that?"

Sophie told him about the clubs and the parties. "Jet Set Carl, that's Stureplan's most powerful party planner. But he's pretty slimy to girls, to be honest."

The final comment set off a ringing through Jorge's head.

Catch the giant.

41

JW got up early. Felt his own inner tension tremble. He knew the schedule; today was the day. If everything went well, they would get access to the big guys. The ones with direct connections to the cartels in South America. The ones who could grease the big gears. The ones who would give JW a rocket career in the C business.

He was sitting by himself in the hotel restaurant's breakfast section, waiting for Abdulkarim and Fahdi to come down while drinking coffee and reading a British newspaper. Felt unusually restless.

He'd spent over sixty thousand kronor the day before. Clothes, bag, shoes, food, strip club in Soho. Later that night, they went to Chinawhite—where bottle service cost at least five hundred pounds—and did some serious damage. For once, they couldn't be the ones to deliver the other China white. The sick part wasn't that he'd spent the money. It was the thought of what his parents would say if they knew.

He texted Sophie. She felt far away, while she was still the one person who knew him best. The only one he'd revealed his double life to. But everything wasn't revealed; he couldn't man up to tell her about his background. Was ashamed of his simple Sven family and didn't want to drag the Camilla story into things. It made him doubtful. If he couldn't tell his girlfriend, how comfortable was he with her, really?

JW put the newspaper down. Two clear thoughts crystallized in his head. One, that he was going to hang with Sophie more. The second was tougher—that he was going to tell her about his background. But maybe she'd even be able to help him find out more.

Fahdi came down at the ten-thirty mark. They ate together and waited for Abdulkarim.

He didn't come down.

It got to be eleven o'clock.

Another fifteen minutes passed.

Fahdi seemed anxious. Still, they didn't want to wake Abdul. Was there something JW didn't know? Was there something Fahdi was afraid of?

Twelve o'clock.

Finally, JW went up. Knocked on the door to Abdulkarim's room.

No sound.

Knocked again.

Nothing.

Alternatives: either Abdulkarim was passed out after the night's escapades or something'd happened to him. Hence Fahdi's stress. JW thought, Who is it we're meeting today?

He pounded. Put his ear to the door.

Silence.

Finally, he heard Abdulkarim's voice from inside.

JW opened the door.

The Arab was sitting on the floor in there.

Abdulkarim said, "Sorry. I was late with morning prayers."

"You're praying?"

"Tryin'. Sadly, I'm a bad person. Don't always get up on time."

"But why?"

"What you mean *why*?"

"Yeah, why do you pray?"

"You don't get stuff like that, JW, 'cause you a heathen Sven. I bow to Allah. My body against the ground from which it came. Says to me, and all people—niggers or whites, Svens or *blattes*, rich or poor—that Allah, the one true one, it is he who is the one creator and Lord."

Abdulkarim was serious.

To JW's ears, it sounded like qualified bullshit, rehearsed flummery, but there was neither time nor energy to discuss Abdul's life choices. He thought, He's going to discover for himself what counts—cash or Allah.

They were pressed for time now.

Abdulkarim skipped breakfast.

JW, Abdulkarim, and Fahdi were heading north, toward Birmingham. It was going to take two and half hours by car service, a limo with legroom. Abdulkarim didn't want them to be cramped on such an important day.

They were on their way—to the really big players.

They could've taken a train, bus, plane. But this was better, safer, calmer. Above all, more gangsta. Who the fuck's going to bounce around on a bus when there's a limo to be had?

Abdul laughed at the plan for the day's deal. He'd gotten a call from an unknown person. Time and place'd been agreed upon: the main rail station. *"Don't be late."*

They were on their way—into the countryside.

The driver was playing the radio, drum 'n' bass pounding through the back-door speakers. Ultra-British.

He was a young Indian. Abdulkarim'd learned a new English word: *Pakis.* JW thought, Please, Abdulkarim, realize that now isn't the time to use it.

Outside, the landscape stretched beautifully on all sides. Rolling, rich-earthed rural communities with sowed fields. Tranquil rivers flowed below the road.

English Eden.

Spring had come with a flourish. Compared to Stockholm, the air was warm.

Abdulkarim was tired and dozed, leaning against the window. Fahdi and JW exchanged curt commentary and evaluated London's nightlife.

"You ever been with a stripper?"

JW thought about the pornos that were always rolling at Fahdi's. "No, have you?"

"Think I gay or what? Course I have."

"Here in England?"

"Fuck no. They too expensive. Pounder's too high."

JW laughed. "Thought you were the big pounder."

He thought about their relationship. On the surface, it was purely professional, with some pleasant small talk. But JW felt Fahdi was actually a warm guy. He never judged, didn't diss, never made fun of anyone. Fahdi was unpretentious. Happy as long has he had two things in life: a bench press and a piece of ass now and then. The drug business—more because he was connected to Abdulkarim for some reason than that he sought kicks, cash, or clout.

The driver started talking. Mentioned Stratford-upon-Avon and Shakespeare. JW looked out, saw a sign with a town's name, under which was printed THE HOME OF WILLIAM SHAKESPEARE.

They passed Birmingham's suburbs. One-family homes with well-tended gardens. Tightly packed apartment buildings with laundry lines tied up in parallel threads crisscrossing narrow courtyards. Industrial areas that looked like movie sets. JW thought it couldn't get more quintessentially British.

They arrived in the city. The houses were lower than in London but otherwise looked the same. Redbrick houses, narrow one-family homes with stairwayed stoops and long, slim windows, Starbucks, McDonald's, bookstores, halal joints. No trees and no bikes.

The car stopped on a bridge by the train station. Underneath, the trains rushed by at high speeds. The noise was deafening.

They got out. Paid the driver and got his number. Said they'd call him in four hours if they needed a car to drive them back to London.

They took the stairs down to the station area.

Their arranged meeting spot was outside the magazine and bookstore in the station.

Didn't take much to pick out their targets in the crowd—two broad-shouldered men in dark leather jackets, black Valentino jeans, and sturdy leather shoes stood stiffly outside the store. Like, were they in uniform or what? Both looked British: mouse-colored hair, gray complexions. One had straight-cut bangs that hung down on his forehead. JW thought it looked like a Caesar coif. The other rocked a perfectly combed side part.

Abdulkarim walked straight up to them and introduced himself in his *blatte* Swenglish.

No surprise. No smiles.

They followed the men to a minivan. They were directed to the backseat and got in.

The man with the side part, in JW's opinion: right-wing extremist, severe expression. Asked how their trip'd been. JW thought, Definitely a Brit, judging by the accent.

Abdulkarim chatted for a while. When they were driving through the industrial areas, the right-wing extremist got out three strips of cloth and asked Abdulkarim, JW, and Fahdi to tie them on as blindfolds. Then he asked them to sit down on the floor of the minivan.

They obeyed.

Lay silent, blind, on the floor.

The Brits blared loud music.

JW's feeling: one of the few times in his life he'd felt real fear. Who, exactly, were they meeting? Where were they taking them? What would happen if Abdulkarim made a fuss? It all seemed so much bigger and more dangerous than when he'd planned the trip back home in safe Stockholm.

One thing was for sure: They were going to meet powerful, shady boys.

After twenty minutes, Abdulkarim asked, "How long are we gonna lie here like sardines?" The Brits laughed. Told him only a few more minutes.

After around ten minutes, JW could feel that they were driving on a new surface. Maybe gravel, maybe stone.

The right-wing extremist asked them to take their blindfolds off and sit back up. JW looked out. They were surrounded by the British spring landscape as it'd looked on the drive up. They were driving on a narrow gravel road toward some buildings.

Fahdi looked bewildered. Glanced at Abdulkarim, who glowed with anticipation and curiosity, but, most of all, with the possibility of doing big business.

The minivan came to a stop. They were asked to get out.

In front of them was a large stone barn with wood crossbeams in a beautiful pattern; next to that was a house surrounded by numerous greenhouses. JW didn't really get it. This was some kind of mad idyllic countryscape. Where was the gear?

Two men came out of the barn. One of them was enormous, not just tall but fat, too. Still, he had authority, like a heavyweight champ. Carried his weight like a weapon, not like a burden. The other was shorter, with a more slender build. Dressed in a floor-length leather coat and pointy shoes.

Drug lords' customary fetishes: fast cars, expensive watches, hot chicks. They loved diamonds most of all. In the leather-coat man's ear: an enormous rock. His body language was clear: He was the one in charge.

Abdulkarim took control of the situation and extended his hand.

The leather-coat guy said in a difficult dialect, "Welcome to Warwickshire. We call this place 'the Factory.' I'm Chris." He pointed to the enormous man beside him. "And this is John, perhaps better known as 'the Doorman.' He worked as a bouncer for a long time.

Now he's found a more lucrative field. You know, before he used to boot the same people we today supply with gear. Oh, by the way, pardon the uncomfortable ride on the floor. I'm sure you understand our requirements."

Abdulkarim sharpened his English. Sounded, consciously or not, like an American rapper. "It's cool, yo. No problems. We be happy to be here and think it'll be mad profitable to meet you."

Chris and Abdulkarim talked for a few minutes. Exchanged some pleasantries—big business demanded long rituals.

"I really think our I-don't-know-the-word-in-English are gonna be pleased."

Chris said, "*Principals*, that's what they're called. Your boss, that is."

JW looked around. He glimpsed two other people farther off, behind one of the greenhouses. Their shoulders were draped with weapons, clearly visible in the bright daylight. Farther down the road, more people. The place was heavily guarded. He'd started to grip the idea: Maybe operating in the countryside was pretty smart after all.

JW counted at least six greenhouses in a row. Around one hundred feet long and six feet tall. The house itself was big and all the windows were covered by drawn curtains. Barking sounds were coming from the barn.

Chris invited them into the house.

It smelled like cat piss in there. Dungarees and heavy-duty gloves were hanging on hooks in the hall. Chris hung up his coat. Led them into a big kitchen with a rustic feel. It was a strange contrast. Chris, with the massive rock in his ear and what JW thought was a tailored suit, in this skanky house.

He invited them to have a seat. Asked what they wanted to drink. Poured out tall whiskeys for all three of them. Fine goods: single malt, Isle of Jura, eighteen years old. They sat down. John remained leaning against the wall, didn't take his eyes off them.

Chris looked happy. "Welcome, once again. Before we begin, I have to ask you to hand over your weapons." In the middle of his smiling face—JW saw it clearly—his eyes flashed in Fahdi's direction. "And to go through a little security check."

Fahdi looked at Abdulkarim.

A fork in the road—either let up on safety, for once, or go home. Could be a trap, could be advanced narcotics investigators they had in front of them. The casting vote for Abdul was probably that the bling in Chris's ear was real; you could tell. No narc would wear something like that, not just because it was so expensive—it was damn gay, too.

Abdul, in Swedish: "It's okay. We have to play by their rules today."

Fahdi pulled out the gun and laid it in front of him on the table. Chris leaned forward. Picked it up, weighed it, turned it over in his hand. Read what was written across the muzzle.

"Nice. Zastava M57, 7.63 millimeter. Reliable. Almost as click-free as an Uzi."

He popped the magazine. It dropped onto the table.

Then he showed them into an adjoining room.

The two men who'd driven them in the minivan were there. They asked Abdulkarim, JW, and Fahdi to take off their shirts and pants; the boxers they could keep on. They turned around once, slowly. JW glanced at Abdulkarim. Looked like he thought this was the most normal thing in the world—being body-searched by two semi-psychos who'd just forced them down on the floor of a minivan. He assumed the Arab'd been searched before.

They were cleared.

Five minutes later, they were back in the kitchen.

Chris's smile greeted them. "All right, now we've dealt with the formalities. Big men with small guns really stress me out. Yours truly isn't all too big, but damn do I have a big weapon." He giggled and grabbed his crotch. Turned to John as though to get backup.

"Let's sit here, relax, and enjoy this fine whiskey. How's London been treating you?"

Small talk and pleasantries went on for half an hour. Abdulkarim really went in for the part of group leader. Told stories about their nights in London, the places they'd gone to, about the shopping, about London Dungeon, and the guide they'd freaked out. All with genuine enthusiasm.

"London's a real city. You know, Stockholm is like a piss in Mississippi in comparison. But we got a subway."

JW chuckled inside. What were the chances that Chris understood the Arab's talk about American rivers?

After finishing three rounds of drinks, Chris got up and said, "Let's get down to business. I want to show you around. I'm guessing you're curious."

They left the house and walked in a row behind Chris toward the barn.

The figures with the guns over their shoulders could be seen farther off, behind the greenhouses.

Chris stopped in front of the entrance. Barking from inside.

"Like I said, we call this farm the Factory. Soon you'll see why. Before I show you, let me just say that we'll solve your problems. We deliver. Over the past year, we've completed successful transports of over five tons of goods. We know this stuff. You'll understand in a minute."

He opened the door.

They went in.

The stench hit JW, a rank smell of dirt and excrement.

The walls were lined with cages.

In the cages: dogs.

The cages were seven by seven feet, with at least four animals in each cage.

There was fluorescent tubing in the ceiling.

When they entered the barn, they were met by deafening barking.

The animals seemed hysterical. They moved frenetically and yapped at the visitors.

The fur on some of the animals was tattered, worn-looking, and full of sores. Those in other cages were in better shape. Some dogs had long, groomed coats and calmer tempers. A few of the dogs appeared sedated; they were lying in heaps on the floor.

Chris said, "Let me introduce our first product for delivery. We've used it successfully to transport goods to countries like Norway, France, and Germany."

A man dressed in a white doctor's coat and rubber boots approached them from one of the aisles.

Chris greeted him. "Hi, Pughs. Can you show them what I mean?"

Pughs nodded. Opened one of the cages where the dogs were calm and coaxed one with a nicer coat out. JW thought it was a golden retriever.

Pughs grabbed hold of the animal's fur right under the front legs and said with a raspy voice, "I operate. They call me 'the Vet,' but that's just bullshit. I was a surgeon before. Look here." He waved them closer. "I've inserted four bags containing a total of six hundred grams of Charlie under the skin of this pooch."

335

JW leaned in. What Pughs was pointing at didn't look like anything more than a fold between the dog's legs. No scars, as far as he could tell.

"It takes a month to heal and another two months for the fur to grow back enough."

Chris took over. "We've sent out more than thirty animals. It's worked every time. But most of the animals in here are ones we've taken in, straight from South America. That's how we import quantity."

JW turned and looked around before they walked on through the barn. There was a total of at least fifty animals in all the cages. He calculated: If half the animals'd had shit inside, they would've brought in over thirty pounds on them alone. Thirty pounds on the streets of Stockholm—almost fifteen million kronor.

He was impressed; this was massive, Trump-size business in a barn in the countryside.

Pughs pulled the dog back into a cage.

Chris led them on through a door.

They came into another room with high ceilings. There were two large green metal machines on the floor. Two men were working at one of them. JW thought the machines looked like the lathe in the woodworking shop in middle school.

Chris explained. "Our next product. We are producing tin cans. Look carefully. The machines are exactly the same as the ones used by Mr. Greenpacking, for instance. We fill them with whatever the order is. Fly them across the borders."

Abdulkarim asked his first question. He seemed completely taken by all this. "Why you fly the shit over? Boat's not cheaper?"

"Good question. Customs is always breathing down our necks. They know to take random samples on big deliveries containing tinned cans. A couple friends of mine got slammed hard by that a few years back. Still rotting in an iron box right now. Listen, we've got connections with a company in the catering business. They sell food boxes to airlines. The idea is simple. On any given flight, let's say ten of the food boxes contain our cans with our contents. Ten people order special food, most often vegan food. They eat heartily but don't open the tin can that's included with the meal. Instead, they throw them in the trash cart the stewardesses push through the plane after the meal. The garbage—that is, the full cans—is then taken care of by our people working in garbage management at the airport. The icing on the cake is that it doesn't even have to be our people ordering the food. We just hire some Ibiza-bound kids, ask them to order the veggie grub, and it's a done deal. We transported two pounds of amphetamines to Kos that way last week."

"And it never happen that some nasty brat pockets the can, not throw it out like you want?"

"It's happened. That nasty brat never made it home from Kos."

JW was fascinated. This was big, brainy, beautifully bad. And fucking surreal.

It was a drug-packaging industry, transportation insanity, amazing logistical philosophy.

Shit.

Chris led them onward. John picked up the rear.

They walked out of the barn, toward the greenhouses.

Abdulkarim asked Chris about stats. How often did their deliveries succeed? What size loads could they take? How much did they import on their own? From which countries? Whom did they represent?

Chris explained. They imported tons from all over the world. The cocaine came directly from South America. Warwickshire operated as the ultimate price regulator. They repackaged, sold their products from there, spread the risks, selected destinations, kept demand high.

A high-level European supply cartel.

Chris's answer to Abdul's last question: "I thought you'd been informed. We're the extended arm of a syndicate. Doesn't matter which one, but you'll get a good price with us. Guaranteed."

They were approaching the greenhouses. JW discovered that they stretched farther than he'd first thought.

Chris stopped outside one of them and pointed. "We grow all kinds of things in these."

He opened the door.

No humidity washed over them. Instead, it was cool.

JW'd expected a jungle of *cannabis sattiva*. Or, even better, rows of coca plants.

Nope.

In rows along the ground grew small, unripe white cabbages.

Abdulkarim looked like a boldface question mark. He'd shared JW's expectations.

JW caught himself—his mouth was wide open; he was gaping.

Fahdi looked at Chris. Was this a joke, or what?

Chris threw his arms open and laughed. "As anticipated. Everyone reacts like you. Goddamn it, aren't they growing weed? Aren't they growing blow? Forget it. We're growing cabbage. In case you hadn't thought of it already, you haven't seen anything illegal here yet. You've seen dogs. But have you seen ice? You've seen two blokes making cans, but have you seen what they're filling them with? Get the point. We don't take risks. If there's a sting operation here, at least we've got some ability to protect ourselves. We store the actual shit somewhere else. When it's time to put it into animals, cans, or whatever else, it's brought here under the strictest surveillance possible, and everything happens very fast. We've minimized the opportunities for the bobby fuckers to get at us."

Abdulkarim was still eyeing the cabbage patch.

Chris continued: "We're not done in here yet, but it's our third, and largest, product." He pulled a couple photos out of his jacket pocket and showed them to Abdulkarim and JW. In the first photo: a cabbage the same size as the ones in the greenhouse. In the next photo: a somewhat larger plant. In the middle of the plant was a plastic bag, tightly knotted, about two inches high and one and a half inches wide. Next photo: same plant, just a little bigger. The next photo: the plant with the bag again. The cabbage leaves almost completely concealed the bag. The next photo: the finished plant. The bag wasn't visible at all. The last photo: three crates filled with cabbage.

JW understood before Abdulkarim did. "Jesus."

Chris held the photos out to Abdulkarim. "Jesus is right."

Abdulkarim looked at JW.

JW said in Swedish, "Don't you follow? They grow the shit into the plant. Look at the picture with the crates. There's no fucking limit to how much they can send."

Abdulkarim said, *"Allahu akbar."*

Abdulkarim was max-speeded all the way back in the stretch. He lay on one of the seats and sang with a Fanta in hand. Around his nose— coke rings.

JW was lit even before he did a line.

Fahdi tried to communicate with the driver. He wanted to change radio stations.

The meeting at Warwickshire'd ended with Chris explaining some economic conditions. Abdulkarim'd promised they would think it over. They'd said good-bye. Chris'd given Adbulkarim a little envelope—in which they'd found the white powder they'd just consumed.

JW asked why they hadn't just sealed the deal right then. He'd done the numbers; profit would be huge.

"No, you don't get it. Me, I'm not the high boss. Chris is not the boss, either. Tomorrow, the real gangstas meet in London. If you're lucky, you get to come along."

It was the first time during the entire trip that JW thought, There's someone above Abdulkarim.

Two days later, they'd switched hotels. Abdulkarim'd asked JW to wait in his room all day. Something was going to happen; that was blue-sky clear.

JW watched TV, smoked despite the no-smoking policy, played games on his phone. He felt more restless than ever. Tried to read but couldn't. Called Sophie. She didn't pick up. Thought about her, rubbed one out, jizzed in one of the free towels from the hotel. Drank champagne from the minibar, smoked again, watched British TV commercials. Texted Sophie, Mom, Nippe, Fredrik, Jet Set Carl. Played cell phone games again, tapped up a bath but didn't get in. Read *FHM* magazine. Checked out the fine-looking centerfold chicks.

At three o'clock, he went down to the street and bought a Twix and a bottle of Diet Coke. Then he ordered a club sandwich to be delivered to his room.

He thought, Where the hell is Abdulkarim?

When he got back to the room, he sat down on the bed and pulled his legs up. Thought about Camilla. When he got back to Sweden, he was going to weed through all the leads once and for all. Call the police again—he had to know what they were finding out. But right now: focus on the C business.

Finally, at four o'clock, there was a knock at the door.

Abdulkarim was waiting outside. "He wants you to come with. I've told him what we saw. We've discussed everything. Now he wants to hear your opinion. Have you as a calculator. It's time. Time to negotiate. You and the boss."

JW's heart pounded. He understood what this meant.

"You moved fast and straight up, buddy. Remember when I picked you up outside Kvarnen? Fucking lucky you didn't say no. I wouldn't ask twice. You know that? And now you sitting at the deal table with the boss. My boss. Me, not the one sitting there."

JW wondered if he heard a hint of jealousy.

He threaded his arms through the newly bought club blazer and praised Harvey Nichols for the sweet clothes.

Put on the cashmere coat.

Felt ready for anything.

Abdulkarim'd told him what hotel he was going to, The Savoy. How sick was that? The Savoy, one of the world's ten best.

It was in the West End. The hotel's restaurant had a star in the *Guide Rouge*.

JW glided past. Self-confidence was all you needed, just like at home at Kharma. He announced his arrival at the reception desk. Two minutes later, a man arrived wearing a dark glam-cut jacket with a silk handkerchief in the breast pocket. His sported a backslick and a languid style. Unmistakable—a true cocaine king.

The man introduced himself in slightly accented Swedish. "Hi, JW. I've heard a lot about you. My name is Nenad. I work with Abdulkarim sometimes."

False humility. It should really be: Abdulkarim works *under* me.

It was nice to speak Swedish. They chatted. Nenad was only in London for the night. Negotiations had to be quick.

JW saw himself in Nenad—a Stureplan type with the wrong roots.

They had a seat in the hotel lobby. Nenad ordered a cognac, finest XO aging.

Large crystal chandeliers hung from the ceiling. Persian carpets lay under the classically designed leather armchairs. The ashtray was real silver.

Nenad asked questions. JW filled in what Abdulkarim hadn't gotten or had misunderstood. Nenad seemed to have a grip on most of it. He saw the potential, understood the risks and opportunities. After an hour's discussion, he reached an objective: first and foremost to import as big a load as possible, preferably in cabbage form.

JW agreed.

They kept discussing. Prices in England, primarily prices in Stockholm. Storage methods, transport methods, increased market shares.

Sales strategies, dealing tricks, new people to enroll. Payment method to the syndicate: money transfer, SWIFT system, or cash.

JW'd learned a lot from his talks with Jorge. Heard how Jorge's words, views, and thoughts came out of his own mouth.

Nenad liked JW's ideas, the way he spit.

When they were finished, he lit a cigar. "JW, think through everything we've talked about one more time. Tonight at seven, we're negotiating with the other side. I want you next to me. You need to be clear on all the numbers."

JW got up and thanked Nenad. He almost bowed.

"See you later. It'll be fun."

JW felt like he was floating on clouds.

He remembered the moment in Abdulkarim's gypsy cab when he'd first decided to help him sell C. Now—seven months later—he was talking big business with Nenad at the Savoy.

JW was a player.

For real.

Soon they were going to negotiate the world's biggest fucking deal.

42

Two bad things. One, he'd been humiliated. Two, he'd lost his job.

Three good things. He was still a part of the organization—not totally out in the cold. He still had drive—possibilities to get ahead, maybe without R. And three, he was still alive.

Two days'd passed since the events at Fiskartorpet's ski-jumping tower. Mrado remembered Radovan's account in detail. Could cite every word/tone/gesture.

Rado'd stoked his own fire. Demonic. Dictatorial. Deadly.

But nothing'd happened. Mrado'd left like after any other meeting with R. At the end of the dinner, they'd talked about general subjects—cars, bars, laundering, dough.

Still, he'd been crowned a nobody.

There'd been total silence in the Range Rover on the way home. The only thought in Mrado's head: Jokso would never've dealt with a situation like this. Not been so hysterical. Not dumped his best partner.

Mrado went on with his life despite the demotion. Went to the gym. Went to Pancrease. Fought with greater frenzy than he had for a long time. Omar Elalbaoui, pleased. "Good recoil to your punches, juggernaut!" he hollered when Mrado sparred in the ring. That Elalbaoui yelled like that at Pancrease—a sensation.

He ruminated. Should he screw Radovan's orders and run a night along the coat-check route? Before he'd even finished the thought, he realized what a shitty impulse it was. Kamikaze idea.

But, on the other hand, Radovan wasn't immortal. He thought he was Jokso, but just like for Jokso, the carpet could be pulled from under his feet in an instant.

In Mrado's head: the possibility of busting Rado's monopoly.

The idea had to be perfected.

Mrado's thoughts flowed in conked-out currents. But at the same time, on an energy-efficient circuit, the idea was sparking: His strength was in his contacts; he should be able to break Rado, trick the fucking turncoat. If R. was planning to redecorate the Yugo hierarchy, there was a chance someone else'd been given the boot, too. Mrado had to find out who.

He rummaged around rumors. Dug dirt. Ratko knew some. Bobban some. Radovan was in the process of cleaning out the house.

Mrado guessed. Probably not Goran. Not Stefanovic. Could it be his friend Nenad?

Mrado began preparations for breaking out on his own the following day.

He was gonna play like in poker, even though it'd gone to hell the last time at the casino: the *Big Slick*. All or nothing. Mrado'd made up his mind. He was gonna take the plunge—all in.

Mrado versus the Stockholm underworld's single most powerful man. It required planning.

Mrado versus Jokso's heir to the throne. It demanded brainpower.

Mrado versus a tool. Mrado would take home the trophy, but he needed faith even to make himself believe it.

He brought out the notebook that'd been left untouched since he'd gone Latino hunting.

Thought about everything he'd done for Rado just to find that *blatte*. Broken the fingers of the fugitive's cousin. Beaten up his chick. Waited in his car day and night and interrogated bums outside of homeless shelters. Turned the Latino into a human puddle. And what were his thanks? Mrado'd made up his mind—he couldn't let it end with his own humiliation.

At the top of a fresh page in the notebook, he wrote, *Secure my life*.

Started to list measures that had to be taken.

Move. Alternatives: become a lodger, sublet, buy a house through a front man, get a trailer.

He reread what he'd just written. Get a trailer—yeah right. Still, let it stand. He had to brainstorm. All ideas had to be put to paper.

Kept going.

Get a new car.

Get a dog: pit bull, German shepherd, or other attack dog.

Always keep the bulletproof vest on.

Get an even lighter gun. To carry, always.

Get an even better alarm system for the car and potential new home.

Arrange for a bodyguard. Possible people: Ratko, Bobban, Mahmud. Who can be trusted?

Stop training at Fitness Club.

Stop training at Pancrease.

Stop eating at Clara's and Bronco's.

Get a new cell phone and prepaid plan.

Start going to a new gym.

Change habits. Drive different roads to the same place. Change workout schedule.

Make Lovisa move, switch schools, and get an unlisted address.

Get a PO box address.

Write down and collect evidence about what I know about Radovan's business and store it in a safe place. My best insurance policy.

He looked over the list again.

As was his habit, he underlined one word: *Lovisa.*

Most important. Most difficult.

He called her mother, the hate object, Annika.

No answer.

He left her a message. Hoped she would call back despite the mess with family court.

Decided once again. He'd make a go for R. But he had to take it easy. No point in rushing. The preparations were key.

Two days later. Nenad's slow drawl on the phone. "Mrado, are you somewhere you can talk?"

"Yeah, sure. What's up? When did you get back from London?"

Mrado's interest was piqued. Nenad's tone suggested something.

"I got back a few days ago. Things went fantastic there. Anything happen here at home? How's your daughter? Is your line secure?"

Nenad let the last question slip in as though he'd asked about the latest K-1 fight on TV, something totally normal.

"These days? With you and me both marked by the Nova bitches? I don't think so."

"Could you meet me outside Ringen in twenty? It's important."

Dreary weather outside. March's drabness was dragging on for longer than usual. And the area by Ringen was as dreary as the weather. Across from Ringen: the Clarion Hotel's enormous entrance illuminated by colorful spotlights.

It was quarter past three in the afternoon. A Sunday.

Nenad arrived with the fur collar on his coat popped—mink against three-day stubble. Mrado saw something in his gaze he'd never seen in Nenad's eyes before. Mrado thought, Is it panic/fear or just confusion? Something'd happened to Nenad; it was obvious.

They walked into the Clarion.

Nenad talked to a pretty girl at the reception desk. He'd apparently planned this well—had booked a mini spa session.

They walked up a flight of stairs. The smell of chlorine hit them in the hallway.

Registered at another reception desk. Got towels with the Clarion's monogram embroidered in gold-colored thread. Felt slippers. A set of bottles each: shower gel, shampoo, conditioner, moisturizer. Terry-cloth bathrobes.

The door to the pool was fogged up.

They went straight to the showers. Rinsed off. Didn't bother with the regular sauna.

Nenad'd booked nice; a private mini sauna was included.

The mini sauna fit three people on the top and three people on the lower level. Classic wood paneling covered the walls and ceiling. On one short side was a round window facing out to the Skanstull Bridge—ultraurban. Cool.

They each sat down on a towel.

Mrado studied Nenad's face again. That strange something was still there in his eyes, and he looked tired, too. Not his usual, confident self. Something was off.

"Mrado, you're the only one I trust right now."

Mrado cut right to the chase. "What happened?"

"Shit show."

"I'm not totally surprised. All of you is radiating 'shit show.' Let me guess. Rado shit."

"Bull's-eye. I suspected you knew. I've been cut. Demoted. Humiliated."

"Tell me." Mrado, strategic: was gonna wait to drop his own bomb.

"Came home from London two days ago. Rigged the biggest fucking deal ever. You can't even imagine, it's so huge. Then what happens? Rado calls my house at one in the morning. I'm making out with this hot little piece of Östermalm ass I brought home. I go there. To his house, that is. Stefanovic brings me into the lib. Classic Radovan audience. Then I get a long lecture about his fucking ideas, a lot of smack about the new type of organization. Ends with him telling me I'm no longer in charge of the C business and am being demoted in the call-girl sphere. That I'm a fucking nobody. That I can forget about my role in the group. And, you know, I just sat there and took it. Felt the pressure—if I'd put up a fight, it could've ended there. Stefanovic was trigger-happy. Fuck. That's the thanks I get. That cunt. And I just busted my hump in London for that douchebag. Biggest fucking deal ever."

Nenad's reaction as opposed to Mrado's: healthier/angrier/more childish. Mrado envied him. That was the right way to tackle this shit. To lose it.

"Nenad, same thing happened to me the day before."

Nenad's mouth looked like a gaping black hole in the heat of the sauna. Both felt the same way. But above all, they felt relieved not to be alone. Someone to share the shit with. Someone to plan the counterattack with.

They talked for two hours. In and out of the sauna. Sitting in reclining wooden chairs outside the sauna. In the showers. In the pool. Ladled water onto the coals. Let the steam rise. Breathed through their mouths. Analyzed. Scrutinized. Rhapsodized.

Why'd they been demoted? What did the situation look like in terms of potential repudiation? Sit tight or try to strike back right away?

Mrado told Nenad in detail how he'd tried to cut himself a bigger slice of the coat-check cake and about his work with the market division. Which persons might be of help. Who he'd made a good connection with, the Bandidos' Jonas Haakonsen, the Wolfpack Brotherhood's Magnus Lindén, and others. But above all, he told Nenad about the feeling he'd had of a confidence crisis between himself and R.

They'd never before spoken so openly about the situation within the organization. And what was encouraging was that they shared so many views regarding Rado.

By the time they parted ways, they'd established three principles. It was the two of them together now. They would keep their mouths fucking watertight about all this. And the only way out: Radovan's fall or their own.

Let the war begin.

43

Obvious—something'd happened to her.

Jorge'd called the brothel madam at least fifteen times a day for the past two days. The effect: She'd stopped picking up her phone. The rings went unanswered. She'd probably gotten a new number. Before she'd stopped picking up, he'd gotten the same answer every time: "I'm sorry, I have no idea where Nadja is." Fat chance—*mentirosa*.

In summation, the situation was clear: Nadja's disappearance, the terror in the eyes of the hooker in her room, the brothel madam's lies.

The tough question: Was it his fault? The thought ate away at him. Ordinary Jorge's basic philosophy: No one is responsible for anyone else. Life's too short to wait around for cash flow. Serve yourself and let others take care of themselves. Worked for blow biz. Worked for cigarette deals at Österåker. Worked when there were direct material gains for J-boy to collect. But now there was something else driving him.

Jorge saw himself as the Yugos' nemesis. And the war against them entailed dangers for others. He already knew that. They'd threatened to hurt Paola. Now Nadja was gone. Where was she? What did she know?

When he found out what'd happened to her—Radovan would have to pay for that, too. Project R. just became more and more important.

Abdulkarim and Fahdi were back from London. Apparently, they had a massive deal in the works there. Abdulkarim'd called. Been restrained. Still, it was obvious—his voice verging on ecstasy. Bare brief: A shipment would arrive within a few months. He didn't say with what, how much, from whom, not exactly when, not how. Until then, they'd move the grams that Jorge'd recently pocketed via the Brazilian. Plus other smaller shipments coming up. Above all, they were gonna keep expanding the market. More sales channels, corners, enlisted bodies.

Blow was blowing up. Jorge was happy he'd stayed in Svenland. Thought back to when JW'd stood bent over him in the woods. Explained Abdulkarim's grand borough expansion. And now, the kale was being harvested faster and thicker than for a big publicly traded company. A project player's predetermined track.

In Jorge's mind, the money increasingly became a means rather than an end. A potent instrument in the enactment of Project R.

Next phase: work on Giant Karl.

Jorge knew the following: Radovan ran a prostitution business. Nenad was in charge. Girls were imported from the former Yugoslavia and other Eastern Bloc countries. Pure fucking *Lilya 4-Ever*. And there were Swedish women involved, too. Nadja's brothel was a part of the business. The place was run by the brothel madam, Jelena Lukic, and the dude with the hoodie. Jorge'd looked him up: Zlatko Petrovic. Nadja'd had her own pimp or boyfriend—the giant, Micke. The latter's role was somewhat unclear. More interesting: The apartment brothel wasn't the only one in Radovan's whore empire. There were more. Further fucking in finer places with finer females. Nadja'd told him: Swedish men'd partaken in parties whose only purpose was for the poor suckers to dip their wicks. Probably paid Radovan handsomely. Gave the Yugo boss contacts and protection, too. The crux: Nothing pointed straight to Radovan, not even to Nenad. Everyone knew who was behind it, but no one'd seen anything. With one exception: Nadja'd met Radovan at one of the pussy parties. He had to see her. Know more.

According to Nadja, there were two people involved in organizing the parties and fixing up the girls: a Jonte and a Giant Karl.

According to Sophie: a Jet Set Carl—Stureplan's golden god, party pasha, scenester supreme.

According to Jorge: The names were too similar to be a coincidence.

Evening. Jorge, ready to go. Sitting with Fahdi at home in the gorilla's lair. Vodka, Schweppes tonic, and weed on the table. IKEA glasses, half-melted ice cubes in a deep bowl, Rizla papers, and a lighter. On the TV: Jenna Jameson being mounted by two American musclemen, on mute. From the speakers: Usher. Fahdi informed him matter-of-factly, "He first Negro ever with three hits on *Billboard* lists in States.

Racist pigs." Fahdi'd clearly been influenced by Abdulkarim. Generally believed that USA spelled Satan. Took every opportunity to hate on the place.

Jorge's idea for the night was simple. They'd hit the town. Raid Stureplan. Find Jet Set Carl. Then Jorge would have a talk with the guy. Finally: Jorge and Fahdi would each find a blonde. With luck, get to play an away game.

Fahdi kept talking about London. Proudly exhibited his Gucci jacket. Described hot strippers, glam boutiques, thick crowds. Described the gun he'd had there.

Jorge wasn't too impressed. Remembered the arsenal Fahdi kept hidden in his closet. The dude was a traveling army.

They downed their drinks.

Jorge rose. "Should we bring some fun?" He pointed toward the kitchen, where scales and envelopes were spread out alongside Red Line baggies of blow.

Fahdi got up, as well. "For us or sell?"

"Not to sell. I've pretty much stopped selling retail. Anyway, that's JW's turf. We don't compete with our own. When's he coming home?"

"No clue. Had stuff to take care of in England. Staying a couple extra days."

Jorge thought, Fahdi—the guys in *Dumb & Dumber* were smart in comparison. He didn't get the rules of the game. The pyramid: Some sold on the streets, some sold to dealers, and some sold to the dealers' dealers. Nowadays, Jorge was almost on top. But Fahdi had strengths—a certain kindness and, obviously, his muscle power.

They called for a cab. Automatic recording on the other end of the line: "Would you like a taxi to come to ROSENHILLSVÄGEN right away? Press one."

Jorge said, "Why do they always gotta yell the street name double as loud as the rest of the sentence, so you get tinnitus for the rest of the night?" Jorge pressed one.

They went down to the street. Jumped in the cab. The Stockholm night down to town.

Stureplan in full swing.

They got out by Svampen. Looked around. Where to begin?

The places around Stureplan's party aorta had their own particular caste system. Kharma, Laroy, Plaza, and Köket—on top. Richest/brattiest/best. Sturehof, Sturecompagniet, the Lydmar Hotel—next tier. Select/bratty/somewhat older scene. Spy Bar, Clara's—Yugo Mafia/bodybuilder/celeb locus. The Lab, East—had their own clientele. Undici, Crazy Horse—regular honest-to-goodness Sven dank dives.

Easy equation: Jorge and Fahdi had to get into a top-caste place. Hardest. Especially for two male immigrants with the word *blatte* written across their foreheads in neon letters.

They started at Köket. Killer line. Seventeen-year-old girls with threads so bare, they would've caught a chill even on a summer night. Downy Östermalm boys in tailored coats and slicked hair. Older, randy slimesters in even more deluxe coats, same slicked hair. Dudes who spent their entire lives within a one-mile radius. Worked at the stockbrokerage firms that framed Stureplan, ate lunch/dinner at the restaurants on the adjacent streets, Biblioteksgatan, Birger Jarlsgatan, and Grev Turegatan, lived a stone's throw away on Brahegatan, Kommendörsgatan, Linnégatan. And, of course, partied here.

They glimpsed the legendary Toad at the front of the line. Real name, Peter Strömquist. Stockholm profile. Silver spoon–born. Pompous. Had a standing invitation to all the parties any self-respecting brat dreamed of being invited to. Knew everyone and anyone who mattered. Good sign that he was on his way into Köket.

From Jorge's perspective: marginalization accentuated. The human mass was a rerun of the feudal system. Some harbored the right to sweep on past the plebs. Some played princes in the Stockholm territory. Others were kings, like the Jet Set guy. Some sold their souls as mercenaries: the bouncers. The *blattes*, at the very bottom. With luck, they might be able to beg their way in.

Only trick he knew was bribery.

Fahdi cleared the way. Swept the little girls to the side. Five-hundred-kronor bill rolled up in his hand. At first, the bouncer looked at him coldly. Message: Even you must understand that YOU'RE not getting in here. Saw the bill. Eyed Jorge.

Let them in.

Crowded.

The music was pumping, something that mostly sounded like a medley of cell phone ringtones.

At the bar, a group of guys were advancing on two chicks with the help of bubbly in ice buckets. The chicks danced in place. Winked. Let themselves be treated.

Fahdi went to the bar. Ordered two beers.

Jorge made his way down the stairs to the lower level. Past the DJ booth. Tonight, DJ Sonic was playing. Mr. Main Street, who'd become an adorable mascot for the Östermalm brats. The next step on the class ladder in sight. Smiled in recognition at 90 percent of all the dames who walked past.

Jorge recognized faces. No one recognized him. Had Abdulkarim and self-tanner to thank. Despite that, J-boy was still a nigger. Market value: zero.

Grabbed hold of a random girl.

Terrified look.

"Relax, girlie. I'm just wondering if you've seen Jet Set Carl tonight?"

Blank response. She didn't know who he was talking about.

He kept asking around. Fahdi showed up with two beers in hand. Wondered what Jorge was up to.

No point in explaining.

Danced away from him.

Asked more people.

The broads were bronzed. The guys all looked like JW. Jorge walked up and down the stairs. Leaned over and yelled his question into people's ears. Tried to look neutral. Didn't want them to think he was making a move right now.

Kept at it for forty minutes.

Finally, a girl screamed in his ear—could hardly hear her over the music. "He's pretty much always at Kharma."

Jorge tried to find Fahdi in the crowd. Couldn't see him. Tried to call his cell. Couldn't even hear as he punched in the numbers. What were the chances that Fahdi'd hear his phone ring with that background music?

Gave up on him.

Jorge walked out onto the street. Up along Sturegatan. Texted Fahdi: *Going to Kharma. Meet me there later.*

The line looked like an organic mass disguised as human hope. The humiliation was even worse in the freezing cold—racism spat straight in the *cara*.

Right moment. Right look. In the bouncer's hand, the money—five hundred kronor. Eyes locked. The bouncer's hand waved past the line.

Jorge was in. Repeated it to himself: J-boy, you're in.

Perfecto.

He ordered a bottle of Heineken in the bar. Checked out the scene. Recognized some other lucky *blatte* boys with bottle service. Jorge walked up to their table. They didn't recognize him. Still, it was obvious that they felt some sort of camaraderie; they knew they were all in the same seat. In the wrong place and on cloud nine.

They chatted for a bit. Graded girls. Praised breasts. Appraised butts. Jorge treated them to a quick line each. Turned toward the wall. On the back of credit cards, sniff/sniff. It worked.

The world picked up speed. Jorge on top.

Asked the bartender about Jet Set Carl. "No worries," the bar guy replied. "He always gets here around one, stands by the cashiers and welcomes people."

Jet Set Carl: jizz set Carl.

Jorge waited. The immigrant boys by the drink table hit on high school girls from Djursholm—Orange County Scando-style. Culture clash of consequence. Those choice chicks'd probably never even talked to anyone from a non-European country before, except for the token adopted kid in school. The *blatte* boys' viewpoint was simple: All Swedish chicks want me and therefore they're whores.

Jorge watched the play unfold. The guys bought drinks. Did their best. The girls drank and let themselves be treated. Dissed them at the same time. According to Jorge, the niggers' only chance was that one of the tarts got blackout.

The clock struck one.

A guy who could be Jet Set Carl was positioned behind the cash register near the entrance. Dressed in a pinstriped jacket, jeans, loafers with the Gucci buckle. Greeted the beautiful people on their way in.

All the vibes screamed, This dude never lets his self-confidence flag.

Jorge stepped up.

"Hey."

Jet Set Carl turned around, surprised.

"Are you Jet Set Carl?"

The dude did his best to crack a smile.

"Yep. I'm called that by those who know me." Emphasis on the words *those who know me*. Message to J-boy: Whoever you are, you do NOT know me.

"I've heard a lot of good things about you. Not just that you run this place and are a damn nice guy. Other stuff, too."

Jet Set Carl laid his hand on Jorge's shoulder. They were the same size.

"I'm sorry, but I don't know what you're talking about."

"I've heard about you and Jonte. You run some sweet gigs together."

Something in Jet Set Carl's eye. A mischievous gleam. Then he returned to his jovial self.

"Excuse me, nice to meet you, but unfortunately I've got to keep working. We'll have to chat more later. Have a good night."

Jorgelito, snubbed. Still, he'd seen something in the jet set guy's eye.

Jorge sent more texts to Fahdi. Got back: *Blessed night. Allah with me. Going home with a smokin' puma.* Fahdi'd gotten lucky. Congrats to him.

Jorge hung out with the immigrant guys at their table.

The clock struck two. The blow-glow waned. He went into the bathroom. Poured out thirty milligrams of ice. Pulled a heavy line.

The kick kicked in. Energy fantasy. Gunning the highest gear.

Went back out into the venue.

Walked up to Jet Set Carl.

"Can we talk?"

Jet Set Carl put on an obviously uncomfortable face.

"Sorry, I have to work. Can we talk later?" He made a gesture with his hand.

Jorge wanted to talk now. Right now.

Too late.

Jorge felt himself being lifted from behind. He tried to turn around, but his head was fixed in a lock. Broad arms. Bouncer gloves.

He screamed. Was carried. Out.

Thought through the C fog, Where the fuck is Fahdi when you need him?

Jorgelito kicked out. He was a high loser with soiled honor. *Blatte* at Kharma, beware. You're not really welcome here. Spread the word.

But he knew one thing: His dignity would never be shat on again by the Yugos or any of their allies.

The blow-flow he was in—deadly.

Jorge wouldn't give up.

This night belonged to him.

This night belonged to the Project.

The Radovan fag was gonna get it. Jet Set Carl or no Jet Set Carl. Fuck him. Jorge would get his hands on enough info anyway.

He just needed to talk more with Nadja.

Had gotten Zlatko Petrovic's number from Fahdi. Jorge'd tried to reach him several times, without success.

He stood in the middle of Stureplan. In the background: hot-dog hawkers, trashed teenagers, shivering brats, boozy forty-year-olds.

Picked up his phone. No new texts from Fahdi, which meant he'd gotten an away game.

He dialed the number to the pimp, Zlatko.

The signal went through.

Finally, for the first time on this number, someone picked up.

"Hello?"

"Hi, I wanna have some fun tonight."

"Then I'm your man. Got a name?"

Jorge gave Fahdi's alias.

Zlatko replied, "All right. Course we can arrange something."

"Great. I wanna see Nadja."

Silence on the other end of the line.

Jorge said, "Did you hear me, or what? I like that Nadja girl."

"I don't know what you want. But she's not with us anymore. Sorry." The chill in Zlatko's voice was colder than freezer-kept vodka.

"So then where can I see her? She was so good."

"Yo, listen up. Never ask about Nadja ever again. She's not with us. I know who you are. One more word about that fucking Nadja and we'll crush you."

The call was cut off—Zlatko'd indexed red.

Jorge was in a cab on his way to Fahdi's apartment. Racked with angst. Racked with blow.

On his retina: Paola and Nadja. And the others: Mrado, Ratko, Radovan. He was gonna burn them. Avenge himself. Avenge Nadja. Radovan was gonna have to pay with bullet holes in his eyes. Assault in a forest. Paola's contorted face.

Chaotic fragments of reality.

Hate.

Paola.

Hate.

The Radovan fucker.

Pendejo.

The cabbie looked anxiously at him. "Want me to walk you upstairs, buddy?"

Jorge said no thanks. Asked the guy to wait.

Up to Fahdi's. Jorge always carried a set of keys to his apartment— needed to be able to get at the stash, Red Line baggies, and scales they kept there. Opened. Called out. No one home. Fahdi was probably getting what he wanted most.

To the closet.

Jorge knew what he was looking for. Fahdi'd proudly exhibited his gear to him and JW a month earlier. He leaned in.

Rummaged around.

Got hold of the shotgun. Opened it by pressing the safety on the side. Put in two red shells the size of rolls of Life Savers. Stuffed a fist-ful of shells in the front pocket of his jeans. It bulged.

Tucked the shotgun inside his jacket. Wasn't visible at all. Sawed-off barrels were good.

The taxi was purring on the street.

The blow flowed through his veins in a pulsating beat.

He vacuumed up the last white milligrams as the taxi drove off. Unclear if the driver noticed anything.

The cab accelerated on the freeway.

Hallonbergen.

A cold wind blew along the external hallway. He accidentally knocked over a kid's sled that was leaning against the wall. Apparently, there were ordinary families as brothel neighbors.

He rang the doorbell.

Someone pulled aside the cover for the peephole. A voice from inside: "What's your name?"

Sounded like the brothel madam. Jorge hoped that the Zlatko dude hadn't told her anything about his call fifty minutes ago. Fahdi's alias again. There was a password, too. He knew both.

She unlocked the door. It was her, the brothel madam in her strange outfit—the blazer with the slit in the back. Clown-painted. Scary.

Jorge slammed the door shut behind him. Cut right to the chase. "I wanna see Nadja."

The brothel madam stiffened. On her guard 100 percent.

She said in her shitty Eastern Bloc Swedish, "Listen, she not here anymore. If you the one call me hundred million time, you can piss off."

Unanticipated aggression. Determined menace.

J-boy felt close to the breaking point. Pent-up waves of explosive blow-temper crashed against the inside of his skull. This'd be the last time a Serb fucked with him.

Took a step toward the brothel madam. "You fucking cunt. Either you tell me where Nadja is or I'll take you out."

The brothel madam cranked up her volume fiercely. "Who the fuck you think you are?"

The effect of the raised voice: From the shadows, from the hallway, Zlatko appeared.

The brothel madam freaked. Kept yelling at Jorge to scram. That he'd regret his behavior.

Zlatko positioned himself a foot from Jorge. His breath smelled like hell. He said in a calm voice, "What did I tell you on the phone just now? Are you slow? Stop digging around in this thing. Just leave."

Super Serbian–style. Reminded him of Mrado.

He could feel the abuse in his back. Legs. Arms.

Jorge tore out the shotgun.

One shot at Zlatko.

Guts gone. Replaced with a gaping hole.

Ground tripe on the wall behind him.

The brothel madam screamed.

Another shot—her head disappeared. Brain matter on the velvet couches.

The recoil slammed into Jorge's shoulder. Hurt.

Jorge opened the weapon. Stuck his hand in his pocket. Reloaded, two new shells.

From the hall came a man. Sheet-white face. Bare chest. Unbuttoned pants. In shock.

Jorge shot. Missed. Forty-square-inch hole in the plaster wall. A cloud of dust.

He ran toward him. The man stumbled on his sagging pants.

Cried. Begged.

Jorge stood over him. The double barrel against his head.

Checked his pockets. Found a wallet. Pulled out a driver's license.

Read aloud, "Torsten Johansson. You've never seen me."

The old trick remained where he was, sobbing on the floor.

Other than that, the apartment was quiet.

"Give me your cell phone. Get on your stomach. Hold your hands above your head. I've got some stuff to take care of."

The man didn't move. He lay with his head folded between his arms, his knees pulled up in a fetal position.

"Don't you understand Swedish, or what? Do what I told you. Now."

The man stretched out. Fumbled in his pants pocket. Brought out a cell phone. Gave it to Jorge. Put his hands on his head.

Jorge, again: "You've never seen me."

He checked the whore rooms. In one of them was a girl, crouching against the wall, her head between her knees. It wasn't Nadja.

Jorge walked out into the hall. Didn't look at the bodies. Stepped right through the chaos. Into the kitchen.

It was dirty in there. A little table of white wood and a chair with a steel frame and a soft seat cushion. Coffee stains everywhere. Ads from Hallonbergen's pizza joints were pinned on the fridge with free Social Democratic party handout magnets from the 2002 election.

On the table was a laptop. Pretty much what Jorge'd suspected.

Best of all: It was turned on. Jorge sat down on the chair. The computer was plugged into the wall. Question: If he pulled the plug, would the battery kick in or would it die? Jorge wasn't exactly a computer geek. But he did know one thing: If the computer died, there was a risk that it'd demand some sort of password in order to start back up. Could fuck the whole thing up if he couldn't get into it again.

Cocaine-lit assessments: He couldn't stay in the apartment many more seconds. Had he touched anything?

No.

He took the risk—pulled the power cord.

Checked the screen.

God loved Jorge.

The computer was still on.

He ran toward the front door. Through the hall. Was about to grab the door handle, when a phone rang. Sony Ericsson's "Old Phone" ringtone—sounded like an ancient spin-dial telephone. Someone's cell was ringing. Probably the john's, the madam's, the pimp's, or one of the prostitutes'. He checked the john's. Wasn't the one making the noise. Jorge listened. Saw the blood. The clotty substance on the ceiling and floors. Finally heard. It was coming from the pimp's pocket.

He was holding the shotgun in one hand, the computer in the other. Difficult to maneuver. He put the computer down. Groped in the pimp's jacket pocket. The vibrations, unmistakable.

Got hold of the phone. A letter combination on the display: JSC. Only one person it could be—the Carl fucker.

Jorge picked up. "Yes."

"Yo, it's me. Could you put the one with the big tits in a cab to my house?"

Jorge, perplexed. The dude sounded trashed. What to say? Try to imitate Zlatko?

Instead, he mumbled as much as he could. "Sorry, she's not here."

"Damn, that's too bad."

A single thought: Have to say something smart. Something that will lead somewhere.

"Eh, so when is the next big thing happening again?"

"You ought to know, Mr. Fix. The twenty-ninth, in two weeks. The one with the tits really isn't there?" Jet Set Carl was slurring worse than a heavyweight postknockout.

Jorge got a lightning rod–hot idea. "Sorry, no. Hey, one more thing. Had a guy here today who definitely has to come on the twenty-ninth."

"Come on, get real. Not possible."

"Fuck it is. Nenad okayed him. Just wanted to let you know, too. His alias is Daniel Cabrera."

"All right, fine. You need a password?"

"Yeah, that'd be dope. Would you forward it to me?"

"I'll forward it to you. You're talking like a fucking lawyer. I'll text you a word right now. Later."

Jorge put the phone in his pocket. The shotgun under his jacket. The computer in his hand.

Threw a quick glance at the bodies. Felt sick.

Thought he'd be immune after all the video gore he'd watched as a kid. Really, it was just the opposite. He felt worse because of all the shit he'd seen on TV. Or it was just the effect of the blow-rush.

Pulled the sleeve of his sweater down over his hand in order to grip the handle to the front door. Nope, no CSI team would find his thumbprint.

He walked out. Felt Zlatko's cell vibrate in his pocket—the text from Jet Set Carl.

It was dark out.

Hallonbergen by night.

Deserted.

44

JW was on his way to the Isle of Man. Manx Airways flew six times a day. It took a little over an hour from Heathrow to the airport outside Douglas, the main town on the island. As opposed to flying with Ryanair, it was smooth, speedy, stylish.

He was still walking around in a dream state—the quantities that could be shipped from Warwickshire. Pricing and upward curves. The C cycle—a sunny future for the trade. The Arab's ideas would be realized. JW would be a wealthy man.

Two days ago, he'd met Nenad at a hotel in London. The man who was Abdul's superior rocked a totally different style than the Arab. Felt good to meet the mythic/shadowy boss. To get closer to the top.

The negotiations with Nenad and the Brits'd gone well. They sat in one of the hotel's conference rooms. Nenad'd booked a room first, but the Brits asked to switch it as soon as they got there. Nenad ate it up—higher security awareness than Abdulkarim.

The conference room was decorated with rococo furniture. An elliptical table of walnut wood in the middle of the room. Crystal wall lamps spread subdued lighting. Pretty different from Abdulkarim's living room.

The Brits looked like soccer hooligans. Nothing like the style they'd seen on Chris, the guy who'd met JW, Abdulkarim, and Fahdi at the packaging plant. The guy in charge was in his fifties, with gray hair combed back and casual clothes: Paul & Shark polo shirt, Burberry jacket, and Prada shoes. Pockmarked face and calm demeanor. He oozed confident power. The other guy was overweight but hadn't compensated for his size by wearing baggy clothes—gave a slightly ridiculous impression when the Pringle pullover stretched taut over the man's spare tires. But after the initial pleasantries, that impression was wiped right out—the fatso was a bone-hard brainiac. JW sat with his notebook and calculator in front of him. The fatso did all the counting in his head.

They negotiated the price of the wares, different grades, shipping methods, payment systems. They went over the risks versus the proceeds. Customs, narcs, competing networks, companies that could be used as fronts. Ways to guarantee that neither side got ripped off. What would happen if pounds disappeared along the way. Transportation was ultimately at whose risk, exactly?

The Brits were cautious. Their routine felt calculated. After two hours, Nenad asked for a break.

They went up to Nenad's room. Compared their negotiation position with their calculations. The deal Nenad was after consisted of 90 percent pure coke in cabbage for under 350 kronor a gram. Would probably total two containers, with five tons of cabbage per container. The five hundred outermost cabbages would go without C as a safety measure, in case of crap customs and sanitation department checks. Sum: two thousand cabbages filled with ice. Fifty grams per veggie, which is to say: one hundred kilos—220 twenty pounds—of cocaine to be transported by trailer and ferry. Some bribing of the shipping company would be necessary in order to separate the containers from those with only regular cabbages inside, and to keep a special eye on them when the situation demanded, including some bribes to actual cabbage suppliers. In Sweden, they had to cover the costs for driving, for reduced checks of the containers, plus fixed sales and distribution costs. Price tag from the Brits: between thirty and forty million. Price on the street in Stockholm after discounting price pressure: seventy to eighty million. Iiiiiill income.

After an hour and a half in the room, Nenad'd made up his mind. The deal was definitely worth going for. He set a bar for the lowest-possible price, plus a level of security, the highest imaginable.

They went down.

Continued negotiating with the Brits. The mood was good. Beneath the surface, the Brits' attitude glared: You know you can't get a better deal anywhere else. Gave them psychological advantage. Gave them mental strength.

The negotiations dragged on; they kept at it for another two hours. JW got exhausted by all the numbers, appraisals, and calculations. At the same time, he loved the whole thing.

By two o'clock, the two parties'd reached a preliminary agreement. The tension eased up. Nenad shook hands with the older Brit. They looked deeply into each other's eyes—the code of honor sealed the deal.

They would reconvene the next day at noon to confirm that the sale was finalized.

Nenad and JW had a seat in the piano bar at the hotel.

The Yugo ordered in two cognacs.

"JW, thank you for your help. I will convey my praise to Abdulkarim."

"Thank you for letting me take part. It was very interesting. I think we got a good deal in the end."

"Me, too. After our drink here, I'm going to run some numbers by Stockholm and hopefully get the whole deal approved."

"By who?"

"JW, sometimes it's best not to ask."

JW didn't answer. He'd seen the same stiff facial expression on Abdulkarim when his boss'd come up in conversation—the Arab'd never mentioned Nenad, even though JW'd nagged. The layers between the levels in the dealing hierarchy were airtight.

"One more thing. You've never met me. Don't recognize me. Won't call out to me at a bar. Will never mention my name to anyone."

JW got it. Nodded.

"It might get really sad if you do," Nenad said gravely.

"It's cool. I understand. Really. I understand."

The plane was small; each row was only one chair wide.

JW was forced to keep his phone turned off. The restlessness gnawed. He thought about what the police were doing. Were they getting anywhere? Maybe they'd called while he was away. If not, should he call Mom and tell her everything? She felt so remote. Bengt felt even more remote, on his way out of the picture altogether.

Outside, gray British weather. He couldn't even see the ocean beneath the plane, despite the fact that they were flying low.

The pilot reported: fifty-three degrees on the ground.

Gearing up to land, the plane passed through the haze.

It was drizzling.

The island appeared down below. Rolling hills dressed in trees sprouting new leaves.

JW on the Isle of Man. He was going to do this thing.

Douglas was situated on the water. The feeling was fiercely British.

The place was crawling with hotels, banks, and financial institutions. But few people—winter was off-season, only bankers and finance sharks on the streets. They were well dressed, well situated, and well informed about the rules on the Isle of Man—bank-privacy paradise.

Of course there were other spots in Europe that were as good: Luxembourg, Switzerland, Liechtenstein, the Channel Isles. But the downside was that those places aroused suspicion. The tax man and the financial-crime investigators immediately raised their eyebrows when they saw accounts registered in those types of places. The Isle of Man was more discreet, but the regulations were just as advantageous.

The basic idea of offshore jurisdiction: easy to create companies, strong company privacy, even stronger bank privacy, and tax-free, obviously.

JW checked into a small hotel overnight. Top-of-the-line service, every single staff person welcomed him by name. Impressive.

He walked along the beachfront boardwalk on the way to Central Union Bank's headquarters. A meeting'd been booked a month back with Darren Bell, a senior associate. According to trusty sources, Darren Bell was an exceedingly reliable person.

The building he was on his way into was ultraspruced. You could tell from ten yards away. The bottom section was made all of glass. The escalators up to the second level, a couple of enormous ficuses, and the gray Ligne Roset couches could be seen plainly from outside. JW walked through ten-foot-high revolving doors. Announced his arrival at the reception desk.

He looked around. Complex light fixtures of glass and chrome were hanging from thin cables. Marble floor. The Ligne Roset couches—empty. He thought, Does anyone ever sit on them?

No time to ponder. A man emerged from an elevator and introduced himself to JW. It was Darren Bell.

He was impeccably dressed in a gray suit with two buttons, a silk handkerchief in his breast pocket, blue tailored shirt with white stripes, and gold cuff links. The tie had a diagonal striped pattern in red, gray, and blue and was knotted with a tiny super-British knot. The Church shoes were brogues. JW dug his style—it was, simply put, corporate to the max.

JW was less formally dressed. The new club blazer with a white tailored shirt underneath, no tie. Pressed black cotton slacks. Correct but light and totally right—the client should be underdressed in relation to his adviser.

They took the elevator up. Made some small talk. Darren Bell had an Irish accent, flawless manners, and discerning eyes.

The conference room was small, with a view over the bay. Two impressionistic paintings on the wall. It was a foggy day. Darren Bell joked, "Welcome to the typical Isle of Man soup."

Darren asked JW to tell him about his needs.

He explained what he needed. It was impossible for JW to tell him everything about certain things. But the most important stuff he could explain. First, he needed a private account to which he could easily transfer money. Preferably from Internet deposits. Or from cash sent directly to Central Union Bank's office in London. Furthermore, he needed two companies on location on the Isle of Man. The main business of the first company was financial solutions for small and large companies. The other one would lie dormant for now, but it had to be ready to be activated at short notice. Both companies' owner had to be protected by privacy regulations. The companies needed privacy-protected accounts with the bank. Finally, the financial-services company needed to be able to provide documentation regarding loans to a joint-stock company in Sweden. Darren Bell took notes. Nodded. Everything was possible. The island's rules permitted most things; he would work on a proposal. Asked JW to come back the following day.

The next day, JW was sitting with Darren Bell again. The banker was in the same outfit as the day before, except for the shirt. Sank the impression. JW wondered, Why didn't he at least change his tie?

Darren spread out a number of PowerPoint printouts on the table. Numbers, graphic explanations of transfer possibilities, depots, transaction costs. Explained what he'd done over the past twenty-four hours. Two companies in place, with accounts already connected. Complete privacy with regard to ownership, in accordance with the island's legislation. Yet another account, owned by JW, that could only be accessed with the correct number combination. Finally, he presented drafts of financing contracts, loan contracts, deposit contracts, privacy contracts, proxy and brokerage contracts, ready to be filled out. The cost of the accounts: 0.5 percent of the total sum deposited per year, with a minimum charge of one thousand pounds a year. The companies: a one-time fee of four thousand pounds each. Three thousand in rolling fees annually. The loan documentation: four thousand pounds. In total: at least 200,000 kronor for JW to cough up.

JW thought, Darren Bell's got a damn sweet job.

Darren looked pleased. "I think everything's in order, sir. The only thing we need are name suggestions for your companies."

JW stewed in his own glory. John Grisham—you can hit the sack. This was for real. JW'd soon be the owner of his own money-laundering system. Fantastic.

45

Mrado in Ringen's mall. In ICA, the grocery store. Preparing the all-out day he was gonna have with Lovisa this week.

He hadn't slept all night. Only been thinking about this day and his future.

Had to buy groceries. Usually, the cupboards, fridge, and freezer in his apartment were empty. Only the bar was full. But since his right to see Lovisa'd been secured by the court, it'd become important to Mrado to be a good father. A new self-realization: homemade eats weren't his thing. Despite that, he tried to make breakfast, lunch, and dinner when Lovisa was there.

He couldn't remember the last time he'd bought so much food.

Red shopping basket in one hand, grocery list in the other. Difficult to grab the grub and still keep track of the grocery list. One hand busy with the list, the other snatching stuff—which hand would hold the basket? Mrado came up with a business idea: to produce list holders for the shopping baskets. Give the shoppers one hand free to grab goods. Maybe have a clip for the list. Maybe even for cell phones? Ads for sales items on the side. Mrado schemed on.

He kept adding stuff to his basket: macaroni, ketchup, ready-made meatballs, tomatoes—important to have vegetables, too. He was gonna be a healthy father.

Thought about his other list. He had to secure his and Lovisa's lives. Tackle risks. Protect Lovisa. Get her to move. Protect himself. He'd already sold his car and switched phones. This week, it was time to buy a better bulletproof vest, get a PO box address, and research the market for home alarm systems.

His and Nenad's pact felt secure. Radovan was gonna have to take it straight up the dirty—no more sitting pompous for Rado the rectal wreck. He'd regret ditching them. Radovan had to learn, the Serbian way. Go ahead, play tough—but don't let your friends down. Who the hell did he think he was?

Mrado looked for a good dessert. Browsed between the freezer units and the cookie section. Ice cream or cookies, that was the question. No, he couldn't just buy unhealthy stuff. Decided on fruit salad. Chose oranges, apples, kiwis, and bananas. Surprised himself—my God, he was fantastic.

He didn't fit into these kinds of environments. It was strange—the same insecurity that overwhelmed the people he pressed for dough, squeezed confessions out of, threatened with death, he felt in totally ordinary places. In the grocery store, in the pizzeria, on the street. Thought people stared at him, that they saw right through him. Recognized a dirty citizen, a criminal parasite, a bad father.

And still, when he saw them—the people in the grocery store—it was clear that what they needed was to pump up their lives. Feel some voltage, get kicks. Experience the adrenaline rush in the ring at Pancrease. The serotonin level when you broke someone's nose. The cracking sound, like dry boards, when the hand's first two knuckles met the nose bone's cartilage. Mrado knew what it meant to be alive.

He flipped through a cell phone magazine he'd plucked from the rack by the checkout. New finesses: TV in your phone, pay with your phone, porn in your phone.

Someone said his name.

"Mrado, is that you?"

Mrado looked up. Instant indignity. Freebie reading instead of buying. Embarrassing.

"What's up?"

Mrado recognized the guy. Hadn't seen him in ages. Old classmate from Södertälje, Martin. The class's brainiac.

"Martin, good to see you."

"Damn, Mrado, it's been years. Did you go to the reunion, whenever that was?"

The reunion: ten years after Mrado'd graduated from junior high. He'd been twenty-six at the time. At first, thought he'd screw it. Then chosen to show them. The fist champion they'd all hated was still a fist champion. With one difference—now he made out like a king. He'd sat with Ratko at a pub in the area an hour before. Downed three beers and two fat whiskeys. Hadn't felt ripe enough to go without warming up.

"Sure, the reunion. That. What're you up to nowadays?"

Mrado wanted to drop the subject. The reunion'd ended in a fiasco:

Mrado in a fight with two old antagonists. Nothing'd changed—they were still on his back. Hadn't understood who he'd become.

"I work in the federal court," Martin replied.

Mrado, surprised. Martin in a green windbreaker, worn jeans, Von Dutch baseball hat. Looked young, chill. Not exactly the lawyerly type.

"Interesting. Are you a judge?"

"Yeah, I work as a deputy judge at the court of appeals. A ton of work. We're criminally understaffed, toiling like beasts. It's not unusual to pull sixty-hour weeks. We just maintain the rule of law. Nothing important. No siree. Sometimes you wonder about the values in this country. In the States, they value academics completely differently. Nope, the courts of law aren't worth shit. Seriously, it's totally messed up. I would make three times as much if I went corporate."

"Then why don't you?"

Martin pushed back his Von Dutch hat. "I happen to believe in this. Functioning courts, a court system where the best lawyers' work guarantees a constitutional state. The possibility for people to have their sentences and rulings tried in appellate courts. Faster processing times without mistakes, carefully considered and consistent verdicts."

Mrado hoped he wouldn't have to talk about himself. He said, "You should be happy you work with something you believe in."

"Don't know if I believe in it anymore. I mean, we keep pushing the sludge through, but the slime is growing exponentially. Crime just gets smarter and more grisly, not to mention that there's more of it. The police can't keep up. We convict them as fast as we can, but they come right back again after two years, when they've done their time and are roaming the streets again. Often, they commit the exact same crime that we convicted them for the first time. Do they change? Not a piss. Soon the gangs are gonna fucking take over this city. Maybe I should offer my services to them instead. Better pay. Ha-ha. Anyway, what're you up to?"

In Mrado's head: I knew it was coming. What do you tell a judge? Mrado liked the guy somehow. At the same time, he felt it unwise to talk to a law fanatic. If he heard so much as a whisper about Mrado's business, there'd be a hell of a racket.

"I work with teak." Thought, Keep it simple. I do run that kind of company anyway. Less than 100,000 kronor in turnaround a year, but still. The perfect cover.

"Are you a carpenter?"

"Sort of. I import, mostly."

Mrado suddenly wanted to stop talking, stop lying. He added the cell phone magazine to his shopping basket. Started to walk toward the checkout.

"Martin, nice to see you. I gotta go now. Am seeing my daughter."

Martin smiled. Pushed his cap back low over his brow again. Looked trendy.

They shook hands. Mrado got in the checkout line. Thought, The dude convicts people like me every day. Imagine if he knew.

Martin disappeared into the store.

Mrado couldn't stop harping. What if he already knows. What if he was just being polite. Fuck, maybe I should quit. For my own sake. For Lovisa's sake.

At the same time, another voice was screaming inside: If you quit, who are you? If you don't get even with Radovan, who are you? A nobody.

Martin'd lived on the same street as Mrado until the ninth grade. Then he'd moved to a better area north of the city.

He reminded Mrado of his school days. Mrado'd come with his parents to Sweden when he was three years old. Work immigration. Saab-Scania, big industry. Södertälje needed people. Sweden'd cut the visa requirements for Yugoslavians a few years earlier. Södertälje was crawling with Greeks, Finns, Italians, Yugos. The Syrians and Turks came later. Back then, the Yugos stuck together. No difference between Serbs, Croatians, and Bosnians. Tito was their hero. How wrong they'd been. Naïve. Gullible. Thought you could trust the Croatians and the Bosnians. Today, Mrado wouldn't even piss on a Bosnian if he were on fire.

The catchword was *Miljonprojekt*, the state-run Million Program to create project housing and opportunities. Everyone worked hard. Mrado did, too. Every day, he'd beat one person up or get beaten up by a couple of people. They were always aggressive, armed. In bigger numbers. He bit the bullet. Never told anyone at home. Sharpened his knuckles. Learned to take a beating. Above all, learned to give a beating. Shootfighting at the basic level—kick to the shins, punch in the stomach, bite, scratch, aim for the eyes. He'd already become a fight-trick master by then. King of dirty play. A name in Södertälje.

He became respected. Did his own thing. No one got in his way.

After finishing ninth grade, he never saw anyone from school again. Instead, he enrolled in an electronic and telephonic technical program at Ericsson's own high school by Telefonplan. Dropped out his junior year and started working as a bouncer. Then straight up on the Yugo career ladder. And now he was gonna reach the top.

Mrado looked down at the girl manning the cash register. Thought, If I was a real father, I'd have an ICA rewards card. Instead, he pulled out his wad of cash. Sliced some cheddar off the top.

The girl didn't seem to give a damn.

He saw Martin get in the line.

Looked away.

* * *

MEMORANDUM
(Confidential pursuant to chapter 9, paragraph 12 of the Secrecy Act)

PROJECT NOVA
COUNTY CRIMINAL POLICE INITIATIVE AGAINST
ORGANIZED CRIME
Balkan-related crime in Stockholm

Report Number 9

Background Information
The following memorandum is based on reports and reported suspicions from the Special Gang Commission and the Norrmalm police's Financial Crime Investigation Unit in collaboration with the United County Effort Against Organized Crime in the Stockholm Area (collectively referred to below as the Surveillance Group). The methods employed include mapping, with the help of the combined experience of the Stockholm police; the collection of information from people within the criminal networks, so-called rats; secret wiretapping and bugging, as well as the coordination of requisite registries.

The memorandum is being submitted due to the murders of two persons active within the so-called Yugoslavian Mafia (referred to below as the Organization), further described in report number 7.

On March 16 of this year, two deceased people were found in an apartment in Hallonbergen. There are strong suspicions of murder. The Surveillance Group was able to confirm that they were killed using violent force. The Surveillance Group had planned for quite some time to put the apartment under surveillance, as there are suspicions of prostitution being conducted there. The date and time of death of the murdered persons have been established as occurring at some point between 3:00 and 5:00 a.m. on the morning of March 15. The cause of death for both parties was shots fired with a large-caliber shotgun to the stomach and head, respectively. Organic material has been sent to SKL for analysis. The weapon, a shotgun, probably a Winchester repeating rifle, Model 12, .12-80-caliber, has not been identified. Interrogations with people in Hallonbergen have begun. Because of the time of the crime, it is probable that very few people were awake and observed suspects in the area. The Surveillance Group believes that the killings are connected with the internal conflicts within the Organization.

A woman, probably working as a prostitute in the above-mentioned apartment brothel, has also been reported missing since March 13 of this year.

Victims

Zlatko Petrovic: Pimp directly subordinate to Nenad Korhan (in turn subordinate to Radovan Kranjic, described in report number 7), 700712-9131, born in the former Yugoslavia, currently Serbia-Montenegro. Came to Sweden when he was six years old.

Had previously worked as a bouncer and a combat-sport coach. His latest reported income: 124,000 kronor, income from jobs as a combat-sport coach and a bouncer, as well as gambling winnings.

Criminal record is as follows: 1987: assault. 1989: theft, illegal arms possession (served six months in prison). 1990: attempted murder, theft (served six years in prison). 1997: unlawful threats, illegal arms possession, sexual assault (served eight months in prison). 2001: pandering (prostitution), assault (served one year in prison).

Petrovic was considered very violent, especially toward women. Since the end of the 1990s, he was believed to have run one or more brothels in apartments around Stockholm's outer boroughs with Korhan. Active in Hallonbergen from 2002 until his death.

Over the past three months, the Surveillance Group has tried to infiltrate the operation. The infiltrator (X), under the name Micke, previously focusing on the Organization's recruitment base, served as "junior pimp," a so-called whore-watcher, for the prostitute who is currently missing. He has observed a number of suspicious visitors and persons who have approached the prostitute in recent weeks. There is probably a connection between the missing prostitute and the murders. For further information, see X's report, Attachment 1.

Jelena Lukic: The so-called brothel madam, directly subordinate to Korhan, 720329-0288, born in the former Yugoslavia, currently Serbia-Montenegro. Came to Sweden when she was two years old.

Had previously worked as a masseuse and pedicurist. Her latest reported income was 214,000 kronor, income from investments, jobs as a masseuse, as well as gambling winnings.

Her criminal record includes only traffic violations.

Lukic had been active within the sex-trade industry, involved in pandering, since the end of the 1990s. In 2002, her "stable" of between three and four prostitutes was taken over by Korhan, at which time she began to do business with Petrovic, primarily in the above-mentioned brothel in Hallonbergen. Lukic is also believed to have run a so-called call-girl business with seven or eight women, primarily Swedish citizens. The women within this call-girl business have been rented out for representational events with foreign clients, for example, and as escorts during meetings of gentlemen's clubs and at private parties.

Internal Conflicts

The Surveillance Group has gathered information that points to the fact that an internal conflict has developed within the Organization. One man within the Organization, active as Radovan Kranjic's personal bodyguard, has informed the Surveillance Group's sources that a "cleaning out" of certain persons within the Organization has taken place. Mrado Slovovic (described in report number 7) and Nenad Korhan have been "demoted" and removed from their positions in coat-check racketeering, cocaine sales, and the sex trade in Stockholm. Kranjic has decided that these two are to be moved down in the hierarchy and that their duties and areas of responsibility will be taken over by others. The Surveillance Group's working hypothesis is that this has all been done in the interest of eliminating threats against Kranjic.

The Surveillance Group believes that the murders of Petrovic and Lukic are connected to the internal conflict described above. X observed that in the days leading up to the murders, the brothel in Hallonbergen was repeatedly visited by an unknown man. The man also contacted the missing prostitute as well as met her outside the brothel on at least one occasion. What took place between them is unclear, since X was not permitted to remain close to the prostitute during their interaction. The man is swarthy, dark-skinned, and around thirty years old. Since March 13 of this year, the prostitute has not been in touch with X, which is why the police have reported her missing. The Surveillance Group is working with several theories as to the motives behind the murders. One is that Kranjic, because of the internal conflict, wants to prevent Korhan from breaking out on his own and starting new prostitution businesses. Another theory is that Korhan and Slovovic committed the murders together in order to destabilize Kranjic's business empire.

Measures

The Surveillance Group suggests the following measures be taken in response to the report presented above:

1. Continue searching for the thirty-year-old man who met the prostitute on several occasions.
2. Continue searching for the missing prostitute.
3. Search for the rest of the women who are believed to have been active as prostitutes in the brothel.
4. Search for the men who are believed to have purchased sexual services in the brothel.
5. Continue the surveillance work, with a focus on Slovovic and Korhan.

Regarding Budget for the measures, see Attachment 2.

Criminal Investigation Department
Superintendant Björn Stavgård
Special Investigator Stefan Krans

46

Jorge, *qué* angst. Been in bed for a week—like sick or something.

Abdulkarim'd asked, "Ey, fuck's up with you, Jorge? Fever, or what? You gotta keep us rollin'."

He'd run through that night over and over again. Replayed the events in his mind. Play/rewind—play/rewind. Sometimes, frame by frame. Like a video producer.

The shotgun shots'd been unplanned, dangerous. Dumb as hell.

Went over the situation one more time. Hopefully, he hadn't left any DNA on the spot. Had just gone in, popped the Yugo pigs, plucked the laptop and the cell phone. Hadn't touched anything with his hands, even held the door handle with his sweater. Not been in a fight or torn up skin or blood. Had a hat on the whole time—probably hadn't lost any hairs. Should be clean.

The john would probably keep his mouth shut. If he exposed Jorge, he'd be exposing his own habits. No one else in the apartment'd seen him; the whore in the other room hadn't even looked up. Had anyone in the area seen him? At four in the morning? The cops would go door-to-door. Ask every neighbor in all of Hallonbergen. There was a risk that someone'd seen him. But that risk was *pequeñito*. His description would fit thousands of others.

Should be tight.

Footprints were a possibility; the weather'd been sticky. On the other hand, Jorge'd filled his shoes with rocks and dumped them in Edsviken Bay first thing the morning after.

The big danger: that Fahdi would start wondering. Check his shotgun. Discover residue or that shells were missing. Make a connection with the latest front-page news in the underworld.

Everyone was speculating. Theorizing. Analyzing. Abdulkarim suspected some john hadn't been able to pay and was scared of being exposed. Freaked and cleared out the only ones who could mess up his life. Fahdi suspected other Yugos. There were rumors about internal disputes. Division in the bar Mafia. JW suspected other gangs. Speculated about market divisions within the city's organized-crime scene to calm the war between the HA and the Bandidos.

Jorge kept a low profile. It was one thing to live on the lam after a nonviolent escape from a prison sentence for a drug conviction. Totally different to be on the run for a double homicide.

His hope: that no trails led to him.

Nevertheless: Jorge wished he could send Radovan a greeting. Just so the Yugo'd know who was after him and why. Message: This is just the beginning, repayment for whatever you've done with Nadja and what you did to me.

A stroke of good bloodbath juju—the laptop he'd grabbed'd survived his plug pulling. The battery'd kicked in. A stroke of bad bloodbath juju—log-in info was needed to rouse it from sleep mode: control/alt/delete, user name and password. Jorge couldn't get in. Needed help.

Cock.

Maybe he could find some hacker who could do it—break into Stockholm's now most wanted computer.

But not today. Today, he was gonna see Paola.

On his way to see her, the first time since he'd busted out. Longest period they'd ever gone without seeing each other. She'd visited him at Österåker a couple of months before he cut loose. Complained that he'd gotten cocky. Didn't she understand the environment he was in?

Jorge didn't dare boost cars anymore. More scared of police checkpoints than ever. Before he'd shot the pimp and the brothel madam— if the cops collared him, he'd be sent right back inside. Hardly get any add-on for the break. He'd kept it so clean, after all. *Sin* violence, *sin* crime, *sin* anything to pin on him. The worst that could happen was that he had to sit out the rest of his time without the possibility of parole. But now, after the shots'd been fired in Hallonbergen, it was a different story. If they got him, he could be sent away for life. His earlier fear of being busted appeared ridiculous. Now it was serious.

Still, when Paola'd texted him, he hadn't been able to stay home any longer. He needed the calm. Needed the connection with his other half.

How'd Paola gotten his cell phone number? He didn't know of anyone who could've given it to her. Possibly Sergio. In that case, it was a danger. She couldn't have his number, for her own sake. He had to get a new one.

He rode public transportation. Even bought a ticket. No more turn-stile hurdling.

Got off at the Liljeholmen subway stop.

The concrete station had been renovated. According to Jorge: with-out improvement. The train he'd been riding on had Norsborg as its final destination and he needed to go toward Fruängen. Had to wait five minutes for the transfer.

He stood at the end of the platform. Liked the area. The few yards the train often didn't reach when it stopped. A wasteland, an aban-doned appendix, a solitary, forgotten slice of the public transit jungle. Alkies pissing on the tracks, gangs juxing kids for their phones, couples making love, rats and pigeons making shit. Most of all, sprayers attack-ing the cement gloom with their colorful tags. The subway sentinels didn't care; the families with small kids stood in the middle of the plat-form, so they wouldn't have to run if a short train rolled in.

The train to Fruängen pulled in. Jorge got on.

The driver's voice bellowed over the sound system: "This train is going to Fruängen." Jorge recognized the voice, the chill African accent; he'd ridden with this driver before. Jorge laughed out loud. Thought, Is Daddy Boastin driving the cars? Subway man sounded just like the rapper.

Hägersten—Västertorp, to be exact, was approaching. He glimpsed Störtloppsvägen near the public pool. Soon he'd get to see Paola.

The working-class area was idyllic compared to Jorge's Sollentuna hood. The public pool, in yellow brick with marble sculptures out front, lay like a cozy meeting spot in the middle of it all.

He walked toward Paola's apartment building.

Hit the key code she'd texted him.

The elevator didn't work. He took the stairs, thought about JW. Good guy. A friend. Jorge felt close to him. Had opened up to him a few days ago and talked about his debt of gratitude. Told the upper-class slick, "I've never been saved by anyone before. I would've died out there." He could tell that JW'd been moved. "If you hadn't come."

He reached the top floor.

Waited a few breaths.

Rang the doorbell.

And then there she was. Over a year since they'd last seen each other. Tear in her eye. More beautiful than he remembered. Heftier.

They hugged/embraced/cried.

She smelled good.

They had a seat in the kitchen on her wooden chairs. Two posters on the wall: Che Guevara on one and an abstract painting by Servando Cabrera Moreno on the other.

Paola put water on to boil for tea.

Jorge thought her hair gleamed. Black as coal, darker than his, even though his was dyed. He saw her face anew. There were similarities with their father. But something was wrong. Even though the tears'd dried, she seemed sad.

"How's Mama?" The Chilean accent stronger than usual, normal *s* sounds, a softer tone than Spanish Spanish.

"As usual. Her shoulders hurt. Wonders what you're doing, and why."

She poured water into two mugs. Dipped a tea bag in one.

"You can tell her I feel wonderful and am doing what I gotta do."

"Whattya mean 'gotta do'? You're intelligent; you could've finished your time and then started studying."

She fished out the tea bag. Dunked it in the other mug. Was enough to at least add some color to the water.

Jorge thought she did everything so slowly.

"Cut it out, Paola. Let's not fight. I make my choices. Everyone can't live like you. I love you; you know that. Tell Mama I said so, too."

"I accept your choices. But you're hurting Mama; you've got to understand that. She thought you were gonna get it together after school. It doesn't matter that she doesn't understand your world. She gets sad anyway. Can't you see her?"

"I can't now. I have to get my life in order. Things aren't safe now. Nothing's safe."

They let the subject drop. Paola sat quietly for a minute.

Then she told him about her studies. Her life: a boyfriend who wasn't working out, involvement in the literature society, friends who were gonna study abroad in Manchester. A well-organized life. A normal life. For Jorge, it was exotic. She asked Jorge about his curly hair, dark skin color, crooked nose. He laughed.

"You already know the answer. I'm living on the run. Didn't you recognize me?"

She smiled.

In Jorge's head: flashbacks. Him and her at the Liseberg amusement park in Gothenburg when they'd visited Mama's sister in Hisingen. Spent a day in Gothenburg. He, maybe seven years old, Paola maybe twelve. They wanted to ride on the Flumride, the number-one attraction, and had to lie about his age in order for him to be let on. Paola's arms around him in the plastic boat that looked like a hollowed-out tree trunk. Slowly upward. In his ear, in Spanish, so the others in the log wouldn't understand, she whispered, "If you don't promise to be good, I'll let you go." Jorge, terrified. But at the same time not. He thought he understood. Turned around. Paola's smile—she was kidding. Jorge laughed.

"You got so quiet. Are you mad?" Paola asked.

"When we were at Liseberg, remember? We rode the Flumride."

Suddenly, her voice was serious.

"Jorgelito, who're you running away from, really?"

A moment of silence.

"Whattya mean? The Five-Oh, of course."

"A few months ago, I got threatened at the university, and it wasn't by the police."

Jorge's eyes blackened—not the effect of his contacts.

Hate.

"I know, Paola. That'll never happen again. The person who did that is gonna be punished. I swear on Papa's grave."

She shook her head. "You don't have to punish anyone."

"You don't understand. I can't live with myself if the people who threatened you don't pay. I've been fucked all my life. Rodriguez, SS hags, cops. And now the Yugo fuckers. At Österåker, I learned to lay low when necessary but to stand up when it really mattered. I am somebody. Did you know that? I make mad cash. I'm on my way up. I've got a career. A plan."

"You should think again."

"I don't want to talk to you about this. Can't we just chill?"

The tension evaporated as quickly as it'd flared up.

They chatted about other stuff.

Time raced by. Jorge didn't dare stay too long. They finished their tea. Paola refilled the mugs. A new bag this time. Topped it with a little cold water so Jorge'd be able to drink right away.

There was a white IKEA dresser in the hall that Jorge recognized from the apartment they'd grown up in on Malmvägen. High-heeled leather boots, sneakers, loafers, and a pair of Bally winter boots in rows.

"You can afford those?" Jorge pointed at the Bally boots.

"My boyfriend the asshole gave them to me."

"Why?"

Paola smiled again. "You're not too quick, *junior*. Can't you tell? I can't walk around in heels. I'm gonna be a mama."

The subway usually lulled him to sleep. Not now. He was speeded.

J-boy was gonna be an uncle.

Sooooooo ill.

Needed time to digest.

Had to slam those swine before Paola had the baby.

Had to haul in a massive harvest before Paola gave birth.

Her child was gonna get all the advantages a flush uncle could give.

Her child was gonna get an uncle who'd punished those who'd hurt the Salinas Barrio family.

47

Money-laundering schemes were difficult, but JW'd done his home-work. New rules and regulations were constantly being instituted—EU directives, commissions, and reports. Collaboration between banks, financial institutions, and credit card companies. Stricter reporting requirements, increased cross-checks, more questions. The EU pres-sured the Financial Supervisory Authority. The Financial Supervisory Authority pressured the banks. The banks pressured the clients.

Impossible to stay under the mandatory reporting requirement when the amounts got too big. The banks coordinated their systems; a deposit into a certain account at one office showed up everywhere. Electronic registries connected any suspicious transactions.

But JW was a laundry master. He'd made connections, mastered trust, manufactured solutions. His Swedish companies each had point persons at different banks and their own accounts with credit. Smiles and explanations about a cash-heavy industry in English antique furni-ture ought to do it. As long as they believed he was conducting credible business, it was all good.

A hundred grand was packed in his Prada bag when he was on his way to see his two contacts, one at Handelsbanken, the other at the SEB bank.

It'd been a week since he'd gotten back. The system was pure genius. Dirty cash in and two ways to get it out to the island. The first way—through invoices to British companies for phony marketing costs, all payable to his island company's bank account. JW'd gotten the idea from the 2005 Ericsson bribery scandals. The smart thing was, of course, that he wasn't messing with shady deposits, but payments. It looked better, didn't raise eyebrows—an English furniture buyer needs to be marketed in England. His bank contacts would consider it completely natural. And, the second way, in order to diversify his methods—by packing thousand-kronor bills and snail-mailing them to the Isle of Man. Then he had someone there collect the package and deposit the money in the island company's account. It was more dangerous, but you couldn't travel on your own with that much cash. The metal detectors'd react right away to the metal threads in the bills.

The Swedish banks wouldn't suspect deposits that were payments for something. He'd made the invoices himself. Not even a full-time graphic designer could've made more authentic-looking logos for a British marketing agency. He was so damn pleased.

The hard cash turned electronic through the payments made in Sweden or the deposits on the island. The accounts on the island were controlled by his companies. Confidentiality cut off all search routes to the companies. The money was his, undetectable to anyone here. And then, the island companies lent money to his company in Sweden. That was how his finances were actually replenished. Totally clean, white cash. Because the glory of it all was that anyone could be rich on borrowed money. Big Brother wouldn't wonder. The interest rates and repayment requirements were set at market standard. Were even deductible.

At Handelsbanken, he took a queue number, then stood reading the text rolling on the screens. The market was going up. JW'd already bought some shares: Ericsson, H&M, and SCA. A good mix. Ericsson, the telecom stock that'd risen over 300 percent. H&M, the company that soared even during times of recession. And SCA, the serene security of timber. Spiced it up with two smaller companies, one IT company that manufactured routers, one biotech company that developed anti-Alzheimer's medicine. Stocks were another filter to purify filthy change. Capital gains from the stock market were taxed, considered normal, weren't questioned. Incorporated into the system. A future step in the money-laundering carousel—maybe he'd get in touch with a broker to tumble dry even bigger sums.

What's more, the stock market gave him good talking points with his buds. The boyz and stocks, like Abdulkarim and coke. The bigger the money, the greater the buzz.

JW eyed the line; it was worse than at the Skavsta Airport check-in. The fifty thousand kronor he'd taken from the Prada bag burned in the pocket of his Dior coat. JW thought, If anyone stabs me, the wad of bills will catch the blade and save my life.

He thought about the packaging farm in the English countryside. Chris, the guy who ran the place, was still just an underling of the soccer hooligans who were really in charge. He'd been a part of something really big for the first time in his life. It felt so incredibly good and so ridiculously difficult not to tell Sophie anything.

It was JW's turn at the counter.

He stepped up.

Became aware of his hand sweat.

Tried to smile.

"Is Annika Westermark available?"

The cashier smiled back. "Sure. Would you like me to get her for you?"

A miscalculation by JW. He'd hoped to go into Annika Westermark's private office in order to give her the cash there. Not have to heap it up on the counter.

Annika Westermark appeared behind the glass dressed in a dark suit in conservative banker style, just like the last time he'd met her and told her about his furniture business.

JW leaned forward. "Hi, Annika. How are you today?"

"Fine, thank you. How are you?"

JW piled on the entrepreneurial small-business-owner style. "Hell yeah, things're rolling. This month has been very successful, which is really awesome. I've had three interior designers buying a scary number of sofa groups." He laughed.

Annika expressed polite interest.

JW'd already explained to her previously that the payments were for marketing costs in England. Prepared her—his whole business with English antique furniture was built on the right purchases being made in Great Britain, which is why heavy marketing was necessary. She seemed to get it.

He handed over the bills, fifty grand in a plastic folder, while he held the fake invoice in the other hand. Slipped it under the protective glass.

Annika took out the bills. Licked her finger—gross—and counted them. One hundred five-hundred-kronor bills. She looked at the invoice.

Was she suspicious?

She mmm'ed.

JW tried to chitchat. "It doesn't feel all too good walking around with a whole month's worth of earnings in your pocket."

She pushed him a slip of paper.

"There you go, your receipt."

All was cool. She didn't care, gobbled his story right up. A fifty-thousand-kronor cash deposit—nothing strange about that. What she didn't know was that he was planning on depositing another fifty at SEB, and he'd snail-mailed fifty more. In two days, his island company would be 150 grand richer.

He thought, Will she react next month when I come with 250 in payment? Time would tell if it would work.

He thanked her and left.

Norrmalmstorg square, flanked by law firms, felt like an arena. Everyone just had to see how he radiated—what a winner he was.

He started walking toward SEB and hit play on his MP3 player: the Swedish band Kent. Bitter Swedish security: "I am going to steal a treasure. The one hidden at the end of the rainbow. It is mine, it is you." He thought about his parents. How would they react if they found out about the Jan Brunéus business? Would they keep doing nothing? Drown in self-pity and tedium? Maybe they'd act. Do something about the whole situation. The ball was really in their court. To put pressure on the police. To find out what'd actually happened.

He walked up Nybrogatan. A new boutique'd opened where the hairdresser's used to be. JW thought, This has to be the city's most bankruptcy-dense street. No store survived more than a year.

It was noon. He should study and was vacillating about wanting to see Sophie later that night or not, couldn't decide.

Thought, Really, I'm a social genius. *The Talented Mr. Ripley*, Swedish-style. Fit in with the boyz—studied the mannerisms of the upper class, played along, laughed at the right beats, volleyed with their slang. But he also fit in with Abdulkarim and the dealer collective, their ghetto jargon, fist romance, drug finance. Tight with Fahdi—a soft, lethal gorilla. He was smooth with Petter and the other dealers. And he had a special thing with Jorge.

The other day, it'd crystallized. JW and Jorge were hanging out at Fahdi's, as usual. The kitchen table was laden with scales, Red Line baggies, manila envelopes. They were measuring out, scraping into baggies, lacing with granulated fructose—easy way to increase the margins by 10 to 20 percent—while they discussed Jorge's success in the boroughs and JW's London trip.

After a while, Jorge said, "I've never been saved by anyone before. I would've died out there if you hadn't come."

JW thought, It's true. If I hadn't picked Jorge up in the woods—

beaten to smithereens, crushed—the Chilean would've died. He didn't recognize himself, sentimental about having done something that was actually good.

JW grinned. "It's cool. We do everything on orders from Abdul, right?"

"Honestly, *hombre*, you saved my life. I'll never forget it." Jorge looked up. His gaze steady, serious, solemn. He said, "I'll do anything for you, JW. Always. Never forget that."

JW hadn't thought a lot about it at the time. But today, on his way to the bank on Nybrogatan, it came back to him. It made him feel good, somehow, that there was someone in the world who'd do anything for him. It was security. Maybe even true friendship.

He decided to grab something to eat before his visit to the bank. Stepped into Café Cream on Nybrogatan and ordered a ciabatta sandwich with salami and Brie, plus a Coke.

He sat alone on a high stool by the window, looking out. The world of high society was small. He recognized more than every third passing Östermalms chick in the age range of nineteen to twenty-four. Same deal with the Yuppie players around twenty-five—men in suits he usually bumped into at Kharma or Laroy, but then they'd be wearing jeans, open button-down shirts, jackets, sporting coke-craving in their eyes. The only thing that remained the same now—the backslicks. He thought, What world'd Camilla lived in? Stureplan by day or by night?

His sandwich was brought over. JW opened it and discovered his bad luck. Usually, he was an omnivore. When he moved away from home, he quickly learned to like most things, stuff that lots of people nixed: herring, sushi, caviar, pickled onions. Now there were just two things he couldn't handle: capers and celery. Inside the ciabatta: salad and capers. In the salad, celery bits.

Damn it.

He spent ten minutes picking the crap out.

Then he ate quickly while he played a game of chess on his phone.

He drained the Coke, left half the ciabatta, and walked out.

Hi'ed two guys walking in the opposite direction. Club buds.

He continued up Nybrogatan. Saluhallen, the indoor luxury food market, was on his left. JW shopped there more and more these days.

The revolving doors leading into SEB's offices were not automatic. Had to push your way in.

As soon as he was inside, JW groped in his bag for the other plastic folder, another fifty grand.

He took a queue number. The place was almost empty, even though there were ATMs and change machines on the premises.

The stock market feeds on the screens were being updated. JW eyed them.

Then it was his turn.

He glanced around. There could be police or other suspicious types there, but it all looked okay.

The cashier had henna-red hair.

JW asked for his contact person, a woman in this office, as well.

The cashier informed him that his contact wasn't there but that he could pay her instead. It wasn't great, but it'd have to do.

"What's up?" said a voice behind him.

JW turned around. Saw Nippe with some chick. Nippe looked down at the wad of cash that JW'd just handed over to the cashier.

Fuck.

JW checked himself. Put on the calm, unaffected veneer. In his head: Holy fuck, how embarrassing. Nippe saw the stash in the cashier's hands. What was he going to do?

"Hey, Nippe." Looked at the chick.

Nippe introduced her. "This is Emma."

JW sighed heavily.

Nippe looked quizzically at him.

"*Emma only exists in fantasy, but she's looo-oovely.*"

They looked like question marks.

JW gave it another go. "You don't remember that TV show, *Kalle's Climbing Tree*, from when we were kids?" He hummed and ended with another deep sigh.

JW grinned, regretted it right away, was ashamed—he was such a tool.

A loser, a nerd.

Nippe said, "I haven't heard that song before. But hey, so, I have to deal with this stuff. Take care. See ya."

Nippe reached the cashier he'd been in line for.

JW got his receipt of payment from the lady behind the glass.

He started walking out.

Nippe didn't nod when JW stepped out of the revolving doors.

Was a new cold front moving in?

On the way home, he thought about what'd been most embarrass-ing: that Nippe'd seen the wad of cash or his lame joke?

48

Nenad called from a new number—apparently, he'd also begun making security changes in his life. Mrado and he made small talk; then they discussed the murders of the pimp and the brothel madam. What the fuck'd happened? Shot to bits. The perp unknown. Nenad was jumpy. Before Radovan'd cut him off, Zlakto and Jelena were some of his best pimps. The questions bounced between Nenad and Mrado. Radovan wanted to purge his ranks? A john who didn't want marital problems? Someone else?

Mrado's suspicion: Either a panicked john or, worst-case scenario, a competing stable. Could also be the Russians. Could be the HA. In that case, the shots were unmistakable acts of war.

Nenad's problem: What did this mean for him? If it wasn't Radovan's doing, would the shadow fall over him?

Made it even more important to keep moving on their own plans.

Nenad explained his idea: It was like Serbian folk music to Mrado's ears. "You know, I've got a guy under me, an Arab, Abdulkarim. He basically serves up the whole blow banquet on his own. Has reported to me at steady intervals. I've negotiated all the bigger deals, drawn up the guidelines and done the top-down organizing. Right now, we've got an expansion plan that's been a huge hit so far. To deal to the boroughs at cut prices. The others can keep selling one gram at a time at the inner-city clubs or the millionaire parties. A thousand kronor a gram. But we, we sell twenty grams at a time. Seven hundred a gram. Volume. That's what's up."

"You told me that the day before yesterday. What's happening with it now?"

"Good question. How do I maintain control over Abdulkarim now that Radovan's demoted me? Abdul is loyal to Rado and won't listen to me. Won't take orders. Keeps truckin' like I don't exist. But listen to this. I usually don't know what guys the Arab's using, but in London,

Abdul sent a special guy, a real brat actually, to help me with negotiations. Superb guy. Sharp. Has worked for Abdul for less than a year. Knows the C biz well. Reliable. Talkin' to the Arab, says the guy's a wannabe. A bumpkin who wants up. Hungry as hell. Drove a gypsy cab for Abdul just so he could rage with his buds and booze the extra cash in bubbly. Party at Kharma, Köket, joints like that. The boy's playin' two hands. According to Abdul, his friends don't even know who he really is. The whole thing sounds kinda tragic, but good for us."

Mrado sometimes tired of Nenad. So much damn jaw. He pinned the phone between his head and shoulder. Tied his shoes. Realized he didn't have a hands-free.

He didn't want to be at home during these kinds of conversations. Went out.

"Get to the point, Nenad."

"Chill. JW—that's the guy's name—knows everything about the deal I made in London. Calculated every pound and krona. Went over freight routes, useful people, pushers. We can use him."

"Now it's getting interesting."

"He wants the same thing as everyone else—dough. But more. According to Abdulkarim, he's even rigged accounts on some Channel Island. Get this. The dude thinks he's gonna be a multimillionaire. Says something about his ambition."

"I'm with you. The dude'll do anything for dough."

"Bingo! You and me, we lay low. Continue what we talked about at Clarion. Play with the Radovan swine. Pretend to allow ourselves to be humiliated. Abdulkarim'll take over the wheel, drive the blow. Think I'm outta the game. We keep working for Rado, no matter the shit he has us do. You're cut off from the coat checks; I'll be cut off from the blow. When the shipment arrives, Rado'll already have put someone else in charge of the Arab, probably Goran. But that doesn't matter. The point is that our man'll be in the game, the brat boy. Just gotta make sure JW gets an offer he can't refuse. He'll be our Trojan horse."

Mrado walked Ringvägen. Suddenly loved Nenad.

The blow pimp was in ecstasy. "When the shipment arrives—and trust me, it's big as hell, more pounds than you can bench-press, Sweden's biggest delivery ever—then we'll be there. Ready to take back what belongs to us. Ready to roll."

Mrado got chills.

"You're amazing. When do we meet up and talk more, today?"

"Sure, meet me tonight at Hirschenkeller. I'm in the mood for some Budapest grill and a dark brew."

Mrado laughed. Hung up. On the phone's display: a seventeen-minute-long conversation. His ear: red and warm. Too much cell phone radiation, or excitement over the breakthrough?

Mrado was on his way home from the gym. Was gonna pick up Lovisa and go to a children's theater on Atlasgatan in Vasastan. He ate a Gainomax Recovery energy bar.

Mrado and Nenad: new dynamic duo. Butch and Sundance. An unbeatable combination.

They'd talked every day; the planning continued. How would they break Rado? The Serbian Godfather wannabe.

Mrado's headache: Lovisa had to switch schools. Annika hadn't understood what Mrado was talking about. Thought he wanted to mess with her, as usual. What should he do?

Some days, his insomnia almost crushed him.

When Nenad called, Mrado understood what it was about right away.

He hit speakerphone in the car.

"I talked to him today."

"And? What he say?"

Nenad—long-winded master. "We met for lunch at Texas Smokehouse. I just called and invited him. He recognized my voice immediately. But he helped me in London, so maybe that wasn't so strange. I just told him I wanted to talk; maybe he got shook. Thought something'd gone to hell. Anyway, we met up."

"What he say?"

"The dude's a brat wannabe—squared. No, hell, he's cubed. Sure, I could tell in London, but even more now. He said hi to every cute Östermalm tail that sashayed past. Really pretty wild that him and the Arab jive."

Mrado turned off toward where Lovisa's after-school program was. She was waiting by the gate. Mrado's heart skipped a beat. Thought, If anything happens to her, it's over. Nenad jabbered on.

"Come on. Cut to the chase. I gotta go."

"Chill. The JW guy's cool. He's with us. But it'll cost. This is the deal. He'll keep track of the big C shipment. Will report directly to me about any progress. When it's expected to arrive. Where it's expected to arrive. How it'll be shipped. Stored. Who'll be guarding it. When it's time, we'll do the rest. What's more, he'll develop sales channels on the side."

"Sounds fantastic."

"And that's not all. He can rig big-league laundromats. For real. No shitty video-rental stores. No dry cleaners. Real stuff. Numbered accounts. Shelf companies. Tax paradise. Everything."

"Sounds totally fucking amazing. What does he want?"

"Twenty-five percent of the pie."

Mrado almost choked. This JW guy really thought highly of himself. He had to consider.

"Nenad, I gotta go. I'm picking up my daughter. We'll talk later."

Mrado had one night and one day with Lovisa.

Life.

Suck on the JW-boy's offer—candy.

Lovisa opened the gate. Mrado couldn't stand to talk to the teachers. She walked toward his car.

Fuck, why did everything have to be so complicated?

49

He had to keep working on Project R. The visit with his sister'd felt good. Jorge perked up, even though Hallonbergen revisited him every night.

He planned the next step. The last thing that'd happened at the brothel'd been timely. Only right—after all those dull days staking out Radovan's house. Something to work from—had invited himself, through Jet Set Carl, to some kind of luxury whore party. Gotten a password texted to the dead pimp's cell. Written the password down that same night, after he went back to Fahdi's. The apartment'd been empty. Jorge'd put the shotgun back. Wiped off the barrel. Tucked it into the closet. Then he'd thrown the pimp's phone in a trash can, the SIM card in a sewer.

The gig he'd invited himself to was happening today. Questions: What, exactly, was it? He didn't know if he was considered a guest or one of Nenad's underlings. Maybe he'd be expected to guard, arrange, or herd whores. Worse: He didn't know how to get there, the address.

He couldn't care less about the first question. It would sort itself out once he got there.

The answer to the final question: He'd have to shadow Jet Set Carl all day.

Jorge knew the brat king's address.

Rocked his old trick—by 8:00 a.m., he was already sitting in a stolen Saab with tinted back windows. Didn't want to miss Jet Set Carl no matter how early he was. Sipped coffee. Peed in a soda bottle. Listened to the radio.

Maybe getting there as early as 8:00 a.m. on a weekend was exaggerated—the dude didn't come out till 12:30.

Jorge thought, What a life. Jet Set Carl organizes parties, snorts coke, pounds hookers. Never has to struggle. Knows *nada* about concrete. Spoiled, carries daddy's plastic, and has stinking self-confidence like crazy.

And yet it was Jorge's dream—to be just like that. He knew every spliff-smoking *blatte* wanted to be Jet Set Carl. But *negritos* were never let in. They might as well stop dreaming.

Jet Set Carl was dressed in a black coat with a hoodie underneath. Hat. Stan Smith shoes. Jorge couldn't help but notice the similarities in dress with the guy whose guts he'd shot out in Hallonbergen two weeks before.

He started the car. Unnecessary—Jet Set Carl only walked two blocks down to the 7-Eleven on Storgatan. Bought milk and toast. Disappeared back into his building.

Jorge chilled in the car. Ate a chicken salad he'd brought along. Thought about himself: I'm becoming a stakeout pro, even getting used to chick food. Maybe I should start my own biz.

Four o'clock. Jet Set Carl walked out again. Same clothes as before—in other words, not time for action yet.

Jorge got out of the car. Kept a good distance. The hood of his jacket over his head. A pair of mirrored sunglasses on his nose. Jorge these days: pure Fletch, disguise master.

Jet Set Carl didn't venture far. Kept to his own pissed-in territory. Slipped into Café Tures in Sturegallerian, the exclusive indoor mall by Stureplan. Around 750 yards from where he lived. The geography within the golden rectangle was simple: Karlavägen-Sturegatan-Riddargatan-Narvavägen. The area practically had a velvet rope around it.

Jorge sat down at Grodan, the restaurant across the street. Read a newspaper. Drank a Coke. Saw Jet Set Carl through Sturegallerian's large glass windows. The dude was having coffee with an Östermalm *mina*. Maybe the prettiest Jorge'd ever seen.

The Jet Set guy ran his hand through his hair. Greased up his fingers. Jorge wondered how many chicks the player dated at once.

Two hours passed. They hugged good-bye. Did Jorge see what he thought he saw? Did the guy make an attempt to kiss her on the mouth? Did the girl pull back? Unclear.

The Jet Set dude went home alone.

Six-thirty.

Jorge still in the car. Wondered when something would happen. Bored.

Thought about all the hours outside of Rado's house.

Thought about all the people who'd helped him.

The blue glow of the digital clock read 7:00.

The door to the apartment building opened. Jet Set Carl walked out, now dressed more like Jorge remembered him. Same coat as before, but underneath he glimpsed a tailored shirt with the top buttons undone. The Stan Smiths had been traded in for a pair of polished, pointed leather kicks. His hair was slicked back.

The dude walked down the block. Unlocked an enormous car—a Hummer. Vodka ad in white lettering across the sides. The car was an ill marketing tool. Regular SUVs—hit the sack. This monster—broader than a truck.

Jet Set Carl drove south. Jorge stayed a few cars behind him. He could see the Hummer from afar. The hood was three feet above the roofs of the regular Sven vehicles. Jorge thought it was filthy sexy.

They drove Nynäsvägen through Enskede. The Globe Arena was lit up like a giant ball of cocaine. Through Handen/Jordbro. Took a left. Road 227. The darkness grew more compact. Frigid fields lined the road. There was one car between Jorge and the Hummer. Hopefully, it prevented Jet Set Carl from seeing what cars were behind him.

Jorge had a carefully folded suit in the backseat. On a hanger hooked into the back window: an ironed, striped, tailored shirt and a tie. To be safe—if there was a dress code where he was going.

More houses. They drove across a bridge. On a sign: WELCOME TO DALARÖ.

The Hummer took a left after the bridge. The car that'd been sandwiched between them took a right. Jorge at a mental crossroads: Did he dare continue to follow Jet Set Carl? A huge fuckin' chance/risk. He took the chance. Tried not to think about the risk.

They drove on Smådalarövägen.

After five minutes, the Jet Set guy slowed down. Blinked: to the right. Drove up a small gravel path and seemed to stop. Jorge slid on past. Got as good a look as he could. Hard to see anything. No light lit up the road.

He kept driving. The road ended at a cul-de-sac. All around: a golf course. Jorge parked the car. Turned up his hood. Looked around. Got out.

Farther off was a large house. A gravel road led up to it. A sign: SMÅDALARÖ INN. A couple of cars parked outside. Jorge walked back on the same road he'd driven. Kept to the side. Up to the place where Jet Set Carl'd turned off. Jorge clocked right away where he'd gone—a black metal gate blocked off the small road. On one side of the gate was a camera and a big sign: PRIVATE PROPERTY. GUARDED BY FALCK SECURITY.

Jorge kept his distance. Walked up into the woods alongside the gate. Woods—reminded him of what he couldn't forget: Mrado's lashes with the rubber baton. One thing was certain, J-boy never gave up. They'd already had a taste of him. Two Yugo pigs shot to pieces. Look out, Radovan, now Jorgelito's coming to get you.

After shivering in the woods for an hour, Jorge saw a car turn off toward the gate, but he couldn't see if the driver identified himself to the camera before the gates opened.

Then nothing happened for forty minutes.

Nine o'clock.

Dark in the woods.

Jorge saw someone moving inside the gate. Stared. He could see clearly now. Two people. Behind the gate. With baseball hats. Obvious—they were guards of some sort.

Twenty minutes later, the cars started trickling in. Beamers. Benzes. Jags. A couple Porsches. A few Volvos. One Bentley. A yellow Ferrari.

In some cases, the camera recognized the arrivals. The gates slid soundlessly open. The car rolled in. In other cases, one of the guards came out through a side entrance. Exchanged a few words with the people in the car. The gates opened.

The procedure was repeated with each car. At least twenty of them. Jorge knew what he had to do. Tried to see what the men in the cars were wearing. Glimpsed someone—definitely a suit jacket.

J-boy: pro of pros—*divinas*—he was prepared.

Went back to his car. Changed into the dress shirt and suit. Hesitated over the tie. Finally, skipped it.

Drove back toward the gate. Up to the camera. The butterflies in his stomach fluttered like crazy. Sweat invaded the space between his hands and the wheel. His car—the only Saab. Second-rate and suspicious.

Rolled down the window. Looked up at the camera.

Nothing happened.

He remained seated. Tried to relax.

Saab. *Blatte.* No tie.

One of the guards came out through the gate.

Round, pale cheeks leaned down. "Can I help you?"

Jorge turned down the treble on his ghetto accent. "Well yeah. Is there a long wait to get in here, or what? Is the parking lot swamped?"

"Excuse me. This is a private area. Do you have some business here?"

Jorge smiled broadly.

"You can say that again. It's gonna be a niiiice night."

The guard seemed to consider. Appeared affected by Jorge's confidence.

"What is your name?"

"Tell Carl, Daniel Cabrera says hello."

The guard took a few steps back. Talked on a phone or a walkie-talkie. Returned. The patronizing chill was back.

"He doesn't know who you are. I am going to have to ask you to leave the premises now."

Jorge remained ice-cold.

"Are you fucking with me? Call him again. Tell him it's Daniel Cabrera and that Moët is on the way. He can check his cell if his memory's failing."

The guard took a few steps back again. Talked on his phone.

Jorge hoped for luck.

After twenty seconds, the gates slid open.

J-boy was in.

He parked the car alongside the others. Counted five Porsches. What kind of place was this anyway?

The house in front of him was big. Three stories. Pillars around the entrance. Ill Beverly Hills style. Supersized McMansion. Did Sweden have stuff like that? Pretty clear: Yup.

Music could be heard from inside.

A man had just gotten out of his BMW. Walked toward the entrance. Jorge followed the guy, who glanced quickly over his shoulder. Saw Jorge. Ignored him. Kept walking. Jorge caught up with him. Extended his hand.

"Hi. My name is Daniel. This gonna be a good night, or what?" Laughed.

The man looked back at him. "It's usually pleasant. I haven't seen you before."

"No, I just got back from New York after a few years. Damn nice city. Already miss it."

They reached the entrance. Jorge had time to think: I don't even know in what capacity I've been invited. The door was opened from the inside before they'd even reached it. A dude in a suit, with a side part and a strong jaw, held it open for them. Another guard, but better dressed. Greeted the man Jorge'd just been talking to. He slid past. The guard eyed Jorge. Suspicious.

Held out his arm. Jorge stopped just inside the door. The guard asked for his name. Jorge rocked a confident VIP-born attitude. "I'm Daniel Cabrera."

The guard said, "Do you know Claes?"

Jorge assumed he meant the man Jorge'd tried to talk to on the way in. The dude'd just checked his coat, disappeared in through a dark wood door. Jorge chanced it. "Sure I know Claes."

The guard: still suspicious. Called someone on his cell.

Nodded.

To Jorge: "Pardon me. I hadn't been informed that you were invited. Welcome."

J-boy—James Bond, through and through.

The organizers seemed as confused as Jorge was. He'd thought he was gonna work for Nenad. Now he appeared to be a guest.

Just play along.

A coat-check girl came to take his coat. Nice to lose it. It didn't fit in. She asked him for his cell phone. Jorge didn't think about why. Handed it over. Anyway, unnecessary to make a fuss.

He hadn't reacted at first. Not when the old guy, Claes, had checked his coat or when the girl took his. But now he looked at the coat-check girl one more time. A miniskirt so short, the bottom of her ass cheeks peeked out. Black stay-ups that ended in a lace border halfway up her thigh, left eight inches of provocative skin bare. The pink top—not whorishly cheap, but low-cut enough for her cleavage to form an obvious bull's-eye for the gazes of the coat-check customers.

Obvious—this was no ordinary coat-check chick. She was some sort of spiced-up call girl.

Jorge opened the dark wood door through which Claes'd disappeared into the house.

Walked through a hallway. The noise grew. Party music. Giggles and chatter.

At the end of the hall, another dark door. Just as Jorge was about to open it, he smelled cigar smoke.

On the other side of the door.

Unreal.

A roomful of people.

Old guys. Well dressed, many in suits and ties. Some, like Jorge, in suits with no ties, a couple of buttons on the shirts leisurely undone. Others in blazers and slacks. Gray hairlines. Deep wrinkles in their cheeks when they smiled. They all looked to be somewhere between forty and sixty.

A few guards/organizers. All younger. Men. Soberly dressed—blazers, light-colored pants, dark turtlenecks or shirts without ties. Jet Set Carl flitted past, a glass of champagne in each hand.

Striking—all the girls were a variation on the coat-check chick. Miniskirts, hot pants, tights. Tops, tank tops, blouses that revealed more than they covered. Garter belts that showed, fake tits that bulged, stilettos, gleaming, glossy lips.

A girl for every taste. Thin, lanky, tall girls. Superbusty broads. Blacks, blondes, Asians. Girls with gripping gazes. Girls with empty eyes.

Still, not a filthy feel. Jorge was astonished. There was something else—a homey feeling. He pushed into the crowd. Counted heads. At least forty men and as many, probably more, women, and then another dozen or so staff. Pounding music. Glowing cigars in wrinkled hands.

Obviously some sort of brothel business, even if he hadn't quite figured out how yet. Still, the mood was like at a large private party. Purely theoretically: Could've been the house owner's invited friends and their significant others. But not a chance that all these geezers had girlfriends this young. Too good to be true. Or, the house owner's male acquaintances plus some party chicks who'd been delivered to lighten the mood. But there was something more than that in the air.

Jorge looked around again.

The room was large. An enormous crystal chandelier was hanging from the ceiling. Spotlights were suspended from the walls. Speakers in a corner. One part of the room was made up of a bar manned by a guy and four girls. Busy mixing drinks. Most of the men stood in clusters with one another or surrounded by girls. Five girls were dancing right underneath the chandelier—at any other place, their moves would've been considered unnecessarily provocative.

Jorge positioned himself by the bar. Ordered a gin and tonic. Felt insecure. How should he act? What did he really want to achieve with this? WHERE THE HELL WAS HE?

Gulped the drink. Asked for a cigar, Habana Corona. *Buena onda.* The girl behind the bar held up a cigar lighter. Small, extra-hot flame. She pouted. Jorge looked away. Sucked the cigar.

Tried to think clearly. Couldn't let the panic take hold.

Tranquilo.

Did he recognize anyone? Could anyone recognize him? The men: Swedish, well groomed. Posture, poise, attitude. Obvious signals of power. Jorge didn't recognize a single face. So, no one should recognize him, either. The staff: Yugo meatheads and Jet Set Carl, plus some of his peeps, the party organizers. The brats. Jorge didn't think the Jet Set dude would recognize him from Kharma; the guy'd been totally trashed. The biggest risk: that Jet Set Carl was extra vigilant because of the shots in Hallonbergen. On the other hand, he'd apparently chosen to organize this party. *Chico* wasn't the cautious type.

Jorge hadn't seen Radovan or Nenad. He should find out if they were here.

He took it chill—one out of about one hundred people. The guests probably thought he was a guard. The guards thought he was a guest.

Jorge gazed out at the room. Considered his next move. Listened to two men next to him at the bar.

One: darting gaze. Relentlessly checking out the girls in the room. The other: calmer. Took deep drags on a thick cigar. They seemed to know each other well.

"These events just get better and better."

The man with the cigar laughed. "Damn well arranged this year, I think."

"Just look at the women he gets. I'm going crazy over here."

"That's the point. You weren't at Christopher Sandberg's two months ago, were you?"

"No, I don't know him. Was it nice?"

"Wow. Amazing. Christopher is as honorable a guy as Sven here."

"I heard Christopher bought a new house near you guys."

"That's right. On Valevägen. Company must be doing well, because it was a nice shack he landed." The old guy grinned.

"I understand he's been doing a good job in Germany."

"Yes, the market has shot straight up there. Apparently, they've grown by thirty percent in one year."

"Damn. Hey, check out the one in the braids over there. Those are some fucking melons."

"Your kind of cut."

The man with the darting gaze stared. Drooled over the girl. Then he took a sip of his drink. Turned to the guy with the cigar.

"I've been wondering something. I know these parties are safe and all, but how do you know no civvies manage to get in? I wake up at night with cold sweats when I think about the party here last year. I mean, if Christina found out, well, you know."

"Don't worry. He's in with the police. The guys who help him organize this thing are good. The people with the power in our dear police force wouldn't touch these events. According to what I've heard, the guys who run this show would end Stockholm's finest if they tried to interfere. Sometimes police chiefs do naughty things, too. You just have to know what."

"So damn nice. I like this."

The men clinked glasses.

Jorge almost in a state of shock. Was Radovan behind this? If so, he was a fucking genius.

The captains of industry supported by the Yugo Mafia. An unbeatable whore cocktail.

Until tonight—J-boy was on to them.

He stayed by the bar. Tried to see if Radovan or someone else he recognized was there.

After a while, the music was switched off. Someone shushed into a microphone.

The men next to Jorge stopped talking.

The chicks stopped dancing.

Spotlights were directed at the bar.

A man climbed up on the bar. Careful, scared of slipping. Not exactly a young athlete—overweight, suited up, but *sin* tie. Well-combed graying hair. Eyes: In the strange light of the room, they had a milky all-white look.

"Hello, everybody. It's so great to see you here tonight."

The old guy held a glass of champagne in one hand, a microphone in the other.

"As you know, I usually host these parties once a year. I think it's pleasant when just us boys have a chance to get together."

After the word *boys*, he paused dramatically. Awaited the laughter that followed.

"I hope that everyone's going to have a nice night. I'll shut up soon so we can turn the music back on and party all night long. Before I toast the night, I want to take the opportunity to thank those responsible for making this night possible. Radovan Kranjic and Carl Malmer. They organize events like these, among other things. Let's give them a round of applause."

The people around the room applauded. The men def with more enthusiasm than the women, Jorged noted.

The old guy on the bar raised his glass, toasted the night.

Was helped down.

The music blasted out once more.

A couple of daddies started dancing with the girls on the dance floor.

An hour later.

The party'd derailed. *Eyes Wide Shut*, but for real, Smådalarö version. No more talking. December was chasing spring. The old men wanted young pussy. The girls were ready to serve it up. It was obvious this was a marketplace.

Everywhere, old guys had their tongues down young girls' throats. Hands inside bras, fingers between legs, tongues in ears. High school prom, with two exceptions: thirty-year age difference between the make-out partners and only the dudes were paying for the good stuff.

Throughout, the girls were willing.

Clear everywhere: The wolves were wild for fresh meat.

Jorge tried to keep moving. Not end up too long in one spot. Avoid calling attention to himself. Danced for fifteen minutes with a pretty, tall girl with an Eastern European accent and pupils the size of needle pins. High on blow or other uppers. He thought about Nadja. Parts of her story were starting to fall into place. The only thing that didn't jibe was that he hadn't seen Radovan anywhere.

For fifteen minutes, Jorge sat in an armchair and carried on an incomprehensible conversation with a guy involved in financial instruments. Worked reasonably well, despite all odds.

For fifteen minutes, he disappeared into the bathroom.

Picked up the name of the guy who was giving the party: Sven Bolinder. Who was that?

A couple of old guys and girls started disappearing from the room. Jorge, worried. Had they gone home? He asked the Eastern European chick he'd danced with. When she answered—Jorge almost yelled out his surprise—it was more hard-core than he'd expected.

"I guess they've gone up to the rooms. Want to take a peek up there?"

Joder.

The rooms.

The guy who organized the party hadn't just brought the whores. He provided rooms, too.

That was some high-class shit. Nicely done. Commonest, dirtiest, simplest form of prostitution—you go to a place, you pay, and you get a room and a girl—remade to create the feeling: I'm invited to a party without my wife. I happen to meet a hot piece of ass there. I turn her on and we sneak up to an empty room in the house and have a little fun.

He declined her offer. No room for him.

Thought: What've I achieved? *Nada.* No further evidence against Radovan. I have to do something, now. Before everyone leaves to get what they came here for.

He got an idea.

Jorge approached the bartender. Played wasted.

"Excuse me. Is there somewhere I can make a call?"

"Don't think so, sorry. Do you need a taxi? I'll get you one."

"No. I need to make another call. I left my phone in the coat check. Could I borrow yours for a sec?" Jorge waved a thousand-kronor bill. "I'll pay, of course."

The bartender averted his eyes from the money. Continued to mix his drink, crushed ice and strawberries in a blender.

Jorge was playing a high-stakes game. Possibly they had cell phone policies. Or they'd just asked him to leave his own phone in the coat check out of courtesy. It could work.

"It's cool." The bartender handed over his phone.

"I'll step outside and make the call. Have to have quiet around me. Okay?"

"Cool."

Beautiful, J-boy.

Jorge took the cell phone. Turned it around. As expected. Yugos and brats had something in common: They liked high-tech gadgets. No matter which category the bartender belonged to, Jorge'd guessed right. The dude had a cell phone with a high-def camera.

Jorge got going. The men weren't paying any attention. Staff surveillance had decreased as people started disappearing from the party room to the separate rooms.

Jorge pretended to talk. Held the phone a few inches from his ear. Actually, the camera was snapping away—paparazzi-style. Didn't give a shit if the bartender guy wondered what he was doing. Quickly scanned through some pictures. Crappy quality. He didn't dare use the flash. Bad light and distance—the pictures were grainy and dark. Could hardly tell it was people in the pictures.

Didn't work. He deleted the pictures.

Tried to get closer to the armchairs.

Hard to get a good angle.

Decided to take the risk. Held the phone up in front of him. Snapped new photos. Looked again. They were somewhat better, but still hard to make out much in them.

To be safe, he scrolled to the e-mail function. Typed in his own Hotmail address. Sent a picture. Then two more.

Looked up. Saw the bartender coming toward him. Followed by the security guard from the front door.

Fuck.

Sent two more pictures.

Smiled.

Scrolled back to the main menu. Held out the phone.

The bartender yelled over the music. "You said you were stepping out. What've you done?"

"It's cool. I just chatted a little. Ended up staying in here."

The bouncer guy didn't look pleased. "No cell phones in here. Don't you know that?"

Jorge repeated, "I just chatted with a colleague. What's your problem?" Jorge tried to sound self-assured. "Maybe we should talk to Sven Bolinder about this?"

The bouncer hesitated.

Jorge plowed on—it'd worked by the gates.

"Come on. Let's take this to Sven. I'm apparently not allowed to borrow a phone and make a call. Is that what you're saying?" Jorge pointed over toward Sven Bolinder. The nasty old hound was seated in one of the armchairs, closely entwined with a girl who didn't look a day over seventeen.

The bouncer hesitated even more.

Jorge kept pushing. "I'm sure he'd love to be bothered right now."

Tension in the air.

The bartender looked at the bouncer.

The bouncer gave up. Apologized. Walked away.

Jorge acted calm. Inside: keyed up like crazy.

He had to get away from there.

Walked out to the coat check.

When the coat-check girl handed him his coat, she said, "Too bad you're leaving, sweetie," in an accent he couldn't place.

Jorge, silent.

Took the coat.

Walked out.

Didn't see any guards.

He started the car. Drove toward the gates.

It was half-past twelve.

The gates slid open.

He drove out onto the road.

Away from Smådalarö.

Away from the sickest shit on this side of the Pinochet era.

He thought, Captains of industry cavort like kings.

Fuck yourselves.

Jorge's the King.

50

The feel of double-double-gaming was titillating. At the same time, it was strange and demanding—almost too many lies to keep track of. The fact was that JW needed to study his own lies instead of his finance textbook, or else there was a risk he'd let his tongue slip.

People thought he was a backslick brat. Really, he was a regular Joe Schmo pleb who made his money in the dirtiest way possible. Abdulkarim thought he made his money by working for him, administrating the C business. Really, JW was gonna make the big time by betraying Abdul for Nenad.

But whom was he betraying, really? Above the bosses were other bosses. He worked for Abdulkarim, who worked for Nenad, who apparently worked or had worked for someone else. Why all this hush-hush? Who was he betraying if he worked for Abdul but worked even more for Nenad? Of course, someone was behind it all. But who? The Yugo boss himself—Radovan? The Yugo boss in some other faction? Some other gang? JW didn't even want to guess. Anyway, it wasn't his problem, not really.

Two weeks'd passed since Nenad'd made his offer. Conflicting interests were battling inside him. JW was randy for riches. At the same time, he should be afraid of the person, whoever it was, that he was betraying. He weighed his options. The advantages were easy to see. First up, the money. Runner-up, the money. Third place, ibid. Besides, he was living more dangerously than he cared to think about. Why run that race and not get the maximum dividend? No reason. If he was going to live like a drug kingpin, he might as well live large. He'd heard Jorge say it, the gangsta rappers' motto: Get Rich or Die Trying. That was the truth of the day.

The disadvantage was more difficult to calculate. It was constituted by the danger. The person he betrayed would, most likely, not exactly be cartwheeling for joy. The risk of being found out by the police's narcs increased. The risk of being gypped on all fronts increased.

But, he repeated to himself, the money.

It took him two days to think it through. He chose the big shots over Abdulkarim, the high rollers over a B-list Arab, cash over danger. Nenad, in other words.

The arrangements he'd made on the Isle of Man came in handy, even more than he'd thought at first.

The trip to England'd been nice, a relief. JW'd forgotten about his Camilla musings. The reality of Stockholm stressed him out. Sometimes he considered moving home again, when he'd put away enough money.

Abdulkarim was overjoyed about the enormous shipment that was coming; the London deal felt like a success. But it was three months until then. The cabbages had to grow nice and big first. The Arab, JW, and Jorge started preparing the organization for the large quantities that were going to flood the system. They didn't want to cause too steep a price drop. They needed more dealers and stash spots. Above all, they needed a plan for transport and logistics.

Stockholm's underworld was still shaken by the double homicide in Hallonbergen. Everyone was speculating. JW couldn't have cared less about the whole thing. A pimp and a brothel madam shot in a brothel. So what? It didn't have anything do to with his industry.

The next day, he grabbed a coffee at Foam Café with Sophie. The hot Sunday brunch spot for top-cream types. The place was decorated in an Italian Starck style. The day-after dank didn't show. The chicks were primped more than was scientifically possible on a hungover morning. The dudes were cropped, showered, scented, fresh.

JW and Sophie ordered pancakes with maple syrup, bananas, and ice cream. A Foam specialty.

JW posed the question he'd been thinking about for a long time: "Why do you want to meet my other friends so badly?"

Sophie pushed the ice cream to the side with her spoon without answering. JW thought, Why'd she order ice cream if she wasn't going to eat it?

"Hello? I'm talking to you."

Sophie looked up.

"JW, stop. Of course I want to meet them."

"Why? What does it matter?"

"'Cause I want to know all of you. We've been together for almost four months now and I thought we'd get to a higher level after a while. Now I'm starting to realize that this *is* the next level. Not to know anything about you. If you have a bunch of friends that you're, like, hiding from me, it feels pretty weird."

"I'm not hiding them. But they're not interesting. They're lame. Not worth your time."

"I thought Jorge was really nice. We talked for hours. Okay, he's not really like your or my other friends. He comes from a world we're not familiar with. But I think that's interesting. A guy who's had to fight to get somewhere. For most of the people we know, silver spoons've been ladling sweets since birth. Right?"

"Sure, maybe." JW thought about himself. How much did Sophie understand? He continued: "Nippe was wondering who the hustler was you were with at Sturehof. Did you have to go to Stureplan with Jorge?"

"Stop being so lame. Are you ashamed, or what? Stand up for who you are. I thought Jorge was awesome. A badass. He told me about his childhood, actually. Total ghetto, you know, like, there were only four Swedes in his class in elementary school. And I don't even know anyone with parents born outside of Europe. I think Stockholm's, like, a total Johannesburg."

Sophie's words seared. What did she know about him, really? JW wanted to change the subject. Usually, that was his expertise. But now he couldn't think of anything to say.

They sat in silence.

Staring down at the melting ice cream.

51

A week'd passed since the night at Smådalarö. Jorge was lying low. The cops were still on high alert because of the Brothel Murders, as the evening press'd dubbed them. What bullshit—who the hell cared about some übercriminal Serbs?

Jorge hung out at home. Sometimes he had to go out on the street to deal with immediate concerns regarding sales and distribution, but not often. He'd been outside a total of three times.

Abdulkarim was happy as long as the plan panned out—to spread the white gold in the boroughs. Lower the prices. Set the bar. Instead of: "Wanna grab a few beers?" make it: "Wanna snort a few lines?"

It worked. Jorge dealt to eight different contacts in the northern boroughs—from Solna to Märsta. Dudes who knew their turf. Knew the right people. Sold at pubs, pizza joints, discotheques, billiard halls, malls, parks, outside Social Services. And he also distributed to some of the city's southern boroughs.

Jorge: a mini Abdul in his own territory. But he still wanted to avoid being seen.

Petter, the soccer hooligan, was his main man. Kept track of the dealers. Dealt with logistics. Drove around all day with baggies. Called himself "Mr. Icee." The only thing missing was a catchy jingle as he drove past.

Peddled K–12. At house and apartment parties, outside hot dog stands and after-school programs. In common rooms, commuter rail stations, housing-project basements.

A competently cold-blooded coke invasion of the boroughs.

The money rolled in. Abdulkarim was generous. So far, Jorge'd collected over 400,000. Stored half the cash at home in six DVD cases on his bookshelf. Rolled the thousand-kronor bills side by side, like cigars. The rest he buried in a wooded area outside Helenelund—pirate-style.

He consumed some but saved most of it.

Couldn't find peace. Woke up at least once an hour on the hour every night.

Disturbing images from his dreams: couches covered in brain matter, Österåker's walls from the inside, old guys with tongues like erect penises.

Didn't need Freud to interpret that.

Jorge was scared.

If he was put away again, it'd probably be for life.

That wouldn't fly now that he was gonna be an uncle.

He needed to act.

Exploit the positive sides of the situation.

Södermalm, Stockholm's south side. On the way to Lundagatan. Unknown territory for Jorge. The subway stop was Zinkensdamm.

Jorge got off the subway. A forceful wind struck him in the face as he walked up the stairs to the exit.

The weather outside, milder. Spring was on its way.

Lundagatan up. The Skinnarvik Park was snow-free. Jorge knew the rumor: Gay Central Station.

Street number: fifty-five.

He entered the key code he'd been given: 1914. Jorge thought, People have poor imaginations. Almost all building key codes begin with nineteen. Like dates.

Checked the list of tenants in the entry. Ahl—three flights. Jorge was in the right place.

He took the elevator up.

Heard music in the foyer.

Rang the doorbell.

Nothing happened.

Rang again. He heard the music stop.

Someone turned the lock from the inside.

A guy in sweatpants and a wifebeater opened. He had bedhead, round glasses, and mad acne issues. The caricature of a computer geek.

Jorge introduced himself. Was let in.

They'd spoken two days earlier. Arranged a time and place.

Richard Ahl: a twenty-one-year-old kid who studied film at Södertörn College and worked nights at Windows XP tech support. According to him: a crack shot who spent at least eight hours a day in the world of Counter-Strike with a gun in his hand. Richard: online gaming's unknown guru. "You gotta practice if you wanna be a pro. You know how much dough is in this industry?" he asked Jorge after he'd explained what he did.

Jorge couldn't have cared less. He played Game Boy, Max; more advanced stuff wasn't part of his repertoire.

Richard explained, "Counter-Strike, it's the cash cow of the online gaming world. You know, that industry has a bigger turnover than Hollywood." He buzzed on.

Jorge'd found Richard through Petter. According to Petter, the dude was a computer genius. Too bad he wasted his talent on games. The guy could easily hack into the Swedish Security Service, the CIA, or the Pentagon, if he'd only give it a whirl.

The apartment: a studio with a sleeping nook. Hardly any furniture save for a bed. Clothes and magazines all over the floor. Most striking, against one wall: the computer desk, completely cluttered. Two screens, one flat screen and one older model. Floppy discs, CDs and DVDs, cases, manuals, joysticks, controllers, keyboards, magazines, three mouse pads, each with a different pattern, one with a water-lily pond by Monet, two different mice, a laptop slightly ajar, cords, a Web camera, empty Coca-Cola cans, and empty pizza cartons.

A computer geek's natural habitat.

Richard sat down on the chair by the computer desk. "Petter said you wanted some help. Spruce up some pics and get into a computer?"

Jorge wasn't totally sure he'd understood. He remained standing in the middle of the room.

"First and foremost, I need to get into this laptop. I don't have the user name or password, and there's info on it that's very important. Then I need your help to up the quality of a couple of pictures I took with a cell phone camera."

"Right. Wasn't that what I just said?" The dude rocked a cocky style. Knew he was smart. But not smart enough to be humble.

Jorge handed over the laptop that he'd swiped from Hallonbergen.

Richard leaned back in his desk chair. Rolled forward. Opened the laptop. Turned it on.

The computer asked for user name and password.

Richard typed something in.

The computer responded with a text message: *You were not logged in. The user name or password you entered is incorrect. Please try again or contact customer service.*

Richard sighed. Tried new letter combinations.

Nothing happened.

He restarted the computer. Inserted a CD.

Started writing in DOS format.

Nothing happened.

He continued to pound the keyboard frenetically.

Jorge pushed aside a pile of dirty laundry and sat down on the bed. Didn't even try to understand what the computer geek was doing. As long as he could hack into the computer. Looked around. On the walls: posters from the first *Star Wars* movies. Might be originals. Luke Skywalker in a messianic pose, with the light saber pointed to the universe's sky. Yoda with a cane and wrinkled face. Probably artsy pictures. Jorge'd never understood science fiction.

He thought about the girls at Smådalarö. Many of Eastern European origin. Like Nadja. Some'd spoken fluent Swedish. Other were regular Swedish chicks. The mix: Svens, *blattes*, Asians. He understood the imported Eastern women. They were living in the country illegally. Were on drugs. Lived under constant threat from their pimps. They didn't have much choice. But the others? How'd they ended up in the shit?

Richard started explaining. "I can't do it. The info you want is on the hard drive. I've tried to reinstall Windows XP, which is the operating system on this computer, from my own CD. The user name and password are just parts of the operating system, so if I installed a new one, those would disappear, I thought. The problem is that the system's somehow encrypted the info on the hard drive. Installing Windows won't cut it. I have to decrypt. Could take a while."

"How long?"

"Well, I don't have the programs to do it here at home. I have to download them. Play around a little. Need three, four weeks maybe."

"You really can't get it any faster?"

"I don't know. I've got a lot do in school right now."

Jorge thought, Might as well kiss this computer geek's ass a little. He said, "Do the best you can. I'll pay good."

Richard closed the laptop.

"You were gonna look at some pictures, too," Jorge said.

They surfed up Jorge's Hotmail account. Downloaded the photos. Richard opened an Adobe imaging system.

Chose File/Open.

Five pictures popped up on the screen.

The first: Sven Bolinder in an armchair with a young girl on his lap. In profile.

The second: a man in another armchair. A girl sat on the armrest. They were kissing.

Third photo: the back of a man making out with a girl against the wall. No face. Fuck.

Fourth: same man against the wall. His face peeked out from behind the girl's shoulder. Broad smile.

Last one: a fourth man next to an armchair. A girl on her knees in the armchair, one hand over the man's pants, over his cock. He was smiling.

All the photos: terrible quality. Looked like Jorge'd photographed fuzzy ghosts.

Richard zoomed in on the pictures. "What the hell is this?"

Jorge wasn't sure—did the computer geek mean he couldn't tell what the pictures were of, or was he shocked because he did see what the pictures were of?

"Pictures that I need to make clearer. I guess I'm the only one who can see what's going on in them now, huh?"

"Jorge. What're you doing, exactly?" Richard's eyes were wide.

"Relax. I'm no private eye, if that's what you think. I don't even know who these old guys are. It's nothing bad. Just help me out."

Richard muttered. Turned back to the screen. Started clicking on the program's icons and the images.

He fiddled. Changed the exposure. Tested different resolutions, pixel qualities, rendering, contrasts. Enlarged the pictures, changed the color tone, retouched blurred bits.

Worked keenly.

An hour passed.

Jorge wondered how long it would take.

Richard didn't seem to understand. "This? This'll take all night. Once I've started, I don't stop."

Jorge got the hint. Thanked him, excused himself.

They were gonna be in touch the next day at lunchtime.

He left.

Walked down Lundagatan.

In the subway on the way home: thoughts. The nasty, fancy gold guys weren't satisfied with their lives. Had to fuck teenage whores to feel good. Sven hypocrisy demasked. The *blatte* world was more honest. Immigrant Sweden was better. That night, for some reason, he slept okay.

The next day at twelve-thirty, the computer geek called.

"Did you fix the photos?"

"Hell yeah. Looks like they were taken with a three-megapixel camera with flash, at least."

"And."

"I've run the pictures though some databases. Thought you might like that."

"Databases?"

"Yup. Don't you wanna know who the old guys are?"

More than Jorge'd expected. He felt goose bumps rise on his skin. This was big.

Richard went on: "The guy with the chick in his lap, that's Sven Bolinder, the chairman of the board and CEO of one of Sweden's biggest publicly traded companies. The guy kissing, that's the heir to a company. Don't think you'd know it, but it's huge. The oldie against the wall with that nerdy-ass smile is buds with the king and a real high roller. Finally, the guy getting his dick massaged, he was the easiest. That's a Wallström."

Jorge had no idea about the companies Richard'd listed. Big business wasn't his specialty, at least not the legal kind.

But he clocked the basics—they were big-timers.

He and Richard made arrangements. Jorge was gonna go there and pick up the photos in altered form.

He threw himself out of the apartment. Ran toward the commuter rail station.

J-boy: like he'd always said—king of kings. Finance men/brokers/CEOs—beware. Jorgelito: *blatte* of *blattes* you'll wish you'd never met.

Some sort of victory was within reach.

PART 3

Two months later.

Svensk Damtidning

The Princess's Birthday—Glamour Party for the Young Crème de la Crème

By: Britt Bonde   Photography by: Henrik Olsson

Princess Madeleine's birthday celebration at the Solliden Palace on June 10 was the natural early-summer high point for the city's glamorous set. The party was, of course, arranged by Stureplan's new favorite, Carl Malmer, known to his friends as "Jet Set Carl," party planner and personal friend of the princess. Dad, the king, and Mom, the queen, were there, as well as the young crème de la crème of Stockholm's high society. The guests enjoyed champagne and an Italian buffet, after which they danced up a storm to E-Type, who played a special birthday concert. The princess was radiant in her early-summer and perpetually even "Saint-Tropez tan," with boyfriend Jonas at her side. Crown Princess Victoria offered congratulations and bestowed her gift upon little sis—a custom-embossed doghouse, model Mini One, designed by artist Ernst Billgren. All the princess's friends spent a long night together, and at the stroke of midnight a snack was served, the classic national specialty, Jansson's Temptation. After that, the baby princess and her entourage continued to have fun all night long!

The princess's friends Sophie Pihl and Anna Rosensvärd were, as always, in high party spirits.

Carl Malmer, Jet Set Carl, was accompanied by (girl?)friend Charlotta "Lollo" Nordlander. Carl planned the party.

The boyz club, Baron Fredrik Gyllenbielke, Niklas "Nippe" Creutz, and Johan "JW" Westlund, threw down on the dance floor.

The birthday girl, Princess Madeleine, was embraced by her Jonas.

52

JW lived Life. And all the while, Nenad kept in touch regularly. Almost three months'd passed since JW'd made up his mind—he wanted to play in the big leagues, with the big boys. Didn't really understand why the equation demanded his participation, but apparently it was important to Nenad. He'd get his cut of the pie. After some bartering back and forth, they'd landed on 15 percent. If all went well, if the whole shipment made it safely into the country, if sales went off without a hitch at good prices, it would be more than six million. Jesus.

The money-laundering system was the great problem solver. Everything'd fallen into place a little over three months ago. The companies and accounts on the Isle of Man, the companies in Sweden, the invoices, the promissory notes, and the hiring contract. Damn nicely done.

JW dug the system he'd engineered for himself—the placement when JW's C cash was transferred as payment for fantasy marketing costs in England. He designed the invoices for the made-up English advertising and marketing companies himself. They all had the same account number—his own company's account with the Central Union Bank. Nothing strange about that—on paper, his fake business was dealing British antiques. His two point persons at the Swedish banks loved him. Every time they saw each other, JW doled out compliments, made them laugh and listen to his stories about leather armchairs or glass tables with marble legs. Top-shelf trust. Phase one of moving the money—transforming the cash into electronic records—went smoothly. The next phase—concealment—consisted of transferring the money to JW's island company. The company'd acquired a name, C Solutions, Ltd. He liked the catchy C in the name. The money was protected, hidden, secure. No one but JW had the right to know how much and where it was.

The last phase—the actual washing—was genius. C Solutions, Ltd., loaned money to JW's third Swedish company, JW Consulting, Ltd.

Promissory notes had been drawn up by JW's own banker, who, in turn, documented the transactions. Interest and payments were regulated. Advanced legal clauses were in place: Event of Default, Governing Law, Termination—everything according to the Isle of Man's legislation. From the perspective of the Swedish authorities, JW's Swedish company got loans from a foreign company. Nothing shady about that. The contracts were completely in order. Carefully calculated circuit: JW paid invoices to his own company, which, in turn, loaned out the money; then he paid himself interest. JW Consulting, Ltd., was stocking up; there was already half a million kronor in the bank, totally legit. If anyone wondered what the company was using the money for, the answer was a given: It was to cover the initial start-up costs, like a company car and cell phone for JW. In addition, there was the possibility of fake-investing the money and earning profits that would become the company's own capital. Best of all, the interest being paid back to the island company was tax-deductible.

The Swedish company bought the BMW JW'd been coveting for 200,000 kronor, cash—the rest to be paid in installments. Formally, it was owned by the company, but it was at JW's full disposal. The day he picked it up from the dealer was one of the best of his life, even better than the day at the luxury department store in London.

To buy an apartment was trickier. It was rare that a legal person was permitted to own a co-op in Sweden. JW's company couldn't formally pay for it. The solution was that JW Consulting, Ltd., called a board meeting. Signed off on the agenda, decided that three hundred grand would be granted to JW personally.

The effect of all the legal stuff was that, last week, he'd put a 300,000-kronor down payment on a luxuriously renovated one-bedroom on Kommendörsgatan. Six hundred and forty-five square feet. Total price: 3.2 million. It was worth every penny—sure, the apartment wasn't huge, but it was enough. Hardwood floors, high ceilings, moldings, deep windows, and a tiled woodstove gave the right feel. He didn't have money left over to buy sweet furniture, but that wasn't a problem—when the big delivery'd been made, and the dealing was well on its way, JW would go wild at Nordiska Galleriet, Stockholm's premier luxury design destination. Become high-class. Become in line with his image of himself.

It'd all gone so fast. In just a few months, he was living under the same circumstances as Nippe, Putte, Fredrik, and the others. Owned a car and an apartment in the golden rectangle.

It could only get better. Since the spring, he'd averaged 200,000 a month. He and Jet Set Carl were an unbeatable team. Carl planned the parties, invited the people, ran the PR parade. JW guaranteed a full rager and full noses. The money in Sweden was transferred to C Solutions, Ltd.'s account on the Isle of Man, then back to JW Consulting, Ltd. It was a complicated, time-consuming, and expensive process. But when the big C delivery'd been made, it would be worth every penny.

He'd tried to explain the system to Abdulkarim. The Arab understood the magnitude vaguely and wanted in. JW praised himself. He was the man who'd thought to plan ahead—after all, he'd bought yet another company on the island and opened accounts for it. Now that Abdulkarim was interested, there was a possibility of running his business, too. Easy enough to activate the other company and start up an even bigger money circuit. Nenad praised him, too, pronounced the situation first-rate. Demanded an in. JW was happy to oblige. Opened accounts. Fixed contracts. Within a month, the Arab, the Serb, and whoever else who wanted would be able buy their way into JW's system. In: pitch-black cash. Out: pure white fleece.

JW'd always known that Sophie knew Princess Madeleine. But the feeling of being invited, and even seeing himself in the back pages of the royal gossip rag, was a joy comparable to the car purchase.

And Sophie'd stopped asking about Jorge and the others. Maybe it'd been enough for her to meet the Chilean that one time. JW was insecure; sometimes it felt like she was letting him go. Was it because she felt like he was hiding too much? His constant source of insecurity. Should he let her meet his dealer friends? That was impossible. A live gun against JW's temple. Sure, she'd met Jorge and everything was peachy keen, but the Arab's rough manner and Fahdi's crude jokes—never. JW pushed the thought aside. It was a relief that Sophie'd stopped asking. At the same time, his fear that the whole thing would go to hell kept growing. No way it could fall apart now. Not when he was so close to self-realization.

He was waiting to hear from the police regarding new findings about Camilla, but nothing happened. At the end of June, almost six months after he'd given them all he knew, he decided to call the investigator.

He got the cold shoulder. The police explained that he didn't have any actual right to information about the investigation regarding Camilla's disappearance. "Confidentiality, you know." If the police chose to communicate with anyone, it would be with the parents, Margareta and Bengt Westlund, not JW. "Also, in the case in question, no breakthrough has been made, therefore, there is nothing to report."

He remained sitting with the receiver in hand for half an hour, just staring into space. Couldn't believe it. What the hell were they doing? He'd served them the Komvux teacher's head on a platter. Of course, Jan Brunéus had something to do with Camilla's disappearance.

Sometimes he considered sending Fahdi to take care of Brunéus. Exert some pressure of his own to make the teacher talk.

JW ran his C business irreproachably. But as long as Camilla's face was the first thing on his retina every morning, he couldn't find peace.

The following day, he called his mom. He hadn't spoken to her in two months.

"Johan, you never call and you don't pick up when I try to call." The first thing she did was guilt-trip him. No wonder he didn't call more often.

"I know, Mom, I'm sorry. How are you guys?"

"As usual. Nothing changes up here." JW understood. Grief still lay like a lid over her voice.

"I heard from a girlfriend yesterday that there'd been a picture of you in *Svensk Damtidning*. I ran right away and bought the magazine. I was going to call you today. How fun, Johan. At the princess's party and all. Did you see the king?"

"I did, actually. He was happy and seemed nice."

"I had no idea you knew those people."

"They're friends from school. Nice people."

"Dad won one of those lottery things you scrape yesterday. Can you imagine? He scraped three one thousands. We didn't see it at first. We scraped it together. The most we'd won before was three hundred kronor."

"Well, that's great. So, did you buy more tickets?"

"No. We went out for dinner in Robertsfors."

The story made JW happy. As far as he knew, they hadn't gone out to eat, not even to Robertsfors's only decent restaurant, since Camilla'd disappeared.

"Mom, there's something I want to tell you."

Margareta was silent. Could tell by JW's voice what it was about.

"The police have new information about Camilla."

He heard her breathing on the other end of the line.

He kept talking. Told her the whole Jan Brunéus story. When he was finished, Margareta asked how he knew.

He avoided answering.

"Mom, you have to call the police. I know you don't like doing it, but you have to. Find out if they know anything else. Put pressure on them to keep the investigation open. We have the right to know what happened."

"I can't do it. Dad'll have to call."

JW spoke to Bengt. His dad was in a bad mood. JW explained again. It was as if his father didn't want to understand. He asked stupid questions. "Why did she cut so many classes? She must've known that bad attendance would mean lower grades."

The frustration grew. Finally, JW almost yelled, "If you don't call the police, I won't talk to you anymore!"

An ugly threat. Low. But what was he supposed to do?

He apologized.

Bengt promised to call the police.

JW sat on the bed in his beautiful new apartment. He pulled his legs up and hugged them to his chest.

Thought about calling Sophie. Telling her everything about his parents. About Camilla.

No, he couldn't do it.

The next day, he busied himself with the regular: Abdulkarim's project, the C business, expansion plans, the collaboration with Jorge. Preparations with Abdulkarim and Jorge for the big C delivery. The Arab'd deliberately dried up the market. Wanted to press up the prices before the shipment's arrival. It meant more time to study for JW, which he needed. He leaked information to Nenad like a sieve. Called him a few times a week with reports. It was starting to feel normal.

And then, on a day in June, the message arrived: The cabbages in England'd finished growing. They were big and dense enough. In a week, they would arrive, packed in containers.

JW and Abdulkarim'd contracted a real transportation company, Schenker Vegetables, Ltd. They'd booked storage spaces around town where the shit would be stored, conferred with the Brits about price guarantees and quality control, made sure the right drivers handled the load. Organized and planned to the max.

Soon they'd flood Stockholm's boroughs with massive quantities of C.

JW and Jorge'd calculated, contemplated. Organized the dealers in accordance with the new quantities that would be available.

The early summer air was thick with excitement.

Within a few months, if all went according to plan, JW would be a multimillionaire.

***

LINDSKOG MALMSTRÖM LAW FIRM

BANKRUPTCY ESTATE INVENTORY DEED

A. GENERAL INFORMATION

DEBTORS
Stockholm's Video Specialist, Ltd., 556987-2265
The Video Buddy, Ltd., 55655-6897
Registered location: Stockholm

Registered Representatives
Member of the Board Christer Lindberg
Ekholmsvägen 35
127 48 SKÄRHOLMEN

Deputy Eva Gröberg (deceased)
Portholmsgången 47
127 48 SKÄRHOLMEN

ACCOUNTANT
Mikhael Stoianovic

SHARE CAPITAL
100,000 kronor

DAY OF INSOLVENCY
June 10 of this year

BANKRUPTCY ADMINISTRATOR
Göran Grundberg

B. OVERVIEW OF ASSETS AND LIABILITIES
The bankruptcy estate inventory deed shows the following:

ASSETS
(Primarily assets from cash registers, inventories, and current assets in the form of VHS and DVD films)
11,124.00

LIABILITIES

Prioritized debts (tax claims)	174,612.00
FLR § 11	
Nonprioritized debts	43,268.00
Estate's deficit	206,756.00

The estate inventory has been approved by the company's registered representative.

C. INTRODUCTION

GENERAL
Since a while back, I have been investigating a number of companies that are suspected of being a part of a so-called money-laundering scheme. The debtors in question, Stockholm Video Specialist, Ltd. (referred to below as Video Specialist), and the Video Buddy, Ltd. (referred to below as Video Buddy), are suspected of being a part of a group of companies with connection to the so-called Yugoslavian Mafia in Stockholm. Other companies included in the same sphere are Clara's Kitchen & Bar, Ltd., Diamond

Catering, Ltd., and the Demolition Experts in Nälsta, Ltd. The companies are involved in varying fields of business, but the so-called shadow owners are probably the same.

DEBTORS
Christer Lindberg acquired Video Specialist in September of last year from Ali Köyglu, who previously operated a dry-cleaning business on the premises. According to Christer Lindberg, the purchase price was 130,000 kronor. We have been unable to confirm that figure with Ali Köyglu. Christer Lindberg acquired Video Buddy in the course of the same month from Öz Izdan, who previously operated a video-rental business on the premises, under the company name Karlaplans Video, Ltd. Christer Lindberg has informed us that he is unable to recall the purchase price. Öz Izdan has refused to answer questions regarding the sale. According to Christer Lindberg, no written documents were drawn up over the sale.

Christer Lindberg has not been active as director. He has had nothing to do with the accounts, nor played an active part in the decision-making process of the companies in question.

BACKGROUND AND DATE OF COMPANIES' INSOLVENCY
The debt largely constitutes tax liabilities. The companies have probably been run in order to launder money for the shadow owners. Secret accounts have been kept, which reveal that the companies' actual proceeds amount to the following (average numbers calculated based on the first six months of operation): Video Specialist, 52,017 kronor; Video Buddy, 46,122 kronor. The figures reported to the tax authorities between November and March of the current year show heavily inflated profits for both companies. This money has not been derived through the revenues of the companies' business.

In April of this year, tax payments were reduced markedly and appear to have become based on the companies' actual profits. Tax authorities made estimated assessments based on the previous fiscal year; in other words, based on the fictive profits. Insolvency is therefore caused by a lack of funds to pay existing tax liabilities. The date of insolvency for both companies has been fixed for the end of May.

BANKRUPTCY, ETC.

On May 11 of this year, the Enforcement Authority requested that the companies be declared bankrupt. The district court decided to declare the companies bankrupt on May 12. Christer Lindberg had no objection to the decision. He has been called to a creditor's meetings on several occasions. He has not appeared voluntarily. On June 12, the district court ruled that the debtor be collected by the police, at which point Christer Lindberg made an appearance. He testified under oath that he was unaware that parts of the companies' reported income did not derive from the video-rental business.

ALLEGED CRIME

The undersigned is of the view that Christer Lindberg has acted as a so-called straw man for the companies. He has had no insight into operations but, rather, has served solely as the physical person liable for the companies' business on paper. The tax authorities have filed a notice of suspected crime with the Economic Crime Authority and an investigation has begun. The bankruptcy investigation has been carried out in cooperation with the Economic Crime Authority and the National Tax Agency.

Göran Grundberg

53

Summer break'd begun one week ago. His daughter was finally in a safe place—Lovisa and Annika were in Spain for three weeks. Mrado covered costs. A vacation cottage in Bergshamra was also rented, fifteen minutes south of Norrtälje. Genuine feel to the place, red-painted timber walls with white borders. Big lawn for Lovisa to practice her cartwheels on. And cunt Annika and her friends could enjoy themselves any way they liked—play croquet, kubb, badminton. Practically paradise.

Mrado hoped they'd keep clear of Gröndal as much as possible.

It oughta work. The cottage was well equipped. There was a washing machine, a dishwasher, a TV, and a DVD player. Lovisa and Annika would have a relaxing summer far from the city. It was a temporary solution, but perfect for the present.

As for himself, Mrado felt pretty safe. It'd been more than two months since he'd gotten a new apartment. Installed an alarm system. Bought a new car. Got a PO box address, stopped working out at Fitness Club, switched cell phones.

Contracted Ratko as a bodyguard: His old squire was hired to stay close to Mrado at sensitive times. Discover any eventual R. honchos before they had time to act. Screen swarms of lead with his bulletproof vest. Ratko charged a killing, but it was worth it. The important thing was to create the impression for Radovan that Mrado was well protected and that he played in the same league as Mr. R.

Mrado'd looked into whom he could trust. They were informed: Ratko, Bobban, a few guys from the gym. Within a few days, Mrado and Nenad were gonna go live. Show Radovan their version of the term *Serbian solidarity*.

Risk of confrontation. Risk of brutal clash. Risk of injuries.

But Mrado was confident: When the big C load'd been lifted, he and Nenad were gonna be the new rulers.

The market division pretty much worked perfectly. The HA and the Bandidos MC'd buried the hatchet. That alone was a feat from Mrado's end. The Bandidos'd let go of parts of their cocaine market in the inner city and all of their coat-check blackmailing business. Instead, they'd increased the protection racket in the southern boroughs. The HA jacked up booze smuggling in all of middle Sweden but reduced their protection racket in Stockholm. The Original Gangsters kept at the CIT heists. Cut down on blow biz in the projects. Sold heavy in the northern boroughs. The only ones who didn't give a fuck were Naser's gang—difficult to influence.

On the whole, though, the groups were able to concentrate. Focus. Develop new areas. Increase the margins. Increase the profits. Above all, they could keep clear of the Nova Project's infiltrators.

After Mrado's demotion and the problem with the video rental stores, his insomnia took on absurd proportions. He popped pills like a kid ate penny candy. It wasn't okay. He hoped it'd get better once they took on Radovan.

Three fat losses on his tax return. Over 200,000 kronor total.

The solution: He'd sacrifice the companies. The fall guy, Christer Lindberg, the super-Sven, would take the hit. That's what he was paid to do.

And nothing could be traced back to Mrado.

The problem that couldn't be solved was that Mrado needed more clean cash to finance Lovisa's protection in the future. The possibility of buying a new apartment for her and Annika topped the list.

He considered Nenad's idea: Use the laundry genius, their guy JW. Apparently, the brat wannabe'd built beautiful solutions for big-load laundry. That'd be necessary after they'd flipped the massive steal, in any case.

Mrado and Nenad were in intense-planning mode. Two days left until they were gonna present their defection to the Yugo boss.

Why do it before the arrival of the C shipment? Wasn't that unnecessary? Mrado'd discussed the matter with Nenad—there was no other way. It was the Serbian way: Let your enemy know he's your enemy. Mrado and Nenad were gonna play this straight.

Besides, Abdulkarim'd been told ages ago that Rado'd cut Nenad off from the C biz. The Arab'd also been informed about who his real boss was. He'd probably suspected it for a while. The Arab fucker apparently sided with R. Refused even to talk to Nenad, which sent an obvious signal: You're a loser. I'm on my way up. In other words, it didn't matter if Radovan knew that Nenad was going his own way. Nenad'd officially not been given any information for the past three months. Rado and Abdulkarim thought he was out of the running. Their mistake: They had no clue about the leak in their pipes—the JW guy.

The shipment was due at the Arlanda Airport on June 23, in six days. Mrado and Nenad's plan was simple. JW managed everything. Two trucks from Schenker Vegetables were set to pick up the containers. JW'd talked to the teamsters who were driving. They knew the final destination for the containers—not a grocery-store warehouse, but the Västberga Cold Storage Center. JW and a couple of Abdulkarim's other guys were gonna guard the load all the way from Arlanda. The truckers would drop the gear off at the cold-storage facility. Abdulkarim plus honchos would pick up the coke cabbage. And that's where Mrado and Nenad came in. JW'd described everything he knew. The guy was gonna wait in the cold storage facility. Make sure Mrado and Nenad made it inside. After that, it was their job to overpower everyone— probably Abdulkarim and his constant companion, Fahdi, plus the guys who'd helped guard the truck transport. When it came to the JW guy, they'd have to pull a feint. Probably just take him down and tape him up, something like that. If they needed to use heat, no problem.

Mrado looked forward to the attack.

It was showtime—to present Radovan with the fact that he was enemy number one. Mrado and Nenad met up outside Ringen's mall as usual. It was midnight. They took Mrado's new car, a Porsche Carrera. Looked funny—Mrado had to fold himself in half to slide in behind the wheel. Nenad climbed into the passenger seat.

He drove toward Näsbypark, Radovan's home. They were arriving unannounced.

Mrado felt naked without Ratko.

Nenad and he were constantly discussing what was on their minds. Nenad'd just talked to JW: "We're all set to go, but there's a risk that Rado'll get cold feet after what we're about to tell him. Choose to reroute the shipment somewhat. Not much we can do about that except be flexible."

Mrado was massaging the knuckles on one hand, driving in silence.

Nenad said, "Why're you so quiet? We're not going some fucking funeral. This is a big day. New Year's Eve."

"Nenad, you're my friend. You know me. I've worked for Radovan for over ten years. Before that, it was him and me under Jokso. I fought in the same platoon as Radovan. Lived in the same bunker outside Srebrenica for five weeks under massive fire. Today I'm gonna present him with my betrayal. You think I'm happy?"

"I understand. But you didn't start this. Radovan humiliated you first. Without reason. That's not how you treat a brother in arms. After all we've done for him. All those years, sacrifices, risks."

"He hasn't treated me like a brother in arms."

"Exactly. He hasn't treated you with the dignity you deserve. My grandfather told me a story from the war, the Second World War, I mean. Did I tell you the one about the fast?"

Mrado shook his head.

"Granddad fought with the partisans. In the winter of 1942, he was taken prisoner by Ustaša. Sent to a German POW camp outside Kragujevac. Conditions were miserable. They didn't get any food, were beaten every day, didn't see their families. They suffered from diseases—pneumonia, typhus, and tuberculosis. Dropped like flies. But Granddad was tough. Refused to give up. Spring came and Easter was approaching. Granddad and a couple of other prisoners decided to celebrate Easter the proper way. You know, Serbian Orthodox, with a fast. They worked in some kind of tire factory. From seven in the morning until midnight, with a little meal in the middle of the day, usually. A German prison guard found out they were fasting and weren't eating meat, eggs, or milk that day in order to remember the suffering of Jesus. He sought out the camp warden and got permission to order extra food. On the floor, inside the factory where Granddad was working as a slave, the guard set out a feast—ham, sausages, pork chops, liver, fish, cheese, eggs. Granddad was skeletal and starved even before the fast. He was, like, suffering from scurvy, was losing teeth like a six-year-old. The guard yelled at them, 'Whoever eats doesn't have to work all week.' Imagine the temptation, to get to eat themselves full for once. Get to rest. But they'd promised to uphold the Orthodox fast. The guard tried to drag them to the table and force them to eat. One man was too weak to fight. The guard wrestled him to the ground. Pinned his hands back somehow and forced his mouth open. That's when Granddad intervened. He hit the German over the head with an iron rod."

Mrado interrupted Nenad's tale. "Well done."

"Yes, the guard collapsed. As a kid, I always asked Granddad how he'd dared. Know what he said?"

"No. I haven't heard this story before."

"This is what he said: 'I'm not a believer, and I'm not religious. But dignity, Nenad, Serbian dignity. The guard was stepping on that man's honor and therefore also on mine. I didn't do it for Jesus; I did it for honor.' He had to pay, Granddad, for what he'd done. I remember how his arms were crooked when I was little. But nothing could bother him. He knew he had his dignity intact."

Mrado understood. Knew Nenad was right. Dignity trumped everything. Radovan'd stepped on Mrado.

Mrado had to retaliate.

There was no way back.

They were heading into war.

Only one of them could emerge victorious.

Mrado checked a final time. The gun was in his inner pocket.

They passed Djursholm. Almost there.

Näsbypark was as peaceful as ever.

He parked the Porsche far from Radovan's house.

They tightened the Velcro straps on their bulletproof vests. Double-checked the ammo in their weapons.

Walked solemnly up to the house.

It was as dark as it could get outside in June—not very.

Radovan ought to be home. They knew their former boss. Every other Thursday night, the old guy played poker with his gambler gang: Goran, Berra K., and a couple of other silver-haired spenders. Mrado thought, I've never been invited.

The game was usually over by half past twelve. Rado always went home after.

He should be inside the house now.

Mrado and Nenad walked up the gravel path toward the front door. A spotlight came on automatically.

Before they had time to ring the bell, the door slid open.

Stefanovic stood in the opening, with one hand inside his jacket.

He spoke slowly, clear emphasis in the Serbian, "What are *you* doing here at this time of night?"

Mrado replied, "We're here to see Rado. He's usually home about now. It's important."

Stefanovic, electrified. In front of him: the two men Rado'd decided to demote. Lethal. One: assassin, debt collector, human murder machine. The other: cocaine magnate, smuggler, pimp king with a penchant for violence.

The air was thick with explosive energy. One spark and everything could go off.

"I think Radovan's gone to bed. I'm sorry. How about you call tomorrow?"

"No. He will see us now."

Stefanovic closed the door. Mrado and Nenad remained outside. Looked for movements in the windows.

Three minutes passed.

They understood that Rado understood. He would never dare let them into his house. How could he know that they hadn't come to pop him?

Stefanovic came back out.

"He has agreed to meet with you. Please follow me."

Stefanovic guided them in front of him toward the garage—smart. He saw them, but they had to twist their necks to see him. He opened the garage door. Mrado looked in. It was dark in there. Mrado glimpsed a Saab and Rado's Lexus, as well as a Jaguar, a motorcycle, and the Range Rover that'd picked Mrado up for the meeting in the ski-jump tower three months ago.

Stefanovic asked them to wait. Possibly, he'd have time to shoot one of them, but not both.

"Stay here. I'll get Radovan."

They remained standing in the garage. The door was still open. Mrado heard a sound and knew what it was—Nenad'd pulled his gun out of his inner pocket.

Mrado followed suit.

He heard the door to the house open and slam shut.

They couldn't see anyone, only heard Stefanovic's voice. "Okay, we want you to put your weapons away. Cross your arms in front of your chests. We'll come out soon. Thought it'd be best you have your little chat with Radovan in the garage. You know, his daughter is sleeping in the house and we don't want to disturb her."

Mrado kept his grip on his gun. "Forget about it. Nothing's gonna go down unconditionally anymore. Radovan needs to have his arms visible at his sides when he comes out of the shadows. It's simple. The mug on the one whose arms aren't by his side is gonna look like it's been in a colander."

Mrado heard Radovan laugh from the shadows. At least the old guy had his humor intact.

He emerged. Arms hanging. Brave.

Radovan face-to-face with his rebellious ex-minions.

Mrado followed suit.

Stefanovic appeared. Arms straight down.

Nenad did the same.

Four men in a luxury garage. Staring at one another.

Radovan said, "Okay, so, what do you two want at this ungodly hour?"

"Haven't you understood by now? We just wanted to do it eye-to-eye."

Radovan smiled. "I had a feeling it would come. Mrado, you've never been good at dealing when things don't go your way. Which is just one more reason why you can't stay at the top. And Nenad, you've got to learn humility. You two can't just desert me as soon as your duties change. Right?"

Mrado chose not to respond to Rado's provocation. "It's over now. We got ten years together. For Jokso, under Arkan, for Serbia. But it's over now. You don't know what gratitude is, Radovan. You don't know what honor is, or what justice is. That makes you weak. And it makes you a loser."

He caught his breath. Continued, "Things could've been different. You could've built this on the same foundation as Jokso. On respect for your men, and on humility. But you chose to demote us. Did you think we would take your shit? Who the fuck do you think I am? Some Sven who'll bow and grovel and take it up the dirty? Rado, your time is over."

Mrado and Nenad walked out of the garage. If Radovan answered, they didn't stick around to hear it.

54

Successful blackmail tactic in review. Three months'd passed since Jorge got the five photos of the captains of industry. He thanked Richard, the computer geek, with all his heart. Surprised that the dude hadn't demanded he be let in on the action. Rocking the blackmail gig with J-boy was never even up for discussion.

Jorge'd had the photos printed on photo paper. The quality still wasn't super, but it was easier to see who was pictured and what they were doing.

He wrote a letter to go along with the pictures, labored over the words.

"The attached picture was taken of you at Sven Bolinder's party in March. It will be sent to your wife within ten days. In order to prevent this from happening, deposit fifty thousand kronor at account number 5215-5964354 at SEB one week from today at the latest."

Jorge'd been in touch with an old junkie. Had the guy open the account at SEB. He pocketed the debit card and the password himself. Was gonna withdraw the deposited money as soon as possible.

Worked wonders.

The four silver daddies, one of whom appeared in two photos, deposited the dough, no questions asked. Jorge couldn't pressure them all at the same time, since the debit card had a withdrawal limit. Knocked one off the list every other week.

After two months—J-boy'd be 200,000 richer.

Easiest gig in town.

Poor suckers, they knew he'd be back for more.

He hoped Radovan would find out that someone was fucking with them. That someone knew what he was up to.

Abdulkarim kept applying pressure. "You gotta rig your squad. Get more retailers. There's a George Jung–class shipment coming soon."

Jorge'd finally gotten info about the shipment from Abdul. It was blow, of course. A lotta pounds, over two hundred, according to the Arab. Could it be true? If so, it was the single biggest imported load Jorge'd ever heard of. His old homeboys in Österåker would faint if they knew.

The buzz about the double brothel homicide'd died down. Other rumors were festering. War within the Yugo Mafia. Revolt against Radovan. Defectors from the organization. What did that mean for Jorge's hate project?

A few days later, Fahdi told him which Yugos'd left the organization: Mrado and Nenad. Fate's fantastic feats. Those were the very men who were number two and three on his hate list, after their former boss, Radovan. Mrado for the pain. Nenad for Nadja.

The computer geek called in the middle of June. The dude'd dragged out on time. Blamed a CS championship. Jorge thought: *Counter-Strike*—who gives? You should've called earlier.

Jorge'd tried to put a fire under his ass. Was only supposed to take a few weeks; had taken two months. But he hadn't been able to do much about it.

At least now the time'd come.

He picked up the computer at the computer geek's place that very day.

Jorge was keyed up on the way over. Maybe there was stuff on the laptop that would lead to even more cash.

He walked up Lundagatan.

Rang Richard's doorbell.

Stepped inside.

"Hey, man, I don't know you and don't know anything about whatever it is you're up to. Just so you know."

Jorge thought the comment was strange. "What do you mean?"

"Nothing, really. Just thinking about what's on that computer. Some stuff is, um, pretty disturbing."

Jorge just wanted the computer and whatever was on it. "It's cool, *chico*. You want more dough, or what?"

"Dough? No, I just wanted to warn you. So you don't get into trouble."

Jorge didn't know what to expect.

He thanked the guy for his help. Paid. Peaced.

He was tempted to open the laptop on the train on his way home. Stopped himself. Best to wait.

Home in Helenelund. He sat down on the couch.

Opened the computer. Wallpaper: a vast green lawn and a blue sky.

He checked the desktop: not a lot of icons. My Computer, Trash, iTunes, two games: Battlefield 1942 and the Sims. Excel and Windows Media Player were also on the desktop. A couple of folders.

He started looking through the folders one by one.

Afterward, he thought, If I'd known what I'd find, I might've stopped looking.

One folder contained images of weapons downloaded from the Internet.

Another folder contained MP3s.

The third folder: English cheat sheets for computer games.

The fourth folder held the names of the johns, their aliases, and passwords. At least three hundred names. Jorge skimmed through the list. Mostly Svens, but some *blattes*, too. Fahdi was there. Jorge already knew his alias. Abdulkarim was there. Jet Set Carl was there. Jorge didn't recognize the other names—had to look closer into all that. Potential gold mine.

Next folder: draft of the Web site where the brothel advertised. Pictures of women. Snippets of text. Telephone numbers. Jorge scrolled through the pictures. Girls posing in stark rooms with strong lighting. He found two pictures of Nadja. Exposed. Alone. Vulnerable.

The list of names was good. The pictures of Nadja were tough but not crushing. Jorge clocked that this was the way the hooker industry rolled. It was the contents of the final folder, an MPEG file, that made him hurl.

The sickest, most disgusting shit he'd ever seen.

It was five minutes long. Enough for a lifetime's worth of nightmares.

The video's opening scene: a room, harsh lighting, a table.

Two men in ski masks dragged a person into the room whose head was covered in a cloth bag. Judging by the body, it was a girl.

One of the men: dark leather jacket, beefy. The other: dressed in a suit. Both spoke Serbian.

Forced the girl onto the table. Hands tied behind her back. Fought back as hard as she could.

The big guy pulled off the cloth bag. A girl, face swollen from crying. Blond, Nordic appearance. Yelled in perfect Swedish, "Let me go, you pigs!" She kept screaming. Jorge couldn't make out all the words. The beefy guy said something. Hit her on the side of the head. Jorge recognized his voice. It was Mrado. The dude in the suit caressed her cheek. She spit in his face, screamed. A couple chaotic seconds. The girl screamed again, "How the fuck could I be with you?" Mrado pulled a gun. Pressed the barrel into the girl's mouth. She grew silent. The steel scraped against her teeth. She cried. The suit guy was angry. Chewed the girl out: "You'll never spit on me again, you fucking cunt." Unbuttoned his pants. Tore off her workout pants. She lay still. The gun still in her mouth. The man in the suit pulled out his dick. Forced the girl onto her stomach. Mrado with the barrel of the gun against the back of her head instead of in her mouth. The suit guy raped her. Thrust. Faster. Went on for two minutes. Jorge threw up. He'd seen tons of pornos, but this was for real. The suit guy—finished. The girl—shattered. Mrado raised the gun. Looked into the camera. His eyes were visible through the slits in the ski mask. Said, in Swedish, "A warning to all you who're thinking of fucking with us." The last minute. They carried the girl to a chair, her workout pants still around her ankles. Mrado hit her in the stomach, over the arms, in the face. Drops of sweat went flying. Blood went flying. Her eyebrows were torn open. Her lips were busted. Ears swollen. Just shards of her left.

The video ended abruptly.

The girl's appearance reminded Jorge of someone, but he couldn't figure out who.

The only good news: the video's hideousness. It should be ill evidence against Mrado. The dude would regret that he'd beaten up on J-boy. For about twenty-five to life.

That night.

Jorge couldn't forget the MPEG video. Assumed it'd been used as fear propaganda for whores who stepped outta line. Had looked closer at the movie's stats: It was about four years old. Did they run the same trailer over and over again?

A parody of sleep. First he couldn't fall asleep. Then, once he'd finally fallen asleep, he woke up several times an hour. Went to the bathroom. Nightmared. Reminded him of the nights before his escape from Österåker.

He felt like shit. Go ahead, watch porn and be happy—but not rape and abuse live in front of the camera.

Who the hell did the raped woman remind him of?

He groped at memories.

It felt good to have shot the shit out of the pimp and the brothel madam.

Now Mrado, the other guy from the video, and Radovan were next in line. He would crush them.

J-boy's on your tracks.

In the morning, he drank strong coffee. Had to get going. Had to forget. It was Abdulkarim's high holiday.

The huge shipment was arriving.

Jorge was part of the preparations—he and JW were supposed to watch over the delivery. From Arlanda to the cold storage facility.

He was meeting up with Abdulkarim, Fahdi, and JW in an hour to plan.

This was big. What he'd seen in the video the night before was bigger.

But now he had to focus.

The shipment would soon be here.

* * *

URGENT!!

Confidential.

Attn: Inspector Henrik Hansson, Special Missions Unit
Fax number: 08-670 45 81
Date: June 22
Number of pages: 1

Business: Operation Snowstorm, Project Nova

Operation Snowstorm Begins

Operation Snowstorm begins tomorrow at 10:00. All units will gather at Bergsgatan, room 4D, for an internal run-through.

Brief History

Johan Karlsson, who has served as an infiltrator within the realm of Project Nova (under the name Micke), has information that the target group is planning to receive a very large shipment of cocaine. The shipment is expected to arrive at Arlanda with flight B746-34 from London at 8:00 tomorrow. From there, it will be driven in containers by trucks from the transport firm Schenker Vegetables to the Västberga Cold Storage Center. The exact location for unloading is unknown at present.

Plan of Attack

There is a possibility that several high-ranking persons within Stockholm's Yugoslavian Mafia network will be present at the unloading of the shipment of cocaine. According to present instructions, Operation Snowstorm will therefore wait to strike until it is possible to arrest as many of these persons as possible.

We are currently working to gather exact information regarding the time of unloading and will be in touch as soon as we do.

The Special Missions Unit, Project Nova's head surveillance team, as well as Drug Enforcement are included in Operation Snowstorm. This fax has been sent to all officers and unit chiefs.

55

JW and Jorge were sitting in a rented pickup. They were waiting, didn't talk much, were just quiet.

JW'd drawn up the plan. Two trucks from Schenker Vegetables would pick up the containers at Arlanda. The teamsters who drove would go straight to Västberga Cold Storage. They were in the know enough to get that what they were transporting was valuable, but also not to ask any unnecessary questions. JW and Jorge were waiting to follow the trucks. Make sure they didn't go off track, didn't pinch any of the shipment, didn't get in touch with suspicious people. Abdulkarim and Fahdi would meet them at the cold-storage place. When the truckers left the scene it would be time for the Arab, JW, Jorge, and the rest to slice open the cabbages and repackage the coke. Move it, restow it. Rake in the dough.

What Abdul didn't know, of course, was that JW was the biggest double-crosser of the decade. He'd informed Nenad of every single part of the plan. According to their agreement, Nenad would be armed, would take control as best he could, maybe tie people up, including JW, and boost the goods. It would be smooth and easy.

Abdulkarim's time as a player was over.

And no one could blame JW.

It was brilliant.

That morning, Abdul'd held an executive briefing meeting. Gave orders like some sort of drill sergeant. As if he'd ever been in the service. JW, Jorge, Fahdi, Petter were riled up, ready, and, above all, potential cocaine millionaires.

The Arab went over the rules. New prepaid cards in new cell phones were a given. As soon as the goods'd been unloaded, the phones and the cards would be destroyed and Abdulkarim would distribute new phones. They all had to wear gloves—the traditional way of avoiding fingerprints. Fahdi brought a police radio with him in the car—the easiest way of knowing what the cops knew and, if they knew something, where they were going. They had to wear blue jeans and blue cotton sweaters—not a lot of people knew it, but forensic scientists hated blue cotton fiber. It was practically impossible to pin a person to a garment like that, since it was by far the most common textile residue people left behind. They had ski masks in their pockets: if the brass made a crackdown and you were able to get away, it was best that no one saw your face.

Finally, just as they were leaving—and it came as a bad surprise—Abdulkarim dealt his final card: He had Fahdi distribute weapons to Jorge and JW.

"You need these, boys. Like the dudes in England. We're just as good. Now it's for real. If the cocksucking cops try to fuck it up, just go for it."

JW got a black gun. It gleamed. Felt dangerously beautiful. He sat on Abdulkarim's couch and weighed it in his hand. A Glock 22. Fahdi showed him how to work it—the safety, the extra trigger safety, and the magazine. Then he demonstrated the right way to hold it, how to take the recoil.

Jorge got a revolver. Was cool about it.

JW felt torn—a mix of terror and delight.

Jorge was calm. He had dark circles under his eyes and whined about having slept like shit. His hair was straighter than usual. JW thought, Did he forget to use the Afro curler?

They were parked outside the gate by the fence at Arlanda's freight terminal. Waiting for the trucks. JW in the driver's seat and Jorge next to him. The Chilean stared out the window.

The car they sat in smelled new.

After ten minutes, Jorge turned to JW. He looked strange. Pensive, but tired at the same time.

"JW, you got a sister?"

JW took his time answering. In his mind, the chaotic questions piled up: Why did Jorge ask that? Does he know something about Camilla? Did Sophie tell him something?

JW nodded. "I have a sister. Why?"

Jorge replied, "Nothing. Just wondering. I've got a sister too. Paola.

Only seen her once since the escape. Heavy. I carry her with me, always."

JW lost interest. Jorge just wanted to talk. He didn't seem to know the Camilla story. That his sister was missing, that she'd been with her teacher, who'd given her top grades in exchange for sex. That she'd ridden in a yellow Ferrari with an unknown Yugoslavian. That something'd been seriously fucked up.

Jorge was a solid guy. Lived up to the ghetto myth about the hard-core *blatte*. At the same time, he was a good person who'd shown real gratitude toward JW for picking him up in the woods.

JW said, "I carry my sister with me, too. I've got a picture of her in my wallet."

Jorge turned to face JW.

He didn't say anything.

The conversation dried up.

They watched the gate.

JW thought Jorge didn't just seem tired; he seemed stressed-out, too.

After half an hour, the freight trucks drove out. Two of them, with the text *Schenker Vegetables* in green lettering on the sides of the containers. They'd already seen several identical cars and had started sweating. No way they could miss the right cars. Imagine if they followed the wrong shipment. Ended up with a ton of cabbage without C. JW and Jorge both had slips of paper with the license plate numbers in their hands—this time it was the right trucks.

JW slipped into first gear. Slowly rolled after. The trucks drove up the ramp and swung around the terminal, JW right behind them.

The only hole in the plan was the access to Arlanda. Theoretically, the truck drivers could've ripped them off in there. They were the only ones allowed on the loading docks within Arlanda's vicinity. But the risk that they'd have exchanged the goods for worthless crap was minimal. The truckers knew the deal: If they ripped off Abdulkarim and the others, they'd have to pay. According to the Arab, with their lives.

The task was important. Not let the trucks or the drivers out of their sight. Even if the truckers didn't totally grasp what they were driving, it was too many pounds to take even the most negligible chances.

The trucks stopped for a few seconds by one of the parking lots just outside of Arlanda. Long enough for Jorge to jump out of the car.

Check that it was the right guy driving the right truck. If it'd been the wrong guys, they would've forced them to get out of the trucks and into the car. Then driven them to Abdulkarim and Fahdi for the full treatment.

Jorge waved. That meant green light—correct guy behind the wheel in each car.

They kept driving.

It was a nice day. Two lonely clouds in a blue sky.

Jorge seemed preoccupied. Was he scared?

JW asked, "What's up? You stressed-out?"

"No. I've been stressed-out a couple of times. Know how that feels. When I ran from Österåker, almost a mile at record speed, then I was really fucking stressed-out. A sign is that I smell. I smell like stress."

"Don't take it personally, J., but you look like shit," JW said, and laughed. He thought Jorge would grin.

But he didn't. Instead, he said, "JW, can I take a look at that photo of your sister?"

JW's thoughts in anarchy again: What the hell does Jorge want? Why all the talk about Camilla?

JW held the wheel with his left hand. Groped in his back pocket with his right. Pulled out the thin wallet in monogrammed leather: Louis Vuitton. In it he had only bills and four plastic cards: Visa, driver's license, gas card, and a rewards card to an upscale department store.

He handed it over to Jorge and said, "Look under the Visa card."

Jorge pulled out the card. Under it, in the same slot, was a passport photo.

The Chilean checked out his sister.

JW kept his eyes on the road.

Jorge returned the wallet. JW put it on top of the glove compartment.

"You look alike."

"I know."

"She's pretty."

Then silence.

The trucks were driving slowly. Abdulkarim's orders were that under no circumstances were they to speed—the highway to Arlanda was a favorite haunt for the traffic police.

Less than an hour later, they were driving through the southern sections of the city. So far, it'd been smooth sailing.

JW called Abdul. "We'll be there in forty. The trucks've been driving calmly. The drivers are cool. Everything seems to be working."

"*Abbou.* We'll be there in twenty. See you there, *inshallah.*"

Despite their new phones and cards, Abdulkarim'd decided that all numbers, times, and the like would be divided in four. In other words, JW and Jorge were actually ten minutes from Västberga Cold Storage. Abdulkarim, Fahdi, and the others would be there in five. JW thought it was a bit much. If the police were tapping their calls, they were screwed no matter what. Jorge almost seemed asleep in the passenger seat. JW couldn't have cared less about him. He fantasized about the future financial fiesta. He set his goal: When he had made twenty mil, he would stop with coke. The delicious part of the calculation: The goal might be reached within a year.

Fourteen minutes'd passed. The trucks backed into the loading docks, spots five and six, by the cold-storage facility. JW parked the car.

He said to Jorge, "This'll be a chill day. You just be chill, too."

Jorge didn't seem to be listening. Was he focused on something else? What the hell was he up to?

They got out of the car and walked over to the freight trucks. The two drivers'd climbed out. JW thanked them and discussed briefly when they could pick up the cars again. Then he paid them. They got three thousand kronor each, cash in hand. A good mood settled. Maybe they thought it was cigarettes, liquor, or other small-time stuff. The risk that they understood that they'd just driven 100 million kronor in cocaine to, at the moment, the most nervous drug pushers on this side of the Atlantic was minimal.

Jorge got out of the car and took a turn around the loading docks. It was his job to scout out the area.

Petter, who'd arrived with Abdulkarim and Fahdi, walked in the opposite direction. He was also scoping out the scene. Made sure everything was straight.

Fahdi emerged from a steel door on loading dock number five.

He nodded to JW. Made eye contact with Jorge in the distance. Meaning: Everything's been cool here so far.

Abdul opened the container on one of the trucks so that JW could look inside. In the dark he glimpsed a pallet and six rows of boxes.

Passed it. Instead, he groped with his hand in one of the boxes in the pallet behind the first one and picked up a head of cabbage.

Fahdi's stare was fixed on the cabbage.

JW held it in his left hand.

Pressed his right fist down between the stiff white leaves.

He could feel it distinctly—the plastic baggie.

56

Sometimes there's nothing you can do but take the next step—and then the step after that.

Mrado wasn't thinking about all the crap today. Just did what he had to do.

Dressed slower, more carefully than usual. Like a slow-motion scene in an action flick, as if to underscore the importance of perfection.

Not because he had doubts or was scared, just because everything had to be perfect.

The knife: a Spec Plus U.S. Army Quartermaster with an eight-inch-long blade in black carbon steel with a blood groove. Black calfskin sheath, strapped around his shin with two Velcro bands.

He tightened them. Made sure the sheath was in place—it was plastered against his leg. Secure. Without interfering with the flutter of the pant leg if he made any sudden moves.

He weighed the knife in his hand. Sure, it was American, but it was also the best battle knife Mrado knew of. He balanced it. Ran his thumb over the blade's edge.

It was newly sharpened.

Images in his mind: the Battle of Vukovar. Bayonet fight with a Croatian sniper.

Warm blood.

He put on his pants. Thin black chinos: Ralph Lauren Polo, for warm summer days. Cool clothes were good. Light clothes.

On his upper body he wore a white wifebeater.

Looked himself in the mirror. Flexed his triceps. Did he detect some deterioration? Not impossible—he hadn't been to Fitness Club since he was demoted over three months ago. Trained at World Class instead but didn't know anyone there. Pleasure diminished. Attendance declined. Triceps and other muscles didn't measure up. Stung to see it.

He put on a button-down shirt, beige Hugo Boss.

On top: a dark linen jacket.

No holster today. If the cops made a bust, he wanted to be able to toss the weapon somewhere without having to explain why he was wearing a gun holster. Happy that his S & W was so small.

Even happier about the ammunition he had: Starfire, hollow bullets that exploded on impact. Worked extra well in weapons with short muzzles, where the bullet's speed was lower, the expansion at contact greater.

Held the revolver in his hand. It was polished. So beautiful with its stainless steel. The emblem on the side gleamed above the grip. An inscribed text above the trigger: *Airweight*.

Mrado remembered when they'd taken it from him at the ski-jump tower by Fiskartorp. After today: Remorse would be their inheritance.

He put it in the inside pocket of the jacket.

Tied his shoes—meticulously.

Ready for the greatest coup of his life—100 million on the street.

Worth certain risks.

Nenad was waiting in the car downstairs. He'd sold his old luxury car. It attracted too much attention. Now he drove a red Mercedes CLS 55 AMG, a powerhouse with soft curves.

Nenad was dressed in a linen suit. Handkerchief in the breast pocket. Slicked-back hair. A big day required smart clothes. The blow and bordello king never scrimped on style.

The Benz feel inside the car was elegant.

They drove the Södra Länken freeway out of the city. Then west. Toward the cold-storage place.

Discussed the break. The pleasure. Radovan's attempt to push them down.

The old bastard was finished. The new kings of the hill were spelled M & N.

Revolution within the Yugo Mafia drew near. Within a few hours, they would be the coke kings of the city. Of Sweden. Of Europe.

They stopped at Gullmarsplan. Were meeting up with Bobban. Ratko hadn't been able to make it. Mrado wondered why. Wasn't Ratko on his side, or what?

Bobban was waiting as planned outside the bus terminal above the subway station. He drove a Volvo XC90 and was dressed in his usual black denim jacket. Mrado thought, That guy never changes style.

All in place: three men against Radovan.

Not really. Three professionals against a confused and drugged-out Arab, Abdul.

Besides, they had an insider on their team. The Stureplan slick in the know.

They drove in a convoy toward Västberga.

Nenad was playing gym techno on high volume. Pounded his fists to the beat against the wheel.

Power.

An easy match.

A nice day.

Västberga's industrial area could be seen from far away. Warehouses. Logistics centers. Cold-storage units. The businesses in the area consisted of a key factory, low-end IT technicians, car companies, sorting plants, and machine workshops.

Mrado thought about Christer Lindberg. The ultra-Sven who'd had to file for personal bankruptcy in order to cover the tax debts from the video stores. This area was filled with his type of people.

Mrado didn't feel bad for him. If you play the game, you have to deal with the rules of the game, or whatever. The guy only had himself to blame.

They drove toward the cold-storage building. It was enormous. Over seventy units, with everything from over two-thousand-square-foot refrigeration halls to rooms of less than fifty. Meat, vegetables, fruit, mink coats—everything kept better if kept cool. Rumor had it that some units housed organs for the Karolinska Medical Institute.

The building was made of white sheet metal with a flat roof. Drearier than dreary. Streamers outside read WELCOME TO VÄSTBERGA INDUSTRIAL AND LOGISTICS PARK.

They stopped the car outside the fence surrounding the loading docks. Nenad gave Mrado a key. They'd made duplicates; in case one of them went down, the other could make off with the car.

Began to walk toward loading dock number six.

Knew what they were looking for.

Bobban pulled in with his SUV. Parked it outside dock number five. The idea: one car close by and the other outside. If shit went down, they would need alternatives.

Nenad'd also parked a rented Volkswagen by the flagpoles on the front side of the cold-storage building the night before. A third getaway car if needed.

Bobban stayed in his car. Scoped out the area.

Mrado's cell phone rang, a silent vibration in his pocket.

Bobban's voice: "I see him now. He's smoking by loading dock six. Swede. Blue sweater."

"Thanks." Mrado hung up.

Apparently, Abdulkarim'd placed only one man outside. Rookie mistake.

Mrado ran toward the loading dock. Saw the guy from twenty yards away. Slowed to a walk. Didn't want to scare him.

The dude saw him too late.

Mrado, commando-style: slit his throat.

The guy gargled, didn't have time to scream.

Mrado worried about bloodstains.

Pulled the guy in under the loading dock. Hid the body.

Bobban stepped out of the car. Jumped up onto the loading dock.

Could be days before the guy's body was found under the loading dock's overhang.

Bobban remained standing up on the loading dock. Stared in the opposite direction. Kept watch.

Mrado fingered his revolver. Felt the faint outline of the handle's grip-friendly ribbing.

Nenad stood behind Bobban.

Waiting.

The air was clear. In the distance, the sound of two trucks leaving the area could be heard. No people in sight.

The big question: Had JW unlocked the entrance to unit 51 as promised? The little question: How vigilant were Abdulkarim and his boys?

Mrado tested the door handle to the entrance. It was designed so you could drive pallets with foodstuffs in and out—could be opened like a hatch.

Nenad pulled his gun.

57

The load-out was quick.

Jorge's head, like a soup. A mix of fear, triumph, confusion. Disgust.

It was JW's sister he'd seen in the video on the computer.

Raped, abused. Beaten to bits. Murdered?

As soon as Jorge got in the car with JW, he'd thought the Öster-malm brat reminded him of someone. At first couldn't think of whom. Half an hour later, he knew for sure.

Ay, qué sorpresa.

JW's sister—a whore. Taken by the Yugos.

He couldn't bear to say anything.

They'd driven the boxes in on dollies. Ten of them. Heavy and difficult to maneuver. They weren't exactly truckers.

Abdulkarim, revved up. Fahdi, sweaty. JW was calm, for being him. Jorge himself didn't know how he was feeling.

The Arab ordered Petter to keep watch outside. The dude was sup-posed to call if he saw anything shady. The pigs were on their backs like crazy these days.

The cold-storage facility had white walls and steel beams in the high ceiling in which to fasten lifting devices. Abdulkarim swore, wished they'd rented an indoor crane. The floor was made of metal. Smelled like cold fruit. It echoed.

Cool temperature in the entire space.

Two doors, the one they'd come in through and one at the other end of the room.

Four pallets were *sin* C—the ones that'd been farthest out. That was their safety margin if customs'd taken a random sample—always a chance they only checked the veggies on the end.

They began to empty the other cabbages.

Jorge and JW tore open the cabbages. Cut them open. Plucked out the small plastic bags with the white powder.

Abdulkarim stood by calmly and watched. Weighed and counted every single bag. It had to be correct down to the last gram.

Fahdi packed the bags into a couple of suitcases that they'd lined up against the wall.

Jorge'd already opened one of the bags. Stuck down his finger. Rubbed it against his gums in the classic manner. Tasted good. Tasted 90 percent.

JW was pleased. The eagle'd landed.

After fifteen minutes in the cold-storage facility, they had three pallets left to unpack.

Thirteen suitcases filled with bags. Bulked with old blankets.

They were almost done. Soon they'd load half the suitcases on Jorge and JW's pickup, and the rest in the car that Abdulkarim, Fahdi, and Petter'd come in.

Abdulkarim, ardent. Every single bag's weight was written down. Added up. Every suitcase had to contain 13.75 pounds of C. To be stored at different hiding places around town. Spread the risks.

Then something strange happened. The door out toward the loading dock opened.

Jorge turned around. Looked at whoever came in. He was still holding a cabbage in his hand.

Was it Petter?

No.

Big guys.

The 5-0?

Maybe.

No.

Men with ski masks over their heads. Both wearing blazers. *Reservoir Dogs*, or what?

Guns in their hands.

Abdulkarim screamed. Jorge pulled his gun. JW got behind a pallet. Fahdi was suddenly holding his gun in hand. Fired shots. Too late. The bigger of the men—and he was really enormous—held a small revolver in his hand. Smoke from the barrel. Fahdi collapsed. Jorge didn't see any blood. The other man, the one with a handkerchief in the breast pocket of his blazer, yelled, "Get down on the floor, fast as fuck, or I'll pop another one." JW obeyed. Jorge remained standing. Abdulkarim hollered. Cursed. Called for Allah. His constant squire was on the floor. Blood was beginning to show. Trickling from Fahdi's head. The man with the handkerchief in his pocket said in drawling voice, "Shut up and get down." Pointed his gun at Abdulkarim. The man who'd shot Fahdi said, "You, too, Latino fag, get down." Jorge lay down. Dropped his weapon. Could hardly see JW behind the packing case. Abdulkarim was on the floor, his hands on his head.

Jorge thought he almost recognized the voice of the man with the handkerchief.

He definitely recognized the voice of the man who'd shot Fahdi.

58

JW sat with his back against a packing case. The floor was cold. His position was uncomfortable. His hands were taped back a little too tightly.

But not that tightly—part of his agreement with Nenad was that they'd tape him so that he'd have a chance to break free. Who wanted to end up on their ass in a cold-storage facility all night?

Even so, the situation'd gotten out of hand.

Shooting Fahdi was not part of the fucking plan. JW had no clue who Nenad's helpers were, but that big asshole'd definitely made a mistake. A horrific overstep.

Panic was creeping up on him.

Abdulkarim was on the floor, with his hands behind his back, duct tape wound tightly around his wrists. But he refused to shut up. The Arab screamed, spat, and drooled in turn.

Jorge was sitting just like JW, against a pallet, with his hands taped behind his back. He stared at JW.

Chills ran up and down JW's spine. The room was chilly. The Yugos were ice-cold.

Fuck.

Nenad and his helper unpacked the last of the cabbage. Opened it just like Jorge, JW, and Fahdi'd done. Crammed the baggies into the suitcases. Skipped the weighing and tasting. Ignored the Arab's screaming. Didn't even look in JW's direction.

Jorge kept staring. But not at the men in the ski masks, who were in the process of stealing over two hundred pounds of C. He was staring at JW.

"You told them, didn't you?"

JW thought, How could Jorge know?

"You, you fucking idiot, got 'em here, and you don't even know who they really are."

"What are you talking about? I have no idea who they are."

JW turned his head. Looked over at Nenad. He had a cabbage in his hand. Carefully slit it open with a box cutter. Took care not to cut the bag. A couple of spilled grams—maybe ten thousand kronor. Nenad didn't seem to give a shit about JW and Jorge's conversation. Maybe he didn't hear it—Abdulkarim's curses were distracting.

Jorge said in a low voice, "Fahdi for sure ain't the canary. Why'd he let someone in who'd shoot him in the face? Abdulkarim? No, he'd never drag anyone into this who'd shoot his best friend. So, who can it be? Petter or you—'cause it ain't me. And you said something a half hour ago that I'm thinkin' about now. You told me to be chill. I've never heard you talk like that before. Why'd you say that anyway? How'd you wanna affect me? You're fucked, JW, man."

"Shut up."

JW looked straight ahead. Turned his eyes away from Jorge. The Chilean was smarter than he'd thought. But what did it matter now? In a couple of minutes, Nenad and his man would be gone. JW would break free and maybe help Jorge with the tape, then disappear. Jorge, Abdulkarim, and Fahdi, if he was alive, would have to make it on their own—sorry, boys, that's life.

There was one case of cabbage left. The Yugos worked quickly. JW closed his eyes and waited for them to skip out.

Jorge hissed again, "Listen to me, JW."

JW ignored him.

"Fuck, man, listen. You workin' with those hustlers? You know who they are? You know what they done to your sister?"

59

Experienced, efficient, evil. They cleaned the Arab out. And the best part of it: By extension, they were sinking Radovan.

Mrado and Nenad, the dynamic duo, didn't take shit. Pinched the blow bags till it stung the old toad.

Abdulkarim used to work for Nenad and was now directly under R. He couldn't have suspected Nenad knew shit about the C deal, since the Yugo boss'd shut him out. Dumbass.

Despite all the planning and JW's information, Mrado was still slammed with some surprises: One of the Arab's helpers was the Latino he'd beaten up eight months ago in the woods north of Åkersberga. What was he doing in Västberga Cold Storage? JW'd said that a Latino was working alongside him on this gig, but he'd never mentioned his name.

It was a bizarre collaboration. Mrado thought, Either the Jorge dude's hired help for this one gig or else he's been working for Abdulkarim the whole time. In that case, he's been working indirectly under Nenad the whole time, and, even more indirectly, under Rado.

Ironic but not impossible. The Latino knew a lot about C. Wasn't strange that Abdulkarim'd wanted to recruit the guy. Not strange that Nenad didn't keep track of every clocker who worked for the Arab, either. And if Nenad'd known, it wasn't strange that he hadn't mentioned it to him: Nenad couldn't know that he'd taught the Latino a lesson he deserved.

Mrado thought, The Latino only has himself to blame. Humiliated by me a second time. And now by sitting with his hands tied and watching his Arab employer snot all over the floor. What a joke.

They had less than one crate left to unload. Mrado stood by the suitcases, Nenad by the packing crates. Lifting out cabbages. Making incisions with a knife, carefully, precisely. Unnecessary to cut anything that shouldn't be. Mrado picked up the bags. Filled the last suitcase.

The ski mask was uncomfortable.

Abdulkarim spat on the floor. Refused to stay calm. Yelled curses in Arabic. Mrado guessed, it was something like: I'm gonna fuck your mother/sister/daughter. The pool of blood around the gorilla on the floor grew big. JW and Jorge sat with their arms taped, each with his back against a packing crate. They were staying calm.

Everything'd gone according to plan. JW'd done a good job. The kid could be trusted. Like Nenad said: The guy wanted up. Would do anything for cash. He'd informed Nenad and Mrado exactly where, when, and how the Arab and his crew would receive the blow. Said all they had to do was drive there, cut down that one lookout, and step right in.

Almost too easy.

In three or four minutes, they'd be done. Mrado and Nenad in one car. Bobban in the other. If shit went down, they had an extra escape car parked safely on the other side of the cold-storage facility. Ready to roll instead of the others cars if the situation blew up.

Within six months, when the whole load'd been sold off, they'd be 100 million richer.

Fresh as fuck.

That's when he was hit with the day's second surprise. The JW guy got up. His hands were obviously untied. Mrado'd cut the guy's tape so it'd be possible to break free. Unnecessary, he realized now.

Why had he gotten up?

Abdulkarim'd understand that something was off. That JW'd collaborated with Nenad.

He said something.

Mrado glanced over. Nenad looked up, interrupted what he was doing. Held a head of cabbage in one hand, the knife in the other.

JW was holding a Glock in both hands. Pointed at Nenad at only four yards' distance.

Jaw clenched. Eyes like slits.

The guy hollered something inaudibly slurred.

What the fuck was the brat up to?

Mrado listened closer.

"Nenad, you pig. If you move, I'll shoot you. In the head. Promise. Goes for you, too. If you move, Nenad dies."

Nenad dropped the cabbage. Tried to look relaxed. It rolled away over the floor. He said to JW, "What's the deal? Sit down."

JW remained standing as he was, arms raised.

Mrado made some high-speed calculations: Was JW losing it, or was the kid sharper than they'd thought? Did he plan on raking in the whole load himself? And if so, how good was he with a gun? Would Mrado have time to pull his S & W before this loon fired off a shot at Nenad's head or chest? Conclusions: Whatever the JW guy was up to, it was a sticky situation—not a good idea to make any sudden moves. The distance was too short; JW seemed too steady with the gun.

Mrado stood still.

"Answer one question, Nenad. Very simple."

Nenad nodded. His eyes could be glimpsed under the ski mask. He didn't look away from the barrel for an instant.

"What's the color of your Ferrari?"

Nenad was silent.

Mrado slowly moved his hand inside his jacket to pull his gun.

JW said again, "If you don't tell me what color your Ferrari is, I'll shoot."

Nenad stood still. He seemed to consider.

The gun in JW's hand, his finger on the trigger. Game time.

Nenad said, "I used to have a Ferrari. What do you care? But it wasn't really mine. It was leased."

JW raised his head slightly.

"It was yellow, if you're wondering."

JW's eyes changed. Furious. Wild. Unpredictable.

"Tell me what you did to my sister."

Nenad giggled. "You're messed up."

JW clicked off the safety.

"I'll count to three; then you'll talk. Or else you're dead. One."

Mrado gripped the gun inside his jacket.

Nenad said, "I don't know what the hell you're talking about."

JW counted: "Two."

Mrado didn't have time to act before Nenad started talking.

"Oh, now I know who I thought you looked like the first time I saw you in London. Couldn't think of who. I guess I just couldn't imagine you were the brother of a whore."

Mrado thought, Why is Nenad even talking to the guy? Insanity.

"She was fine, your sis. Made good money. I even hung out with her for a few months. She was the freshest call girl we had. I promise."

A pause for effect.

Silence in the cold-storage facility. Even the Arab was completely still.

"She was a little too cocky, though. When she started with us, she was still a student and knew her place. Apparently, it was her teacher, an old regular of ours, who tipped her off about our way of making dough. But after a while, she got uppity. Tried to pull some funny biz. We couldn't tolerate that. As you must understand."

JW stood still. Arms straight out. Gun in a firm grip.

"How'd you find out, by the way?"

"Fuck that. Pig."

Mrado tore out his gun. Raised it toward JW.

He didn't care if Nenad was making some sort of confession to JW. The situation had to end. Time for him to do some yelling.

"JW, put down your gun."

Pointed his gun at the brat.

JW's gaze skipped. Probably saw Mrado out of the corner of his eye. Deadlock. Triangle drama. Mexican standoff.

If JW shot Nenad, he would fall, as well.

Did the guy understand the situation?

"JW, there's no point. If you hurt Nenad, I'll blow your head off. I'm a better shot than you are. Maybe I'll have time to pop you before you even pull the trigger at Nenad."

JW remained standing.

Mrado felt how the polyester of the ski mask itched.

Nenad clocked, kept quiet.

Mrado said, "Put your gun away and we'll forget about this."

Nothing happened.

Abdulkarim started screaming.

That's when Mrado was hit with the third surprise of the day. The worst one.

The entrance to the loading dock opened again.

Cops stormed in.

Two shots went off.

60

Jorge in the midst of the chaos.

JW'd fired. Mrado'd fired.

Nenad on the floor. The police crawling like ants. Despite that, the shot toward Nenad'd spooked them. Confused. Mrado's shot at JW'd missed. JW on his feet. Unharmed. The cops'd stormed in at just the right moment to distract the Yugo.

Tear gas in the cold-storage facility.

Mrado shot wildly at the cops.

They took cover. Interrupted. Hollered commands. Made threats.

Jorge behind the packing crate.

JW next to Jorge, a box cutter in his hand. Cut off the tape around Jorge's hands.

Jorge rose to his feet. They looked at each other.

Eyes stung like hell.

They ran toward the back door.

The cops clocked the situation too late. Focused on Mrado, who still had the gun in his hand.

Jorge unlocked the door.

He and JW ran out into a hallway.

No cops.

A fluorescent light was flickering farther down.

They fumbled around in confusion.

A ladder leaning against a wall.

Up.

They climbed toward the ceiling, a hatch.

Took the rungs three at a time.

Heard cops bursting into the hallway.

Jorge looked down. Opened the hatch. They yelled from below, "Freeze, police." Jorge thought, Fuck you. J-boy's been around the block and has some golden rules: Never stop. Give it hell. The pigs'll *se pierden*.

They got up on the roof. The sheet metal was flat and gray-colored, as if it'd once been white. The sky was clear.

JW seemed out of breath. Still held the Glock in his hand. He probably didn't have any bullets left. Jorge in better shape, despite the lack of exercise lately.

They ran across the roof.

JW seemed to have a direction. Took the lead.

Jorge yelled, "Where we goin'?"

JW replied, "There's supposed to be a car, a Volkswagen, parked out front, by the flagpoles."

Cop cocks poured out of the hatch in the roof, positioned themselves. Took up the chase.

Autotuned voice over a megaphone: "Stop where you are. Put your hands over your heads."

JW raised his gun, pointed back toward the men. Idiot move.

Jorge heard the cops yelling, "He's armed."

He ran faster.

Breathed through his nose.

The smell of his own sweat.

Not stress. Just exertion.

No stress.

Continued over the roof.

The megaphone again.

JW held the Glock in his hand. Turned back to the cops. A sharp sound was heard. Was he the one who'd shot?

Shit—Jorge hadn't thought he still had bullets left.

Another shot sounded.

JW fell. Grabbed his thigh.

What the fuck were the cops doing?

No time to think.

He rushed on alone.

Harmony in the runner's stride.

Jorge with flow. Jorge with rhythm.

In a trance: All he knew was how to run.

Remembered his loops around the Österåker rec yard. Remembered his homespun rope tight over the wall.

Ran so fast.

Toward the edge of the roof.

Didn't even look down.

Just jumped. True to habit.

Farther fall than from the Österåker and the Västerbron bridge.

A cracking sound in one of his feet.

He saw the Volkswagen.

Fuck the pain.

Limped up to it.

Broke the window. Opened the door.

The driver's seat, covered in shards of glass.

He tore out the ignition wires from under the wheel.

He could hot-wire a car better than anyone.

The king.

The car started up.

Adiós, losers.

EPILOGUE

Paola should've given birth by now.

Jorge lit a cig, leaned back. A rickety lounge chair. A beach umbrella with a Pepsi ad on it.

His foot felt considerably better.

Ko Samet: not one of the most popular islands. Farther up the bay than Ko Tao and Ko Samui. No Swedish charter trips, no German mass tourism, no families with children. Instead: cheap bungalows, solitary beaches, and backpackers with greasy hair. On top of that: single middle-aged men and Thai whores.

Half his stack exchanged into dollars was packed into the shoulder bag next to the lounge chair. The rest in an account at HSBC. The bank with offices all over the world.

Suited him well.

The beach was almost empty of people.

He groped with his hand to make sure the bag was still there.

He thought back.

He'd made it. Jorgius Maximus. Driven the car like a maniac despite his sprained ankle. Obvious comparison: like the escape from Österåker, except no planned escape route. They were less than a minute behind him. He drove into Midsommarkransen. A lot of houses and narrow streets. The cops couldn't keep him in sight like on the freeway. He ditched the car by Brännkyrka Gymnasium. Boosted a new one in under thirty seconds. They didn't clock shit. The Miracle Man strikes again. Shook the cops. Outbrained the 5-0.

First thing he did after that: drove to Fahdi's apartment. Had the keys on him. Limped into the bedroom. To the closet. Took out the shotgun he'd used in Hallonbergen. Stuffed it in a paper shopping bag. Limped out.

Had second thoughts. Back into the bedroom. Grabbed the assault rifle and Fahdi's other weapons, too. Wrapped them in his sheets.

Fahdi was a friend. If he survived, he wouldn't have to do more time than necessary.

Went into the kitchen. On the kitchen table were, as usual, scales, Red Line baggies, manila envelopes, mirrors, and razor blades. Three hundred grams of blow in different dime bags.

Jorge put the bags in the paper bag.

Rummaged. Turned the place upside down, soundlessly. Gloved hands. Didn't leave a trace. Found what he was looking for: the keys to the storage units.

Down to the street. Boosted a new bucket.

Threw the sheet with the weapons into Edsviken Bay.

Drove around for the rest of the day. Shurgard Self-Storage in Kungens Kurva, Högdalen, Danderyd. Emptied the stash spots.

The next day: the stashes in Rissne, Solna, and Vällingby. Total harvest: 2.7 pounds of blow.

The following three days were hectic. He sold it all off at a *loco* dumped price. Seven hundred a gram. Flew as fast as frosted bottles at a beer garden on a warm spring day.

Got a half-assed passport. Dished way too much for it, but there wasn't any time to play cold.

Ordered tix on a charter flight to Bangkok. Chanced it.

It worked. No one checks passports too closely on an outbound flight.

He left the country within four days of the fiasco in the cold-storage facility.

Not the way he'd planned it.

If it was a boy, Paola'd promised him she'd name him Jorge. A real Jorgelito. Even if he could never live a Sven life, at least Paola could. Let Jorgelito grow up in peace. Without Social Services hags, racist teachers, cock-sucking cops, and Rodriguez. Jorge would create some structure, would send every cent he could to his sister's baby.

A pale European man walked down the beach hand in hand with a young Thai woman.

Jorge closed his eyes. He'd had enough of johns, but still had a few left to pop.

Thought about JW back in the cold-storage facility. JW hadn't wanted to understand at first. Jorge'd kept pushing. "I've seen your sister raped and beaten in a movie. By those guys. You gotta believe me." JW stared straight ahead. Mumbled, "Shut up, Jorge. Shut up already." Jorge kept going, whispered just loud enough for JW to hear him clearly, "Believe me. You've picked the wrong side. I get it if you can't rethink this. You've invested in these guys. But your sister was some kind of prostitute. Those Yugo Mafia guys've murdered her." It was then that JW seemed to react. He turned to Jorge. Said, *"Shut up before I fucking club you."* Nenad and Mrado still didn't seem to care about JW and Jorge—they were slicing cabbages, pouring bags of blow. Abdulkarim kept screaming. But Jorge could tell he was listening now. "JW, I've been watching those guys for months. I know what kind of business they're in." Jorge told him quickly about the brothel in Hallonbergen. He didn't mention the shots at the pimp and the brothel madam. Instead, he described the whore party out at Smådalarö. The way the johns carried on, the way the girls looked, who was there. Underscored the latter by telling him about the parking lot outside the enormous mansion. The luxury rides in a row. And that's when JW suddenly got in a hell of a hurry.

Jorge stubbed out his cigarette in the sand. Enjoyed the heat. The sun gave him a real tan. Nice not to have to deal with the nasty smell of the self-tanner. Except for that, his appearance was back to normal. Straight hair, trim body, no beard. Only his broken nose reminded him of Jorge Nuevo.

Safe.

At the same time, he had to keep moving.

The cash wouldn't last forever.

Maybe worth going home soon. Get more kronor.

Meet Jorgelito.

* * *

The sound of a key scraping in the lock. The double doors opened.

Margareta began to cry. Bengt looked strained; his eyes were glued on the floor.

The CO closed the door behind them.

Margareta's face had the same color as Österåker's walls: bone white.

JW sat on the other side of the wooden table. Margareta and Bengt sat down. Margareta's hands reached across the table and met JW's. Held them tightly.

"How are things, Johan?"

"It's cool. Much better than jail. I can study here."

Bengt kept staring down at the tabletop. "And what kinds of jobs did you have in mind?"

JW thought, He will never forgive. Bengt: the honest Swede in a nutshell. And, yet, he came. Maybe Mom made him.

"I'll get a job."

Bengt didn't reply.

They talked more about other stuff—the food in the prison, the lawyer's visit, and JW's schoolwork.

They discussed the final days of the trial. The prosecutor'd tried to get JW convicted for attempted murder. He'd told his parents about the drugs. But the bullet to Nenad—never. Wished he'd been better with a gun—he'd only hit Nenad in the shoulder. The court'd believed his explanation, that he'd been scared when the cops stormed in, scared by Mrado's threats, by Fahdi's death, that he'd let a shot slip. Without the intent to kill or even harm.

The court bought that stuff. JW confessed to his involvement with the cocaine. His line throughout was that he'd been there only to help boost the gear. They lowered the sentence a few years on account of that and of his age. Still, he'd have time to rot, to decompose ten times over, before he was let out.

The boyz'd turned their backs on him. Pretended like they never knew him. That was to be expected. Those who wade through shit would rather not look down—too nasty. But he'd set his hopes on Sophie. Without success.

There was only one thing left to do—create an okay existence for himself on the inside. He could always sell his money-laundering scheme to other inmates. Do business as usual.

His parents didn't mention Camilla. And JW refrained from telling them. The cops wouldn't get much out of Jan Brunéus. He probably hadn't done anything illegal. JW carried the burden alone. Spared Margareta and Bengt from the truth. That made him sleep a little less badly.

Margareta said, "We got a postcard last week that was alarming, I think."

JW's interest started churning. "From who?"

"Didn't say from who. But it was signed *'El Negrito.'*"

"So, what'd it say?"

"Not much. That the person was having a nice time in Southeast Asia, the beaches were beautiful, that there was coral. And then he said he sent three hundred thousand kaley hugs from his island to yours."

JW looked indifferent. "Huh."

"Johan, is there something strange about that?"

"No, just a friend of mine who's having a nice time. He doesn't even know I'm in prison. When I get out of here, I'm going to head to the sun, too."

Bengt opened his mouth. Closed it again.

Margareta turned to him. "What, Dad? Were you going to say something?"

Bengt looked at JW for the first time today. JW stared back and thought, Maybe this is the first time ever that my dad's really looked at me.

"When you get out, you're not going to the sun. You're going to get a real job. Far from Stockholm."

Bengt lowered his eyes to the table again. He didn't say anything else.

The silence was heavy in the room.

"Johan, can't you describe what a day is like in here?"

JW let his mouth run. In his head, he let go of Bengt. Gave Jorge eternal thanks. Three hundred thousand deposited into his account on the Isle of Man. The Chilean was a good person. Didn't forget who'd picked him up in the woods, even though JW'd betrayed them all, gone behind Abudlkarim's back, sold his soul to the Yugos. Jorge must've understood that JW'd double-gamed them, but he'd also understood that JW didn't know whom he'd been dealing with. That he'd been naïve.

Visiting hours were over.

The CO led his parents out.

Margareta cried again.

JW remained seated at the table in the visiting room.

Knew what he was going to do with the money.

Didn't know what he was going to do with his daddy issues.

* * *

The rec yard at Kumla, a maximum-security prison: close-cut grass, no trees. Cement blocks with a polished surface and relatively fresh metal rods—the outdoor gym. Mrado and the other Serbs were pumping iron.

A silent agreement governed. The morning was for the Serbs. The Arabs bulked postlunch.

Life on the inside was better for him than for many others. In the joint, he was someone. His reputation protected him. Still, the climate was harsher than he remembered it from his last turn. Understood his own and Stefanovic's lectures in a hands-on way. The gangs ruled. The mobs governed. Either you were with them or you were fucked.

What ruined everything: He was gonna lose Lovisa. Annika'd made the case right after the dope sentence'd fallen against Mrado. Demanded sole custody and visitation for one hour once a month for Mrado in a shitty little visiting room with a chaperone present. Strangled him psychologically. Killed him slowly.

Mrado's luck was that Bobban'd ended up in the same place. Someone to talk to. Someone who had his back.

How could the Nenad fucker've been dumb enough not to see the resemblance between the JW guy and that whore he'd been pumping a few years back? Everything'd been so perfect. They would've ruled. Spat Rado in the face. Sold blow for millions.

And now: Radovan continued to maneuver Stockholm's most powerful network, to control the coat checks in the city, to sell C, to push smuggled booze, to sit in his worn leather armchair in Näsbypark, to drink whiskey and just smile.

Fuck.

This wasn't Serbian justice. One day, Mrado would have his time with Rado. Rub out his smile. Slowly.

A half hour left till lunch. The other Yugos went inside. Mrado and Bobban lingered.

Bobban sat down on a cement block that served as a bench press.

"Mrado, I heard this morning. They've put a price on your head."

Mrado'd known that it would come. Rado didn't forget. Had to uphold the code.

"Who told you?"

"Some dude on my hall. Sven. Doing time for armed robbery and assault. He heard it from some Latino hustlers."

Mrado sat down next to Bobban.

"Latinos?"

"Yeah, it's weird. High price, too. Three hundred grand."

THANKS TO:

Hedda, for putting up with me, for all the help and inspiration. Love.

Elis, for all the reading, the rewarding discussions, and ideas.

Sören, for the support and guidance. Sven, Helena, Göte, Yvonne, and Lars, for comments and criticism.

Pappa, for insight, and Mamma, for hope.

All the rest of you who read and commented: Jacob, Johanna, David, Anna, Birnik, Dennis, Bosse, Daniel, Hanna, Jael, Mirjam, Lars, Jesper, Jenny, Johan, Pawel, and many more.

Wahlström & Widstrand: Pontus, Annika, Gustaf, and all the rest.

Sanks.